Felicity Savage

Music to Die By

FIRST KNIGHTS HILL PUBLISHING EDITION, JULY 2011

This is a work of fiction. Names, characters, places and incidents either are products of the author's imagination or are used fictitiously. Any resemblance to actual persons, living or dead, events, or locales is entirely coincidental.

Knights Hill Publishing ISBN: 978-1-937396-03-9

www.knightshillpublishing.com

Printed in the United States of America

Music to Die By

Part 1: Unfair Game

"Let's talk about you," I snarled. "It must've been the first time. So did it excite you?"

Gen stood on my left, hunched over his Ibanez as if he were trying to protect it from the crowd. He wore his uniform of jeans and a plain black t-shirt. Sweat fell sparkling from his curls. When I tore into the chorus, he raised his head and bellowed the harmony into his own mic. He had the best voice of any of the boys, a raspy tenor that harmonized nicely with my own voice. I was more of a shouter than a singer, and inevitably got Janis Joplin comparisons, although I preferred to think of myself as the female Layne Staley, without the heroin problem. I had enough problems as it was.

Our faithful supporters swayed an arm's length in front of me, chaotically out of step. About three-quarters of our guest list had showed up by the time we went on stage. It does mean something to be headlining. And it didn't hurt, either, that Ace's High was so small that this modest crowd was a capacity one. We couldn't take all the credit: Dew Over, Bloodthirsty Fakers, and Vanilla Camp had left a residue of punters who were determined to get full value for money, curious about a band with two gaijins in it, or simply willing to give us a try. Some of them had trickled away during our first number, but others lingered. They even clapped.

Unlike Gen, I didn't just stand there. I covered the whole stage – which wasn't difficult: I could only take two paces before I bumped into Gen or Tad, our bassist. I struck poses, touched myself, danced with the mic stand, and interacted with the boys. My bottle-green top hat shadowed my face in the hot, shifting spotlights. When I finally doffed it, applause went up. I mugged, did a clownish shuffle, then hooked the hat on my mic stand and started dancing in earnest. I wore my cowboy boots, my lucky talismans, harness brown with turquoise, gold, and white flames. Their heels made me tall enough to see four or five deep into the crowd.

"Let's talk about you," I ranted, "and the little places you call home."

Tad planted his left foot on a wedge speaker and banged his head as he churned out the bass solo. A pair of black cat ears poked out of his flying hair. At home he also had floppy white bunny ears, tall grey donkey ears, and a magician's hat with stars and moons on it. He liked to wear that one with a gold kimono.

"It was the only thing you've ever done! I hope, oh yeah, I hope it was a good one."

I extended the end of the phrase into a melodic scream, jammed my mic onto the stand, and let my head fall forward as Gen took over for the outro. Through the curtain of hair that slid in front of my face, I saw constellations of cigarette ends explode in the outer darkness as the technique freaks applauded. I straightened up and gestured broadly, helping the spotlight on Gen to make its point.

Joaquin crashed both hands down on the keyboard of his Korg. An instant of silence, and then the applause kicked in. I stepped back to the mic and thanked the crowd.

"For those of you that we haven't got to know yet, Joaquin's the tunesmith." In his place behind the Korg, Joaquin bowed. "I write the lyrics. They let me do that because I can't play an instrument."

Tad grabbed my mic and said, "I've got an idea, Shanti. You can have my job and I'll have yours."

I grinned and said over the catcalls, "Shut up, Tad, I'm busy showing off my Japanese."

This got a huge laugh, as usual. To the extent I spoke Japanese, I spoke it like a native. For that I could thank my sense of pitch, but more to the point, as Joaquin could have explained, once you have a second language, it's no big deal to acquire a third one. As a kid in Paris, I'd gone from zero to fluent in French in a year, and as an adult in Tokyo, it had taken me only slightly longer than that to learn Japanese. I still had plenty of holes in my vocabulary, but they didn't show onstage.

"Now guess what, you lucky people, we're going to do a song off the new album. U-Turn Day, out next Saturday from Cold Coeur Records. Available from your local clued-up independent music store, or buy it on our website, where we're streaming select tracks for your listening pleasure. Now here's another dirty little sample." I leaned into the mic. "When I first started writing lyrics for Gorot, I didn't want to write about the same old thing. You know. Lurrrve."

Nina, Joaquin's wife and our recording angel, dodged across the Bermuda Crescent in front of the stage with her digital camera. Our Shimokitazawa gigs rarely got rowdy enough for the crowd to venture into that buffer zone between us and them. Even when they did, they retreated when the music stopped.

"But I've learned a lot since I've been in this band," I said. "I've realized that I have more to say about life in general than I ever knew."

I saw him.

His blond hair shone in the dark. He was leaning against the wall about three people behind Nina. At this distance I couldn't see his eyes.

"A lot to say," I repeated. "A lot to say."

I had nothing to say to Ned Gallant, now or ever.

But maybe it wasn't him. Maybe it was just some coworker of Nina's who hadn't been on the guest list, or one of the European drifters Joaquin collected.

Tad glanced sharply at me. I couldn't tell if he was alarmed, or just trying to prompt me, but it reminded me why I was here, why I'd written the song I was currently supposed to be introducing, and how I'd felt while I was writing it, in my tiny studio apartment with my headphones on, pushing rewind over and over again on the rough mix: as far from Ireland as I would ever get.

"Recently," I said, "I realized that I even have something to say about love. And this is it. 'Heartbreak.'"

I signaled to Joaquin with one hand behind my back. The silence lengthened: one, two, three, and the first plaintive piano notes floated out over Tad's bass line. Shingo tapped on the rim of the snare, a sinister rhythm like a clock ticking. Until its closing seconds, this song required no more of Gen than filler duties. "Heartbreak" was that rare thing in our repertoire, a slow burner designed to prove that I could actually sing, and that was appropriate, because it was my song of liberation.

"Struck dumb by a closing door," I sang, cupping my mic in both hands for a bit of distortion, "face down on the bathroom floor. Here's a dirty little sample, better keep it to yourself. I've lived, I've been, I've seen…"

Joaquin's line swelled, surging towards maximum volume.

"I've sunk, I've swum, I've fallen in between…"

Someone whistled deafeningly.

"And you, you think that you'll remain in my memory like a stain, but you'll fade like everyone! You were never here!"

Sweet, languid Jonathan had been the lead guitarist of the first band I was ever in, back in New York, and I'd thought he was the love of my life, until he turned out to be a cheater and a liar. When he cheated on me, I hadn't just dumped him, I'd left the country. Top that, asshole. I'd won, but it had taken me another four years to write him, literally, out of my heart.

And in the meantime, I'd discovered something strange and surprising, better than sex and almost as good as music.

Friendship.

I'd once had a boyfriend. Now I had four boy friends who meant more to me than Jonathan ever had.

I'd written "Heartbreak" for them, and if the lyrics didn't really reflect that… well, my lyrics always turned out kind of dark.

I couldn't lose them. I couldn't, but my own words sounded like a dire prophecy as I sobbed, "Stupid enough to not quite see the temporary nature of everything behind your eyes!"

It was Gen's moment. Unexpectedly, he launched a gargoyle of a riff that climbed on the back of Joaquin's piano line and reached for the stratosphere. We'd heard this variation in rehearsal, but never live. I signaled to Tad and went for a repeat of the chorus. Gen's riff toyed with my voice, then folded up and flatlined into a distorted hum that grew louder and louder until it swallowed Joaquin's last notes.

After that, our last number was an anticlimax. I thrashed around the stage, but I couldn't stop looking at that spot over by the wall. In a montage of underexposed stills, I saw him draining a can of beer, taking off his knit cap, and putting two fingers in his mouth and whistling. So it had been him.

"Encore! Encore!"

For once I wished our supporters weren't quite so faithful.

"Encore!"

I bowed for the third time. Behind me, Joaquin hissed, "What are you waiting for?"

"No encore," I said through my smile.

"Fuck off. What's wrong?"

With the show officially over, we could take a minute to confer. I went back to Joaquin, mic in hand. His face was scarlet and his hands hovered on the keyboard. "OK," I told him, "I'll do an encore. But not 'You're No Fun.'"

"Don't give me this shit. If you don't want to do it, why did you want it on the set list?"

"Joaquin, I can't fucking do it!"

Joaquin's jaw tightened. He seized the mic from my hand and plunged around the Korg, shaking the cord clear. "OK, we'll do another track from Xenophobia," he said out of the side of his mouth. "They've heard the whole album many times, but what the hell."

He arrived at the front of the stage in a single stride with his smile on full. A storm of clapping greeted him. Everyone knew he was the brains of the band, and although he seldom took a producer's bow, they felt he deserved it. He thanked them in English, Japanese, and French, and waited for the applause to subside. I hovered at his side, trying to look supportive rather than apprehensive. He said in Japanese, "We are delighted that you come all the way to Shimokitazawa to see us. I mean, it's the middle of nowhere, eh?"

Laughter.

"We hope you will come all the way to Hokkaido to see us, too! We can't reimburse you for the airfare, but we think it will be worth it. They say that Sapporo is a beautiful city. Myself, I've never been there, but I'm looking forward to it. Yes, ladies and gentlemen, Gorot is going on tour!"

I did what I had to do, which was lead the applause. When we were debating whether to tour for U-Turn Day, I'd been anti. I didn't know why I even bothered, since Joaquin always got his way in the end.

"Some of you are familiar with Kinderbox," continued Joaquin, naming another of the acts he produced for our label, Cold Coeur Records, which he also owned. "We tour together. We will look for you next week in Sapporo! Hakodate! Aomori! Morioka! Yamagata! Sendai! Fukushima! And Utsunomiya! But if we don't see you there, we hope to meet on Tuesday the twelfth of March at Oasis in Shinjuku, where we plan a party for our homecoming. It is also the release party for U-Turn Day! Yoroshiku onegai shimasu. Also," Joaquin added rapidly, "we have gigs upcoming throughout March, please check out the information on the flyers. We're running late, but we will do one more song for you tonight. 'Dreamstomper.'" Throwing me a look of triumph mixed with a challenge, he hopped back behind the Korg.

Numbly, I waited for the piano loop to roll out of the speakers. In the interval of rustling silence I cleared my throat. "This one's for everyone who got lost along the way," I said, wishing Ned Gallant had.

Backstage, Nina handed out bottles of Crystal Geyser. Joaquin upended his over his head, splashing everyone. "To Cold Coeur Family Volume I!" This, unbelievably, was what our tour had come to be called. Infected by his mood, the other boys slavishly acted like they'd all been excited about it from the start. The manager played along, too, opining that it would be just the ticket to launch us into the big time. Joaquin followed him into his office to sort out our cut of the door. After retrieving our kit from the stage, Gen, Tad, and Shingo piled into the cruddy little restroom down the hall and jostled for access to the tap.

I gulped water. As soon as Joaquin squared the manager, we were due to join up with our faithful supporters and head to an izakaya. Ned might turn out to be someone else, and it wouldn't be the first time. My fight-or-flight reflex often went off at the sight of a blond head and a pair of blue eyes. But if it had been him…

Pushing a hand through my damp, tangled hair, I went out the side door and said hello to my friends. There were about two dozen people left in the house, and I didn't know all their faces, let alone their names. Back in Gorot's early days, the same people had come to all our gigs and we'd gone to all their gigs; now we had friends and fans, and it was getting harder to tell which were which. I clocked the blond guy hovering near the exit.

I went back through the grey room, past the manager's office and the restroom, looking for another way out. There was an emergency exit, but it was padlocked.

I retrieved my shoulderbag, threw on my coat, and ducked back through the side door. I didn't have a plan. All I knew was that I had to keep Ned away from the band. I couldn't be sure that he wouldn't approach me in front of them, and I was even less sure of my own ability to deny to his face that we'd ever met. I wasn't even sure that would be the best line to take. He might react unpredictably.

"Shanti, you're not skipping out?" Nina said in astonishment.

"You're on PR duty, gorgeous," I said. "Oh, I left my hatbox back there. Could you take it home with you? I'll come over and pick it up tomorrow or sometime."

I beelined to the exit, calling goodnight to the technicians who were shutting down the equipment onstage. As I passed the blond guy, he took an abortive step towards me. I pushed through the door into February. His footsteps echoed mine on the stairs. Out on the street, the rest of our supporters were hanging around in groups, smoking and chatting. I shouted to them that I had an early start tomorrow and inconsistently turned left, away from the station. He caught up with me. I kept walking. At the 7-11 on the corner I turned again. He matched my strides. A cold, dusty wind blew around us.

"Fuck, this feels weird." His voice was deep. I'd subconsciously been expecting him to sound like a child. "But it feels kind of natural, too, doesn't it?"

"Well, it's been a while," I said, head ringing.

"A while?" He laughed. He looked like none of the men I'd mistaken for him over the years. He was still blond, and his eyes were still that eerie blue – but he was no longer small or pale or skinny. His skin had seen a lot of sun, and he hulked over me with shoulders as broad as the axle of a small car. He'd turned out as big as Nigel. But his accent no longer sounded like Nigel's. It had softened dramatically. "I guess you've added the art of understatement to your repertoire. It's been half our lives. No, more. I was twelve, and your birthday is before mine, so you'd have been thirteen."

He spoke as if he didn't remember exactly. This confused me.

"So how's Alastair doing these days?"

We were turning corners at random, and although I couldn't remember crossing the railway tracks, we must have done, because we were now descending the gentle hill on the far side of Shimokitazawa station. Shuttered boutiques lined the narrow street. Here and there, golden light from the windows of a restaurant shone through a screen of trees. The wind numbed my face; it seemed to have penetrated to my bones and slowed down my brain. Ned and I were talking. How had this happened?

"Alastair lives in the States," I said. My brother had spent his early twenties trying to be an artist; now he was the assistant manager of Windrose & Sons, a 150-year-old gallery in Boston's Back Bay that sold objets d'art and antiques from all over the world, true to its origins as a clearing-house for plunder from the Orient. He and his girlfriend Maisie lived together in Somerville with her second-hand Volvo, his BMW 6-series, and two Weimaraners, and he seemed happy. "He's doing OK, I guess."

"Figures. He was bound to land on his feet. And June? Still painting, is she?"

"She moved back to France years ago," I said. Our mother had nothing to do with it. Ned would have no reason to track her down, nor could he learn anything from her he didn't already know. "She lives near Bordeaux now. It's la France profonde, the true France. She keeps chickens and goats. And yeah, she's still painting her heart out."

Ned laughed. "You know something funny? All this time I thought your family was still in Thailand."

"You're kidding! We only stayed there for six months."

I remembered promising Ned that he could come with us. Promising it would be all right. But I was only thirteen and it wasn't my decision to make.

Ned would probably have hated Thailand, though. We did. After Ireland, it had been so hot that I felt like I'd stepped onto another planet. I remembered the energy draining from my thirteen-year-old body, the sunlight so bright that my eyes hurt, and a hundred and one permutations of boredom and anxiety. That was nothing to how June must have felt. She'd dragged us halfway around the world to the one man who had to take us in: our father. Malcolm Ogilvie had settled in Phuket. He was a poet – we'd owned an actual book of poetry by him at one point – but he subsisted on the generosity of hotel and bar managers who gave him odd jobs. From his point of view, having the three of us descend on him must have been the worst trip of his life, especially since he had a live-in Thai girlfriend.

Somehow, we all managed to cohabit in his disgusting bungalow for five or six months. That was how long it took June to accept that she'd made a mistake. She fell back on her brother Red, my corporate lawyer uncle in Philadelphia. And just like that, as if the first thirteen years of my life had been a dream, I'd suddenly had the life of a privileged American teenager.

Not for long, though. Unlike Alastair, I hadn't been able to keep it up.

"As for our father," I said, "he's dead."

It was Ned's turn to exclaim, "You're kidding!" And in his smile I saw a hint of schadenfreude that chilled me to the bone.

"He hanged himself about ten years ago," according to the letter that the Thai girlfriend had sent June. It had been wrapped around a small teak box that contained Malcolm's ashes. "He left a typical, self-pitying note. Saying he'd failed everyone and he was sorry. Talk about wasted sentiments. *We* weren't."

Ned hissed between his teeth. I thought I'd succeeded in shocking him. But he said in the same easy tone as before, "Funny thing is, *I* live in Thailand now. On Koh Samui. I go across to Phuket all the time, and I used to ask around for you, but no one's ever heard of you or your father."

Shit.

"Ned, how on earth did you end up in Thailand?"

"I'm an architect," he said, and went on expansively, in the strange nonaccent he'd acquired. "Koh Samui is booming. The tsunami created a lot of opportunities. New regulations, new land up for sale. I've got my own business, building villas. Referrals from all over. The clients appreciate having someone on the ground to see their projects through to completion: they don't want to deal with the Thais themselves. They're racist fuckers, as a rule. But I believe in doing the best work possible."

"Wow."

"I'm building my own house, too. It's still under construction. I've been working on it on and off for the last four years. But it's going to be fucking stunning. I can show you some photos if you're interested."

Laughter bubbled up in my chest. Ned was a builder. I didn't know why this struck me as so funny. I said, "Cool. Did you study architecture at school?" I wanted to find out where he'd spent the twelve years that were still unaccounted for. Why couldn't I just ask?

"Sure, I learned on the job. That's the best way. Hands-on experience. You've got to be focused, though. Thailand is full of Westerners who just drift from beach to beach…" Ned shook his head.

"Oh, we've got them here, too, except they don't come for the beaches. They come for the jobs."

"Still, I can't criticize that lifestyle. I lived on Bali for a while. Bummed around Indonesia, Malaysia, India." We reached the level crossing at the bottom of the hill. The barrier was down, the warning bell pinging. "I guess I was looking for something, but I didn't know what it was," Ned shouted as a train rushed past. "Maybe it was just a decent living," he added, laughing.

"Look," I said, pointing to a record shop on a side street. "They sell our albums. We've got our own label, and we're hooked up with an independent distributor."

"Oh yeah? Way to go!"

"Jesus, Ned, what *has* happened to your accent? You sound almost American."

"You sound fairly American yourself, Shanti."

"Well, I went to school on the East Coast. High school in Philly, and then NYU." No need to mention that I hadn't graduated, committing myself to rock 'n' roll instead of to the library.

"Get a load of you. I didn't go to university at all. After you left, my grandmother showed up and took me back to Denmark with her."

"Denmark!" That was it, of course. He didn't sound American. He sounded ever so slightly Scandinavian. The legend came back to me all at once: the mother who did a runner when Ned was three, leaving Nigel to raise him whilst making a go of his business, Allihies Ceramics. I even remembered Ned telling me where she'd come from. Somewhere like Norway, but without the funky mythic associations. *Denmark*. "I didn't know you even had a grandmother!" I said.

"Neither did I, until she walked in and told me to pack my stuff. I had a terrible time adjusting in Copenhagen. Couldn't get my tongue around the language. I used to think about you and Alastair jabbering away to each other in French. How did you do it? I picked up enough Danish in the end to get by, but as soon as I got out of school I buggered off. I used to go back as often as possible to see my grandmother, though. I owed her, didn't I?"

"She must be an amazing lady," to have put up with you, I added to myself.

"She was. She died last year."

"Oh Ned, I'm so sorry."

I caught his flickering glance of contempt. He didn't believe I was sorry, although when I said it, I *had* been.

We rounded the corner onto the plaza. I veered towards the station entrance and started up the stairs. Ned climbed beside me. He was explaining how it was that he could jaunt off to Japan at his pleasure, with zero hardship or sacrifice, but I wasn't really listening, because I knew it was just a bunch of excuses. I was wondering if I could lose him in Tokyo's fiendishly complicated rail system. "Have you got a ticket?"

"I need to buy one, do I? Where to?"

I thought quickly. "To Shibuya, but the tickets are priced by distance. It's a hundred and twenty yen."

I watched him shoulder through the milling crowd to the ticket machines, scoop change out of his pocket, and examine every coin before putting one into the slot. I had a prepaid Passnet card. I thought about dashing through the wickets while his back was turned. But there was only one platform. I'd have much better odds of losing him in Shibuya, where the JR, Tokyu, and Keio Inogashira train lines and the Ginza, Hanzomon, and Denentoshi subway lines all looped around each other in a multistorey knot.

As we came out of the wickets at Shibuya, I plunged ahead of Ned into the horde pouring down into the Mark City building. He seized the shoulder strap of my bag. "You don't mind if I hang onto you? This is fucking mad. I've never seen anything like it in my life. Feel like I'm about to be swept off my feet."

"Yeah, it's crazy, isn't it," I said, teeth gritted in frustration.

But then again, if I'd cut and run I would have looked guilty. And he'd just turn up again at our next gig, wouldn't he? My only hope was to brazen it out and get rid of him by some means as yet beyond the reach of my imagination. Leave him as completely as possible in the dark.

Yet every minute he was finding out more about my new life. I showed him how to buy a JR ticket and we rode the Yamanote line south, squashed shoulder to shoulder between drowsy drunks and noisy ones. At Gotanda I got off. He got off. We left the station and walked along a dark street, embroidered on one side with snack bar signs, which led back along the foot of the Yamanote line embankment. There was no traffic. Gotanda was an undercover town, buttoned up during the day and sleazy by night, with the highest concentration of love hotels south of Shibuya. You never bumped into anyone you knew here, which was why it suited me.

Among the office buildings on this side of the station towered a few elderly apartment blocks. I came to the dinged elevator doors at the foot of my building and turned to face Ned, feeling panicky. "Well, now you know where I live."

"Pretty ritzy." He craned his neck to look up at eight floors of concrete balconies.

"At least it's supposed to be earthquake-proof," I said.

"Oh sure, that would be a concern in this country."

We stood between the morgue-like walls of mailboxes. Was he waiting for me to invite him in? Did he plan on crashing *at my place?* No. No. No. This was not happening.

"Whereabouts are you staying, Ned?" I said bluntly.

"I've a couple of mates living in the city." He looked away from me. There was a trace of anger in his voice. "They came to Japan to work and save money, and they're spending it as fast as they make it, but they're good lads. I'll introduce you at some point. Mike's got a job in the public school system; Gavin works for one of these English conversation schools, same as you. They're raking it in. So they've a house, not just a crappy little apartment, in Nakano. You know where that is?"

Five minutes west on the Chuo line from Shinjuku. A goodly haul from here. But nowhere would be far enough.

"I can stay with them as long as I want. It's party central, but I'm not fussy. You've no need to worry about me on that score!" Ned chuckled, an unamused masculine sound that reminded me of Nigel.

"Ned, how did you find me?" I blurted. Immediately, I had a sensation of having taken a misstep. "I've often thought about you, but I had no way of knowing where you were."

He looked at me for a long minute. I concentrated on not letting a muscle of my face twitch. At last he said, "I searched for your name on the internet. Googled you, and up you popped. Your band's website. Pictures and everything."

I'd known it. I'd *known* it.

"So I knew it was you. Of course, it had to be you; there can't be two people in the world named Shanti Hazard."

Oh God. To hell with staying true to myself. I should have changed my name.

"That was about eighteen months ago."

So I'd been living in jeopardy, my illusion of safety hanging by a thread, for more than a year.

But how could I have talked the boys out of putting up a website? How could I have forced them to leave me off it? I was the face of Gorot, literally – Tad had used a picture of me for our logo, and they were always pushing for more pictures: pictures of me walking on the beach, drinking coffee, laughing out loud – pictures that would make me seem like someone you knew. I vetoed all but the blurriest live shots. That had made me feel better about the website, as did the fact that not much of the information on it was in English. But what difference did that make when my name was out there?

"I thought about getting in touch there and then, but you know how it is. Life gets in the way. By the time I finally got around to it, I thought I might as well just pop over and see you. So I got a Japanese mate to translate the squiggly bits for me, and here I am!"

"And how do you like it so far?" I keened softly through my chattering teeth.

"Well, I'll tell you. It's bloody confusing and it's bloody cold." Ned lowered his voice conspiratorially. "And do you get the feeling that these people don't know how to relax? This is according to my Japanese mate at home, but the culture here is fucking totalitarian. The level of social control is such that the people can't make their own choices. If they could, maybe they'd choose to be a bit more free!"

"I like it here because I fit in," I said, provoking a cry of disbelief from him. I explained, though it felt futile: "I didn't do very well as an American. It's much easier to be a foreigner."

"Well, in that case, then, I know what you mean! It was a nightmare living in Denmark, as I said. Looking like them but not speaking their language, not knowing their TV shows or their songs, not knowing shit about their fucking history and not caring. But when you're a Westerner out East, no one cares where you supposedly come from. No one asks why you've got a funny accent. You don't have to pretend to be something you're not. You can be yourself, can't you?"

Ned's face lit up as the words tumbled out. I didn't want to agree with him about anything, so I said nothing.

"Shanti, this is the kind of conversation I want to have with you! It's not everyone who understands, is it? But you're on my wavelength. You've had the same life experiences. You were *there.*"

Feeling dizzy, I steadied myself on the mailboxes.

"I just want to talk. No games, no bullshit." He looked eagerly into my face. "I just want us to be open with each other."

"Yeah, OK," I said faintly, "but can we do it some other time? I'm dead on my feet, and if I don't get indoors, I'm going to die of hypothermia."

"Oh well, then, I won't keep you," he said, drawing back with unsettling rapidity. "We couldn't have *that,* could we?"

Safely upstairs, I raged around my apartment, crying. My apartment was too small to rampage around very effectively, but I had a routine: I bounced on the bed, punched the walls, and threw my stuffed fox, Henri, at the bookcase. After fifteen minutes I was calm enough to sit on the floor, wiping my eyes, and realize I was hungry. All I'd had since lunch was some fries at Mickey D's before the gig.

I topped some bread with processed cheese slices, stuck it in the microwave, and put on a CD while I waited for it to ping. *Appetite For*

Destruction, a mood-improver tested under the harshest experimental conditions. I also switched on the heater. What else? I double-checked that the door was locked. Welcome to the jungle… I took a turn around the apartment, picking up the things I'd knocked down. Picture of Alastair and June on the beach at Biarritz, check. Picture of Alastair and Maisie at Fresh Pond with their dogs, check. Picture of me and Alastair with Uncle Red, Aunt Phoebe, and their daughter Katie, our only cousin, as pretty as a carrot in a plastic bag, check. No pictures of Ireland. June had only ever taken photographs as references for landscapes. But she'd given Ned a little Kodak for his eleventh birthday, I recalled. Defying her example, he'd mostly photographed us, instinctively placing human beings in the center of the universe…

As I washed up my plate, a fresh wave of fear hit me. I forced myself to complete the motions of drying the plate and putting it away. Then I turned off all the lights and the music, went to the window, and parted the curtains. Nothing on the balcony except my laundry carousel. In the distance, clusters of red eyes winked in the brownish night sky: the aircraft warning lights on the tops of the skyscrapers in Shinagawa and Shiodome. I stepped outside in my sock feet. Peeping over the balcony wall, I could see down into the alley that ran around the back of the building. A couple of bare-armed women escorted a salaryman out of a snack bar door and bowed him on his way. Their voices tinkled like a distant music box: goodbye, goodnight, come back and see us some time.

I went back through my apartment, putting on my sneakers en route, and pattered along the windy corridor to the fire escape. By going down a flight and craning around the corner, I could get a view of the sidewalk outside the building's entrance. It was deserted. The light from the lobby fell on bare concrete. As far down the street as I could see, nothing was moving.

But I couldn't stay out here all night! I couldn't defend my perimeter while I was *sleeping!*

I went back into my apartment and sat on the floor with my arms around my knees. After a while I tore off my clothes and flung myself into bed. But it was no good. I rolled over and looked at the clock. Five to midnight. I jumped out of bed and packed some overnight things into my bag.

Gotanda station was full of rings of salarymen bowing goodnight. I threaded between them, caught the Yamanote line south, changed at Shinagawa, and boarded a southbound train on the Keihin-Tohoku line. The press of bodies kept me upright. Wielding my bag, I fought my way off at the second stop, Omori. This was the southern fringe of Tokyo, where the city bled into the Kanagawa sprawl. A couple of kids were playing guitar pop outside the supermarket, off-key and out of tune.

Cutting through Omori's dowdy little red-light district, I hurried south through the narrow streets. Despite the proximity of the railway and the small factories that lined it, this neighborhood qualified as livable by Tokyo standards. Not many family homes remained among the new apartment buildings and lowrise blocks of condos. Floodlights gave a lurid tint to the greenery that overhung yard walls. Streetlights dimly illuminated the corners. Still, I was very conscious of the darkness. A couple of times I thought I heard footsteps behind me, but when I stopped to listen, I heard nothing except my own breath.

At last I rounded the windowless corner of the Armageddon Institute, as we called it – we had no idea what it manufactured, although trucks rumbled in and out of the gates all day. The Keihin-Tohoku tracks glimmered through a chink of fence at the end of the street. I ducked into a tiny cul-de-sac, leapt up a flight of steps flanked by potted trees, and rang the bell.

Tad opened the door. "Oh boy. We'd pretty much given up on you for tonight."

I smiled weakly and stooped to untie my sneakers.

"That's Shanti, is it?" Joaquin appeared at the end of the hall. "You have something to say to me? Let's hear it." He slouched against the jamb of the door. "Although I have to tell you that your childish behavior really pisses me off!"

The relief that had already started to take hold of me soured. If I'd thought about it at all, I'd hoped that a couple of hours of booze and adulation would have put Joaquin in a conciliatory mood. Evidently not. It did him credit, in a roundabout sort of way, that he still felt the need to justify himself, but I no longer wanted to argue with him about the tour or anything else.

"Sorry I ditched the afterparty," I said meekly. "Did it go OK?"

"No thanks to you, it went better than OK! Didn't it, Tad?"

Joaquin was still blocking the entrance to the dining-room, so I hung a left into the kitchen. Herbs on the windowsills, pots hanging from the undersides of the cabinets, appliances crowding the counters, dishes soaking in the sink – the comfortably chaotic ambiance made it feel like one of those kitchens that someone has been adding to for twenty or thirty years. In fact the clutter was all Nina's. She and Joaquin had been living here with Tad and his father for almost three years now, their rent in abeyance the last time I checked, still surfing the collapsing wavefront of their personal charm. Tad's father worked nights as a taxi driver. He wasn't home right now, judging by the strains of King Crimson yowling from the boombox on top of the fridge.

Nina, bless her, never objected to me at any hour of the day or night. Brushing back a strand of her short blond hair, she looked up from the textbook she was highlighting at the table. "How about a coffee, Shanti?"

"Lovely, I'll fix it." But she was at the sink before me, filling the electric urn.

Tad sat down at the table and flipped the pages of her textbook, blatantly eavesdropping.

I edged up beside Nina and whispered, "Is Joaquin really mad? Because I'm not. I still don't think the tour's a good idea, but…"

"I *told* him we should have held a vote," Nina said, which was as close to criticizing Joaquin as she'd ever get.

"Shanti, here's your money," Joaquin said entering the kitchen. He handed me an envelope. I stuck it in the back pocket of my jeans.

"One of these days I'll break even."

"Count it. You have three thousand yen in profit there. I didn't charge you for anything we ate or drank at the afterparty, although I should have." Joaquin sat down at the table, pushed his arms out before him, and yawned. "Cherie, I'll have some of that. We have a lot of important decisions to make, and not much time left to make them. The travel arrangements still need to be finalized…"

"We'll have to rent a bus at this rate," Tad said. "The latest addition to the lineup is Chiharu," he told me. "Gen's girlfriend."

"His ex," Nina said, trying to soften the blow for me.

"She came to the afterparty and played some of her new songs," Joaquin said. He grinned at me. He was still drunk. "I think in future I'll hold all my auditions at izakayas! The material is catchy and it's only guitar and vocal, so it will be easy to produce. Maybe a maxi-single… Of course, we'll have to see how it holds up to the audiences on tour."

"And whether she can afford your fees," I said. In his incarnation as Cold Coeur Productions, Joaquin fleeced wannabes to pay for Cold Coeur Records mastering and manufacturing.

Joaquin chuckled. "I'm fond of Japanese girls. They never quibble about money!"

Nothing I could do to soften that blow for Nina.

"In fact, I'd like to substitute Chiharu for Shanti on tour." Joaquin's bloodshot eyes gleamed. "But unfortunately it's impractical. Unless, Shanti, you want to stay behind?"

I dropped into French. "You know what? I was dead set against this tour. And I still think there is no way we're not going to end up in the red, and that's all right for you, because you'll make it back by charging Kinderbox and Chiharu for PR and marketing and God knows what else—"

"Naoya and the others are very excited about it, and without them, you're quite right, we couldn't do it. Let me tell you about a concept called economies of scale." Joaquin stood up.

"Joaquin, I'm not finished!"

"I need to smoke if I have to listen to you. Tad?"

"Sorry, I'm all out."

"I think I've got enough for one jay." Nina went to look for her bag and came back with a miniature glassine bag with a few black crumbs in the bottom.

"This is fucking ridiculous." Joaquin rolled a joint the size of a cocktail straw, moved over to the stove, and switched on the fan in the hood. The joint stuck out between his fingers like a skinny white accent acute. "This fucking country."

Tad said nothing. When Joaquin offered him the joint, he shook his head.

"If you're really desperate, you could always go to Center Gai or Roppongi and score off the Iranians," I needled Joaquin. "Then when you get caught, we'll be rid of you for at least ten years."

He extended the joint towards me. "You should," he added, anticipating my refusal. "It might help you to relax!"

I shook my head. Switching back into French, I pointed at the thread of smoke winding into the hood of the stove. "See that, that's what will happen to the money you're spending on this tour. But…" Ned's face loomed in my mind, those bright blue eyes too near together, too close. "Oddly enough," I said through gritted teeth, "I've started to think it would be nice to get out of Tokyo for a while."

"You're such a terrible loser, Shanti!" Joaquin leered at me triumphantly.

"Don't worry," Nina said, hugging me one-armed as she clonked the coffee pot down on the table. "It *will* be fun. Tours always are. The best gig Joaquin ever had in Europe was tour manager for Jemme… twelve countries in two weeks. We had a blast."

She lit a handful of incense sticks. Tad's father probably wouldn't have known the difference between the smell of poor-quality Turkish hash and the smell of Twilight Rose #36, but you can't be too careful.

Curled in my sleeping-bag on Tad's floor, I berated myself.

What's the point of being in a band if you don't want the whole world to hear your songs? I'd been asking myself this fairly obvious question for as long as I'd been involved with music. When I sent Alastair a copy of *Xenophobia,* he'd made all the right noises, but I knew it had given him sleepless nights, and he was right.

I should have ditched Gorot a long time ago. But I'd got pretty good at reassuring myself, and one way and another, I just hadn't been able to tear myself away.

I couldn't tell Alastair that Ned had found me, and it was all my own fault. I *couldn't.* Somehow, I'd have to contain this catastrophe so that he never found out.

I managed to go to sleep, but I kept waking up, jolted by glimpses of a figure standing motionless outside the Armageddon Institute, watching the house through the hours of darkness. It grew light outside, and I opened my eyes on rainbows: Tad had hung a geodesic prism in the window of his room, so that the morning sun filled the room with streaks of color. But when I fell asleep again, it was still night.

Around ten o'clock, my nightmares drove me out of my sleeping-bag. I took a shower, and was making coffee when Tad's father wandered into the kitchen with a pair of garden shears in his hand. Mr Kuroiwa lived in the annexe at the back of the house. At some point, Joaquin and Nina had edged him out of the master bedroom upstairs, either by design or because they weren't culturally equipped to deal with his politeness. A tolerant man with a quiet sense of humor, Mr Kuroiwa worked for thirty years at the same company until the lifetime employment system turned out not to be. Now he spent the same ten, twelve hours at a stretch behind the wheel of his taxi. He was also a racegoer and a heavy bettor, which made me feel less guilty, for some reason, about taking advantage of his kindness. I bobbed my head. "Good morning, Kuroiwa-san."

"Morning," he greeted me. I suspected he didn't know my name. "Going out to prune the azaleas. Spring wind's blowing. That old plum tree should be blooming any time now."

I hadn't noticed, but the windows over the sink were rattling in their frames, and the branches of the plum tree in the fun-size garden leapt in the sunlight. They looked bare, but I believed him, and for an instant I could almost believe that it mattered.

As soon as the door closed behind him, I went to get my coat. We'd used up the bread on a midnight snack of fried-egg sandwiches. I'd nip out and buy some before the others came down for breakfast.

The wind caught me on the doorstep. It seemed to toss the pale clear sunshine around the cul-de-sac. Mr Kuroiwa was right, spring was coming. The sky had a hint of color in it, and the polluted city air smelt almost fresh. I bounced down the alley and around the corner.

"Shanti."

Ned pushed off from the wall of the Armageddon Institute, almost exactly where I'd seen him in my dreams. My grip on reality seemed to falter. "Jesus Christ, how long have you been out here?"

"Half an hour?" He gave me a hangdog grin. "I was going to knock on the door, but I thought I'd give it a bit longer. Didn't want to wake up the neighborhood."

The red and white parka was the same as yesterday, but he'd changed his jeans from blue to black and he looked like he'd had a better night's sleep than I had.

"Wasn't positive I had the right house, anyway," he admitted, looking around at the variegated palisades of shrubbery. "They don't go in for street numbers, do they?"

Of course, he needn't have followed me last night. He could have taken Gorot's mailing address from our website and worked it out with a map. Finding any given address in Tokyo was a challenge even for natives… but Ned was nothing if not dogged, was he? A third possibility occurred to me: he could have followed me last night, returned to his friends' house in Nakano by taxi, and then come back.

I kept walking on autopilot. Ned kept pace with me. "Heading home? I thought we might hang out today. We could do some of the tourist spots. I reckon you've never been to Tokyo Tower, have you? Gav and Mike haven't, and they've been here for years."

I went into Family Mart and bought a loaf of sliced Pasco while Ned wandered up and down the aisles, asking me what things were. As we reemerged into the sunlight I said brightly, "I might as well let you know, my schedule is pretty crazy. We've got a rehearsal in a couple of hours."

"You know, it's funny," Ned said after a moment. "Of all the things I thought you might have turned out to be, *rock star* wasn't even on the list."

"It still isn't," I said.

Short of an outright confrontation, I couldn't stop him from following me back to the house. Mr Kuroiwa squatted over his pot plants beside the steps, a cigarette hanging from his mouth. He greeted us without surprise. He was used to uncouth strangers turning up at all hours. But Ned couldn't have known that, so maybe it encouraged him. He didn't ask me whether he could come in. He just did it.

"Shoes off, Ned," I said between my teeth.

"Whoops. I was forgetting."

Oddly, he seemed bigger and clumsier with his shoes off – or it might just have been that he was too big for the Kuroiwas' dining-room, which was almost entirely taken up by a table covered with books, junk mail, Gorot flyers, sheet music, CDs, magazines, pencil diagrams on scrap paper, ashtrays, Joaquin's and Tad's laptops, and the dismantled guts of an effector that Joaquin had been working on last night in hopes of selling it online. I went into the kitchen and dropped the bread in its Family Mart bag on the counter. "Well, do you want some coffee?" I said ungraciously.

Tad came into the kitchen with a towel knotted over his hair. "Good morning," he said, staring. Tad spoke English almost as well as Joaquin, with an equally heavy, but very different accent: *Guu' moningu.*

"Ned," I said, "this is the guy whose house you're in."

Ned surged forward to give Tad a high five. "I saw your show last night, man. You were fucking fantastic."

"Always helps when we get a good crowd." Tad tossed his towel onto a chair and returned Ned's high five, grinning. "First time you've seen us?"

"First time I've seen Shanti in sixteen years."

"No way!"

Gritting my teeth, I explained that we'd been childhood friends. *Friends* was a stretch, of course. How had Ned maneuvered me into covering up for him like this?

"Sixteen years," Tad marvelled. "Did you recognise her easily?"

"Oh, she hasn't changed at all."

"So what was she like as a child?" Tad gestured Ned to a chair and sat down across from him.

"Well, she was into a bit of everything, I'd say. Of all things, it never would have occurred to me she'd become a rock star!" Ned cleared his throat. "I don't mind saying I was fucking impressed last night. You've got an aura of greatness. I could tell you believe in yourselves."

I choked on my coffee. I was twenty-nine, and the only thing I believed in was the brutality of the world and the music industry in particular. Tad was two years older than me, a veteran of the Tokyo indie rock scene, but he was vulnerable to flattery. I saw his social grin turning real, and knew exactly what was coming next. "I used to be in Fuct Of Life. You haven't heard of us, but we opened for Saxon, Fastway, such dinosaurs... Well, that was ten years ago. Metal isn't so popular anymore. But Gorot isn't metal. We're pure rock 'n' roll."

"Yeah, man," Ned said, grinning. "Yeah."

When Joaquin and Nina came downstairs I steeled myself to trot out the childhood-friends line again, but Tad assumed the responsibility of introducing Ned to them, and he did it so well that Nina jumped to the conclusion that Ned was to be made to feel at home, while Joaquin grunted and ignored him. We ate breakfast and migrated into the dining-room. Joaquin and Tad multitasked on their laptops while Nina told Ned about teaching English in Japan. I could see that it was nice for her to have a non-musician to talk to for a change. I contributed a few English-teaching anecdotes of my own, swilling coffee to counteract the sense of helplessness that was making me feel sleepy.

At noon Shingo, our drummer, sloped in. By now Ned had worked himself so adeptly into the ambiance that his presence passed without comment. Shingo eyed me. "What happened to you last night?"

"She had a diva moment," Joaquin answered for me. "But she's over it now."

"Entirely reconciled to the inevitable," I said with a poker face. "While reserving the right to say I told you so."

Shingo laughed and stretched his legs out. "So, any further word from Hori-kun?"

Tad shook his head. "I'm emailing Naoya now."

Naoya Kobayashi had been in Fuct Of Life with Tad, back when dinosaurs walked the earth. He'd also been the vocalist in Ravisher, the first band that Joaquin and Tad started together, and the lead guitarist in Dufek Intrusion, the second one. Finally he'd left to start his own band, citing creative differences with Joaquin: the stuff they'd been doing was too upbeat for his tastes. That hadn't stopped him from persuading Joaquin to produce Kinderbox for free, though, and they'd released their album on Cold Coeur Records.

"Hori-kun is their drummer," Nina explained to Ned. "He's afraid if he comes on tour with us, he might lose his job."

"Ha," Tad said. "And if he lose, he never gets another one." Hori-kun was Joaquin's hash dealer, and an enthusiastic consumer of his own product.

"Anyway, Shingo said he'll double for him if he can't come. He's a total star, aren't you, Miya-chan?"

"Musically, I've wanted to dispense with Hori-kun for some time," Joaquin said. "But he's so useful in other ways!" I watched Ned. He was faking amusement, but he didn't seem to know what Joaquin was talking about. "But I'm also thinking about the driving," Joaquin added more seriously. "If Hori-kun doesn't come, that's one less person with a license. And we have too few drivers as it is."

"I just want to know whether I have to learn all their songs or not," muttered Shingo. Seeing Tad's Lucky Strikes on the table, he took one and lit up. I dug my fingernails into the seams of my jeans.

"If you're needing a driver, I might be able to help you out." Ned spoke up. "I've got my international license."

I sat bolt upright.

"We aren't hiring," said Joaquin, to my unspeakable relief. Chuckling, he added, "If you're content to do it for free, then by all means, let's talk!"

"Sure, I wouldn't expect a penny. I'd do it for the chance to see the country. What kind of a rig do you have?"

My stomach twisted, coffee-sour. "Do we really need another driver?" I said in French. "You, Tad, Nina – "

"It's me, Tad, Shingo, and Naoya only," Joaquin said, sticking to English. "Nina failed her Japanese driver's license test."

"I screwed up," Nina confirmed with a brave smile, and I couldn't say anything, because that happened to her sometimes: she had these periodic, inexplicable lapses.

"Yes, they say even a corpse can pass it, but she failed. Heh! So we're looking at four drivers for two vans, and all of us must perform every night. Have you ever tried to play at your best after driving for five hours? It's not pleasant. We could use a roadie, in fact." Now Joaquin spoke directly to Ned. "We have two vans: one of them fairly new, that belongs to the other band that will be travelling with us; the other one – it's mine – fairly shit."

"I've driven a decommissioned army bus across the Himalayas," Ned said proudly. "And when I say decommissioned, there was a reason for that. I had to take the entire engine to pieces several times before we reached Nepal."

Nina giggled. "That sounds like ours! We lived in a bus for a while. In Germany. We called it The Autobahn Racer."

"Ours was just called This Fucking Thing."

"It's a very attractive offer." Joaquin's voice seemed to come from a distance, and his frowning face might have been painted with crushed jewels on wood. "But we're driving up to Hokkaido the day after tomorrow. And we'll be on the road for ten days. Are you sure you can commit for that long? Don't you have other plans?"

"Nothing I can't reschedule!" Ned chuckled.

I said, "But Ned! What about your business on Koh Samui?"

His brows flexed in annoyance, then smoothed out again. "I've a business partner. Jeremy Loh, he's half Chinese. I'd trust him with my wife if I was married. He'll look after my projects for me. Don't you worry, when I make a promise, I keep it."

"On that basis I can't say yes, but I can't say no, either." Joaquin frowned and tapped a rhythm on a back issue of *Voicer,* one of the freezines where we advertised. Tap, tap, *and he played upon the table, and his name was Aiken Drum!* I shivered. Abruptly Joaquin said, "Where's Gen? Fuck, it's twelve o'clock already, and I have to be in Shinjuku at three."

Joaquin worked part-time as a sound engineer at Oasis, a club in

Shinjuku where Gorot performed once a month. The gig paid peanuts, but we cherished it.

"Somebody call Gen," Joaquin ordered, looking at me. "In the meantime, since our guitarist is not here, we can't rehearse, so I'll show you the van, Ned."

Unwilling to let them out of my sight, I trailed them out of the house and around the corner, away from Family Mart and the little neighborhood park. Joaquin had rented a space in a privately owned four-car parking lot, its corrugated iron roof festooned in dead kudzu. From a distance I watched him reverse the van into the street. All four men looked under the hood, then squatted to peer under the chassis. They made a comical group. Ned seemed to take up as much space as the other three put together, Shingo was equally tall but half as bulky, Tad was a brown wisp. Average them out and you got Joaquin, with his medium build and medium brown hair sticking up in a dozen cowlicks. From all the way down the street I could hear him lecturing Ned about the broken heater, the possibly defective steering column, and whatever other problems had manifested recently.

Gen's cell phone rang in my ear. "Moshi mosh'!"

"It's me. Did you forget you were supposed to be here at noon?"

He apologized breathlessly. "I'll be there in fifteen minutes. You guys go ahead and start without me."

He knew we couldn't start without him, but he persisted in acting as if he was dispensable, because the alternative would have been to act his age. "Gen," I said rapidly, "just to warn you before you walk into a crazy situation. This guy I know from Ireland turned up at the house this morning, and he's trying to get himself taken on as our roadie. I… Gen? Hello? Hello?" He'd hung up on me.

The van crawled past me with Joaquin at the wheel.

"Ned thinks he can fix the heater right now," said Tad, returning on foot.

"I wonder what it feels like to have that much time on your hands," Shingo said.

"Speaking of which, Miya-chan," I said. "How are you swinging the time off? Tad's going to quit his job…" I still thought that was a mistake, but at least Tad was only a temp in the hot-desk realm of IT, and he could easily get another job. Shingo was a fully fledged salaryman. *"You're* not quitting your job, are you?"

"I'm going to take my legally mandated two weeks of vacation time per year," Shingo said with mingled pride and defiance.

"Will they let you?"

"Can't stop me. I didn't take any vacation days last year, and the last time I called in sick was the twentieth century."

The van plugged the cul-de-sac so neatly that we had to squeeze past it to reach the house.

"Tools," shouted Ned self-importantly from underneath the dashboard. "I need a Phillips, an all-purpose wrench, and a pair of pliers."

"We've got tools in the studio, but they won't be the right size. I'll ask my dad," Tad said. "It'll give him something to do while we rehearse."

We'd tried at first to stay out of the studio when Tad's father was at home, but this rule had inevitably fallen by the wayside. We rehearsed with everything plugged in but turned down. Shingo played with three towels stuffed into the bass drum and muffle rings on the toms and snare. Thanks to Joaquin and Tad's DIY soundproofing, you could hardly hear us outside the house. When we were cooking in the studio late at night, we resorted to headphones and a set of electronic drum pads, and when we were recording, we just cranked it up as loud as necessary and crossed our fingers.

"I've got an idea for a new song," Joaquin said.

"We just put out a new album!" I wailed.

"Well, I haven't worked it out yet, but here's the basic idea…"

I'd never known anyone who could touch Joaquin as a songwriter. He might have become a one-man band like Trent Reznor, or just another Pro Tools whiz, alchemizing bands that sucked live. But with this band the energy came from our synchronicity, and what worked live worked equally well in the studio. Nowadays, Joaquin often just dumped his ideas on us and let the chemistry take over.

Within the infamously narrow specs of the four-minute rock song, there are only so many ways you can flip the script. Gorot had two tempos, fast and heavy or slow and bluesy. This wasn't either, or rather it would be both. Joaquin's new idea involved an inversion that put the chorus first, in the form of an intro where we all had to come in at once, behind the beat. The verse was a simple turnaround played by Joaquin and Tad, with a final B flat chord creating the expectation of a key change. Then Gen and Shingo would burst in and annihilate the key altogether. The song would explode like a dirty bomb, shattering the beat into a maelstrom of guitar noise, where I found a long note like a plutonium contrail in the sky.

But my voice wasn't cooperating. All that talking after the gig last night, followed by a crying fit, followed by more talking: a recipe for cranky vocal cords. I couldn't concentrate, either, for thinking about Ned, who still hadn't left the house, as far as I knew. Could he find out anything from Nina to use against me? I blamed the late night I'd had.

"Diva diva," said Joaquin.

"Fuck youuu," I sang, high C.

We kept at it for a while after Joaquin went off to work, but there was a limit to how much we could do without inadvertently starting to memorize our mistakes. At last Gen said he had to go.

"Oh God, what time is it?" I croaked. The studio had no windows, or rather Tad and Joaquin had covered its one window with acoustic foam.

"The Celeste Trio is playing Newport Café at six thirty." Gen zipped his guitar away and unplugged his stomp box.

I thought fast. "Can I come?"

"You don't like jazz," Tad said.

"Yes, I do—" if the alternative was leaving here with Ned. I couldn't very well stay over *again*. Christ, Tad might invite *Ned* to stay over, they'd got on so well!

We found Ned talking to Nina in the kitchen. "Zen and the art of van maintenance," she giggled. "He fixed the heater. A miracle."

"It was only the wiring," said Ned modestly.

"Tell you what Shanti, let's ask him along," said Gen. He switched into English. "Ned-san, do you like to hearing jazz?"

Of course Ned did.

With tears of frustration in my eyes, I darted back upstairs and stuffed my overnight things into my bag. Tad appeared in the doorway. "Don't forget your hatbox. It's downstairs by the front door." I could see he was thinking about coming with us, but I didn't encourage him.

Twilight had deepened into windy darkness by the time we plodded up the steps into neon twilight and a swarm of touts, tourists, club kids, US servicemen, and prostitutes. There's Roppongi for promiscuous party people; there's Roppongi for big spenders; there's Roppongi for ravers; and showing through the cracks, there's Roppongi for you and me. We climbed a flight of outdoor stairs to Newport Cafe, a landmark that dated back to the Occupation. Gen plus guest could get in for free. To my disgust, he offered to pay for Ned, who had the grace to refuse.

This place attracted a certain segment of the expat community, older English teachers and the less wholesome element of the financial crowd. Ned perked up immediately at the sound of English. I remembered how I used to flag after a long day of listening to incomprehensible conversations, and how long it had taken me to reach the point where I noticed other gaijins instead of noticing when there weren't any other gaijins. Would Japan defeat Ned for me, just by being so damn Japanese? It seemed like a lot to hope for, I acknowledged to myself as I edged through the crowd, following Gen and his gig bag.

"Gen! I thought *I* was late! Hi Shanti, long time no see." Chiharu Ota shimmered out of the crowd, fey in a lace dress and yeti boots. Gen's girlfriend – his ex? Not even a month ago I'd been keeping him company while he got drunk and groaned that she was neurotic, she was driving him crazy, he wouldn't even want her back. Now here she was again… and now I understood why he'd been reluctant to let me come tonight, and why he'd invited Ned. *For me.*

Meanwhile, Ned had bottled off in the direction of the bar.

"So Chiharu, I hear you're coming on tour with us!" I gushed. "I can't wait to hear your new material!"

She ducked her head. "It's really personal. I'm kind of shy about getting on stage with it. But you have to put your heart into it, or what's the point, right?"

Onstage, the Celeste Trio was twiddling its way through some number that I could identify only as jazz. The paunchy man in his late fifties, seated on the central stool with a guitar on his knee, in a paisley shirt and jeans, with wavy black hair floating to his shoulders from either side of his bald spot, was Gen's father. Though he was a pro, Hiroyuki Tajitsu had never lifted a finger to further Gen's musical career. I knew how I felt about that, and now I wondered how Chiharu felt about it.

I went to the bar and ordered a glass of white wine. Ned had drifted into a corner. "Come on up front," I shouted. He shook his head and I rejoined Gen and Chiharu at the side of the stage, but I couldn't relax, much less share their absorption in the music. I kept glancing over my shoulder to check what Ned was up to.

Talking to a giraffe-faced white guy in a suit was what, the first time I looked.

Talking to a black guy with scraggly dreadlocks was what, the second time.

Half a tune later I looked around again. Now Ned was talking to a pair of fat white girls who seemed to be Scraggly Dreads's friends.

"Gen. Look."

Gen looked and laughed. "He's getting some action!" He shook his head in exaggerated admiration.

"Is that your friend from Ireland?" Chiharu squealed. "He's gorgeous!"

"Gorgeous? *Ned?"* I peered through the crowd, trying to see Ned objectively instead of as a practical joke superimposed on the skinny little boy I used to know. He and Scraggly Dreads appeared to be exchanging phone numbers. "What is he up to," I breathed.

"Maybe it's something to do with his business in Thailand," Gen said. "Maybe he's lining them up as renters."

"He doesn't rent houses. He builds them."

"I thought he said he rents them out, too, on behalf of the owners when they're not there."

I summoned a smile. "OK, forget it."

Gen did a Japanese shrug, raising his chin sideways and then looking away from me. I realized he was playing dumb to punish me for Chiharu's comment about Ned. It wasn't fair - when I'd lived through shit he couldn't even imagine! I'd told him parts of it, and he'd barely reacted at all, as if he thought I was trying to impress him.

Ned rolled up through the crowd. "Not bad!" He looked pleased with himself. "Not a bad place at all, this, is it? Got a friendly atmosphere."

I gritted my teeth. He could just have asked this morning, and Joaquin would have given him Hori-kun's phone number. But he'd been on his best behavior - and now he was letting his hair down. In the middle of fucking Roppongi.

When Hiroyuki Tajitsu came offstage, we converged on him, but he brushed our congratulations aside. "Hello, Chiharu. Gen, I'll give you a ride home."

Gen shuffled his feet and muttered, "Can't. I mean, Chiharu needs a ride, too."

Where to? The Tajitsus lived in Yokohama, and the last I heard, Chiharu lived on the opposite side of the city, out in the wilds of Saitama prefecture.

"Oh, all right," Hiroyuki Tajitsu said. "Come on then, both of you. I'm parked in Nishi-Azabu."

"See you soon, Shanti!" Chiharu trilled. Gen didn't look at me.

My temples throbbed as they vanished out of the door. The sound system boomed. Keep on rockin' in the free world...

"Cool, cool. So how did you hook up with Joaquin and the guys in the first place?" Ned shouted. "Did you know them before you came to Tokyo?"

"No, I got to know everyone through Tad," I said listlessly. "I came here with a teaching job at one of the big chain schools. Tad was in one of my classes."

"Tad was taking English classes? But his English is perfect!"

"Yeah, he didn't really need to be there. But remember, this was four years ago..."

"My man! Shanti, this is - this is Geoff." Ned introduced the giraffe in a grey suit, who had desperate eyes and bad breath. "He's lived here for five years, but he doesn't speak Japanese. I told him about you. Gotta hear her… Say something, Shanti, go on!"

"So what is it, hash or speed? Not smack, I hope," I said in Japanese, smiling.

By the time we finally emerged into the street, I'd passed into a sort of stupor, mentally exhausted by the effort of holding my act together. "Here." I scrabbled in my bag. "Let me pay you for those drinks."

Ned rolled his eyes. "I'm not *that* cheap. Your shout next time."

Whatever he wanted from me, I thought for the umpteenth time, it wasn't money.

"Well, I guess I'll see you on Friday," I said when we reached one of the aboveground entrances to the station.

Ned stood below me on the first step. Girls in anklebreaker boots eddied around him and down the stairs, shrieking. "There's a whole week until then." He raised his face with a grin, looking exactly as he had at twelve, when he would swallow some horrible insult from Alastair with a smile that denied it: *I'm all right, so everything's all right!* "We could do something together tomorrow, or Tuesday. You don't have a rehearsal *every* day, do you?"

"Pretty much," I said. In reality, we'd probably schedule at least one weeknight rehearsal this week, although I foresaw that we'd do less rehearsing than arguing over the set list for our shows.

"Ah then, you can afford to skip one! I'd never live it down if I went home without seeing anything: Tokyo Tower, the Ginza, the Imperial Palace… "

Was he incapable of sightseeing on his own? Well, actually, I thought, watching his eyeballs jerk in a vain attempt to make sense of the crowds, he might be. "Sorry," I said. "I've got to work. But what about your friends? Gavin and Matt - uh, Mike? Couldn't they show you around?"

"They're already putting me up. I can't really ask them…" Ned stepped out of the way of a boisterous party of gaijins. "To be honest, I don't give a shit about Tokyo Tower. I came here to see you." His smile was rueful, but the blue eyes sparkled edgily.

It was up to me now to steer us out of danger, and the only way I could think of to do that was to give in and agree to hang out with him tomorrow, which was what he wanted. I took a couple of steps backwards, telling myself that I couldn't just walk away from him. As I turned on my heel, I confronted baggy jeans, an oversized down jacket, a gold-filled smile: the face of salvation.

"Hey sister how you doing, check it out. Dub Paradise! One free drink."

"We've still got an hour before the last train," I shrieked. "Lead the way, brother!"

There was nothing sleazy about Dub Paradise, a hole in the wall with a shitty sound system held together by duct tape and devil-may-care African attitude. The DJ mixed dancehall tracks with commercial rap; cornrowed Japanese girls danced with homeboys from the US naval bases. I gyrated in front of the speakers. When a tall black man invaded my space, I grinned at him, and moments later we were dancing together. I sneaked a glance at Ned, hoping he was impressed by my carefree display.

My steps faltered. He was sitting at the bar, and he hadn't rearranged his features quickly enough to prevent me from seeing the look on his face. It wasn't hatred. It was a mixture of fascination and disgust. I'd occasionally seen a similar look on the faces of people standing near the stage at our shows. *What a mess that girl is,* that look said. *Someone should put her out of her misery, quick.*

I dreamed I was locked in my apartment. I got up and ran to the front door, but no matter which way I turned the knob, no matter how hard I shook the door, it wouldn't open.

In dreams there's always a failsafe. You get too scared and you automatically wake up.

If only it were the same in real life.

In the spring of 1989, Alastair had installed a lock on his bedroom door. *Two* locks, one on the inside and one on the outside. Crummy little bolts like the ones on toilet stalls, they'd never have held up to a battering. Alastair had just been making a point: he was fifteen and he wanted to be left alone. So why had he needed a lock on the outside of the door, too? Answer: it was Nigel-bait. By that time, the two of them had been communicating in a code of silences and veiled insults, and according to Alastair's interpretation of the rules of the game, installing a lock on the outside of his door was the equivalent of giving Nigel a free throw. If Nigel had taken the opportunity to lock him in, that would have translated into a moral victory for Alastair.

Unfortunately, Alastair had the rules of the game all wrong.

It wasn't a game.

It was a war.

Don't forget about the sea, don't forget about the light on the... on the waves...

No. Could I get another syllable in there? I backtracked to 00:40 and listened again to the scratch vocal that I'd recorded for the rough mix. At 00:52 I pulled my headphones down around my neck and scribbled: *Don't forget about the light on the breakers,* and I already had the next bit—

The airplane's wheels bounced on the runway.

Brain spinning like a paused CD, I stuffed my gear into my bag. A flight attendant's voice welcomed us to Sapporo.

It eats at you, it claws at you, takes its due in flesh!

This was the song Joaquin had started writing on the day Ned first came to Tad's house. Sinisterly emphatic, punctuated by bursts of feedback-corrupted fury that would startle you out of your skin if you weren't ready for them. It eschewed all the emotional shorthand of the genre. Joaquin wanted to use it as our encore on tour: proof that we were capable of outlandish originality, a taste of where we might be going in the future.

Gen differed. He thought our encore should be "Guardian Angel," the last track on *U-Turn Day,* a sizzler with a long guitar break that gave him room to show off. In the end he'd got his way, but not because Joaquin had changed his mind… just because I hadn't written any lyrics for the other song yet. I knew the others thought I'd deliberately abetted Gen's cause. The irony was that I hadn't. I agreed with Joaquin that this earpopping oddity left "Guardian Angel" in the dust, and if I could have met the deadline, I would have. I'd been trying all week, but strangely enough, my concentration wasn't there.

It gave me some bitter satisfaction that inspiration had finally struck on the very day we left for Hokkaido. But as we shuffled down the corridor to the baggage claim, all the music drained out of my mind, leaving nothing but thoughts of Ned.

I grabbed my suitcase off the belt. It practically pulled my arm off. I'd limited myself to one hat - my electric blue Panama - and I'd carried my hatbox as hand luggage. But I'd had to check the suitcase that contained the eight separate outfits I'd planned around the hat, or rather seven of them, because I was wearing the first one: a swirly gold satin skirt with my cowboy boots and a blousy grey camisole. I had a sweater as well as my coat on top for warmth.

Chiharu lifted her guitar case off the belt. Her clothes all fit in one small rucksack. In an Indian cotton skirt over jeans and a black sweatshirt with ANARCHYISM written in Gothic script along the back hem, she looked like the zeitgeist itself beamed down to earth amidst the dowdy provincials and business travelers.

"Well, it looks like no one's luggage has gone missing," said Nina. "I just talked to Joaquin. He's running late. But it would be a hassle for him to park, so shall we go outside?"

Musicians are like goats: the more of them you put together, the harder it is to get them moving in the right direction. Around the Kinderbox boys, Tad and Shingo tended to forget they were supposed to be responsible adults, and Gen had no sense of responsibility to begin with. Nina and I herded them out of the baggage claim area, past the deserted customs desks, and through the arrivals lobby, managing not to lose anyone to the souvenir shops selling Royce chocolates and everything that could be printed with the image of a black bear. Outdoors, the air bit into my throat like raw spirits.

"Smells like New York," said Nina, zipping up her coat.

"Yeah," I said. "Snow."

No snow was falling, but the blinding grey sky beyond the concrete overhang presaged it.

The smokers had time for a cigarette before the van swooped up to the curb. Joaquin was alone. I waited for him to kiss Nina, but he barely spared her a glance, chivvying us into the van, making us take our shoes off on the step. Overlapping offcuts of dark red carpet covered the metal floor, and the tinted windows had been fitted with curtains. This was Ned's doing, Joaquin said. But where was Ned?

Shingo and his long legs got the front seat. The rest of us had to sit on top of our bags and each other. I could have sworn the engine was straining. The others were practically weeping with hilarity. Even Gen, who normally held aloof from our silliness, wondered aloud whether there wasn't some legal limit on the number of people you could pack into a Hi-Ace Custom.

"Listen! It's now three o'clock," Joaquin shouted. "The staff of Klub Kounterweight will be there at four. The doors open at six; Chiharu is on at six thirty. We'll go straight to the club. Ned, Naoya, and Yves are there already. Any questions?"

"What's the advance sales situation?" said Shingo. As he was sitting next to Joaquin, he probably thought the rest of us wouldn't hear. I was right behind them, however.

"Don't ask," said Joaquin, grimacing.

I scrutinized what I could see of his face in the rearview mirror. Horizontal creases rucked his forehead, and his eyes were red-rimmed. For the last month he'd been negotiating with venues, having flyers printed and shipped, arranging media spots, liaising with the local acts who were to open for us at some of our dates, settling our differences over the artwork for *U-Turn Day,* sitting in on the mastering process at Grand Rocks in Akasaka, haggling with the manufacturers, and fine-tuning the split between label funds and our tour budget. To top it all off, he'd just driven from Tokyo to Sapporo with no one but Ned to spell him. Yeah, I'd say he was under pressure.

Leafless trees lined the highway on both sides. Dirty ice choked the black brooks trickling along creases in the snow. We rolled through a northern version of the same strip mall you can find anywhere in Japan: pachinko parlors, car dealerships, Sports Depo, Toyotires, Sega World, Book Off, Fish Land, Seiyu, and dozens of sprawling ramen restaurants, every parking lot harboring a flotilla of new cars. White motes swirled past the windows of the van. It was the first time I'd seen snow since my last Christmas in Boston, and it amplified my apprehension. Bad weather limits your options.

By the time we got into Sapporo, it was snowing heavily, the eddies blowing horizontally down the grid streets between the highrises. Unlike in Tokyo, where sidewalks blossom with umbrellas at the first hint of a drizzle, people were trudging along with their heads bare to the snow. Joaquin pulled the van into a deep dead end. There was a McDonald's and a Marui department store on the same block. We were downtown.

Ned emerged from a doorway and greeted each person to scramble out of the van with a grin and a punch on the shoulder (for the boys) or a flirtatious stagger of mock emotion (for Nina and Chiharu). My limbs were inexplicably heavy; I felt drowsy. I waited in the van for Ned to follow the others upstairs. He didn't. Reluctantly, I got out.

Not even an hour into the tour, and I was already alone with him.

Snow crystals glittered on Ned's hair. Joaquin had passed him the van keys, and he bounced them in his palm. "Told you, when I make a promise, I keep it."

"Look at this snow," I said. "I've never seen anything like it. It doesn't stick. It doesn't even seem to hit the ground. It just drifts around and around."

"Like us," said Ned.

"Oh God," I said.

His mouth tightened. Steadily, he said, "So how was your flight?"

"Fine," I said. "Listen: what do you think of this?" I felt as if I had to give him something to appease him, and all I had was a song. "No one else has heard this one yet." Clicking my fingers and swaying my hips, I sang, "It eats at you, it claws at you, takes its due in flesh! It lives in you, consumes you, but this is for the best. This game was never meant to be fair! OK? That's the chorus. This is the first verse. Don't forget that moment, that special moment, don't forget that wonderful light in your eyes…"

"'This game was never meant to be fair.' What's that supposed to mean, then?"

I squinted up into the snow, hoping for a new flash of inspiration, a wholly formed and plausible lie. But the sky was as blank as the inside of my head.

I couldn't do anything right. I missed several cues during soundcheck. Joaquin shouted at me, and I shouted back at him until shame overcame me. The staff of Klub Kounterweight were watching us: the manager, the sound engineer, the DJ, and a bartender. I forced myself to apologize to Joaquin. "Let's run through it again." We had to be perfect, or if we couldn't manage that, we at least had to be polite. In America, people take you more seriously if you yell at them every so often. In Japan, you keep a lid on your emotions if it kills you. When we were stressed out, Joaquin and I sometimes forgot to play the game their way. But this wasn't Tokyo, where you can get away with anything. This was Hokkaido, where anything can happen.

Klub Kounterweight's system was a hodgepodge of ancient Marshall stacks and newish Yamaha cabinets that we had to shift around in an attempt to control spillage from the stage. The mixing board was a toy in cracked beige plastic housing with minimal functionality. Given the same budget, I'd have invested in a 24 channel mixer instead of cabinets powerful enough to compete with the FOH speakers, but that would have made no sense for a place like this. The graffiti on the concrete walls commemorated bands such as God's Guts and A Piece Of Shit. The bartender had spiky blond hair and padlocks dangling from his earlobes. The sound engineer had probably pushed all the sliders up to the top of the mixing board sometime last century and left them there.

But one of the nice things about sharing a bill with Kinderbox was that Naoya, who knew his channel fader from his parametric equalizer, could mix our set, and Joaquin could mix their set and Chiharu's. It saved us a bit of money, too. We'd rented Klub Kounterweight outright. We were paying for the bartender, but not the DJ or the sound engineer.

That they were here at all made me wonder if there'd been some misunderstanding, if they were trying to pull a fast one, or if the engineer had come to warn Joaquin about some peculiarity of the board such as that it only worked if you poured vodka on it. I wasn't surprised when Joaquin, organizing a McDonald's expedition after the soundcheck, invited him and the manager along. I waited for Ned to loudly declare how much he was looking forward to a Big Mac, and then said I wasn't hungry.

Thirteen pairs of shoes thudded down the stairs. Left alone with the bartender, I breathed more easily. I wandered over to the merchandise display we'd set up on a folding table and rearranged the stacks of flyers, questionnaires, t-shirts, and CDs. We'd decided against commemorative t-shirts, so there were just the three familiar ones: white with the ice-blue and black Cold Coeur graphic of a heart dripping icicles; yellow with the Kinderbox logo of an exploding teddybear (Naoya's alias was The

Suicide Bomb Bear, and the title of their album was *Suicide Bomb Bear Attack!);* and grey with the Gorot logo in white. The latter was basically the same as our sticker, a stylized version of my own face, which I was already sick of.

I wasn't sick of *U-Turn Day,* in fact I was still desperately in love with it, so I picked up a copy and handled it like a talisman.

1: Propaganda
2: You're No Fun
3: It Doesn't Matter (Genocide)
4: Heartbreak
5: A Drop Of Poison
6: Over Here
7: Kimi Ga Akuyaku [lyrics in Japanese, cowritten by me and Gen]
8: Même Un Baiser [Joaquin had helped me with the lyrics]
9: I Would Die For You
10: Guardian Angel

And the jacket art had come out better than anyone expected. It was a photo of the five of us seated on the sofa in Kuroiwa-san's annexe. The television cabinet intruded on one edge of the picture and the bookshelf on the other. Above our heads, a swirly black *Gorot* obscured the pale brown floral wallpaper. The carpet at our feet was littered with newspapers folded to the racing pages, back numbers of *Gallop,* and betting slips. We all wore jeans and t-shirts, and we were barefoot. Gen, Tad, Joaquin and I lounged on the sofa, with me in the middle, legs casually slung over each other's thighs, heads on shoulders, arms around waists. Shingo sat on the floor at our feet with one of Gen's legs over his shoulder. If you looked closely, you saw that Shingo was holding my left foot in his hand, his fingers interlaced with my toes. We all wore enigmatically tranquil expressions. On his lap Joaquin held a placard drawn with magic marker to resemble a road sign: *U-Turn Day.*

Nina had used up the whole battery of her camera on shots where one or more of us looked uncomfortable or was laughing. It's hard to project enigmatic tranquillity when you're embracing people you'd never normally touch. But in the end, we'd calmed down, and she'd got this shot: all five of us gazing serenely at the viewer, as if it was normal for us to sit around draped all over each other. It had been Joaquin's idea to parody the cliché of band members lounging on a sofa and glowering at the camera. Like most things Gorot, the concept had bloated into a parody of a parody, silly enough to bridge the cultural humor gap or die trying. But what did we have to lose? We were already commercially untouchable.

And now the decision to go through with it was starting to look like the best one we'd ever made. We'd bombed Recoman's distribution network with posters. A couple of days ago, traipsing around the local stores to bribe the staff with freebie stickers and cellphone straps, Tad and I had seen that every single store had chosen to put the poster up. And we'd seen customers walk past it, stop, and actually backtrack to make sure they'd seen what they thought they had. This was in Shibuya. Half by accident, we'd accomplished the impossible. We'd created an image that was shocking people.

We still had a few dozen posters left. I suggested to the bartender that I put one up in the stairwell. He temporized. Admittedly, it wouldn't have gone with the shadowy mug shots that were already there.

"So what kind of a crowd do you normally get in here?" I asked.

"Depends. Local kids. Depends on the band, y'know?"

"It's a nice big space." Translation: it was too big. You'd have to pack forty or fifty punters in here before it felt crowded.

I wandered up to the stage and stood behind the lead mic, visualizing how I would project all the way back to the bar. Then I went back and asked for some hot water.

"No hot water."

I'd wanted to make tea. "OK, a Pernod Classic."

"No pernod."

"Hell." I normally never drank before gigs unless it was pernod (I had a theory that the anise was good for my throat). Alcohol in general dries out the vocal cords. "All right, a vodka tonic."

Everything in Hokkaido seemed, to my Tokyoized eyes, to be slightly oversized, and that turned out to include cocktails. "That'll be six hundred yen," said the bartender.

I blinked. The bar take for the night was ours, and even if it hadn't been, free drinks for the talent were a standard perk. Did he mean to say that the night hadn't technically started yet?

But I hadn't the heart to argue. I handed over the coins and sat down behind the mixing board, nursing my glass. I'd quit smoking a year ago. Now I wanted a cigarette so badly I could taste it.

Chiharu kicked off her set to an audience of us, plus three guys who turned out to be a freezine editor and two of his friends. By the time Gorot went on, the crowd had doubled in size. We were about to perform half a dozen blistering, stomping, life-altering tracks off *U-Turn Day,* plus a couple of highlights from *Xenophobia,* for six people and the void at the back of the club.

I'd been here before, but it never got any easier. To make matters worse, Naoya and Yves, the Kinderbox rhythm guitarist, had turned their amps up, which meant that Gen and Tad had to do the same. They knew better, but no guitarist I ever met could ignore a challenge to his amplification. It's a guy thing. Stuck in between them, I could hardly hear myself, despite my earplugs. Then Naoya, forgetting everything he knew about stage monitoring, boosted the vocals so high in the mix that my mic started emitting squeals of feedback.

Our last number was "You're No Fun." It was the best song on *U-Turn Day;* there was no way we could leave it off the set list this time. "A mediocre novel I've already read! A joke with no punchline except in your head!" Defiantly, I growled the lyrics with all the rasp I could coax out of the small of my back. "A person who should be, should already be dead! You're no fun, no fun."

I strained my eyes to see into the corner where I'd seen him last. He wasn't there. A few seconds later I spotted him in the back of the club. Nina was with him. She'd put down her video camera. They were tangoing. Who'd have thought it? Ned could dance. I couldn't see very well past the lights, but I could see that Nina was all floppy with laughter as he dipped and whirled her.

I'd let myself get distracted. I struggled back into the groove and came in half a bar late.

The silver lining… well, there wasn't one. We might only have attracted seven legit punters, but a handful of Joaquin's indie label contacts and reporters had also turned up. As I wobbled offstage, a girl accosted me. "Great show! You guys have this incredible energy."

"There's an old American saying," I told her. "When all else fails, turn up the volume."

"This is Junko from North Wave 82.5," Joaquin said. "Have you forgotten you're guesting on their indies show with Naoya tonight?"

Onstage, Ned lumbered around with coils of cable looped over his elbows. He was taking this roadie gig seriously.

I'd always been shy of publicity, for reasons that turned out to be good ones. But during the North Wave broadcast, I had a revelation: publicity could be a lot of fun. The DJ seemed genuinely interested in the Cold Coeur story, not just the gaijin angle, and I had a ball with the guest callers. They ended up asking me to record a promo spot after the show. "North Wave 82.5 rocks," I said in English, and added in Japanese, in my huskiest tones, "I wanna be with you forever."

"I wanna be with you forever," Naoya intoned in the taxi, on our way back to the hotel. "You've got such a sexy voice, Shanti. Why don't you have a boyfriend?"

He was all innocent curiosity, the darkness disguising his bloodshot eyes. At some point he'd managed to get very drunk. He'd disguised it well enough on the air, but as we walked out to the taxi I'd seen him stumbling.

I laughed. "Are you applying for the position? There's no wait list." What on earth would I do if he took me up on it? Small and compactly built, with chunks of his hair dyed blond, Naoya worked a Bambi act that played intriguingly against the groaning dissonances and suicidal inversions of Kinderbox's music. Once you got to know him, the ambiguity vanished. He was a fuck-up coasting on the remnants of his boyish charm.

"No, no, not me." Naoya cackled. "I wanna be with you forever," he sang, and subsided into his corner of the seat. Just when I thought he'd gone to sleep, he said, "Ned's a standup guy, isn't he?"

"When he makes a promise, he keeps it," I said glumly.

"You can say that again." Naoya laughed so hard that he coughed. "Hey, is it OK if I smoke in here?" The driver said it was. Naoya shook a cigarette out of his packet of Marlboro Reds and lit up. With admiration and envy, he said, "There's one guy who's not going to be out one yen for expenses. I bet he'll turn a profit. Nice work if you can get it..." His cigarette fell from his fingers onto the floor. This time he really had gone to sleep.

I wanted to pick the damn thing up and smoke it. I ground it out with the toe of my sneaker. I was going to leave it there, but the salt-and-pepper back of the driver's head reminded me of Tad's father. Guiltily, I transferred it to the ashtray.

Dashing into the hotel in a swirl of snow, we dodged bellboys in red monkey jackets and crossed an ocean of red carpet, beneath ornate etched glass light fixtures that had probably looked modern in the 1930s. We'd got a night's stay here thrown in with our air fares. It would be our first and last taste of luxury on this tour, and the boys were taking full advantage. The moment Yves opened the door to us, I smelt weed.

"Make sure you put that towel back," Joaquin's voice floated out.

Yves squatted and rearranged a rolled-up, dampened bath towel along the bottom of the door.

"You guys are toking up in a hotel," I said. "I do not *believe* this."

"Shanti, for once in your life, could you just relax?" Joaquin lay on his stomach on one of the twin beds, typing on his laptop. Chiharu sat cross-legged beside him. Ned was in front of the TV, bracketed by Sato-kun and Kiichi, the Kinderbox lead guitarist and bassist, who were speaking English for his benefit, shouting each other down as they explained the pecularities of Japanese TV. They'd warmed to him more in one day than they had to me in four years.

"This is just unacceptable," I said. "It's crazy. I could smell it in the hall."

"Yves," said Joaquin in French, "could you go out into the hall and make sure there is no odor? Merci."

It turned out there were no radios in the hotel, nor had anyone thought to bring one. Tad, however, had gone down to the parking lot to sit in the van and tape the broadcast. "So you can listen to yourselves tomorrow if you like."

"No way! Ego trip!" exclaimed Naoya. "With the commercial breaks in and everything? Authentic, my man." He plucked one of the joints from Sato-kun's hand and inhaled deeply. "Whoa, this is good shit."

I said, "I'm sorry I fucked up the gig! OK? Now is it too much to ask that we stick to legal substances while we're on the road?"

"*You* didn't fuck up," Joaquin sighed, and Chiharu echoed him.

I scowled. "Where's Nina?"

"Oh, I think she's gone to sleep," Chiharu said. "We're sharing: you, me, and her. They gave us a couple of triples because we have odd numbers of boys and girls." She giggled. Why was she in such high spirits, after the disaster at Klub Kounterweight? Well, it hadn't been as bad for her as it was for us: she had less to lose.

"No odor," Yves reported, coming back into the room. His small black eyes blinked unnaturally fast. He was half French, but he'd grown up in Tokyo, so he always seemed more Japanese. Originally recruited by Joaquin for Dufek Intrusion, he was now more Naoya's man than he was Joaquin's: a lifestyle choice rather than a musical one. Not that there was really all that much to choose, I thought bitterly, between Gorot and Kinderbox for debauched imbecility.

I turned my back on Joaquin and went to sit on the carpet beside Tad. "Is there anything to drink apart from beer?"

Ned rose and presented me with a plastic glass of clear fizz. "Gin and tonic. Your favorite, is it not?"

"Thanks," I said coldly. After a moment, he went back to his place in front of the TV.

"Kanpai. You haven't eaten anything today, have you?" Tad shoved a bag of senbei towards me.

"Who brought it, anyway? Naoya?" I said with my mouth full. "It just better not have been anyone who was on the plane with us today!"

"Huh? Ned brought it from Thailand."

Nice work if you can get it.

"I knew that," I said. As I spoke, I remembered that night at Newport Café. I'd thought Ned was looking to score. I'd had it backwards. He'd been looking to sell. "I hope he came well supplied, because this lot are going to get through it," I said blackly.

"He's got E, too. Not many takers for that here. But…"

"Joaquin's promised to help him move it," I guessed.

"The profit margin on that shit is through the roof."

"For a cut. Jesus."

Tad laughed, without much humor. "Well, if this tour doesn't… I hate to say it, but we might need insurance."

Shingo offered him one of the joints. He took it and inhaled deeply. Passing the joint on to Naoya, he nodded at the rest of Kinderbox. "They've got to deal with their stress somehow. After tonight…"

"No kidding. I could kill Joaquin for booking us into a dump like that," I said tiredly.

As if I'd flicked a switch, Tad's face went expressionless. Whoops. It had slipped my mind that in Tad's world, you did not criticize Joaquin.

Well, it wasn't as if criticizing Joaquin would do any good, anyway. He'd got us into this mess, but no one could get us *out* of this mess. That was why the others were laughing it off so determinedly. What other option was there, after all? We couldn't stomp off home, bitch to our other friends, and get over it. We were in Hokkaido.

"And besides," I said, "I don't see you setting an example for the younger generation." I turned to include Shingo in that. He was sprawled in an armchair behind us, smoking a cigarette. "Our supposedly mature thirty-somethings!"

"I'm here to get away from my mature thirty-something life," said Shingo with a lazy smile. "How about *you* follow *my* example?"

I said, "You know why I can't relax around this shit? It's because I don't like to see the people I like get fucked up. Yeah, I know, you can't get the hard stuff in Japan—"

"Yeah, you can," said Tad.

"Whatever, but you can get it a lot easier in New York. When I was in my band there, the bassist was a junkie." I eyed Tad's fingers, which sparkled and clanked, like everything else on him, with a wolf's head, a death's head, a sort of signet with a plain black stone. "He wore rings just like yours." I didn't think Zeke had been making an ironic statement with them, he'd meant it, but that had been his tragedy. He meant everything so deeply. "He took them off to perform and put them back on afterwards, just like you do. Only, he ended up losing every one of them. He got so fucking skinny they just fell off. He was my best friend, but we had to fire him from the band. We told him to clean up and then call us. Well, he didn't clean up. He overdosed. It was me they called from the hospital."

"And then what happened?" said Tad.

"Oh. He died." I forced a shrug. "So we hired another bassist."

"Well, that wouldn't have happened in Japan," Shingo said, uninterested.

I got up and blindly skirted the room to the bathroom, where I locked myself in and drank off the rest of my G&T in one gulp. When I came out, I went over to Gen, who was lounging in the corner behind the TV. He made room for me on the carpet.

Gen didn't get the Asian flush, unlike Tad whose brown face glowed like a rose after two beers, but there was a telltale narrowing of those oblong eyes. Tonight's disaster had hit him hard, I thought. Unlike some of the others, he was taking this adventure seriously.

"What's wrong, Shanti? You're not drinking!"

"Well, you've got a bottle all to yourself. You can fix me something."

"Mademoiselle's wish is my command." He picked up a plastic glass, frowned at it, and very carefully dumped the dregs of the last drink it had held behind the TV.

"I don't want straight vodka," I said, sighing.

"What do you want, then?"

You, I thought. No, kill that thought. Help. Help.

He picked an inch-long roach out of the cap of the vodka bottle. After several tries, he got it lit and held it out to me.

I almost took it. I was so tired of staying on my guard, so tired of keeping my wits about me. But then I looked at Ned.

He was still in the group around the TV. The boys were still going out of their way to include him - and not just because of his sparkling personality, as I now knew. He guffawed obligingly at their bad English. But tension resonated like a low-frequency hum from his rounded shoulders.

I shook my head, reached for the vodka, and poured myself an inch. "You know I don't do that shit, Gen."

"Ah, I forgot. Sorry."

"You don't have to be sorry. It's just..." I sipped the vodka. "it's just that I grew up with it. My mother, the guy we lived with in Paris," *Nigel,* "basically all the adults I knew..."

"But Nina and Joaquin didn't grow up with it."

"No, they didn't. I did. And so I saw very clearly, the way that children do, what it does to the judgment of otherwise rational adults."

After a moment Gen said, "OK, but Ned grew up with it. Just like you."

"Well," I said, "I don't think he values rationality as much as I do." When I'd said this my heart started to pound, as if I'd made a confession of some kind.

"Rationality is overrated," Gen said. "Give me passion. Passion! That's the trouble with our… our society… our generation. We're ruled by logic. We think everything through. Talk everything through. And then, by the time we're done… we've talked ourselves out of it. Whatever it was."

This speech made me look around for Chiharu. Joaquin had fallen asleep. Chiharu still sat on the bed beside him, quietly sipping her drink and watching TV over the others' heads.

I opened my mouth, then shut it again. Gen had sunk back into his own world, eyes almost completely closed, head nodding in time to music I couldn't hear.

I finished my vodka, slid across the floor, and tapped Chiharu's knee. "What room are we in? If Nina's asleep, I'll need a key to get in. Do you have one?"

"Oh Shanti, it's still early!"

"The voice needs her rest," I said expressionlessly.

"Oh… OK." She shifted around to dig in her pocket. Joaquin raised himself on his elbow, blinking and pawing the bed to make sure his laptop hadn't walked off. Chiharu giggled.

I looked away… and saw Ned stepping over people's knees towards me. I was too slow off the mark to avoid his gaze. His blue eyes were clearer than they had any right to be, unless he'd only been pretending to knock back the cocktails. I hadn't been pretending. I'd had two strong drinks, three counting the one at the club. My reflexes were shot.

"Think I'm going to turn in, actually," he was saying. "If I don't get some sleep I'll have us off the road tomorrow."

Chiharu leaned across Joaquin, holding out a keycard. "I'll be up soon."

I was putting on my sneakers and picking up my bag, trying to figure out how to stop this sequence of actions, and then I was out in the hall. Ned closed the door behind us. The carpet muffled our footsteps.

Nothing bad can happen to you in a hotel, I told myself.

"Well, it's a relief to see Joaquin recharging his batteries," Ned said.

"Yeah."

"He's fucking driving himself into the ground, no pun intended. This morning he was nodding out on the highway. I had to take over and let him sleep. That's why we were late getting into the city: I had to keep pulling over to the side to read the map." Ned chuckled in that unamused way that reminded me of Nigel. "You're all as bad as each other. Well, except *you!* What time is it now? Half past two? And we've to be on the road at nine. It would be earlier if it was up to me. I don't like the sound of that route through the mountains, and in this weather…"

"Yeah, but no one thinks about that kind of thing when they're having fun," I said.

"That's a fucking understatement. We're going to see some very green faces in the morning." Ned laughed. "Now if it was myself, I'd have chosen another night. A breakfast buffet is a terrible thing to waste."

I tried and failed to suppress a snicker. Me and Ned laughing together! What was wrong with this picture? Answer: I was drunk. That wiped the smile off my face. "So what's the deal, Ned?" I heard myself saying. "You don't indulge when you're working?"

We were standing in front of the elevators, but the call button wasn't glowing. Neither of us had pressed it. I reached out and stabbed it.

"Oh, I indulge," Ned said. "Not every fucking night. I'm not one of these people that treats it like… It's not a crutch. And if you let it become a habit, it controls you, not the other way round. But it helps. Sometimes, it helps to take the pain away."

Mercifully, the elevator came before I had to produce a reply. This time I remembered to press the button for the fourteenth floor. Six… seven… the indicator light crept upwards. Ned slouched against the brass handrail and blew out a breath. Staring at the floor, he rolled his left shirt sleeve up to the elbow, then started on his right sleeve. His forearms were chunky with muscle, tanned golden, matted with equally golden hair.

Sticky drops of sweat crawled down my back under my bra strap.

"Joaquin was raised in a strict Catholic family," I said. "You'd never think it, would you? But he has seven brothers and sisters, and one of the brothers is a priest."

The elevator doors opened. The fourteenth floor looked exactly like the fifth floor. We turned the corner past the identical dried flower arrangement in an illuminated alcove.

"But Nina's not Catholic, is she?" Ned said.

"Oh… not that I know of. They met in Paris when she was doing her junior year abroad." Like me, Nina had never graduated, committing herself to life on the road with Joaquin instead.

"They're a grand couple, aren't they?" said Ned.

I heard myself saying, "Do you have a girlfriend, Ned? In Thailand, or…"

He shot me a searing glance out of those blue eyes. "I had. Petra. She came to the island to study yoga and meditate. She was a lawyer. Needed a break from the urban jungle."

Had. "So what happened?"

"She went back to Munich at the end of last year. It was never going to be a permanent vacation..." Ned smirked. "She's got a husband, albeit separated, and two daughters."

I had to stifle a laugh. I'd been picturing a Thai gamine with caramel skin and a quick smile, someone like my father's girlfriend who'd called herself Mandy or Candy… not a German lawyer running away from her own life. Petra was probably a good bit older than Ned. And – I did the chronology in my head – she'd left him a couple of months after his grandmother died in Denmark. A couple of months before he came to look for me. It wasn't really funny at all.

We'd reached the door of my room. I inserted the keycard in the lock, but hesitated to turn the handle. Ned was volunteering more details. I covertly scrutinized him. I'd done this before in my struggle to figure him out, but this time, for a moment, I really did see him afresh: just a boy adrift in Asia, not as tough as he looked and not as sophisticated as he should have been. "You deserve someone less messed up than that," I said when he paused for breath.

"It's easier to pick up the pieces of someone else's life than to put your own life together."

"You know, that's very true." I stared at my own hand on the keycard that I would use to lock him out, just as I'd thrown a crummy little bolt, years ago, to lock him in. Technology progresses, we don't. "But the best therapy of all," I declared, "is when you care about someone else," I was thinking about Alastair, "so much that you want to be a better person, so that you don't hurt them. So you can do as much for them as they do for you."

"That's exactly what I think! We've always been on the same wavelength, haven't we, Shanti?" Ned exclaimed. He was standing at an angle to me, so close that I could smell his aftershave – a sharp wintergreen scent, expensive without a hint of elegance, like his clothes.

He was still talking, but I found it increasingly difficult to follow what he was saying. He was standing too close to me, one arm casually braced on the wall behind my head. My whole body started to tremble. I stared at the center of his chest and concentrated on taking deep breaths. I dimly understood that I was listening to a tale of woe. Petra, Ned's "business partner," some guy named Jeremy, no, Jeremy *was* his "business partner," and what? Jeremy's girlfriend had a dream in which *my father* appeared to her and told her that I was waiting for Ned to get in touch with me, and when she told Ned about it, she'd asked to look at his hand. She did palm readings. That rang some kind of a bell, but what did it have to do with psychic dreams? Anyway, she'd looked at his palm and said that his heart line had basically gone crazy, intersecting with his head line in two new places, *here* and *here* –

Ned's palm was densely crosshatched with lines. I couldn't see the one he wanted me to look at, much less understand what this whole story was leading up to. "Ned, I'm sorry. I think I drank too much. I'm going to be sick." I ducked under his arm, threw my weight on the door, and fell inside. Not caring whether or not he could hear it, I fumbled in the darkness for the chain and pushed it into its slot.

I stood inside the door for a couple of minutes, scarcely breathing. From around the corner came the soft chitter of the TV, and blue light flickered on the walls of the little foyer. At last I judged that Ned must have gone away.

Even if he hadn't, to hell with him. With the door locked, I felt better already.

I padded around the corner. Nina was sprawled in an armchair in front of the TV. On the small table beside her were her cell phone and three? four 500 ml beer cans.

In the blue firelight of the TV, I sidled closer to her, holding my breath.

Faint snores came over the ringing in my ears. I smothered a hysterical giggle.

Goddamn it, I was trembling.

I changed into my t-shirt and sweats, collected my MP3 player and notebook from my bag, and locked myself in the bathroom. I'd wanted a bath, but the running water might disturb Nina, and anyway, I had something to do. I switched on the light, sat down on the tiles beside the toilet, and fumbled my headphones onto my ears. *Play.*

It lives in you, consumes you, but this is for the best! This game was never meant to be fair.

And the last verse, which I'd thought of at some point during the evening while I was thinking of something else: *Memories, sinking, something glitters on the edge of your vision… Whispers of weakness, sweat-soaked on a winter night…*

"Maybe he doesn't remember," I'd said to Alastair when we were talking about Ned once, speculating about what might be going on with him (if he wasn't dead). "Maybe he doesn't remember anything…"

"Oh, I should think he remembers everything," Alastair had said. "That's what pain does. It helps you to remember… trivial things, at least. I can shut my eyes right now and see the hood of the Land Rover. The specific pattern of the drops of rain. Or the cobwebs in the corner of the barn."

Alastair meant the half of the Gallants' barn that Nigel had used as his pottery studio. It had two big kilns in it. When he was firing a batch, the smell would sometimes drift down the hill as far as our cottage.

Fuschia Cottage belonged to a Monsieur Duvalier, a friend of June's who used to come to West Cork to paint, but nowadays was rich enough to live in Provence.

The day we moved in, Nigel came down to say hello. "The fourth Madame Duvalier, I presume?" he said to June. He was swinging a bottle of wine by its neck.

"Unfortunately not," said June. "The great man prefers brunettes."

"Thank God. In that case, welcome to West Cork. I'm your neighbor. Singular. You haven't any others for a mile either way. Allihies Ceramics; you'll have seen the sign as you came in."

Singular. But I was very picky about English at that time, since I could no longer be entirely sure I was getting it right, and I said, "There's a boy in the garden."

"Ah," said Nigel, carelessly. "That's my son." He was still looking at June. "Anything I can do for you…"

Within a couple of months, they were sleeping together.

Nigel taught June the business of art. County Cork had something that neither County Sligo nor Paris did at that time: an abundance of craft shops. The tourist trade was booming, and in one of the many ironies of life in West Cork, souvenir production was more or less monopolized by the resident expats. The pretty watercolors that June now began to turn out daily, working from photographs, brought thirty and forty pounds apiece. In the summer, she and Nigel would drive around all day in his Land Rover, calling at every town and village from Glengarriff to Clonakilty, dropping off paintings and pottery and collecting their earnings. I remember one night when she blew in the door, spun me around by the hands, and threw handfuls of money over my head as if she'd robbed a bank. "Angel, we're rich!" I scooped up the money and chased her with it, remembering a once-upon-a-time snowball fight in the Place du Tertres. Ned joined in the scuffle. In the process, several banknotes ended up getting torn / lost / pocketed.

Ned paid for that, of course, and I think I did, too. Yes, I did, but not for a couple of days, because Nigel had to catch me on my own. By that time, I'd almost forgotten the ten-pound note I'd slipped up my sleeve. Ned must have squealed on me, I realized, and the grain of the butcher block table in the Gallants' kitchen, the smell of ancient fryups, became the indelible texture of my hatred.

With pain, it makes no difference whether you earn it or not.

When did it start? About six months after we moved into the cottage,

I think. Until then, Alastair and I had assumed that it sucked to be Ned, but *we* were safe. We were wrong.

It was Alastair, not me, who caught it first. I can't remember what he'd done. It didn't matter. Nigel always had some justification, but his criminal categories were absurdly broad - lying, carelessness; "So what have I done this time? Oh, I know! I've been breathing," Alastair said once..

But that first time, he didn't say a word or make a sound.

Nigel dragged him into the barn and manhandled him to the floor. Alastair hunched, folding his arms over his head, as if he'd been told what to do, while Nigel knelt over him, hitting him mostly on the rear end but also around the kidneys. He used the flat of his hand.

"He never really hits you," Ned whispered to me.

We'd hidden in the other half of the barn and now we were spying through chinks in the wall of the loft where Nigel stored the hay for their goats. It's true: pain helps you to remember things. Even when it isn't your own pain. I remember the mindless maa-ing of the goats outside, the sharp smell of the hay, and the awful sensation of simultaneously trying not to sneeze and not to throw up. Ned whispered, "If Alastair was a grownup, he'd make him fight man to man. Then he'd get smashed to a pulp! But my father doesn't fight kids."

At least, not that year, he didn't.

At twelve, Alastair was small for his age. He and I were sometimes taken for twins.

At thirteen, he shot up.

By the time he turned fifteen, he'd hit five feet ten, which would be his adult height. He still had a lot of filling out to do, but he was shaving twice a week and his voice had settled to tenor.

He was still a kid.

But Nigel seemed to forget that.

And that's how we got a chance, a single solitary chance, to swing the war our way.

Needless to say, we let it slip through our fingers, because we still didn't understand that we were at war.

How could we have been so naïve? Answer: there were rules. Children have a natural compulsion to believe in rules. Even Ned. He cheated at every game we ever played, but he had his own set of rules for life, and we accepted them, because he, after all, had managed to survive under Nigel's regime so far.

He never really hurts you.

Yeah, right.

It was snowing in Hakodate, too, so heavily that all the cars had their headlights on.

"Like an explosion in a fucking soapflakes plant," Ned griped, straining to see through the crescents opened by the windshield wipers.

After tunneling and winding through the mountains, the road had followed the coastline south for hours. A thin rind of inhabitable land curved between the forested slopes and the sea. We'd driven through towns with glass buoys heaped outside doors and crows dancing in the fog around ancient factory buildings. In between the towns, the road ran parallel to an endless black beach segmented by black groynes. Grey rollers glowed dimly in the blizzard. The bluffs had been reinforced with concrete quilting and jumbles of tetrapods. These were actually erosion defenses, but I'd made a fool of Ned by "explaining" out loud that they were fortifications to prevent enemy landings. He'd believed me until the others burst into laughter.

Slowed down by the snow, we were running three hours late. The long drive had given me a sense of detachment, but now I felt as if I was falling, watching the ground come closer.

An illuminated streetcar swayed around the curve in front of Hakodate station. We fishtailed around the curve after it. Shop windows glittered beneath the arcade roofs covering the sidewalks. Was this downtown? If so, Hakodate was lagging about two decades behind Sapporo in the globalization race. "We're heading straight to the venue!" yelled Joaquin into his phone over the music that filled the van.

Tad was on the phone, too, translating and relaying directions to Ned. The commercial veneer on this main drag turned out to be shallow. Turning off, we drove among warehouses and the abandoned premises of small manufacturers. The snow distorted the outlines of buildings and scrambled the graffiti on weathered billboards. In a parking lot crisscrossed with slushy tyre tracks a tall figure stood under a vinyl umbrella, phone to his ear.

I screamed in delight, forced my sneakers onto my feet, and jumped out of the van before Ned could brake. I pelted through the snow, skidding where it had been churned up. "Oh, Yuki! Yuki, I'm so glad to see you!"

He probably hadn't been expecting a hug from me, but he handled it well, giving me a squeeze around the shoulders before holding me off. Simultaneously trying to hold his umbrella over my head, he shouted, "As crazy as ever! You're going to annihilate them, Shanti! They've never seen anything like you up here!"

He'd cut his hair. It used to hang below his shoulders, and he would tie it back with a bandanna or a keffiyeh. Now it framed his face in damp black wisps. But he was dressed with familiar flair in a long brown leather coat and pink jeans printed with dragons, flapping wet over pointy red cowboy boots. It was no coincidence that he and Tad had a similar sense of style: Yuki used to work at a boutique in Daikanyama, selling vintage leather and gear by designers no one ever heard of, and that was where Tad had found him when he was browsing for stagewear in the days of Ravisher.

Yuki had been Gorot's first guitarist. I'd always thought he belonged in Tokyo like a flamingo in a zoo. But he came from way the hell up north in Hakodate, and at the beginning of last year, when his father died in a traffic accident, he'd moved back here to live with his mother. It had all happened so suddenly that we felt like Yuki himself had died on us. And then we'd recruited Gen to take his place. We'd kept in touch with Yuki, but only sporadically, until we started planning Cold Coeur Family Vol. I. His emails tended to be funny and off the point, so I had no idea how he'd been making his living here, far less whether he was happy. I did know that he had a new band, Alcazar del Norte.

"You kept saying you'd come back to Tokyo, Yuki. You kept promising. Pig!"

"And in the end you guys had to come to me. I know." He stuffed his umbrella into my hands and loped across the parking lot: "Tad! Joaquin! Hisashi-fucking-buri, guys!"

The Saturday Night Club occupied the fourth floor of the building we'd parked in front of. There was a dance club on the third floor and a bar on the second floor.

"When it comes to nightlife in Hakodate, this is it," Yuki said. "There is nowhere else!"

"And what's more, it's Saturday night," exulted Tad. "Do we have great timing or what?"

"Your timing sucks ass!" hooted Yuki. "This is the worst blizzard since nineteen sixty-four."

"On some level you have to interpret that superstitiously," said Gen.

"Hey, don't worry, man!" Yuki burst into laughter so infectious that everyone joined in. "Up here, we don't let a little bit of snow stand in our way!"

The elevator deposited us in a corridor heaped with junk and other bands' instruments. We found the bands themselves inside the livehouse. SNC probably had the same square metreage as Klub Kounterweight, but it was a cube, not a glorified tunnel. Insulated concrete beams traversed the ceiling three metres above our heads. The speaker stacks reached almost as high. Crowd control barriers anchored with breezeblocks stretched across the front of the stage. A wire cage protected a forbidden zone around the ramshackle eyrie at the back of the club where a bearded man was fiddling with a video camera on a tripod. "You must get some serious moshpit action here," I said, trying to sound impressed.

"We cart them off on stretchers," said Yuki. "Well, that only happened once, actually, but it was at one of our shows. Best publicity we ever had!"

He introduced us to his new bandmates, three guys on the young side who all came off as repressed and/or scared of gaijins. Trying to put them at their ease, I asked them who their influences were. They apparently couldn't think of any. One of them finally came up with Judas Priest. "Oh, Tad," I hissed, "help!" But he was too busy making friends with the other band on the bill to come to my aid. Parrot-coiffed and aggressively friendly, Mad's Ultra were down as the opening act. Kinderbox were going on after them. Alcazar del Norte had the eight o'clock slot, and then it would be our turn.

Push the genre envelope as you might, there was no way to put Chiharu on a bill with two acts influenced by Judas Priest (three if you counted us), so she wasn't performing tonight. She had her own show at a different venue tomorrow, while we would have a day off.

While Kinderbox ran through their soundcheck, the rest of us hung over the technicians' shoulders, chatting them up. The bearded guy in the eyrie turned out to be the owner. He stuck around long enough to shake hands and wish us good luck in American-accented English.

"That guy is connected to hell and back," Joaquin said reverently, watching him leave.

It was true that SNC had a starstudded schedule (probably because there was no competition in town), but the flyers littering the table outside the wire cage were all for local acts: The Exorcists, Moyen Kick, Blasted Gals, Goner… "Goner," I giggled. "Doubtless."

"It's not a band, it's a shop," said Tad, glancing at the flyer in my hand.

"It's *my* shop," said Yuki with a crooked smile.

"You've got a shop?" I covered up my lack of Japanese reading ability with enthusiasm. "You mean you own it and everything? Oh, my God! Guys! Did you know Yuki's an entrepreneur?"

"Didn't *you?*" said Tad.

"I'm sure I told you," said Joaquin.

If he had, it must have gone in one ear and out the other while I was agonizing about Ned. Ever since he reappeared in my life, I'd been paying less attention to my life itself. It was as if I had a constant murmur of white noise in my head. The white noise wasn't Ned himself;

it was the game we were playing, the incalculable possibility that he was preparing some move I wouldn't even see coming.

I looked around and saw him helping Nina unpack our merchandise. "Clothes hangers!" he was saying. "Clothes hangers! I knew we'd forgotten something!" At the sound of his voice, something strange happened to my vision: it went all sparkly, as if there were mica scattered over everything.

We went onstage with the house lights down, checking the sound levels and the stage lighting at the same time. Since we were running so late, this was our only chance to rehearse "The Hound of Heaven," the biggest of our *Xenophobia*-era punk anthems, with Yuki.

Everyone (except Gen, I worried) had been looking forward to this reunion. Even though we were playing together for the first time in a year and a half, Yuki didn't flub a note. Scattered applause followed the last crescendo. As we hurried offstage, I saw that Mad's Ultra and the rest of Alcazar del Norte seemed to have duplicated themselves. There were twice as many parrotheads and pallid chain-smokers drifting around in the semi-dark as before, and now half of them were girls. Whoever was on the door had started letting in the public, or what passed for the public in a town where everyone had gone to school together.

We sat crosslegged on the floor of the tiny kitchen across the corridor from the stage door and ate instant ramen and soba. Disconnected samples of Mad's Ultra's opening number escaped the livehouse door. After we finished eating, we went to watch the rest of their set. A gaggle of high school boys clung to the crowd control barriers, shoving each other. Now and then an older yoof with a mohawk took a running jump and slammed into them, showing them how it was done.

Kinderbox took the stage, cranking up the fuzz and crash. We lurked in a corner, obsessively counting heads. We'd paid a flat box fee, and we needed to sell fifty tickets to break even. I slurped a vodka tonic. Was I making the same mistake as last night? No. Tonight, I wasn't going to stop at one drink. I was going to nudge my blood alcohol up until I got into the zone where nothing, not even Ned, could distract me.

I was returning for the third time from the window in the wire cage that served as a bar when Alcazar del Norte made their entrance.

Yuki raised his arms, and every female in the place shrieked.

"Oh my God," I said.

He wore a black ten-gallon hat, which he now doffed and twirled like Lucky Luke the Cowboy crossed with Gene Kelly.

"My hat," I whispered.

Well, OK, it wasn't *my hat* in the sense of being a hat that I owned.

But it was my trademark. My gimmick. And he'd nicked it. What's more – I'd noticed this before, but hadn't thought anything of it – he was also wearing cowboy boots!

I brushed my hand over my hair, thinking panickily of my electric blue Panama nestling in its box in the kitchen, waiting to snuggle onto my head. Waiting for me to twirl it on one finger and clap it back on with the brim down low in front, just like Yuki was doing right now with his hat.

Shit.

I ran my hands over my outfit. Black chiffon blouse over a black lace cami. Kneelength bias-cut skirt of rough hessian. Green fishnet tights. My boots. The ensemble needed the Panama. It wouldn't work without it.

I shoved my drink into Gen's hand and slid out of the club. Down the stairs, out into the snow. What if Joaquin had locked the van? This was Hakodate, not Shinjuku: he hadn't locked it. Shivering with cold, I climbed into the back, rooted out my suitcase, and stripped off everything except the black lace cami, which had shoulder straps wide enough for it to pass as a top. I put on my old 501s. Then, for warmth, I added my brown hoodie with the front zip. Nothing to be done about the boots – I *couldn't* go onstage without them.

I dashed back upstairs and reclaimed my drink from Gen. He looked me up and down. I shrugged.

The black hat worked for Yuki, I had to admit. A visual kei idol manqué, he wielded his guitar like an angel with a sword. And the hat made him into a dark angel, a mythic figure with the top half of his face in shadow, a gunslinger of the endless northern night… The songs that his rhythm guitarist cowrote were just homogeneous noise with a beat. Yuki had always been a crap singer, and he still was. He got round it by growling in a death metal voice instead. But his guitar playing justified the whole caper, teetering on the borderline between extravagance and insanity. That was the sound you could hear on *Xenophobia.*

Oh God, I thought, why did we ever change? *U-Turn Day* sounds like a fucking Bryan Adams record compared to this. They're going to hate us! This is Yuki's crowd, not ours!

I tugged Joaquin's shoulder and shouted in his ear, "Let's do the new song!"

"Impossible! We haven't rehearsed it with the lyrics."

"But we've rehearsed it plenty without them! And I sang the lyrics for you in the van!"

Joaquin seemed suddenly to take in how I was dressed. "All right! But no backing out at the last minute!"

"Don't worry about that! I want to do it as our opener!"

"You – OK. OK, Shanti. You're the one who hasn't rehearsed, so it's your call. By the way, have you got a title for it?"

"Yeah." I said. "'Unfair Game.'"

"**M**inna-san, konban wa."

Silence.

I was melting. No hat to shade my head. No kooky outfit to distract attention from my face. Just me, and the boys behind me, and the strangers waiting in the dark beyond the crowd control barriers.

Two red LEDs glowed in that darkness, brighter than cigarettes. Nina with her video camera. And the bearded owner, up in his eyrie.

"We're Gorot, here all the way from Tokyo. This is Gen Tajitsu on guitar! Joaquin Gorot on keyboards! Tad Kuroiwa on bass! Shingo Miyazaki on drums! And I'm Shanti Hazard!"

Dutiful applause.

"Now here's another one off our new album, available over there, just tell the lovely Nina you want your copy of *U-Turn Day,*" I pattered. "'It Doesn't Matter (Genocide).' Listen closely to the lyrics and you might pick something up."

Shingo brought his sticks down.

I threw the mic stand to the stage and posed with one hip cocked, beating time on my thigh with a loop of mic cord. Tad's bass line rose and plateaued. Gen's guitar landed on it with a scream like a fighter jet, and my voice rose for the moon.

And somewhere in the next five or ten minutes, they turned into *our* crowd. The house shook so hard it felt like the woofers in the FOH stacks had tripled and quadrupled in power. Drunk on the love as much as the vodka tonics, I dropped to my knees and crawled along the stage, yelping into my mic. The boys balancing on the crowd control barriers reached out to me. Sweat dripped into my eyes as I looked up into a smile like a gift from a distant galaxy. I let him grab my hand and pull me to my feet. "These people, not quite people, not like people," I growled. "A million stories that no one wants to hear – "

He was reaching for me. I dropped to my knees again, writhing to the thud of the kick drum, and slid my free hand around his shoulders. *Crash!*

"A million memories of another wasted year," I sang, and let my mic fall to my side. He strained across the crowd control barrier, and I leaned forward and kissed him on the mouth. He was just a high-school boy with a hard tongue that tasted of beer. The crowd yelled deafeningly. *CRASH!* I pulled back and sang, "A million voices mumbling into deaf ears!"

"The Hound of Heaven," ended up feeling like an interruption. The crowd applauded Yuki, but when I stalked back to the center of the stage alone, they screamed.

It was almost eleven o'clock when we finally staggered off. I leaned against the wall of the corridor, where a landslide of broken furniture partially blocked us from view of the punters piling into the elevator, and slurped Pocari Sweat, which tastes like it sounds. It has electrolytes, however, and I needed to rehydrate.

"Shanti-san! Omedeto, omedeto. Great gig!" Yamanaka-san, the bearded owner, loomed in front of me.

I realized we'd probably have to cough up more money for running late. "Oh no," I said dazedly. "I mean, that's me, but he's the one you want to talk to."

Joaquin had his arms hung around Yuki's and Gen's shoulders. With Tad and Shingo at the ends of the C, they were swaying and yawping into each other's faces. Even Japanese guys get over their complexes about hugging at times like this.

"It takes it out of you, huh?" said another voice, this one speaking perfect transatlantic English.

"It sure does." I looked the speaker over without moving. Asian-American? He had a smooth round face and a goatee that made him look like a youthful Chinese sage. He was wearing a navy V-neck sweater over a white t-shirt. "Call it a hunch, but I don't think you're from around here?"

"Does it show? Yes, I'm from Tokyo. Just up here on business."

The *yes* where a native speaker would have said *no* told me that he was Japanese, but he must have spent a long time in the USA. I pointed to the CD in his hand. "Congratulations. You saved two hundred yen by buying it direct from the source."

"Great jacket art. I can't think of any Japanese bands that would risk it."

"We're sixty percent Japanese. Anyway, what's so risky about it?"

He cackled, and then, for an unexpected instant, we were smiling into each other's eyes. Huh! I thought after he moved on to talk to Joaquin. Well, it was nice to know that somebody got the joke.

There was no afterparty as such, but all the bands drove in teleconferenced convoy to Lucky Pierrot, a 24-hour hamburger restaurant that served booze. Raucous toasts were made and the boys ordered heavily. When the waitress reappeared, buckling under pineapple curry, crab au gratin, and squid spaghetti, I excused myself. On an impulse I headed for the front door instead of the toilets.

The snow had stopped. When the cold air touched my face, my

nausea subsided.

I floundered to the edge of the parking lot and stood beside Joaquin's van. The illuminated signs of strip mall businesses appeared to float unanchored in the air, receding to a humpy line of darkness. The edge of the world always seems to creep closer at night. Snow caked the privet hedge at my knees. I hadn't been paying attention on the drive; I hadn't a clue where we were, except that this wasn't the way we'd come into the city.

Footsteps crunched on the snow. I whirled.

Ned plunged up to me, panting with excitement."That guy, the one with the goatee that came with Yamanaka-san? You're not going to believe this. But he turns out to be A&R for Apex!"

"Oh shit," I said. "Oh my God, no fucking way. What's he doing in Hakodate? He said he was on business—"

"I think he was here to check out Alcazar del Norte." Ned grinned. "You've got to get back inside. He's been asking Joaquin all about you!" He grabbed my arm and started to drag me between the cars. He was gripping me just above the elbow, the place where policemen grip criminals on TV. I stiffened, my hand closing on my cell phone in my pocket. Full of excitement, Ned didn't seem to notice my resistance. "It's up to you to charm him now before he gets away!"

"Please let go of my arm," I said coldly.

Ned stared at me. "Am I hurting you?" His fingers flexed, tightening.

"Not as such." I glanced at the doors of the restaurant. We were close enough that I could see the vending machines and the uniformed girl at the front desk. "It's just that, you know. I've been in Japan for a while now, and I'm not used to being, uh, touched anymore."

"Oh, sure." He laughed and released my arm. I took several steps back. "I saw when you hugged Yuki. The poor guy was completely freaked out. Didn't know how to react. It's a very cold culture, isn't it? You'd think there was something wrong with affection."

"It's a personal space thing," I said, retreating another step.

"I understand that." But his face said something different. "I guess you'll just have to charm your man with your sexy voice, then," he joked, and if it had been a little darker, I would have been completely fooled.

"I'll do my best. It would help if I knew his name?"

"Whoops! Didn't catch that."

"Never mind. He looks like the young Confucius, so I'll just call him Master." What would Confucius do? *The Way is that which does not move* – or maybe that was Lao Tzu. Whatever. *Nothing.* The answer was nothing. I could beat Ned, and charm this Apex guy into the bargain, by simply doing nothing.

I barged into the dry heat of the restaurant, and heads turned.

At the end of our stay with him, Yuki came to the port to see us off. He stood in the parking lot with us for a few minutes, cracking lame jokes, and then we got back into our vans and drove under the orange visor of the car ferry. Long-haul trucks filled the car deck with exhaust fumes.

I raced upstairs and hung over the railing of the passenger deck. "Yuki!"

His van was still parked at the edge of the dock. Slouched against the driver's side door, elegant in pinstriped jeans and a red sweatshirt that hung off his narrow shoulders, he was checking his cell phone. He looked up and waved. "I miss you already!" I still felt terrible about what we'd done to him.

The noise of the ferry's turbines deepened. A trench opened between the hull and the dock. Yuki waved one last time and climbed into his van. "Don't forget us, Yuki," I screeched, "don't forget us…"

"Anyone would think you were parting forever," said Joaquin, coming along the walkway. For once, he was alone. He settled onto the rail beside me, rubbed his face with his hands, and yawned. "Ouf, I'm tired. Too much sleep and solid food!"

"Joaquin, what do you think? Is Apex really interested in us?"

"They're interested in making a quick buck." Joaquin popped flakes of orange paint off the railing with his thumbnail. They fell invisibly into the wave curling back from the ferry's hull, two storeys below. "Don't tell any of the others yet, but he said he'll come see us at Oasis when we get back to Tokyo. I don't know, it might mean something." He jammed his thumbnail hard into the paint and then snatched it back, a drop of blood springing out. "Merde. You should remind me to be more careful with my hands."

Chiharu came bounding along the walkway. "Jo! Jo, oh, there you are. You've got to come and see the games center. Some of the machines are so old, I remember them from when I was little."

"When you were little? You're still little," Joaquin joked.

Jo? *Jo?* I thought.

"Come on, Shanti," Chiharu entreated me.

I shook my head. "I'm going to stay out here in the fresh air. You guys watch out for those one-armed bandits."

The sun stabbed the sea like a welding torch, too bright to look at. As we chugged out of port, the wind picked up. Halfway between Hokkaido and Honshu, I went to get my electric blue Panama and threw it into the sea. The wind carried it so far that I lost sight of it before it hit the water.

"Thank you! Thank you! Thank you and goodnight!"

Backstage, I fell onto the sofa – there actually was a sofa at Mick's Carrot, a dark blue pleather one with rips gaping foam – and poured Crystal Geyser down my throat. Someone tossed me my brown hoodie. I pulled it over my face. Someone else tried to pull it off.

"She's having a diva moment," said Joaquin, "better leave her alone."

Goddamn Joaquin.

I kept the hoodie over my face, and eventually their voices swirled out of the room. I could practically feel the buzz washing back every time the door banged.

"Are you OK?"

Goddamn Gen.

"My plan is to just lurk back here until it's time to leave," I said into the stale darkness of my hood.

Mick's Carrot, the biggest little live house in Utsunomiya, had been our fourth gig in as many days, our last stop before going home. And tonight we weren't sleeping on the floor of anyone's apartment. As soon as we'd done socializing here, we were going to drive to Kusatsu, an onsen in the mountains where Shingo's company maintained a getaway facility for its employees. Since this wasn't the high season, his boss had agreed to let us stay there. There were some advantages to having a salaryman in the band. Lest we expect too much of the place, Shingo had warned us that it was beyond basic – but we were used to that.

"Joaquin's promising you'll come and sign CDs," Gen said.

I sat up and put my hoodie on properly. He was pacing around the table, fingering the empty beer cans and string wrappers. I said, "Are we *selling* any CDs? Or is Joaquin giving them away to self-styled reporters?"

"He's giving them away. Ned's selling them."

I laughed, not really thinking it was funny. Ned did have a knack for moving product. And not only *his* product, either. Joaquin had recently announced that our merchandise sales had gone up by something like 50%, and proceeded to gloat over Ned's acumen, as if he'd discovered him all by himself. But Ned's sales manner always struck me as painfully false – I could practically see the strings where it was tied on – so I avoided the merchandise table when he was there.

Let's see, who *wasn't* I avoiding? It had been a rough few days.

"I've had about all I can take." I sprang upright. "Thank God this tour is nearly over."

Gen accompanied me up the back stairs, past the recording studio that Mick's Carrot operated on the first floor. By day, the parking lot would have been full of cars. Now the wind blew unimpeded over the asphalt. Outside the fence, the Sunday night crowd crawled along Orion Street. Utsunomiya had the reputation of a yakuza town, but Chiharu, who'd grown up near here, had assured us that that was all a lot of media hype. As far as I was concerned, it was just another claustrophobic Japanese city, bundles of overhead power wires everywhere, drooping to the tops of high walls.

Side by side, Gen and I stomped around the inside of the parking lot fence. I thought of a dozen things to say, but discarded them all. It had to come from him.

"I should pay more attention to what you think," he said suddenly. "You don't miss much, do you? And you never trusted her."

I sighed. "I figured all along that she was using you. But to be fair to her, I don't think she… uh… planned on this."

"I never thought she'd fall for his superficial bullshit." Gen's vicious tone didn't suit him. "Can I have a swig of that?"

"Help yourself. Finish it."

He took the Crystal Geyser bottle from me and chugged it as if it was beer instead of water.

"It just kills me to see you like this," I said. "If you're still in love with her…"

Looking at me, yet seeming to look through me with his oblong black eyes, he spoke with unexpected intensity. "You're so sweet, Shanti. Sometimes I feel like I'm the only one who gets to see the real you. Why is that?"

"Because you're the only one that's younger than me, so I don't feel like I have to prove how mature I am," I said with a little laugh.

"Shanti! Yo! Gen! Hey!" Balancing cardboard boxes of merchandise on one knee, Ned shouted across the parking lot, "We're out of here!"

I slept through the drive to Kusatsu and woke up to a new sense of the largeness of the night. Joaquin and Naoya had parked under stooping hornbeams. The air smelled dark green. The silence flattened our voices. We straggled uphill to a highrise that looked like my building in Gotanda, only older and crummier, with shrubbery crowding the steps. Shingo flourished a set of keys.

Our "room," on the first floor, was a small apartment with a kitchenette, a bathroom where everything including the toilet had OUT OF ORDER signs, and a bigger tatami room where we spread out our sleeping bags.

"Who's for a bath?" Tad was practically hopping up and down with enthusiasm. "They're open at the main hotel until three in the morning."

Gen said quietly to me, "I don't think they are. How about some fresh air?"

"You mean, 'Keep me company so I don't have to get drunk by myself.'"

He showed me the bottle of cheap wine stashed in his coat pocket.

We slipped out of the apartment thirty seconds behind the bathing party. Casting around the parking lot, we hit an earth path into the trees. It circled around two more dormitory buildings and wound down to the bottom of the hill to join the driveway, then the main road. The full moon hung overhead. Looking up to our right, I could see the main hotel building, a checkerboard of yellow squares. An almost vertical forest overhung the road on our left. On our right, the trees soon gave way to diminutive fields with bungalows behind them, a post-agricultural hamlet more squashed together than its typical Irish counterpart, the fields even smaller and planted with vegetables, the houses ensconced in topiary and ornamental shrubs. A lane snaked away between them, towards the mountain ridge behind the fields.

"Can you hear what I hear?" I said excitedly.

"A waterfall. Of course. There's always a river in the mountains."

We took the turning through the hamlet, tiptoeing past the walled gardens. A dog started barking. We broke into a run. Past the last farm, the road plunged down into a morass of weeds. Laughing, we plunged with it, across an unpaved stony bit and into the forest.

The path turned uphill. Following the hollow hiss of water, we ducked under the whippy arms of laurels and dogwoods. The slope grew steeper. "I think we must have taken a wrong turn," Gen said.

"Oh, come on. We have to find the river!"

The path had turned into an obstacle course. Moonlight tangled in the branches above us. Stumbling uphill in the dark, we had to use our hands and knees as much as our feet. I forgot about the tour; I forgot about Ned. Breathing hard, I scrambled around a massive oak whose downslope roots clawed empty air. Ahead of me rose an almost sheer wall of earth. It looked like there'd been a mudslide. Saplings jutted out at right angles, retaining a grip on the earth so tenuous that I barely dared put my weight on them. When I reached the top, the forest still blocked out the sky ahead, but the noise of the waterfall was now coming from below. Somehow, I'd managed to climb right around it.

"Gen!" I danced on the lip of the mudslide. "That last bit's tricky!"

"Catch," came his voice, immediately followed by the wine bottle flying end over end out of the darkness below. "Now watch me make a fool of myself." He jumped, caught a branch that must have been a foot out of his reach, and hauled himself up, lifting his whole body weight with his arms. I laughed and clapped. He swung up to a higher branch, found his footing, and wobbled out along it, his feet on a level with my face. Then he jumped, crashing through the foliage, legs scissoring, mouth wide.

"Fantastic!" I cheered. What really touched me was that Gen had been willing to make a fool of himself in front of me. Maybe when he lost Chiharu, he'd also lost some of the prickly pride that always held him back.

He picked himself up, grinning. "Where's the waterfall? I can hear it, but where is it?"

We ploughed on through the undergrowth, following what seemed to be the remains of the original path. The noise of the water grew louder. When Gen stopped suddenly, I cannoned into him. I squeezed up beside him and saw that we'd almost walked into thin air. We stood on an earthy overhang about a metre above the… river? It was just a stream, tumbling over boulders to a final smooth stretch. A reflection of the moonlight trembled on the water like piano keys played by an unseen hand, producing no music, only a continuous low roar.

The stream had scooped a big chunk out of the bank where we stood, but to our left was a small clearing that seemed to be the intended end point of the path. A signboard gave the name and history of the place – I assumed; it was too dark to see the characters. There was even a wooden bench. We sat down and held the wine bottle up with all four hands in a parody of a toast.

"Kanpai!"

"O-tsukare-sama!"

Gen lit a cigarette. It smelt vile, tainting the rich earthy fragrance of the forest, yet my mouth watered. "You're making this really hard for me," I told him with a mock scowl.

"Haven't you learned anything on tour?"

"Yeah, I have. There is life after hats."

Gen laughed. "I was hoping for something a bit deeper than that."

"Hey, that is deep. That's so deep it could be a lyric. Or a tattoo. I might suggest it to Sato-kun. But let me rephrase." I took a deep breath. "Life goes on, even after everything has gone to shit. Life just fucking goes on."

"Now that's profound," Gen said, teeth flashing in the dark.

Abruptly, I stood up. Oh God, maybe this hadn't been a good idea, after all. You can liberate your spirit, but then your emotions come along to stomp all over the picnic.

"Shanti?"

"I'm all right," I said crossly.

"Shanti." Gen's arm went over my shoulders. I jumped, sticking out my hands to fend off what my subconscious took for an attack, with the result that my arms were open as he turned me to face him, and they went around him, and his mouth came down on mine. Now that it had happened, I knew what to do, or rather my body remembered how to go through the motions. He tasted of Marlboros and wine, and he smelled of sweat and that dusty ozone whiff that people get from handling high-voltage equipment. He shoved his hands inside my coat and under my hoodie, plucking my camisole out of the waistband of my Levis. I flinched from his cold fingers, and broke away. I tucked my camisole back in.

"Sorry," I said nervously.

He took me in his arms again. I tensed for more aggressive fumbling, but it didn't come. He gently pressed my forehead down to his shoulder. "It's OK. Come on, tell me. What is it?"

I stared blindly over his shoulder into the forest. Through the moisture in my eyes, I saw Ned watching us through the trees, his face in shadow, the silhouette of his body rigid and slightly hunched. I squeaked in shock.

"It's OK," Gen breathed, patting my back.

"I just don't think I can do this," I said inattentively.

"You don't have to do anything you don't want to." He stroked my hair.

I pushed him away. "You're just upset about Chiharu," I said. "Joaquin's claimed her, so you thought you'd claim me… but I'm not Joaquin's in that way." As soon as I said it, I thought: Jesus Christ, I probably *did* have to say it.

"Why does this have to be some kind of payback?" Gen took a last swig of the wine before capping the bottle and jamming it back into his pocket. "Why can't I just be attracted to you?"

I stood hugging my coat around me, staring at the spot where I'd seen Ned. Of course, there was nobody and nothing there except some twisted branches. In a sense, this was a wake-up call. I hadn't known just how badly Ned had got to me, how deeply he'd wormed his way into my mind.

"Come on." Gen touched my elbow. "They'll be wondering what's happened to us."

Just like that, my relief morphed into anger. "I'm in your band," I said. "You should have thought about that before you—"

"I'm sorry, OK?"

"OK." But a heartbeat later, I realized that it wasn't OK. "Listen, I'm not going to let anything damage this band. I slept with the guitarist of my band in New York… hell, I lived with him. So when we broke up, that was the end of the band. And I'm not going to make that mistake again. I love this band too much. I love you guys too much. As friends."

"I said I'm sorry! I had no idea you'd take it this badly."

"No, *I'm* sorry," I said wretchedly.

In silence, we scrambled down the mountain and back to the road. Gen swigged from the wine bottle as he walked. Furtively watching him, I noticed that he'd lost weight on tour: his high cheekbones protruded skeletally, and his springy black curls looked somehow unnatural, like a wig on a corpse. Oh God, I thought. He's not the one that's screwed up. We are. Hour by hour, day by day, we're screwing him up worse than his father ever could.

I woke up in the middle of a rumpled sea of empty sleeping bags. I didn't remember going to bed.

But I remembered everything else.

Oh fuck, fuck, fuck.

I was alone. All was silent, that mountainous silence that I could maybe never get used to.

I crawled out of my sleeping-bag, found my aspirin, and took two with a swig of green tea from a carton on the living-room table.

When Gen and I got back last night, the others had been carousing hard enough not to have noticed we were gone, or to comment on our return. My head still hurt.

I ate some leftover rice crackers and peanuts. I hadn't undressed, so I didn't need to dress. I had no clean clothes left, anyway. I felt sticky and grotty, my hair desperately in need of a wash, but the shower in the bathroom was OUT OF ORDER. Well, we were at an onsen. Was that where everyone had gone? The Cold Coeur Family took the art of getting value for money seriously. And the Japanese contingent, at least, took onsens seriously. They'd probably think three or four baths was the minimum acceptable return on ¥2000.

Picking through the debris on the table in search of something more to eat, I found a note. It was addressed to me in English, the schoolboy printing obviously the work of a Japanese hand.

Dear Shanti, meet me by the river. 1 pm. Same place. Please.

Oh Gen! For fuck's sake. Why couldn't he just let it go? Come to that, why hadn't he just sent me a text message? He could be so roundabout when it came to the simplest things. He – I dug my phone out of my bag – oh. I didn't have a signal. I guess the coverage was patchy up here.

It was almost two o'clock.

I stuffed my phone into my pocket, ducked out of the apartment, and hurried back the way we'd gone last night. It took more of a nerve in daylight to traipse through the hamlet, where several picturesque relics were pottering in their gardens. In the hard grey light from the cloud ceiling, the scenery looked less Irish: no hedges, no rocky crags rearing out of the grass, and the grass itself was the wrong color, as were the trees: volcanically green, not bleached to a muted sea-green by fog and rain and wind. I sped uphill along the forest path. With every step, I felt increasingly convinced that Gen's note had been some kind of a cry for help.

Muddy and panting from the last part of the climb, I burst into the clearing.

Ned shambled towards me, his hands in his parka pockets and a hint of embarrassment on his face.

Now that it was daylight, I could read the plaque behind him. It said simply: *Danger. No throughfare beyond this point.*

I'd seen him watching Gen and me last night, and I hadn't believed I'd really seen him. Without even noticing it, I'd slipped back into my old habit of convincing myself that there was nothing to be afraid of.

I took his note out of my pocket and uncrumpled it. "You forgot to sign this," I said with a little laugh.

"Did you not know it was from me?" He turned his face away, but failed to hide his grin. He knew he'd fooled me. "I thought you'd recognize my handwriting," he said.

Motherfucker, this isn't your handwriting, I thought. I was with you in Miss Kelleher's class. I watched you sweating over those curly capital *S*s and *I*s and the *p*s and *q*s like upside-down musical notes. I know your handwriting and this isn't it. You deliberately disguised it.

"So where have all the others gone?" I said.

Ned did an elaborate look around the clearing. Oh, he was enjoying himself hugely. "Most of them are somewhere in these woods, I think. But then again, they could be miles away. They went to pick bamboo roots, or was it bamboo shoots? This is the season for them, apparently. They took both vans, but those of us not entranced with the scheme got dropped into town... I walked back. It's only half an hour by foot."

"Who else got dropped off? There was nobody at the apartment."

"Sato-kun. Kiichi. Tad. They were going to buy souvenirs."

"Yeah," I said distractedly, "it's a big deal here. Whenever you go anywhere, you've got to buy boxes of manju and senbei and chocolate and God knows what for everyone at home. I guess today is their last chance."

So I could expect no help from that quarter.

In the daylight, the trees around the clearing glowed the livid green of spring, and I had to change my mind about the stream again: it *was* a river. Gushing over the boulders, spraying off them in white fans, the water had a chaotic beauty. Between the last boulders, the torrent rolled over in a smooth black lip that trembled continuously, as if on the verge of speech. A dead branch hung in the spray, twisting in a pattern that never quite repeated itself.

I faced Ned at a comfortable distance. Not a *safe* distance – I had no illusions there – so I braced myself, preparing for a crazy flight through the woods. I was smaller and nippier, but the tangled undergrowth would diminish that advantage, which meant he'd stand a good chance of catching me. I didn't want to take that risk unless I absolutely had to.

"So what did you want to talk about, Ned?"

He looked taken aback. At last he reached into his parka pocket. "Basically, this." He brought out several sheets of paper folded together. "I'm not the creative type, so maybe I'm missing the point, but I just don't understand why you thought this was... all right." His voice thickened on the last words. Clearing his throat, he unfolded the papers and passed them to me.

With mingled astonishment and relief, I recognized my own handwriting, a scrawl like a strung-out version of French copperplate, with hooked *p*s and *q*s that testified to the efficacy of Miss Kelleher's old-school teaching methods.

Let's Talk About You

Did it excite you?
Was it the first time?
It must've been the first time
So did it excite you?

Was it the best one?
I'm sure it was a good one.
It must've been a good one,
I'm sure it excited you

So let's talk about you
And the little places you call home (2x)

Let's talk about you
Silent, sobbing, guilty, and alone

I know it was the best one,
Powerful like a pointed gun,

I'm sure you had a good time,
'Cause you knew it was the first time
Did I excite you?
That peculiar stain,
Did it disturb you?
And I'd thought it was a good one

(chrs)

The only thing you've ever done
I hope it was a good one.

The words stretched and hooped in my head, and I heard the thundering bass line and ingeniously deployed snares that made "Let's Talk About You" a keeper. There's no such thing as lyrics that stand on their own.

You're No Fun

August days wasted in the city
August nights, tedious and swollen
You're no fun
A mediocre novel I've already read
A joke with no punchline except in your head
A person who should be, should already be dead
You're no fun no fun

August days and nights counting up the charges
You're the criminal, murdering my life
You're no fun… (chrs)

If you thought being good was good enough
If you thought that sincerity mattered
If you thought being good was good enough
If you didn't get why you were here
August days, all these days, tedious summer holidays
You're no fun… (chrs)

Just a little bloodbath
Just a little bit of fun
But you couldn't even laugh
No fun, no fun, you're not the one, you're no fun

I never finalized my lyrics. They evolved constantly, word by word. That was one of the joys of gigging.

The last sheet was especially dense with crossings-out and scribbled corrections.

~~Ned's Game No Way Out~~ Unfair Game

Don't forget that moment,
That special moment,
Don't forget that wonderful light in your eyes

Bone is not as strong as it looks
And I can't remember how long it took,
While you try to keep your feet on the ground
The noose still tightens with that awful sound

Don't forget about the sea, don't forget
The light on the breakers,
Don't forget about the lost days dreaming
Of what sleeps beneath the waves.

Memories, sinking, something glitters
On the edge of your vision,
Whispers of weakness
Sweat-soaked on a winter night

It eats at you, it claws at you,
It takes its due in flesh
It lives in you, it consumes you,
But this is for the best
This game was never meant to be fair

We didn't print our lyrics in the CD liner notes. And "Unfair Game" wasn't on any CD, anyway. So where had Ned got the lyrics? I didn't have to ask, because I knew. The sheets of paper were A4. There were shadowy rectangles around the words. I was always leaving my bag around. It had never occurred to me that anyone would pinch my notebook, photocopy a bunch of pages, and – put it back? Had he? Yes, he had, because I'd seen it when I took my phone out.

"What?" I said lightly. "You don't like my rhymes?"

He drew the photocopies out of my hands. "I'm not a rock critic." A dull flush discolored his tan, his emotions getting the better of him. "I'm just the fucking roadie, but I'm entitled to my opinion. I've only chosen these as representative samples. But this is what I'm talking about." He underlined the outro of "You're No Fun" with a finger that shook slightly.

"Well, I'm sorry you don't like it," I said. "But you're in the minority. This is the song that's selling *U-Turn Day.*"

"That's what I mean! You're selling *this.* You're making money off *this.*"

"Oh God," I said, "don't make me defend the artist's prerogative."

"You call this art?" He shuffled rapidly through the photocopies, shaking his head as if he could hardly bear to look at them. "I call it self-promotion. Oh, it's a nice little hustle you've got, pretending to be shy of publicity. While you're dishing your life story to anyone who'll listen."

"You know what, Ned? Don't assume, because it makes an ass out of you and me." *Just a little bloodbath,* so maybe that had been a lapse of judgement, but at the same time it was only an image. Ned had to be aware that he could hardly lay claim to the authoritative interpretation. "It may not be art, that's for our listeners to judge. Everyone's entitled to their opinion, including you. But I'll tell you what it isn't, is autobiography."

We stood there facing each other.

"What is it, then?"

"I just write about stuff that's important to me."

"And never mind that you're trespassing on someone else's privacy, is that it?"

He wasn't listening. A chilly trickle of panic seeped through my gut. "Listen, Ned, no one's ever asked me, so what's this song about? It *never* happens. Not even the guys have ever asked me, you know, in a serious way. And that's—"

"Because they don't fucking understand English."

"No. They don't ask because they don't give a damn. That's artistic freedom in the twenty-first century. No one gives a damn, so you can say anything you like." *So I did.*

"If I wasn't hearing this with my own ears, I wouldn't believe it." Ned inhaled sharply through his nostrils. "I don't know, Shanti, it may not mean anything to the majority of your listeners, but it sure as hell does to me. I ordered your first CD off the internet, you know. By the time I got to track three or so, I felt like someone came up to me and punched me. Couldn't believe my fucking ears." His face was reddening again. "You've taken my life and used it to further your pitiful excuse for a career! I really did think better of you."

"It's songwriting," I repeated. "Haven't you ever listened to the radio? It's got nothing to do with reality. It's got nothing to do with you."

"Oh, yeah, 'Ned's' what's it, 'Ned's Game,' that's got nothing to do with me. I appreciate your decision to leave my *name* off!"

"What the hell do you want?" I said. "Royalties? We're not making that much fucking money!"

I tensed my knees, watching the center of his body, shifting my weight forward. In my mind I was already plunging down the mountain.

But Ned just shook his head with a ponderous show of sadness. "What do you want, she says. I can't believe… I never thought we'd end up fighting like this."

In his voice I heard the forlorn drifter I'd written a song for. Too late. I wasn't going to fall for his little-boy-lost shit again. I waited.

He rolled his shoulders and turned his head from side to side, cracking out the kinks. "I'm all for nature." He glanced up at the ridge that loomed over the treetops. "But fuck, I'd get claustrophobic if I had to live here year-round."

"I would, too," I said.

"Don't understand this mania for onsens, either. They're nothing but gigantic fucking bubble baths without the bubbles. Give me the sea any day… My house in Samui? It's right on the beach. It's not finished, hasn't even got a roof, but I sleep there now and again. The weather's warm enough most of the year. Crime's a worry, but I'm a light sleeper. As a matter of fact, I've been diagnosed with insomnia."

"Tad had insomnia," I recalled, "when he was working on a contract for Microsoft. He was under so much stress. He got some prescription sleeping pills. They seemed to work."

"I don't like taking pills. I'll smoke a joint and that usually sends me off all right, but if it doesn't work, I just hop in the truck and drive down the road to my house. I can always get to sleep if I can hear the sea."

"I sometimes have trouble sleeping, too," I said.

"You've repressed everything, haven't you?"

"When I want therapy, I'll ask for it," I said brittly.

"I had therapy. Did I tell you that? Two years. My grandmother paid for an English-speaking analyst. Waste of money. I spent the entire time staring at the wall."

I didn't know what he wanted me to say, so I shrugged and said, "I would have done the same in your place."

"I kept my mouth shut for *you!*"

I blinked and took a step backwards.

"Meet me halfway. That's all I'm asking. Meet me halfway!"

My bravado crumbled. The part of myself that was still daring me to taunt him I now recognized as insane. Very slowly, I sidled back towards the scooped-out part of the bank where the path started. "Therapy hasn't caught on in Japan," I said. "Which is kind of a pity, because I know a lot of people who could use it. But personally, I don't believe in—"

"Nor do I! That's what Petra could never understand."

Petra? Oh, yeah: Ned's ex, German lawyer, mother of two.

"She couldn't understand that the problems I have, they're not the kind of problems therapy is set up to address." Ned was talking fast, almost gabbling. "I keep trying to put it behind me. For a long time I thought I *had* put it behind me. But then it came back. It's nothing you can treat with a pill. My head just fills up with images that just sit there, like fucking statues in a temple, until I want to burst in there like Indy Jones and blow it all away. And I can't talk to anyone about it." His voice grew louder, as if he thought I wasn't listening. "I told you! The analyst in Denmark. There's no one in the world I can talk to - except you..."

I backed up again and hit a snowbell bush that was just coming into flower. Tiny white blossoms kissed my hoodie like an attack of stars. "I don't want to talk about it," I whispered.

"But we have to talk about it."

"What about Alastair?" I said dully. "Why not him? Why me?"

That rush of color flooded Ned's face again. Even with his tan, his coloring was so fair that his emotions were frighteningly visible. "Alastair? He's got his Ivy League degree, hasn't he? He's got his prestigious job. He doesn't have any problems. He's getting along just fine."

"And I'm not?"

"No, you're not. Your life is screwed up beyond belief. Sooner or later you've got to come to terms—"

"It's no use!" I shook my head. "Ned, it's no use. Listen, I'm sorry you didn't have anyone, but Alastair and I have been talking about it for years. So anything that you can say to me, you can say to him." Sheer terror inspired me. I dived my hand into my pocket and speed dialed by touch as I brought my phone to my ear. We'd gained a lot of altitude, so I had a signal. "You can tell him whatever you were going to tell me. We can all talk about it together." Lamely, I laughed.

Ned grabbed my phone away from me, squinted at the screen, then switched it off. "Fuck. You were going to call him."

My arm stayed stupidly extended, my fingers stinging. "Can I have that, please?" I sounded ridiculously formal.

"You really love this phone, don't you?"

"It's got my life in it."

"Sure. Everyone's got their life in their phone these days. That's why I left mine in Thailand. If I ran into trouble at customs, although that would never happen… if they confiscated my phone, it might cause a fucking war. The names I've got in there."

"Speaking of customs," I said, "I can't believe you dared to take your uh, merchandise through—"

"Normally, I wouldn't be taking it through myself. But don't worry, I've never been stopped yet."

"Oh yeah? What's your technique?"

"I'm Caucasian and I travel business class." He shrugged, weighing my phone in his hand. "So, do you reckon life wouldn't be worth living without this hunk of plastic?"

"I wouldn't say that. Life's always worth living."

"Mine's not."

He spoke so matter-of-factly that I blinked, unsure if I'd heard right, unsure how to respond even if I had. At last I said, "Give me my fucking phone, Ned, it's not funny anymore."

"Nah. Don't feel like it. Not today."

He raised his arm. I jumped at him, trying to pull his hand down. He grabbed my arm. At the same time, he casually hurled my phone over my head, into the river. It would only be fair if he went in after it, so I pushed him in the chest with all my strength. It felt like pushing an impossibly heavy door. He stumbled half a step backwards. I pushed him again. He still had hold of my left arm. With a practised movement that I didn't know how to counter, he bent my wrist up and swung me around, making me take one big running step past him and another step into the air.

The world stood on end. I didn't even have time to scream before I hit the water.

My feet whirled over my head. Which way was up? I couldn't get a breath that was all air. The current tumbled me between the boulders, banging me into them and shooting me past them so fast that I couldn't grab onto them.

The battering came to an end.

The water all around me seemed to stretch and stop, as if I'd been flung into some crazy Galilean experiment where there was nothing to choose between rivers and girls when it came to falling.

Night has fallen.

Evenings at Fuschia Cottage are safe, since June is here, but that's not enough to compensate for the fact that Nigel's here, too. They're downstairs fixing an elaborate curry. The cottage has a modern kitchen, whereas the farmhouse only has an ancient range that you have to feed with briquettes. Why doesn't Nigel spring for an electric cooker? Then they could cook up at the farmhouse by themselves. And eat by themselves, too! No bistro here, no boulangerie, no tabac, but I'd rather go hungry than eat anything Nigel's touched, I vow to myself, as I always do. In reality, I've started to grow, so I won't be able to stop myself from having seconds and then filling in the corners with sweets from my shoplifted stash.

It sounds like they're well stuck into the plonk already. June's screams of laughter mingle with the low rumble of Nigel's voice. They're having une grande fête down there, a party for two. I try to block them out by concentrating on the game of Scrabble I'm playing with Ned.

But Scrabble with Ned is always an exercise in frustration. "That's not a word!" I scream. He hangs his head and gathers his tiles in again. I become obscurely furious with him for giving in so easily. "Alastair! Alastair!"

Alastair is hunched up at his desk with his back to us, drawing, tapping his pen on his teeth, kicking the leg of his chair, drawing, kicking, tapping. I've snooped in his desk, so I know what he's drawing: comics – except they're not comics like *G.I. Joe* or *Judge Dredd*. Each page tells a whole story: *The Life Of Sebastian, The Mosquito King, The Clockwork Necromancer*. I'm not very impressed by his art skills, but I've agreed not to tell June that he's drawing at all. I understand why it's got to be a secret: he doesn't want her to think he's copying her.

As a condition of letting me and Ned into his room, he forbids us to look over his shoulder. You can't even stand in a position where you might be looking, so I stay on the floor and scream at him.

"Look how he spelled *zephyr!* That's wrong, isn't it? It's *ph,* isn't it? Isn't it?"

Alastair ignores me. I persist until he jumps up, white with rage. "Look it up in the fucking dictionary! Fucking hell!"

"It's OK," says Ned, laying out the letters with a smile. "I've got another word."

"You didn't have two Rs! Ned, you took another R when I wasn't looking! Put it back, put it back!"

Nigel's voice comes through the floor. "Kids! Keep it down! We're not bloody interested!"

Nigel is very sensitive to noise. When he's not the one making it.

I can hear June laughing. She thinks he's so funny. I scream at Ned, "You cheated! You always cheat! It's not fair!"

"Fucking hell," shouts Alastair. He takes one stride across the room, picks up the Scrabble board, and throws it into Ned's face, tiles and all. "If you can't play by the fucking rules then don't fucking play!"

An instant of silence. Then: "I'll speak to them, love," and Nigel's heavy footsteps on the stairs. The cottage is so small that he's upstairs before any of us can move except Alastair, who throws books on top of his drawings to hide them. Nigel pushes the door open, its splintered edge catching the carpet. His enormous shoulders fill the doorway and his head blocks out the light on the landing. He brings the smell of curry and pot into the room. Alastair stands with his hands at his sides. I crouch where I am, paralyzed by the impulse to flee. Ned crawls around the floor, picking up the Scrabble tiles. "Alastair, old chap," says Nigel. "Don't use that fucking language at home."

Get it? He's joking. With Nigel, everything is a joke. Alastair is supposed to hear *fucking* and think Nigel is on his side. How can Nigel think that, when he's bruised and bled Alastair half a hundred times? Well, maybe it's not so farfetched. Ned has suffered worse, and *he's* still on Nigel's side.

Alastair is rubbing the palms of his hands up and down his jeans, as if he's rubbing off sweat.

Nigel looks at his son picking up the game pieces, shakes his head and sighs. Then back to Alastair. "If you want to make anything of yourself," he says softly, "you have to be better than they are. You have to be fucking perfect."

Sometimes I think Nigel is trying to turn Alastair into a creature like himself. Sometimes, in my darkest moments, I think he's succeeding.

"As soon as you let them see a trace of weakness, they'll be on you, pulling you down." He gazes into Alastair's eyes, exerting his hypnotic power, which is considerable. "You have to learn self-control."

Alastair says in French, "Ç'est drôle, coming from you."

"Sorry, old chap. Didn't catch that. Come again?"

Smiling, Alastair says in English, "Nothing."

"Very good. But try to keep the bloody volume down. Understood? Feeding time in half an hour, give or take." Nigel lumbers out of the room, retreating while he's arguably ahead. He's ridiculously protective of his dignity – but I won't understand this until many years have passed. Right now, it doesn't seem ridiculous at all. Nigel's dignity is a minefield extending for an indefinite distance around him. It's safer to keep away from him altogether. But how can we keep away from him when he's *in our house?*

I pick up the pencil we've been using to keep the Scrabble score and stab the carpet between the outspread fingers of my left hand, picturing a princess, twelve years old and pathetically beautiful, stitched with knives to a wall.

"Don't worry, Shanti," says Alastair in French. "He daren't touch us any more."

"You would have caught it when you said *nothing.* If June wasn't downstairs."

"No, I wouldn't," says Alastair with confidence. "He'll never lay a finger on either of us again. He's afraid she'll blow him out if he does."

Catch it. Blow him out. Both of us have fallen into the habit of using these grotesque euphemisms. Although I'll lose my accent and learn yet another language in the years to come, I'll never be able to entirely scrub this idiom out of my mind. It originates from the same place Nigel does. Sheffield, I think.

What does Nigel see in June? Probably the same thing everyone does: an exquisite face, a spritely figure, and a sense of joie de vivre that often makes her seem more childish than her own children. What does June see in Nigel? The obvious, I suppose. Towering strength, clever hands, the ability to hold a whole pub rapt with his wit. But she's not as enthralled with him as she used to be.

We're too old to tell her what's going on. Too big, too proud, too shy, too fond of secrecy. Our years in Paris killed our instinct to run to her with our problems. All four of us, including Nigel, have tacitly conspired to keep her in the dark, which is probably the main reason that it's always felt like some kind of nightmarish game. But now she has an inkling what he's capable of. And it can't be a coincidence, I think, that they've been rowing a lot recently.

Tonight is a rapprochement: a disappointment.

But Alastair reminds me, "We're *winning.*" The confrontation with Nigel has energized him. He sweeps his sketchbook and pens into his desk, then seals the drawer with a piece of sellotape positioned just so, which is supposed to deter me and Ned from snooping. "She's going to blow him out pretty soon, no matter what. Don't you recognize the signs? I do. He's nearing his expiry date. Still, that's no reason not to help the process along." All this in an intense whisper. This is the way he used to be, and I relax imperceptibly. For a little while, at least, I've got him back, fully engaged and on my side. "Aiken Drum at supper? That'll wipe the smile off his ugly face."

Aiken Drum had been one of our family songs when Alastair and I were very small: *And he played upon the razor, the razor, the razor, and he played upon the razor, and his name was Aiken Drum!* And he played upon the windscreen, the windscreen, the windscreen - you get the idea. The sort of thing no one much older than five could enjoy. But a few months ago, we resurrected Aiken Drum and refined it to take advantage of Nigel's sensitivity to noise. June is immune to it, which makes it an ideal trick to play on him when she's there, as he has to simmer in silence.

Grasping after the impetuosity of happier days, I sing under my breath: "He *was* a big fat *ee*jit and his *name* was *Aiken Drum!*" I tap the skirting board with my fingernails in a skittering rhythm. Tap t-t-t-*tap!* It's the sound of lights coming on in the night, a constellation of deliciously scary possibilities. Years later I'll rediscover this thrill onstage, riding the high of my own audacity, reveling in the flip side of the terror that keeps me coming back for more.

Alastair, moving across the room, taps the chest-of-drawers: tap *tap,* and he's past. You can't even be sure you heard anything. A third outburst of tapping makes us both look around at Ned, who's kneeling in the corner by the wardrobe.

"I wasn't cheating," he says as soon as he has our attention. "I wasn't."

"Oh, who cares?" I say in exasperation.

"No, Shanti," says Alastair. "You let him get away with it every time; that's why he keeps doing it."

"I do not let him get away with it! But he never owns up."

"That would be a start." Alastair rounds on Ned. "Why do you keep saying you weren't cheating when we know you were? That's what interests me. What's the point of denying it? No one believes you. Including *you.*"

"I don't mind if you believe me or not. I wasn't." Ned lowers his head. His fist, with Scrabble tiles peeking between his knuckles, creeps out to one side and taps on the wardrobe.

Alastair and I look at each other with a wild surmise.

Long before we came into his life, Ned had reinvented the classic survival strategy of the weak – keep out of the way when possible, take your punishment "like a man" when it's inevitable. Under our influence, he's learned to shoplift, play truant, and lie with a straight face… all the "French" tricks that Nigel detests in us. But ultimately, our objectives and Ned's are incompatible. We want Nigel and June to break up. Ned is terrified that they'll break up. That we'll move away and leave him all alone with Nigel again. His dearest dream is that Nigel and June will one day get married. And so he's always stopped short of joining in Alastair's practical jokes, or even in the games we play, such as Aiken Drum, which are supposed to "help the process along."

Of course, there's also another reason he doesn't join in – a much simpler one. He's a scaredy-cat. His desire to please Alastair has never outstripped his cowardice.

Until now?

The possibility of a temporary operational alliance arises before my eyes, lustrous and scarcely credible, like a fairy castle on the horizon. I telepathically beam a question at Alastair, who nods.

"Like this." He taps one heel on the floor, taps one shoe against the other, and simultaneously clicks his thumbnail against the nail of his index finger, all without being seen to move a muscle. "You've got to be covert."

Ned taps his knuckles on the floorboards beyond the edge of the carpet. It's a Moroccan one we brought with us from Paris, brightly striped and fraying at the ends.

"Too loud."

Tap, tap, tap.

And he played upon the floor, I think, and let out a hysterical squeal of laughter.

"That's more like it," says Alastair in satisfaction.

What do you think about when you're dying? I should have guessed. You think about swimming.

The distance between thinking and doing is the distance between life and death. Or between death and life. For a split second that lasted forever, I struggled to want to live badly enough to make my limbs work. At last I popped to the surface. I breathed and coughed and choked and my legs gave way. I fell over again.

I'd been standing up. The water was less than five feet deep.

I rose into a floating crouch and stayed there, just breathing, for a few minutes. The world had grown very small. Eventually I registered desirable qualities in the distance: dry, flat. I half stumbled, half swam that way, tripping on the stones that lurked underwater. Waist-deep, knee-deep, and then I was falling down all over again on a little pebbly beach.

I threw up. The nuts and crackers I'd eaten for breakfast, and a lot of water.

After that I just lay there.

The trees rustled overhead. A bird craked. The breeze whispered softly over my body. Nothing had ever smelled as homelike as the loamy scent of the dead leaves mushed among the stones that my cheek rested on.

At last it dawned on me that Ned might guess that I wasn't dead and come looking for me. I'd crawled out of the water on the other side of the river. He'd have to climb down the mountain, wade across the river, and then find a way upstream on this side. But I'd lost all reckoning of time. He could be here any minute.

I wobbled to my feet.

The pebble beach led back to a clearing like the one at the top of the waterfall, only tidier and better furnished, with a wooden picnic table and a tanuki-proof metal litter bin. I turned for a last look at the waterfall. A billowing white sheet, it didn't look as high as it had felt. Thirty feet? High enough. The water had to be fairly deep at the bottom, or I wouldn't be alive. But it spread out into a wide, placid green pool with mossy rocks at the edges. The overflow burbled away downhill, bereft of all impetus.

A nice place for a picnic on a summer afternoon.

A nice place for a fatal accident.

If Ned didn't manage to kill me, the irony might.

A path opened off the far side of the clearing. I started down it, but had difficulty walking in a straight line. I stopped and tipped my head left and right. Warm water trickled out of my ears. Idiotically, that was when I realized that everything I had on, including my sneakers, was sopping wet. And as soon as I knew I was wet, I also knew I was *cold.* It was late in the afternoon. Beyond the mountains, beyond the clouds, the sun must already have gone down.

Where did this path lead? It wasn't going uphill, but it wasn't going back to the road, either. Not if the road was still where it had been this morning.

I kept on walking. There was nothing else to do. Besides, while I concentrated on putting one foot in front of the other, I didn't shiver so badly.

"Shanti!"

My head jerked up, but my voice didn't work.

Tad came towards me. "Have you been swimming in your clothes?"

"Kind of," I managed to croak.

"Ha. Mmm. OK. It's only about ten minutes back to the dormitory."

"Not sure I can walk that far. I'm cold."

Tad frowned. Then he muttered, "Oh, we've known each other long enough." He shrugged his leather jacket off, letting it fall on the path. He was wearing a black sweatshirt from Pantera's 1992 Japan tour. He stripped that off, too, with his t-shirt inside it. "Raise your arms. Good girl." Clumsily, he pulled my hoodie and camisole off over my head.

Of course, my bra was wet, too. "Don't look," I croaked as I undid the hooks and stuffed it in my pocket. I struggled into his t-shirt and sweatshirt, which smelled of cigarette smoke. "OK, you can look now. Put your jacket back on. You can't walk around like that."

At last we emerged from the trees. Across a broad hillocky lawn, the hotel rose eleven storeys tall, its windows glowing in the twilight.

"You'd better go in and take a bath," Tad broke the silence. "As hot as you can stand. Get your core temperature up. The shower at the apartment doesn't work. Besides, I don't know if the others are back yet. They were going to eat in Kusatsu, but..."

He knew I wouldn't want them to see me in this state. I appreciated the thought, but all I could say was, "No bath. I just want to lie down."

"And who's going to sing at our homecoming show if you catch pneumonia?"

"Not sure I can sing, anyway. My throat is fucked." I would have started crying then, if I'd had any strength left.

"What... no, never mind. Let's just get you warmed up." Tad steered me across the parking lot, through a herd of tour buses, into the hotel. Old ladies in yukatas and young couples with children gave us funny looks and scuttled aside as we crossed the lobby. Tad neither flinched nor commented on this. He pushed the elevator call button. "The baths are on the B2 level. I've got the key to the apartment; Joaquin gave it to me when they dropped us off in town. I'll get some dry clothes for you and bring them over."

"Thanks. Uh... Tad?"

"Yeah?"

"Were you looking for me? Or were you just out for a walk?"

"Just out for a walk? In the mountains? In March? Not this city boy."

The elevator in front of me pinged open. A phalanx of old ladies swept me in.

Women of all shapes and sizes thronged the cavernous baths. I washed my hair with the cheap herbal shampoo that came out of the dispensers. Every time I opened my eyes, I caught someone staring. I always got stared at in onsens, but...

Reluctantly, furtively, I examined my body. I irrationally feared I'd discover a broken bone, an open wound, something missing. I was still in one piece. But the shadows of bruises floated under my skin, seeming to flow with the light when I turned my limbs. My left elbow sported a huge graze that was still oozing blood. I sprayed it with the hand shower until it stopped bleeding.

I almost went to sleep in the largest bath, with the water lapping my chin and the echoing murmur of conversation around me. Eventually I got too hot and climbed out. The roar of hairdryers filled the locker-room. Stark naked, I approached the attendant and received the plastic bag of clothes that Tad had left with her. I blanched at the awful realization that he'd sorted through my dirty laundry in order to find a (relatively) clean set of underwear.

When I came out of the locker-room, I spotted him in a massage chair at the end of the hall. "Thanks for waiting."

"You're still wearing my sweatshirt."

"I'm hungry," I said vaguely.

"Do you want a five-course traditional dinner?"

"Uh..."

"Good, because I bought food on my way back from town. We can eat at the apartment. None of the others are there, or at least, they weren't fifteen minutes ago."

They still weren't. After so many hours in the fresh air, the frowsty pong of the apartment turned my stomach. I huddled on the shabby tweed sofa, staring at the blank television screen without seeing it.

The others were in Kusatsu, but where was Ned?

Wandering up and down the river, looking for my drowned body, or my living body to drown it a second time?

Tad fixed two mugs of Nescafé instant and stuck a convenience store bento into the apartment's ancient microwave.

I wordlessly accepted the mug of coffee he gave me, but didn't drink it. I just wrapped my hands around it for warmth. Now that I'd started thinking about Ned again, I couldn't stop.

My life's not worth living.

How fucked up was it that I was *worried* about him now?

The microwave pinged. Tad handed me an extra set of disposable chopsticks and sat down beside me. Tonkatsu with rice, pickles, and lemony sweet potatoes. I swallowed a few mouthfuls, then put down my chopsticks and climbed the step into the tatami room where we'd all slept. I dropped to my knees and pawed through the futons. Shingo and Yves, who were neat freaks, had packed up their stuff, but everyone else's belongings were all over the place. "Tad, could you put the light on?"

"What are you looking for?"

"Ned's backpack. It's not here."

"Course it is." Tad came and joined in the search, folding futons as he went. Within minutes we'd tidied up the room. "OK," he admitted. "It's not here."

Numbly, I sat down on the sofa again. "He must have been here. How did you miss each other? How did he get in?"

"We're on the first floor." Tad nodded at the windows that gave onto the balcony. Our washed-out reflections floated in the glass. After a minute Tad went to draw the curtains. "Do you feel like telling me what happened?"

I barely heard him. An even worse thought had struck me. Ned might have got up early and hidden his backpack somewhere on the hotel grounds. No one would have noticed it was gone. And if that was what he'd done, he'd been planning to disappear all along.

So much for *you're the only one I can talk to.* So much for *my life isn't worth living.*

He'd intended all along to kill me.

On cue, I started to shiver again. I wasn't cold anymore, so what the hell was wrong with me? I drove my knees together and gripped my elbows, trying to stop my body from shaking itself to pieces. Tad shoved the table aside and knelt in front of me. "Shanti, talk to me. I saw when you took your top off..."

"I thought I t-t-told you not to look."

"Your elbow was bleeding."

"Th-th-that's the least of it."

"Did Ned..."

Oh God, what if he thought Ned had raped me? I couldn't allow him to think that. But I couldn't think of a good lie. I couldn't even think of a bad one.

When I'd told him roughly what happened, without any context to make Ned's attack on me rationally explicable, not that it had been rational in the first place, I folded over double, wrapping my arms around the backs of my knees. To hell with coping on my own. I needed to talk to Alastair.

"Are you all right?" Tad worried aloud. "Do you want me to call an ambulance?"

"No. I'm f-f-fine. Just can't stop shaking."

"Is there anything I can do? Anything. Just say the word—"

"It m-m-might help," I said into my knees, "if you w-w-would hold me."

Was that my voice? Did I say that? Jesus Christ, I must have hit my head as well as everything else. Before I could take it back, Tad said in a choked voice, "Oh, Shanti."

He laid his arms over my back, his chin on my shoulder.

"That's not helping," I muttered.

"OK." He prodded and nudged me until I was lying on my side. Then he stepped onto the sofa and lay down behind me. He slipped one arm under my head and tentatively crooked his other arm over my waist.

"What if the others come in?" I said.

"I'll say I'm giving you first aid. Think they'll buy it?"

"I don't want them to know what happened."

"Then I'll explain that we're having a torrid sexual relationship. Better?"

"I think I'll just pray they d-d-don't come in." I closed my eyes. After a moment, Tad lay down again and put his arm back where it had been.

It had been ages since I spooned like this with anyone. Four years, eight months, to be precise, the length of time since I broke up with Jonathan. Tad held me, his cheek against the back of my head, his arm staying chastely around my waist, and I gradually stopped trembling as a warmth that was different from simple physical heat spread through my body. He could be anyone, I thought. It wouldn't matter.

"Shanti?"

"Yeah."

"I thought you'd gone to sleep." His breath tickled the back of my neck. The arm around my waist tightened as if he thought I might start trembling again. "One question. OK?"

"Go on."

"Was it an accident?"

I couldn't help laughing. "Are you kidding? He tried to kill me."

I didn't expect Tad to believe me. It was such an extreme claim that it could be taken as parody, another way of saying *Hell if I know.* But I felt him nodding slowly. "From day one, I figured that you guys had some kind of history. So I've been keeping an eye on him."

Oh God. "You mean… you came looking for me – for us – on purpose this afternoon?"

His voice was annoyingly calm. "This morning he was the last one out of the apartment, except for you. We tried to wake you up, but you were so out of it, we decided to just let you sleep. I came back in to hurry him up... And he put something down on the table. So I… I made out like I had to get something from my backpack, and when I passed the table, I saw it. *Dear Shanti. Meet me by the river."* He paused. "I didn't mention that I'd seen it. I didn't know for sure it was him who'd left it there. But then… the others went off to dig bamboo roots, and we were looking around the souvenir shops in town. Kiichi and Sato-kun went off one way, and Ned went off another way. And I was wandering around by myself. And I just started thinking…" Tad trailed off, shifting position against my back.

I thought about sitting up so I could see his face, but I didn't want to see his face. I didn't even want to hear this.

"I just kept thinking: this doesn't feel right. So I came back to see if you were here. And you weren't. It was about three o'clock. I waited for a while. But in the end, I decided… it's a nice day for a walk." He laughed, mocking himself.

Now I really wished we weren't having this conversation. For as long as I'd known Tad, he would always opt to believe the best of people, and run a mile to avoid being confronted with proof that they didn't deserve it. But put together, maybe Ned and I constituted a proof that he couldn't run away from, like an independently verified scientific experiment.

Dread crept up on me. I'd been counting on him not to take my story seriously.

"Well, this cat has nine lives. Uh, maybe eight now, but that's still plenty," I said brightly. It was my turn to try to kill the conversation. "I didn't drown, I didn't break anything, and you'll be happy to hear that my throat feels fine now. I think it was just raw because I threw up. So I'll be able to sing tomorrow!"

He lifted his arm from my waist, and I felt a tiny pang of regret. Now that I'd claimed to be fine, I didn't need to be held anymore. That was how he'd interpret it. Wouldn't he? But he didn't sit up, so I didn't move, either.

"I don't give a damn if you can sing tomorrow or not. I just want to be sure that you really are OK."

"It matters to *me* that I can sing tomorrow."

"OK. Fine, it matters to me, too. But I'm also worried that you may be hurt and not know it. Adrenaline can mask pain."

"My adrenaline wore off hours ago. Unfortunately."

"So you are in pain."

"Not really."

"Where?"

Why couldn't he just shut up and hold me? "My ribs," I said reluctantly.

"Shit!" Tad sat up. "I'm going to take a look. OK?" He tweaked at the hem of my sweatshirt. I flashed back to Gen's hands slipping under my clothes last night. Did Tad know about that? No, he wasn't that observant. And he'd been busy watching Ned.

I rolled over and buried my face in the smelly sofa cushions, mutely arching my body so he could work my sweatshirt up to my armpits.

"You're covered in bruises."

"They haven't come up properly yet. It takes at least twelve hours."

"You sound like you know what you're talking about." Very gently, Tad prodded my ribs. Then he began to stroke around my ribcage with a touch as light as silk. "Does this hurt?"

"Tickles."

"Does it hurt when you breathe? I should have asked that before."

"No."

His hands swept gently down to the low waistband of my jeans, up my spine, and around the hollows of my waist. The light swooping movements hypnotized me. "You're bruised, but there's no swelling," he murmured. "If you'd cracked a rib, it would swell up. Looks like you're in the clear." His hands stilled. Something tickled my back, a slightly sharper prickle. Then his breath heated my skin. He brushed his face over my back as delicately as he'd stroked it with his hands. The prickling touch of his hair electrified my nerve endings. He pressed his lips onto my spine, and I gasped aloud. "Tad, please stop."

"Really?"

"Yes. Please," I rolled onto my side again and grabbed his sleeve, afraid to look into his eyes. I pulled him down beside me and pulled my sweatshirt back down where it ought to be. "Please," I whispered. "Just hold me."

"Gladly."

He gave me his arm for a pillow, just like before, but now that sense of calm was gone. I wasn't trembling anymore. I was quivering with tension. After a moment, he took my free arm and pushed my sleeve up to my elbow. He began to stroke my forearm with the same delicate swirling movement, using just his fingertips now, and damned if it didn't have the same effect on me.

He strained against my back, and I could no longer ignore what was pressing into my buttocks.

I wrenched away and sat up on the edge of the sofa. Tad swung his feet down to the floor. "Whew," he said. He cleared his throat, reached for a cigarette, slipped his rings back on. (When had he taken them off? I would have felt them on my skin, but I hadn't.) Same old Tad, who I'd never been remotely attracted to. So what had he just done to me?

Post-traumatic reactions can manifest in strange ways, I told myself.

But what was *his* excuse? He wasn't saying anything. Tad, who could laugh off anything this side of the apocalypse, wasn't saying a word.

"Oh hell," I said, watching the blue flame leap out of his Zippo. "Can I have a cigarette?"

"You quit."

"Tad."

"You only just survived, and now you want to throw your life away? Mottai nai."

Sensing that he didn't really mean it, I took a Lucky Strike from the packet on the table and plucked the Zippo from his fingers. The smoke tasted foul. I inhaled grimly. "Nothing makes you feel more alive than flirting with death," I said. "That's what smoking is all about, isn't it? I'm alive, I'm *alive,* and I want to keep on feeling this way."

Tad did the Japanese version of a shrug, tucking his chin down and narrowing his eyes. "So have you decided what you're going to do about Ned?"

The nicotine was making my head spin. I couldn't think. I'd been way too open with him.

"I don't think I can do anything about him," I said disingenuously. "I mean, he's gone."

"For now. Apparently. But what's to stop him from trying again?" Cigarette clamped between his lips, Tad got up and went over to throw the half-eaten bento in the trash. "You could go to the police, I guess. But I don't think it would do any good. It's your word against his, isn't it?" He ran the faucet to wash our chopsticks, even though they were disposable ones. "Not that *I* don't believe you. I do."

There was still some corner of him that *didn't* believe me. I seized on this glimmer of hope. But before I could decide how to exploit it, the door crashed open. The Cold Coeur Family crowded in, filling the room with noise, dumping earth-stained plastic bags on the table. Tad exclaimed over the bamboo roots they'd dug up - great hairy brown things like the fangs of trees. I flopped back on the sofa and dragged on my cigarette.

Joaquin's eyebrows went up. "Tad, how many times have I warned you not to give her cigarettes? It's bad for her voice."

"Hey, we came here to relax," smiled Tad. "Anyway, it's just one. Right, Shanti?"

"That's right," I said, and lost whatever I'd been going to say next as I remembered I was wearing Tad's sweatshirt. What would I say if anyone noticed?

"Hey, guys." Nina looked puzzled. "Where's Ned?"

I pretended to be as mystified as anyone, and Tad took his cue from me. Where could Ned have gone? We couldn't imagine. The only thing we knew for sure was *how* he'd gone. Without a car, the only way out of Kusatsu was good old Japan Railways.

As for *why,* that fueled the conversation for the rest of the evening. A consensus emerged that he must somehow have got into trouble in Utsunomiya last night. In panic, the smokers made a move to flush all the baggies of weed and half-smoked blunts they were holding. Then they changed their minds and decided to finish the shit off instead.

I contributed as little to the discussion as possible. "I'm resting my voice for tomorrow," I claimed. Snuggled in my sleeping-bag, I let the conversation wrap around me like a cocoon.

But when midnight came, I got up and moved to the door. It wasn't difficult to catch Tad's eye. "I need to borrow your phone," I whispered when he reached me. "OK?"

"Sure. But..."

"I need to make an international call. But I've got a phone card, so it won't show up on your bill."

"Are you going to call your mom?"

"No. My brother."

Part 2:
I Would Die For You

Kabukicho is Shinjuku's legendary backside: a dozen square blocks of sex shops, host clubs, hostess clubs, soaplands, Chinese massage parlors, snack bars, pachinko, mahjong parlors, illegal gambling dens, cocktail lounges where they lure you in with discount coupons and then hit you with a ¥10,000 table charge, movie theaters, gay bars, revolving sushi restaurants, and theme cafés for tourists, all basking in a fifty-year glow of hysterical media coverage. Judging by the movies, you'd think you could hardly move here for bullets. In fact, the police did a pretty good job of chasing the yakuza out to the suburbs in the '90s, but now the Chinese gangs have moved in. So Kabukicho is as seedy as it ever was, and Oasis, a drab little den on the Ni-Chome side of the lights and noise, is as obscure as ever. You can validate your indie credentials just by a) knowing about it and b) getting here in one piece.

The owner, Hibi-san, is a local legend. He played in one of those underground late-seventies metal bands that no one appreciated at the time but later turned out to have influenced a whole generation of musicians. He first opened Oasis as a bouquet to the heavy metal community – a bouquet appropriately reeking of spilled beer, smoke, vomit, and piss. The club languished when the Shibuya sound was big and everyone wanted to be the next Pizzicato Five, but with the comeback of pure rock 'n' roll, it gained a sort of specious retrospective cachet.

But even before that, when Joaquin was just a random gaijin with no job and no money, Hibi-san had taken him on as assistant sound engineer / odd-job guy. He'd probably seen it as suitably offbeat to have a white guy tending bar. He got credit from me, however, for being the first person in Japan to recognize Joaquin's talents. He'd sponsored Joaquin's first working visa, fudging the figures with an easygoing contempt for authority. When Joaquin incorporated himself as Cold Coeur Productions, he'd taken over responsibility for his own paperwork. But still, if it wasn't for Hibi-san and Oasis, Gorot would never have existed. So Joaquin continued to work here once or twice a week, even though the pay was crap. And when we were deciding where to hold our homecoming gig, we'd really had no choice.

By seven o'clock, the crowd had overflowed from the club onto the stairs. I threaded through on my way back from buying cigarettes, feeling like a very slow comet with a disruptive gravitational field. People I'd never seen before in my life were breaking off their conversations to watch me perform the fascinating feat of going downstairs. The balance of the crowd was inside, catching the band that Hibi-san had slotted into second place on the bill, a fourpiece called The Sticks with a white Australian drummer. The Aussie had commented that somebody must be trying to create a new subgenre: Bands With Gaijins In. This might actually have been close to the truth. Hibi-san had grown cynical in his old age.

A hail of sonic pebbles beat on my ears as I pushed through the club door. Confucius, the Apex A&R rep we'd met in Hakodate, whose real name I'd learned but forgotten again, had shocked us by showing up. Now he was talking to Joaquin, Shingo, Chiharu, and Hibi-san himself. I stood on the fringe of the group and lit a cigarette. Joaquin didn't even notice. He was bluffing nonstop to stay in the conversational game with Confucius and Hibi-san. They were talking about - what else? chart trends. How the industry was in for a "rationalization" now that Oricon, the Japanese equivalent of Billboard, had started tracking the sales of major internet music stores. How an even greater rationalization would ensue if download sales counted, too.

"Cold Coeur doesn't sell downloads," I piped up. "We give them away. That's how we grew our fan base. By giving people music that isn't shit. Operative word, *giving.*"

"Tais-toi," Joaquin muttered out of the side of his mouth. Of course, the very idea of free downloads was anathema to anyone who worked for a major label.

They moved onto the ringtone market, which is bigger than the download market in Japan. I was asked what ringtone I had on my own phone. "You're going to love this," I said, pulling out my phone.

Confucius laughed aloud. "It's the theme tune from that show. *The Dukes of Hazzard!*"

I nodded, grudgingly impressed. "I once had a boyfriend who used to hum it whenever I came in the room." In retrospect, maybe that's when I should have known that Jonathan wasn't the love of my life.

Chiharu laughed politely as she handed my phone back. I sneaked a glance at Joaquin. He hadn't noticed. Nor had Shingo or Hibi-san. None of them had noticed that my phone had lost all its dings and scratches, as well as the string of sandalwood beads that it used to have for a strap.

I'd spent the whole afternoon going from store to store until I found the same model as the one that Ned had thrown into the river. I hadn't been able to find a similar strap, but I'd bought a USB cable, gone to an internet café, and downloaded my old ringtone. I'd known it would be worth it to get the details right.

It had also helped me to kill the day. We'd left Kusatsu early this morning. As soon as we got back to Tokyo, everyone had scattered to go home and change their clothes, take a shower, do whatever they had to do before tonight's show.

Everyone except me.

The odds were good, I thought, that Ned, too, had come back to Tokyo. And he knew where I lived.

So when Joaquin dropped me off at Shinjuku, I'd gone into the station with Shingo, Naoya, and Yves - but as soon as they were out of sight, I'd come right back out again.

Sooner or later, I'd have to go home. But right now, I wasn't thinking that far ahead. Right now, nothing mattered except getting through this gig. Even without a major label A&R rep in the audience, this would have been a big show. Close to capacity. On a fucking Tuesday night.

Talking to Alastair last night had helped me get a handle on my emotions. My body was another story. When I woke up this morning, I'd been so stiff I could barely move. That had worn off to some extent, but when I took a shower at the internet café, I'd seen that my bruises had turned resplendently purple. There was one on my left shoulder, high enough to be revealed by a scoop neck, so I'd gone back to the coin locker where I left my suitcase and changed into the dress that I'd bought at Yuki's shop, Goner, in Hakodate. A vintage lace shift, cut in half at the waist and sewn back together with a ribbed khaki waistband, it was very mini, but a pair of ochre tights and my cowboy boots hid everything that it didn't cover. To complete the look, I'd fixed my hair in an updo, riveted in place with several dozen bobby pins, with tendrils hanging loose: a more adult version of my trademark Sing Sing hairdo. Still unsure if there really was life after hats, I was reaching back into my past for inspiration. I'd also taken more trouble than usual with my makeup, smoothing base over my end-of-tour breakout and shading my eyes with dark pink so that they appeared mossy green, not their usual hazel. If I looked hot, it wouldn't matter that I felt like shit.

That was the theory, anyway.

The Sticks jangled towards a climax. The crowd started to get rowdy up front. Good old Oasis.

Confucius twinkled at me. "Great atmosphere. Reminds me of Hakodate. Only this time, we're all here for *you.*"

I heard myself answering, but I didn't know what I was saying. To my dismay, Joaquin let me carry on the conversation. He'd probably decided that by letting me display the limits of my professional polish, he could shrewdly play into Confucius's expectations.

"We just finished our first tour..." I straight-armed sweat off my face. Had that really been me, worrying about stiff muscles? "It was great, yeah, Tohoku and Hokkaido, all those cities. We'll have a crack at the Kansai area next time. Now that's a scary prospect. So anyway, we got back to Tokyo this morning... we were feeling kind of flat, you know, the way you do. But I tell you what. I saw those skyscrapers, over there," I gestured at random, "and I've never been so happy to see anything in my life."

Applause.

"We're kind of a motley crew. We've got three different *continents* represented in this band. But this is where everything came together for us, here in Tokyo. And so... coming back to Tokyo felt like coming home." I drew breath and yelled, "We're *home!*"

Laughter and clapping.

"This is the craziest fucking city in the northern hemisphere. This is the craziest fucking livehouse in Tokyo. And Hibi-san," I could see him bouncing around at the back by the sound booth, "you're the craziest old fuck on the planet! We love you!"

I caught Joaquin's eye, and we launched into "Over Here." Miraculously, none of our problems had seeped into our music. We were telepathically tight, and we had more confidence than ever before. Every note found its target. But in all honesty, that was mainly because the punters were making themselves into such big fucking targets. Half of them were our faithful supporters. The other half were ciphers. Swaying, sitting, standing, shouting along wordlessly with the easiest bits of the lyrics, they were doing what we wanted because they wanted to. Now that's love.

For the last week, I'd been trying to get a mental fix on the fans who were buying *U-Turn Day.* Now I felt like it should have been obvious to me all along. They were here.

Here in Tokyo.

These people had believed in us before there was anything to believe in, because that's what Tokyo is all about.

"So over here I'm dying of the details," I sang. "I'm lost between the lines. I'm demanding back something that was never mine. Hey yeah, over here."

"I know why Ned ditched the tour," Gen said.

I stiffened nervously. We were sitting on the steps of an office building at the other end of Kabukicho. I'd drunk too much beer at the afterparty and barely managed to get outside before I threw up. The mild night air smelled of smoke, yakisoba and garbage: here in Tokyo, spring had sprung at last. I swigged Crystal Geyser in an attempt to rinse the taste of bile out of my mouth. Shanti Hazard, rock star. "So why did Ned ditch the tour?"

Gen looked knowing. It wasn't an expression I associated with him. "Well, Joaquin was pushing Ned to maximize their profits. And they couldn't agree on the split. So Ned took off, and Joaquin never got his cut from the last two or three shows. Ara, ara!"

I felt dizzy with relief. "Serves Joaquin right for being greedy," I said lightly.

Gen nodded. "Ah, but Joaquin had his reasons. We - Miya-chan and Naoya and me - talked to him before the show tonight. What do you think? Listen, we sold nearly all our merchandise, didn't we? Which is fifty percent to the band, fifty percent to the label. That's how we've always done it. So each of us is clearly entitled to ten percent of those net sales. But he's not going to give us a single yen. He says he's 'recouping' it." Gen shook his head. "In other words, the tour went way over budget. He paid for it out of label funds, without telling anyone. He planned to cover the shortfall with his cut of Ned's profits. But that didn't happen, so now he's using our money to—"

"Well, hang on," I said. "If he supplemented the tour budget out of label funds, then there *weren't* any profits. And that's not Joaquin's fault. I know he's a devious SOB, Gen, but he's willing to do anything to support our music… he's willing to sell drugs to support our music. And personally, I respect him for that." Oh hell, why was I defending Joaquin? "If you don't want him to make executive decisions, you should be more involved in the financial side of the label."

"I know, but he's just so unprofessional!"

This wasn't about the money, of course. But I couldn't think of a damn thing to say that would make Gen feel better. More to the point, what I was going to say to Nina? I, too, had seen Chiharu sitting on Joaquin's lap at the afterparty. *Everyone* had seen her.

Kabuchiko streamed past us: gals tanned as dark as their Vuitton handbags, scouts with baggy black suits and anime hero haircuts, smelly schizophrenics lugging their belongings in shopping bags, young couples with the lovelight in their eyes. A pair of Chinese thugs (identifying marks: leather bomber jackets and stonewashed jeans belted at the waist) squatted under the vast neon sign across the street. An African tout worked the corner, intercepting salarymen. His lilting Japanese floated over a refrain of *Irrashaimase, irrashaimase* from the door of every izakaya and clip joint in earshot. Poor human race, I thought. Poor Gen. Poor Nina. Poor me.

"We're heading into a window of opportunity," Gen said. "We've got the major labels sniffing around—"

I couldn't help myself. "Do you think Apex are really interested?"

"They're one of the Big Three. If they weren't interested, they wouldn't have been there."

I hugged myself. "Wouldn't it be absolutely incredible if we scored a P&D deal?"

"That's the bait." Gen brought his hands together. "And you're already in the trap."

I couldn't see what he was getting at. "We approached Apex two years ago," I told him. "Before you were in the band. Back then, we were just like any other bunch of wannabes trying to land a record deal. And they treated us like any other bunch of wannabes: don't call us, we'll call you. But now - well, everything's different now. We've got the label. We got this far all by ourselves, didn't we? We can tell them to take a running jump if we feel like it. But I know Joaquin's happy that he got to make his pitch to Confucius."

Pre-internet, there was basically no way for an indie label to break out of its home market other than some kind of P&D - pressing and distribution - deal with a major label. Now, indie bands can exploit the internet for publicity, but one thing hasn't changed: You still have to have money to make money. If Cold Coeur Records could score a P&D deal with Apex, it would untie our hands financially, and we'd get shelf space in the major chains. I knew that was Joaquin's dearest dream.

An even dearer dream than I'd known, if it was true that our tour had drained the CCR coffers.

"I lost my job, Gen. I just found out today. They've given all my classes to the guy who was covering for me while we were on tour. I'll have to look for another job, but if Apex decided to support the label—"

"This is exactly what I'm talking about," Gen said. "You just don't get it. You and Joaquin are so focused on the label. But what if they're not interested in the label? Kinderbox, Three Fridges, Bon Kyoki And Sayaka, Love The Movie, That Takahashi, The Deadenders, Apebelle... and Chiharu." He reeled off the list in a flat voice. "What if they're not interested in any of them? What if they're only interested in Gorot?"

"What's your point?" I snapped. "That it's going to be all my fault if they're not interested in Chiharu, and she drops out of sight again, and you'll never get to see her, even hanging all over Joaquin? Shit, Gen, you are a masochist."

He sat beside me like an ice sculpture, smoke dripping silently from his cigarette, bony knees showing through the rips in his jeans.

I sighed. "Sorry. I shouldn't be taking my stress out on you."

"I'm ashamed of myself." He spoke slowly, staring at his sneakers. "I particularly wanted to talk to you tonight... and I got sidetracked. But there's something I have to say."

"What?" I said edgily.

"Sorry." He still wasn't meeting my eyes. "That's all. Sorry."

"Is that really all?"

"You were right. We can't let anything affect the band."

If he only knew.

I forced a smile. "I think we're going to be OK," I said. "I mean, wasn't tonight an awesome show? We annihilated them."

He smiled back at me, his relief profound and visible. He stood up and slung his gig bag over his shoulder. "I'll see you home," he offered.

Home.

Oh, shit.

I had to quit being a coward. My building wasn't in some creepy deserted area. It was practically within sight of the station. I'd have had to go home sometime. And what better time than now, when Gen was with me?

Laughing and bumping into each other, we meandered along the sidewalk below the Yamanote line, sixty degrees of geometric concrete bas-relief on our left, a queue of taxis on our right. As we crossed the street to turn the corner by the Rigolette Hotel, Gen took my hand, saying nothing, just squeezing it, a warm pulse that went straight to my heart. I allowed myself to think that this time maybe it wasn't about Chiharu. Maybe we really were going to be all right.

Two blocks off, my building reared tall and shabby on its corner. A man stood in the tiled forecourt between the walls of mailboxes. Doubts spun through my mind, while my feet kept moving. An unJapanese slouch, but you can never really tell... hair cropped short, glinting around the edges in the dim light, but it might be dyed... fitted denim jacket, not a bulky parka...

I didn't trust my instincts. I didn't believe my eyes until we got closer.

Close enough for him to see us, too.

He started forward, reaching out with one hand. The other hand stayed in his pocket. Gen said, "Shit. That's Ned." I stood paralysed.

He shouted down the street, "Hey, Shanti! Got something for you!"

"Hey," I shouted back weakly.

He started towards me. He still had his right hand in his pocket.

I wrenched my hand out of Gen's, turned, and ran.

"Shanti!"

"What?" Gen caught up, running awkwardly with his gig bag on his back. "What? It was only Ned!"

"Run," I gasped. We had a head start of almost a block. My bag bumped against my hip and my cardigan flew out behind me. Hitting the T-junction, I dived straight through the traffic, cars braking on either side of me, with Gen a couple of paces behind. We swerved back towards Gotanda station. But now people thronged the sidewalk, slowing us down. A dark swell of panic ate into my mind like the leading edge of an eclipse. Ned would catch up with me, and then... Would Gen's presence deter him? Or would he just murder Gen, too?

"Shanti!" His shout cut through the sidewalk clamor. Too close. "Hey, Gen, man! *Shanti!* What are you scared of?"

His voice landed like a whip on my shoulders, driving me on. I dodged to the outer edge of the sidewalk, where the crowd was thinner, and led Gen at a jog up the line of stationary taxis. Now the kanji on the arch of the station entrance glowed in sight, *JR Gotanda Station,* and now they were overhead. I fished my Suica passcard out of my bag as I ran... and skidded to a halt. All the automatic wickets showed red *Do Not Enter* emblems. It was a quarter past one. That flood of people had just come off the night's last train.

Gen panted, "What's going on? Why are we running?"

I was too breathless to answer. We dashed out the other side of the station and halfway into the zebra crossing. Wildly, I glanced around at the traffic, the neon signs for snack bars, fast food, fast cash, English conversation, blank faces. I grabbed Gen's sleeve and pulled him back the other way. A denim and blond blur converged on our trajectory. I put on a burst of speed. The automatic door of the first taxi in line swung open. I dived in, Gen right behind me. The taxi accelerated even before the door shut. Ned reeled back to the sidewalk, his face contorted with rage. The taxi swung under the Yamanote tracks and glided around the roundabout, beneath the splayed knees of the pedestrian overpass.

I hunched over my thighs, catching my breath.

The driver was a woman. Fortyish, heavyset, she'd pulled her black hair into a short ponytail that gave an indefinable impression of a crew cut. "Going anywhere in particular?" she said neutrally.

Gen looked at me. Where *were* we going?

"I... Please give me a minute." I couldn't have said it if the driver had been a man. But she'd intuited what was going on, I thought. She'd opened the taxi door a little bit early, two seconds before Ned would have grabbed me. "OK," I said. "Back... Back the other way. Can you do a U-turn?"

She swung around the block instead. We cruised back under the tracks and out onto my side of the station. I wanted to scoot down to the floor of the taxi and curl up in a ball. Instead, I pressed my face to the window. So many people. But Ned's height, the breadth of his shoulders, his blond hair, and even the rigid forward thrust of his head combined to pick him out. He was standing outside the station, looking at the screen of his cell phone. In the moment before he was out of sight, his head came up and he gazed around, as if he belatedly sensed that I was nearby.

I sank back into the seat, smoothing its pristine white cover. Gen sat stiffly upright, facing forward, his hands folded over his gig bag. I'd infected him with my panic, I'd made him run, and he wasn't going to forgive me for that. The distance in his profile forbade me to explain or even apologize. I tried, anyway, knowing it was hopeless.

The taxi slid to a halt in front of the Armageddon Institute. "Don't stop the meter," Gen said. "I'm going on."

"What?" I said. "Come on. Come in with me."

"No, I'd better go home. Got a lot of stuff to work on, stuff I noticed on tour..."

I swallowed. "Well, let me pay for this leg, anyway. It's going to cost you a bundle to get to Yokohama."

"I'll get Dad to pay for it." He gave a tight painful smile, and I knew the pain wasn't something I'd caused, but it was something I might have healed. Now I'd thrown that chance away.

Correction. Ned had taken it away from me.

The taxi drove off. I skittered down the cul-de-sac and rang the doorbell. The night felt large and wild at my back, raucous with the passing of a freight train.

Tad opened the door. He was still in his stage gear, a transparent yellow shirt over a brown tank top that said *Doctor Scythe,* jeans laced up the sides with leather thongs. Scandinavian progressive rock blatted around him. "This isn't the best time, Shanti." His eyes flicked past me, then back to my face, as if he wanted to make sure I'd come by myself.

I couldn't believe it. "You're kidding. You mean I can't come in?"

"I didn't mean that! I just meant... OK, come in. But..."

As I stooped to take off my shoes, I heard Joaquin and Nina's voices over the music in the kitchen.

"Oh no," I whispered. "Are they..."

Tad shook his head. "Let's go upstairs. I don't want to get involved."

"I didn't *try* to fail it," Nina was wailing, almost screaming. "I just blanked. You know what that means? I blanked, I choked, OK? I screwed up!"

"I know you screwed up, because this is what I told you at the time!" Joaquin roared. "You were not qualified to come on the fucking tour! Yes, I was pissed off with you, and I had reason for it!"

Nina screamed wordlessly. I started down the hall. Tad grabbed my arm. From behind the closed door of the kitchen, Joaquin shouted, "Tad, take her upstairs." Nina screamed again. "Or no, fuck, just get her out of here—"

"It's Shanti," Tad shouted.

I wrenched open the kitchen door. Joaquin fell back. Dirty guitars lashed out of the CD player on the counter. The TV on top of the fridge added a layer of fuzz. Nina sat at the table. Her hands came down from her face, revealing teary blotches. "Oh, Shanti. It's sweet of you to want to help, but we have to work this out for ourselves."

"Do you hear her? Get out!"

"What, so you can convince her she's in the wrong? So you can make her apologize, when *you're* the one that - that—" I switched into French. "That's been cheating on her?"

Joaquin switched into French, too. "You don't know the first thing about our relationship."

"I want you to be happy!" I screamed.

"And so you come tearing over here in the middle of the night? My God, this is fantastic! You're only our colleague, not our counsellor!"

I laughed loudly. "You're doing it again. Everyone else is always to blame, not you! Oh no, you never make any mistakes!"

"You think I'm perfect? Shall I tell you something? I'm sick of it. Sick of being perfect for you. No, Shanti, shut up!" Joaquin's eyes shone feverishly. "You want me to be perfect, and Nina, too, so that you can continue to believe in some kind of Hollywood ideal of love. But I am sorry to tell you that we are not perfect, and neither is love! It's not even permanent! And if that's what you believe in, then you believe in nothing." He repeated the word as if it tasted bitterly good. "Rien, rien, *rien!*"

"Are you trying to tell me I shouldn't trust you?"

"I'm trying to tell you that this is between me and Nina! It has nothing to do with the band. And that reminds me, we have a meeting with Apex on Thursday. Everyone must be there. It's necessary that we have a band meeting first, tomorrow I suppose, to discuss what we want from… from…" Joaquin rubbed his hands over his face. "I can't think about it right now."

"A meeting with Apex! But that's great," I said.

"It wouldn't be news to you if you hadn't ditched the afterparty, *again.*"

"Look, I drank too much and got sick. But I'm sorry. OK?"

"Apology accepted." Joaquin dropped back into English. "Now get out."

"Don't pick on her," Tad said. "She's only trying to help."

"I'm only trying to help," I echoed. "Nina, if you want to talk. I'm here; I'll be here."

She shook her head. I flinched from the sight of the tears trickling down her cheeks. "Maybe a while ago I would have wanted to talk. But not now. Jesus H. Christ. Not *now.* I'm kind of… we're in the middle of resolving some major relationship issues here."

I let Tad hustle me out of the kitchen. Their voices started up again as we went upstairs. "I knew she wanted to talk before," I whispered frantically. "She needed me, and I wasn't there for her! I just couldn't deal with everything at once. So I *avoided* her!"

"She'll need you again. She's the type who always needs someone."

"Are you on his side?" Even as I said it I thought: Stupid. Tad was always on Joaquin's side.

"I'm not on anyone's side."

I went ahead of him into his bedroom and reached up for the cord of the fluorescent ceiling fixture. In Japanese houses, even the bedrooms have fluorescent ceiling fixtures. Tad had tacked a length of Indonesian batik over it, which softened the light. He'd dumped his dirty laundry from tour all over the floor. Unedited footage of our Hakodate gig flickered on the aquarium-sized monitor on the triple-decker desk. On the bed lay a guitar, the Fender clone that Tad had had since high school, with two of its strings sproinging loose. "Are you going to start playing six-string again?" I said.

"I'm going to try and convert it into a baritone. When we did 'I Would Die For You' tonight, I had an inspiration that it would sound really good if I played the bass line on a baritone. You can get this kind of clangy tone, like you hear in some of Korn's stuff." He picked up the guitar. "All I have to do is take out the nuts, tighten the trussrod, adjust the height of the saddle…"

I listened to him, but I was also listening to the music leaking up the stairs, listening for anything that made it through the guitar frequencies. Tad put his conversion-in-progress down, lit a cigarette, and slumped into his desk chair. "Have a seat," he said vaguely.

The only place to sit was the floor. I leaned against his bed and fished out my Marlboro Lights. Without commenting on the fact that I was smoking, Tad pushed his ashtray to the edge of the desk nearest me.

It was a green ceramic frog with a cartoonishly distended mouth. I tapped my cigarette on its lip. "You were right. I shouldn't have tried to intervene. What a fucking mess."

"Don't give yourself too much credit."

"Do you think they're going to… to… split up?"

"I couldn't say. It's too complicated. They've been together so long. I don't know what it's like to be married for ten years. To be married, period." Tad shook his head. "You threw up. Are you OK now?"

"Yes… and no."

"Here." He plucked a half-drunk bottle of ginger ale off his desk and passed it to me. "It's a bit flat, but try to drink some. It'll settle your stomach."

I picked shyly at the bottle's cellophane sleeve.

"It was weird," he went on, casually. "Nina took off, no one noticed until she was gone, and then the next thing I knew, you and Gen had vanished, too. Did he take you home?"

I took a deep breath. "He walked me to my building… and Ned was there. Outside. Waiting for me."

Tad's chair swung around, bumping the desk. He stared at me. "What did you do?"

"Ran away."

"I should have been there. *I* could have seen you home. "

"You were helping Joaquin pitch the label to Confucius. That's your job. What happened, anyway? Joaquin said we've got a meeting—"

"You tell *me:* what happened?"

"Nothing. Literally, I told you. I ran away. So did Gen." I sucked on my cigarette, turning my head away. I felt like I might physically disintegrate if I had to talk about it. Ned pounding after us through the crowd, *what are you scared of?* A kaleidoscope of blank faces. Zem gaijin, zey no respect Japanese culture. Gen's shame.

I didn't want to see that kind of shame on Tad's face. What was I doing here?

"He really does want to hurt you." Tad sounded stunned. "What are we going to do?"

"I don't know," I lied. "Can I stay here tonight, anyway?"

"Stay here? Of course. You don't have to ask." Yet he sounded uncertain. He set the green china frog on the floor between us and lit a fresh cigarette. "I wonder, though… I hope… I mean, it's just my dad. I don't want to involve him. It's kind of awkward…"

I nodded and stood up. "I totally respect your dad," I said, remembering the taxi driver who might have saved my life and Gen's. I'd always unconsciously thought that taxi drivers were unimportant in the grand scheme of things, and that had bled over into my attitude to Kuroiwa-san. I'd been carefully polite to him, but in the same way you're polite to sales assistants. He deserved better. He deserved not to be used by me as an obstacle that Ned would have to get through. "I shouldn't have come here. I'm sorry, Tad. I wasn't thinking straight." I picked up my bag and moved towards the door.

"Where are you going?"

"Home." In all honesty, I hadn't decided yet. I opened the door and started down the hall.

Tad got in front of me before I reached the stairs. "Stay here as long as you like."

"I can't."

"Why? You were going to stay here tonight."

"I've changed my mind. I can't put you in danger."

"Let me worry about that."

"What if Ned comes here? I can't promise that he won't!"

Tad smiled. "I hope he does."

"Your dad. I can't put *him* in danger."

"I said, let me worry about that."

"All right, I won't go home. I'll stay in a hotel."

"A hotel." Tad shook his head. "You're still in shock. I'm trying to analyze this whole situation, and I know you can't afford to stay in a hotel for more than a couple of days. And it might take longer than that to… to… resolve the situation."

No, it wouldn't. But Tad didn't know that, and I hated myself more than ever for being too open with him, yet not telling him everything. "Listen, I'm not a completely evil person, OK? I couldn't live with myself if anything happened to you or your dad. If that sounds inconsistent, when I came here—"

"You came here because you knew you'd be safe here! And you *are* safe here. I know the ambiance sucks right now, but..." He glanced over his shoulder again, making sure we were alone. "Stay. Please, Shanti. Stay."

If you're going to go, go! I told myself venomously. Don't let him talk you out of it!

But he prodded me back into his room, and I put up only a formulaic resistance. So maybe I hadn't really planned to go. Maybe I'd just staged my exit to force him to bear the responsibility for my decision. I sat down on the floor again and miserably drank ginger ale.

"Good," Tad said. "So that's decided. Like I said, I'm trying to analyze this situation; it's an interesting challenge." He grinned. "But I have to say, it would be a lot easier if I knew *why* Ned wants to hurt you."

"Can't tell you that," I muttered.

"Go on. Whatever it is, I've already imagined something worse."

Wanna bet?

I put down the ginger ale, raised both hands to my hair, and started dragging out the bobby pins that held it up, as if that might relieve some of the pressure in my head. One of them caught a painful strand, and I wailed aloud, losing patience and grabbing the rest of my hair as if I could pull all the bobby pins out at once. "Now I remember why I never put my hair up anymore."

Tad caught my wrists. "Stop it. You can't just take it off. It's not a wig." He flexed his eyebrows comically. "Unless you've got more secrets than I know about."

I breathed shallowly, not meeting his eyes. He was too close. My voice edged into a higher register. "I just can't get these fucking bobby pins out."

"Shall I take them out for you?"

"I guess."

"All right, just stay there." He released my wrists and hopped up on the bed behind me. I turned to see him shifting the six-string and his tools to the foot of the bed. He sat down crosslegged, his knees nudging my shoulders. "Don't move, or I might stick you."

His fingers worked deftly through my hair, extracting the bobby pins. It felt strange: he was handling my hair more gently than I ever did.

"I liked this hairdo." Tad's voice broke the light trance I'd fallen into. "You looked... elegant tonight."

"Elegant? That's not really what I was trying for."

"And that's not really what I wanted to say, either." He added another bobby pin to the pile on the corner of his desk. "I wanted to say..." He hummed a couple of bars of the Clapton chestnut. "You looked beautiful."

"That's my job," I deflected the compliment. "So you think it was the right move to end my relationship with kooky headgear?"

"Definitely." He pulled out the last bobby pin. I rotated my neck, tumbling my hair past my shoulders. Tad slid his legs off the bed so he was sitting next to my shoulder. "To be honest, though? I don't think you need the kooky outfits, either." He gestured at my dress. "In Hakodate, you just wore jeans and some little top."

"That's pretty funny, coming from you." I touched his transparent yellow sleeve.

"Yeah, yeah." He grinned. "You guessed it. I just don't like you stealing the limelight."

I relaxed. "Well, I happen to like this dress, but I don't plan on sleeping in it. So can I borrow a t-shirt and some sweats?"

"Sure."

He was up to the elbows in his bureau drawer when the music downstairs stopped. The silence stretched like a soap bubble. I saw black spots before my eyes.

Joaquin's voice rose in an indistinct shout.

"Can we put on some music of our own?" I said loudly. "Drown them the fuck out."

"Now you're thinking strategically." Tad dropped folded clothes in my lap and leaned over the desk, clicking away the gig footage. "Let's see. GNR? The Manics? Dir en Grey? The White Stripes? Muse?"

"Don't tell anyone I said this, but do you have anything a bit mellower?"

"OK, how about this? VAST. It's some American guy. I haven't listened to it all yet, but it's got a lot of Gregorian chant samples."

"Sounds good," I said. And it did, churchy white noise stealing out of the speakers, drowning out whatever was happening downstairs. I let my head fall back against the edge of the bed. After a moment I opened my eyes. Tad was watching me. He looked away. I stood up with the folded clothes under my arm. "I guess I'll go downstairs and change."

"Into the line of fire? I'll just turn my back, if you like."

"Last time you said that, you cheated. But OK. I trust you." I retired to the far corner of the room and turned my back on him. I wriggled out of my tights and into his sweats, then let my dress fall to the floor. I drew breath, turned, and closed my mouth.

Tad sat on his bed, watching me. "Yeah, I'm cheating again. Those bruises look a lot worse than they did last night."

Standing there in my horrible padded Japanese bra (I'd bought new underwear in Shinjuku this afternoon) and Tad's sweatpants, I glanced down. On my way over the waterfall, I'd caromed into the boulders so fast that I hadn't known exactly where I hit. I knew now. I couldn't see my own back. But I could feel it.

I grabbed Tad's t-shirt off the floor and tugged it on. "Can we go to sleep pretty soon? It's been a long day. And we've got a band meeting—"

"Yeah, I've already confirmed with Shingo for tomorrow night."

"What's the deal, anyway? Confucius must have said *something.*"

"He's a pro, he has six hundred ways of saying nothing. I guess we'll find out more on Thursday… At least I don't have a job at the moment, so you and Joaquin won't have to go by yourselves." Tad rose, stubbed out his cigarette, and stretched. "So. We took all the sleeping-bags on tour, and right now they're in the washing-machine. You didn't bring yours?" He made it a question, although he'd seen me arrive with nothing except my shoulderbag.

"It's in a coin locker in Shinjuku. With the rest of my stuff." I fidgeted.

"Then I guess you'll just have to share with me."

We moved his guitar onto the floor. I hopped into bed, scooted over to the wall, and buried my face in the pillow. It smelled toasty, *bassy,* like the color of his skin. He turned off the overhead. Then the desk light clicked off and the topography of the mattress shifted as he lay down. The bed was a three-quarters width, so we weren't embarrassingly close together. Oh, who was I kidding? I was so embarrassed I hardly dared to move a toe. I opened my eyes. The darkness wasn't complete. He'd turned off the computer monitor, but left it booted to play VAST. Various LEDs leaked red and green shadows across the room. On the ceiling, my mind superimposed not the fleeting scenery of the sidewalk in Gotanda, not echoes of Joaquin and Nina's fight, but overlapping circles of heat.

Tad yawned. "Goodnight, Shanti."

"Goodnight."

I was back in Kusatsu, back in the water at the bottom of the waterfall. My limbs wouldn't obey my thoughts. I was drowning. And it felt so good. As hot as an onsen bath, the water swirled around my body, a zillion little bubbles kissing my skin. I wanted to moan in ecstasy, but my lungs were full of water: I couldn't make a sound.

I woke up.

Tad's hand stilled momentarily. Then he went on stroking my upper arm. Gently, so gently, his fingers were tying a knot of heat in the middle of my body. In a drowsy trance, I rolled over and allowed my fingers to run up his arm. He raised up on one elbow, shoving the futon aside, and pressed his mouth onto mine. I tasted his wildly crooked eyeteeth, his lips that felt softer than they'd ever looked... We broke apart to tug each other's t-shirts off, and then his body slid on top of mine and he was kissing me again, and I wrapped my arms around his shoulders, and he worked his hand under my head, and I opened my legs, and his hipbone dug into the bruise on my lower stomach, and I yelped, "No."

He reared back. I shook my head frantically.

"No. Stop it, Tad. I didn't mean it."

"You don't want to…? Then what are you doing in my bed?"

"OK, I'm sorry. I guess I sort of… but no. No."

"OK, I guess that was pretty fucked-up," he muttered. "Mind if I put the light on?"

"Do you have to?"

"I want to see you."

I covered my eyes. My eyelids turned dark red. I heard Tad's Zippo and smelled cigarette smoke. He was sitting up against the triangular piece of wall at the head of the bed, a Lucky Strike in his fingers. Still the same old Tad. Naked to the waist, but still the same old Tad. That was what I'd been afraid of.

"You're beautiful." He was staring at my chest. I couldn't even remember taking my bra off.

"Tad, this is me! Me, Shanti!"

"I know that."

"So..."

He sighed again. "Would you believe me if I said I couldn't help it?"

"Oh, for fuck's sake." I tried to tuck the futon over my breasts. It didn't reach, as Tad was sitting on part of it.

"Well, there's never been a good time to say this, but I'm going to say it now." He reached out and picked up my hand. Then he switched into English. "I love you. I – how can I say it? I really, really love you. I've loved you since three and a half years ago. Uh... that's what I wanted to say."

My hand fell from his. "We've only known each other for three and a half years. Almost four, I guess."

"Yeah, well, it doesn't feel like *only* to me."

I realized the music had gone off. I couldn't hear anything from downstairs. I hoped the front door was locked. *I love you I love you...* Why not *daisuki?* Or *ai shite iru?* Why had he said that in English? Had he really had a crush on me all this time? No. I didn't believe it. He was messing with my head to break down my resistance. "Why tell me now?" was all I could think of to say.

"Well, I guess I was afraid you'd run away, and I'd never get even one kiss."

"I *can't* run away," I said in surprise. "Not with Ned out there."

His eyes widened, and I knew beyond a shadow of a doubt that he'd forgotten why I was here. He'd forgotten that Ned was trying to kill me. With that insight, I suddenly trusted him even less.

"You're right," he said, smoking nervously. "What shitty timing. I hope you don't think... you know, if there'd been a clean sleeping-bag, I wouldn't have... I just couldn't stand it... but you don't have to. I hope you understand that you're not under any kind of obligation to me."

He was blushing. I hadn't known he could blush. The yellow slant of light from the desk molded his shoulder and the right side of his chest. Ridges of muscle shadowed the forearms dangling over his knees. All those years of playing the bass. And the six-string before that. As a teenager, Tad had been the bad boy who dyed his hair and played in a band instead of doing his homework. *Guitars and girls,* he'd told me once, summing up his high school career, *but the guitars won.* Not for the first time, I thought that I probably saw him differently than any Japanese person could. By my standards, he didn't have a trace of bad boy in him. He was just too nice.

I couldn't let him beat himself up like this, as if he'd exploited me in some kind of sordid sex-for-shelter transaction. I had to convince him that I hadn't been his victim. The irony was that I'd had a choice before, but now I really didn't.

I laid my cheek on his knee. He didn't move. I rose to my knees and pressed my face into the crook of his neck. He stubbed out his cigarette. Then he went still again. I breathed on the hollow behind his ear, then lapped the salt off his skin with my tongue. I licked down to his collarbone. He shoved me away. "Don't. That feels too good."

"Let me."

"No."

"Why not?"

"You're…" He touched the bruises on my ribs. "You're injured."

"You weren't thinking about that a minute ago."

"Let's just go to sleep." He flailed for the light.

"Fine," I said angrily. I flung myself face-down on the bed and waited for the light to go off. It didn't.

Tad knelt beside me and whispered into my ear. "Shanti, I'm sorry. I'm such an asshole. I didn't want to hurt you. I'm so, so sorry."

I rolled onto my back. "Is this a language problem? Why am I not getting through to you? You didn't hurt me. Fucking Ned hurt me. You're the only one I can rely on. I trust you," I couldn't let myself think about what I was saying, "you're my best friend, and… and…"

I'd said something wrong. Even from this angle, I could see that his face had closed like a window. I guess there's one advantage to hooking up with your best friend: you know all their expressions already.

"If you trust me, then why aren't you telling me the truth about Ned?"

"Because I can't."

"OK. I get the point. You don't want to talk about your past. That's OK. That's your right."

He was angry with me, and he had every reason to be. But one of the first things I'd learned as a performer is that anger is like electricity: you can use it for anything.

Tad pushed up on his elbow and looked down at my face. "I never thought this would actually happen." He was grinning idiotically. "I guess I'm in Ned's debt. Think he'd take it the wrong way if I thanked him?"

I had been feeling pretty good myself. I never would have suspected that Tad could make me feel so… well, *safe.* But at the mention of Ned's name, my euphoria evaporated. I had to fake a smile. "You could have made it happen before. You didn't *have* to wait for me to be injured and incapable of resistance," I teased him.

"I was afraid of screwing up the band. It's the first thing everyone says. Don't have sex with your bandmates. Not that I've ever been tempted before, I mean, Joaquin's a great guy, but he's not that cute."

"I've never had sex with a guy who *wasn't* my bandmate," I confessed. "Or a musician, at least. My body is my instrument, so I guess I only feel safe with guys who understand how important musical instruments are. Believe it or not, I was a virgin until I was twenty-two."

"Oh, Shanti." He hugged me. His voice vibrated through my bones. "I love you. You know that? Huh, huh? You know that?" After a moment he rolled onto his side and changed the subject. "It's almost four o'clock. Let's hop in the shower before my dad gets home."

We got half-dressed, tiptoed along the dark hall, and listened at Joaquin and Nina's door. Not a sound. All the lights had been turned off in the studio and downstairs. My heart thudded as I peeked into the kitchen. I half expected to see Nina sprawled on the kitchen floor, blood puddling around her body; I would skid in it when I tried to approach her - but the shadows were empty.

Tad switched on the light in the front hall and sorted through the outerwear on the hooks. I squatted down to count the shoes in the genkan.

"Nina's shoes are all here," I said, looking up. "But Joaquin's Adidases aren't."

"Nor is his jacket. Well, maybe he took it upstairs. And the sneakers." With a sigh, Tad let his armful of coats fall back in place. "Nothing we can do about it. Let's have that shower."

As in most Japanese houses, the bathroom at the Kuroiwas' was entirely tiled, with a showerhead on one side and a tub built in on the other. We didn't bother with the tub. Even so, the air quickly got hot and foggy. Suddenly, for whatever reason, I knew there was one thing I couldn't go on concealing from Tad. I'd already concealed it too long.

Reaching for Nina's shampoo, I said, "Did I mention my brother's coming to Japan?"

"Is he? No way! That's great."

I dolloped shampoo into my palm and started to work it through my hair. "He's arriving on Thursday."

"That's the day after tomorrow. It's the day we're meeting with Apex."

I nodded, eyes closed against the suds.

I'd called Alastair from Kusatsu and told him everything. He'd immediately promised to get on the next flight to Tokyo. But while we were on the phone, he'd surfed some online travel agencies and found out how much that would cost. This afternoon he'd called me back. Somehow, he'd convinced Oswald, his boss, that he needed to make a business trip to Japan. The catch was that I'd have to hang on, as he put it, for another forty-eight hours.

Why did everything with Alastair always have to turn into a complicated strategy? I'd had to put my own feelings aside before I saw the answer. It wasn't about saving a couple of thousand bucks. It was about deflecting suspicion. Alastair still hoped to convince not only Oswald, but also his girlfriend, Maisie, that nothing was wrong.

Well, it looked like he had that covered.

But I'd never been as slick as Alastair, and I hadn't been able to hang on for even a few hours, and now Tad knew too much.

I kept my eyes closed and rinsed the shampoo out of my hair. The sound of falling water filled the bathroom.

"Where's he going to stay?" Tad said at last.

With me, had been my plan. "At a hotel, I guess. He has some contacts in the city, but I don't think they're on 'come and crash on my floor' terms. I mean, it's the art world, not the indie circuit."

"No problem. He can stay here. Wait, his wife's not coming, is she?"

"They're not married. Just living together. But no, she's an actress. She's in a play. She can't get away." I dashed my wet hair out of my eyes. "They never go anywhere together. Alastair travels a lot for business. Hong Kong, Singapore – I've gone out there before to meet up with him, browse around the shows and do the night life with his art dealer buddies. But Maisie always stays home."

Tad somberly ran a washcloth up and down one arm. "What do they have in common?"

"Good question. They love each other, I guess."

"Well, as long as there's only one of him, we can fit him in here. What's one person more or less in this house? My dad will take him for a musician. And as for Joaquin and Nina…" Tad sighed. "It might be good for them to have someone they don't know to stay. It'd stop them from getting into another fight like tonight."

I thought Joaquin and Nina might not be in trouble at all if they'd had a few more opportunities, over the last ten years, to get into fights like tonight. But they never did. There were always fifty people inside Joaquin's perimeter, because that was the way he was, and Tad was right: one more wouldn't make any difference, even if it was Alastair.

And through the fog of my own misgivings, I saw that having Alastair to stay here might, in fact, be a good thing. Because Alastair might be able to accomplish what I couldn't. He might be able to convince Tad that nothing was wrong.

"I'll tell him," I said. The water beat down on my head, sluicing over my shoulders and breasts. What a difference there is between water in its natural state and hot water coming out of the showerhead. Yet it's all the same stuff. A treacherous killer with a hold over us. "He'll appreciate it. He's going to be on a tight budget."

"So, no sightseeing, I guess. No Kamakura, no Nikko, no Kyoto, no Mount Fuji."

"No onsens," I said, trying to turn it into a joke.

"No festivals. No kabuki. No temples."

I gave up. "No."

Alastair's plane was late. He emerged from the Nothing To Declare channel in jeans and an olive parka, towing a gigantic suitcase, looking pale and tired. As we hugged, I saw a cluster of aggravated razor bumps on his chin. Or were they spots? Like me, he often broke out when he was under stress. The scar above his right eyebrow stood out, white on white, the jagged shape of Bantry Bay.

"You guys look so much alike!" exclaimed Tad. "You sure you aren't twins?"

"Who's this?" said Alastair.

As Tad came forward, I saw him through Alastair's eyes: a skinny little Asian guy in red Converse, black jeans, and leather jacket over a khaki t-shirt with a Soviet kitsch emblem of a tractor. He'd pushed his sunglasses up on top of his head, so they raked his hair back in a spiky cinnamon halo. The skull earrings, the knuckles clustered with rings, the smile so wide, trying too hard …

Alastair stuck out his hand. "I'm Alastair Hazard, pleased to meet you."

"Pleased to meet you, too!" Tad pumped Alastair's hand. If he smiled any harder, the lower half of his face would fall off. "I'm Tadashi Kuroiwa, but everyone calls me Tad. Did you have a good flight?"

"Not really. Business class isn't what it used to be. The book I bought at the airport turned out to be crap, and I can't sleep on planes."

"Neither can I!"

"Alastair, we've got to get into the city by five o'clock," I broke in. "I expect after fourteen hours of sitting down, you're just about ready to sit down some more, aren't you? Good! We can talk when we're on our way."

As we maneuvered through the crowd, Alastair said to me, "This is the guitarist, right?"

"No!" My face burned. He knew the whole story, I'd told him. How *could* he? I caught his eye and realized that he thought it was funny. And it *was* funny, of course; it just didn't feel that way to me. I said in martyred tones, "You're jetlagged, aren't you? Tad's the bassist."

"But a bass is a kind of guitar. Only it have four strings instead of six," said Tad, giving Alastair an excuse to drop it.

"I know that," Alastair said. "I thought you were the six strings guy."

"No, that's Gen Tajitsu," Tad said after a moment. "I know Japanese names are difficult, but once you meet him, you'll have no problem to know I'm not he."

"I'm looking forward to meeting the whole gang," Alastair said. "Which reminds me, Shanti, what's all this about meeting your lawyer today? What kind of trouble are you guys in?"

Trouble! I laughed, as he intended me to, which must have further confused Tad. Pick your flavor!

"We're being courted by a major label," I told Alastair as we watched the orange boilersuits pack luggage into the hold of the limousine bus. "We have a meeting with their reps at seven o'clock. So we fitted in another meeting before that... You have to have good representation, it's the one thing that really makes a difference in this business." Joaquin's words, not mine. "So the six strings guy's father is a jazz guitarist, and he fixed us up with his lawyer. Sorry, I know the timing sucks."

"Why do they call this a *limousine* bus? It looks like a Greyhound dressed up for Halloween."

"God knows. Welcome to Japan. Alastair, what's with this enormous suitcase?"

"Rather have it and not want it than want it and not have it," Alastair said vaguely. "Courted by a major label? Correct me if I'm wrong, but isn't that a good thing?"

"Yeah, but we've got our own label." I was uncomfortably aware that by *we,* I meant *Joaquin.* "So what we want is for them to get behind the label. It's pretty common: if you see an indie release in a chain store, it's almost guaranteed that they've got some kind of tie-up with a major label. And it's also guaranteed that someone's getting screwed. And it's almost always the artist. But we've got one advantage, which is a record that's selling... excuse me while I freak out. We're number 96 on the indies chart, and I still can't quite believe it."

"Our songs have airplay now," Tad broke in. "If you turn on the radio you might hear Shanti. Very late at night."

"Yeah, so they've got something to gain, and we've got nothing to lose." Again, I was uncomfortably aware that Gen, for one, might not see it that way. Why else had he tackled his father for help? It couldn't have been easy to persuade Hiroyuki Tajitsu to get involved, even to the meager extent of setting up a meeting with his lawyer.

We climbed onto the bus. Alastair got a window seat, and I sat beside him. Tad sat across the aisle. As the bus ground into motion, an interminable announcement came over the PA, and by the time it was over, we were speeding along the East Kanto Expressway.

"Neat how the walls curve in at the tops," Alastair said. "I guess it's to cut down on noise pollution." He glanced across the aisle at Tad. His head was tipped back, his mouth open, hands slack in his lap. Alastair turned to me. "Hello," he said softly.

"Hello."

"I knew you were all right, but I... well, never mind what I pictured. You really are all right. Thank God."

"I know I should have told you earlier."

"You certainly should."

We'd been over all this on the phone, but I said again, "Sorry."

"Never mind. I'm here now. And you're all right; that's what matters. Incidentally, what's *he* doing here?"

"Tad? I think he's bodyguarding me."

Alastair stifled a laugh. I could see he'd already dismissed Tad. I wanted to tell him that might not be a good idea, but Tad had made a disastrous first impression, and once Alastair formed his impressions, he seldom reappraised them. It was the downside of being so smart.

"So..." He gestured with both hands. "Dites-moi. Dites-moi tout."

Alastair's face underwent a barely perceptible change when he spoke French: his lips seemed to harden, his eyes to grow warier, a layer of polish flaking off. The same thing was happening in my mind, now that he was here.

I took a deep breath and started from the beginning.

Alastair listened without interrupting. As a child, he never used to listen at all, but now I could feel the pull of his attention like a vacuum cleaner, sucking up every word. This was the worst thing that could possibly have happened to him. I felt terrible about inflicting it on him, but it was too late now, so I held nothing back. I told him everything I'd already told him on the phone, filled in the gaps that had been created by my self-exonerations, and finally summarized what Ned had told me of his movements over the last fourteen years, concluding with his job on Koh Samui. "It's nothing to do with Malcolm," I added. "Except maybe indirectly."

"I should say it is to do with Malcolm. Obviously, he's been stalking us all these years." Alastair expelled a loud breath. "I didn't want to freak you out about it. But I knew your band's website was going to get us into trouble. I've kept my name off *our* website, as you may have noticed. Google me and you won't get a single result. No letters to the editor. No published articles. I've never even participated in a conference above the informal academic level. Oswald has never been able to figure it out. I'm the last person you could accuse of having a shy and retiring nature, and I'm committed to the business in every other way."

"Believe me," I said, "I blame myself, too."

"Oh, for chrissakes. I didn't mean it like that."

"Well, it is all my fault. I'm admitting that right now."

"No. It's not your fault. It's just the way the world is nowadays. When we were kids, the internet didn't even exist. But now… Anyone can find out anything. Except the truth! But he already knows *that.*" Alastair fell silent. I studied the pamphlets in the mesh seat pocket. At last he said, "I wonder if we could buy him off."

I made a noise in my throat that wasn't quite a laugh. "We could try. If this deal with Apex comes off…"

"I could sell my car, and a couple of artifacts I've got around the place…" Alastair tapped his first knuckle on his chin, deep in thought. "I wish we knew more about these buddies he's staying with. Do they a) know about and b) approve of his career as an amateur drug pusher?"

I held back a nervous giggle. "I don't know anything about Gavin and Mike, but I'm not sure *amateur* is the word for Ned. On tour, if there were any fans that wanted to score, he'd just tip them the wink and they'd kind of migrate over to him, and he'd get their numbers and hook them up later. It was so slick, everyone was in awe. Of course, he was also hooking up my bandmates, most of whom are total dope fiends, so it behooved them to at least pretend…" My giggles escaped. "Oh, Alastair, do you know what I was thinking the whole time? Ned's finally discovered the secret of popularity."

"Premium ganja?"

"Yeah."

"I mean, nothing harder?"

"Well, that's my favorite difference between Tokyo and New York. Heroin's a career drug, and there aren't many opportunities here for career drug users." I made a mental exception for Hori-kun, the Kinderbox drummer. "I've never seen any signs of coke anywhere.

Speed is pretty big, but it's got a skanky image. It's the drug of choice of provincial biker gangs… the Japanese equivalent of trailer trash. It's not rock 'n' roll, tu comprends?"

"So Neddo knew his market."

"Well, I think anything he brought in, he could have disposed of it. Just because the supply is so limited. The customs are pretty effective, and there aren't many people that want to risk twenty to life in a Japanese prison. I don't think Ned cares about the risk. But I think in his own mind, he makes a distinction… I heard him talking to our guys once. He was very down on heroin: 'That shit can *kill* you.'"

Alastair barely smiled. "They didn't even look at my luggage. Just checked my passport and waved me through."

"Well, you're an American citizen. And you flew in from JFK. They probably figure if Homeland Security didn't find it, it's not there."

Alastair sighed. "No, I didn't."

"Didn't what?"

"Didn't fly in from JFK." He met my eyes squarely. "The truth is, I'm not here. I'm in Shanghai. There's a fair on: the rather oxymoronic New China Antiquities Fair. It started yesterday. I flew to Shanghai. Met up with a couple of guys I know from Hong Kong. They introduced me to some of the local players. The event really is new this year, kind of a trial project, so a lot of people are playing wait and see. Attendance was pretty sparse, but there are some local exhibitors that have never shown anywhere before. Tang bronze, Ming ceramics, assorted loot from the ongoing sack of Tibet… we've got a bunch of collectors who go apeshit for anything Tibetan. So I shook hands on a couple of deals. Stayed out all night being feted. Then back to the airport. Voila."

"No wonder you look wiped out," was the only thing I could think of to say.

He shrugged. "Oswald and I had already more or less decided I should go. The fair lasts a whole week. And Shanghai is a big city. So I just have to put in another appearance on the last day, and no one will know I wasn't there all along."

"Wait a minute! So you've only got a week?"

"Five days. But Shanti? If we can't solve this problem in five days…"

"I know, then we're really in trouble," I said glumly.

"If worst comes to worst, I'll think of some way to stay here until it *is* solved. That's a promise. OK?"

I felt absurdly comforted. I wanted to tell him how much it meant to me, the contortions he'd gone through and the lies he'd told for me, but I knew he would criticize my gratitude as premature. Alastair was a results kind of guy.

"What did you tell Maisie?"

"Same thing I told Oswald." He turned to the window to hide a smile of satisfaction at the way his plan had worked out. The incurved walls had vanished. The rain shrouded the distance in gloom. The expressway soared on tall legs across the endless acres of Monopoly-board sprawl, seeming to dip and rise in the distance, and I had the answer to the question that had rankled in my mind for the last two years: how much did Maisie know? The answer was *nothing*. Alastair had told her nothing.

We reached Tokyo in an unearthly premature twilight. The rain clouds had settled down onto the towers of the city, obscuring the skyline. All the neon signs had come out, and they seemed to float unmoored in the fog, glowing every color in the universe, spitting diamonds at close quarters. The expressway marched from Ginza to Yotsuya, high above the streets, between glass and steel dinosaurs with neon crests.

"I thought Tokyo would be like Hong Kong without the bay," Alastair said. "But it isn't, is it? Hong Kong is a vertical city. This is like some kind of multidimensional matrix." He was glued to the window.

Tad woke up and fumbled his hand out across the aisle.

The bus dropped us in front of the Keio department store on the west side of Shinjuku station. "We'd better take a taxi," Tad said. Pulling Alastair's suitcase, he dodged out of the bus shelter, into the rain and the crowds.

I caught up. "What about Alastair?"

"He'll have to come with us. Unless you have a better idea?"

"Sorry," I said to Alastair. "You are now witnessing my total inability to visualize impending logistical conflicts." Inside my head I couldn't help blaming Tad. If he hadn't insisted on coming with me to Narita, Alastair and I would now have been on our own. I could have ditched the meetings - it wasn't like it would make any difference whether I was there or not. Alastair and I could have gone for a coffee or a cocktail and continued our conversation. Instead, we were scuttling through the rain beneath a jostling roof of other people's umbrellas, every imaginable color, like the neon skyline. Prongs caught my hair and rain splattered my face. Alastair, six inches taller, got it worse.

We piled into a taxi. By the time we alighted in the Scramble crossing outside Shibuya station, it was ten past five and the meter read ¥3,700.

"I see at least one of the legends is true," said Alastair. "I've got it; I changed some money at the airport." He peeled a ¥10,000 note out of his wallet. As we scrambled out of the taxi, he addressed the driver, in English but in unmistakably rude tones: "Anywhere else in the world, you'd have immigrants undercutting these fares. It's called globalization."

"This way," said Tad, and went ahead of us at a jog.

"There's definitely an energy here," said Alastair as we dove through the crowd. If I'd ever told him that Tad's father was a taxi driver, he'd plainly forgotten it. "It gives you a fresh understanding of Ando Hiroshige's oeuvre. Where's Waldo? Where's Neddo? And where's this meeting?"

"I'm not sure." We were plunging along the street behind HMV, where the crowd overflowed the sidewalks and milled in the street. "I thought it was going to be at the lawyer's office, but... Tad!"

Ahead of us, Tad was juggling his umbrella and his phone. "Change of location!" he called back to me. "That was Gen. They're up here—"

We hustled past dingy staircases leading to secondhand CD and record shops: Shibuya's Vinyl Village. "Not where I would have pictured a top-flight entertainment lawyer hanging out," I sighed.

Alastair grinned. "Just remember, if in doubt, don't sign anything." The rain had brought out the curl in his hair, separating it into tendrils around his shining face. With his delicate nose and mouth, he looked like a Pre-Raphaelite angel.

"Gen!" I shouted.

He was balancing on a flight of brick steps that led down to a terrace below street level. We crossed the street and joined him under the building's overhang.

"This is my brother."

"Hajimemashite." Gen barely glanced at Alastair; he was staring at me in horror.

"Oh God." I swiped rain out of my eyes. My hand came away smeared with all the mascara I'd worn to look spirited and pulled-together for Alastair.

"What were you thinking?" Tad spoke to Gen in clipped, accelerated Japanese. "You shouldn't have left Joaquin alone with them!"

"He's not alone with them. Miya-chan's there. Made up a doctor's appointment to get off work." Shoulders hunched, Gen led us into the café that fronted on the sunken terrace.

I spotted a sign pointing to the restrooms. "Thirty seconds, OK?"

"We'll be upstairs."

"God, I feel bad about making you guys late," Alastair said as we edged between the tables with his suitcase.

The sign for the restrooms led into a sort of annexe with more tables. I blinked. "Nina. *Nina.*"

"Ssshh!" She rose.

"How did you know we'd need a bag check?"

She hovered, hugging her old Le Sportsac purse, neither sitting down nor getting ready to leave. She wore a pink sweater and jeans with one of her Indian scarves floating from her neck. A chick lit novel lay next to the coffee cup on the table, but it didn't look like she'd read more than a couple of pages. Her eyes flicked to Alastair and then fastened on my face. "Uh, Shanti, don't mention to Joaquin that I'm here, will you? Please."

"Nina, I've hardly seen you for the last two days. Even though I've basically moved in with you." While we were working on our presentation for Apex, she'd been lying low or hanging out with friends from work. "I thought you were avoiding me - us—" Joaquin. "Oh God, I've got no time, I've got to get to this stupid meeting—"

"Well, that's what *he's* been saying. *I have no time, I have no time.* And that he'd have time to talk after the meeting. So here I am. To talk to him after the meeting. But it's really no big deal." Her gaze slipped off my face, going to the mirrored wall, in which the bottom of the staircase was visible. "It doesn't involve you guys."

Like hell it didn't. But I had *no time, no time*– "We got caught in the rain, I've got to fix my face. This is my brother. Alastair, this is Nina Gorot—"

"I figured." Alastair smiled at her and dumped his backpack in the chair opposite. "You don't mind, do you? We can compare notes on having a rock star in the family. That should stave off boredom."

Nina rolled her eyes. "Wait until you have to sit through their shows, or rather stand through them. You don't know from boredom yet."

In the restroom, I reapplied mascara and concealer. There was nothing to be done about my hair or clothes. When I passed Alastair and Nina again, they were poring over the menu.

I climbed the stairs to the second floor. Our party was ensconced at one of the long tables perpendicular to the floor-to-ceiling windows. Hiroyuki Tajitsu smiled thinly at me - a first. The man beside him, with pouchy cheeks and a barcode combover, didn't look up from the point he was making to Joaquin with a gold pen on the back of one of the copies of our presentation. Thank God we'd prepared several color printouts of all twenty-seven slides. A projection screen obviously didn't figure in today's agenda.

I slid into the last armchair, between Tad and Gen, who looked like he was on the verge of passing out. Shingo, in a snappy pinstriped suit, looked like he was on the wrong side of the table. He'd checked Joaquin's numbers to ensure their plausibility, and now he was contributing more to the discussion than Joaquin or Tad. I realized I was seeing Shingo in full salaryman mode for the first time. And *hearing* him!

Japanese basically has three levels of politeness. I'd internalized the colloquial level, and I could do the desu-masu level, but apart from a few stock phrases, the hyperpolite business level was beyond me. *Gozaimasu, orimasu, osshaimashita* – hearing the deferential verb forms flowing from Shingo's normally foul mouth, I had to stifle a laugh.

It was laugh or cry, because I couldn't understand what they were talking about. The hyperpolitesse and financial / legal terminology combined into a buzz in my head that cast me immediately back to my early days in Japan, and from there back to my first days in school in Paris, like a stone skipping, skipping, and sinking into the foreign waters that I'd learned to walk on, but never plumbed all the way. I focused on Joaquin. Pale and tense, he nodded thoughtfully, as if absorbed in the graphs that the lawyer was drawing. It wasn't very convincing. I just hoped the lawyer didn't spot him.

The lawyer paused and looked questioningly at me. Shingo said, "Tajitsu-san, Asakawa-san, I'd like to introduce Shanti Hazard, our vocalist." He'd forgotten that Gen's father and I had already met on the sidelines of Celestine Trio and Tajitsu Quartet gigs.

The lawyer leaned precariously across the table to present me with his business card. I also had to lean at an ungraceful angle in order to take it correctly with both hands. For a horrible second I thought I was going to overbalance into the coffee cups. "Yoroshiku onegai itashimasu," I muttered, and covertly flipped the card over to read the English side. Shuichi Asakawa, LL.D., LL.M., Partner. In what? Asakawa Jigyo Kyodo. The rumpled suit and plain navy tie, the rapid-fire yet somehow petulant speech, gave the impression of a sales clerk with a bad attitude. Asakawa-san wasn't customer-oriented. Or maybe the truth was that *we* weren't his customers. We were just the product. No, we weren't even that. We were just raw material.

Hiroyuki Tajitsu mildly addressed Joaquin. "You have a tremendous opportunity being handed to you in giftwrap. And you're here with a shopping list? Let me tell you, I've been in this business for twenty-six years. Any other band would be saying, 'Where do I sign?'"

"I realize this," Joaquin's Japanese sounded so French that even I could barely understand him, "but we have certain non-negotiable requirements."

Tad's voice layered onto Joaquin's. Like Shingo, he was being hyperpolite, or was it sycophantic? I distinguished certain phrases because they were the good-Japanese version of Joaquin's non-negotiable requirements: authentic underground sound... creative control… package deal…

Joaquin might be pretending, but I didn't have to. I slouched deeper in my armchair and whispered out of the side of my mouth, "Ne, Gen. What 'tremendous opportunity'?"

"Apex has offered to sign us," he whispered back. "Three albums, *U-Turn Day* to be the first, reissue rights for *Xenophobia,* options, a solid marketing push, a domestic tour, the works."

His words turned up the gain on my world. The twilit street outside the windows, the cups and papers on the table, the smell of dusty upholstery, even the acrid taste of coffee in my mouth, all acquired a new weight of intensity and significance. "Why didn't I know about this?"

"The offer came through Asakawa-san."

"Why him?"

"He's our lawyer, isn't he?"

"Since when?"

"Since today."

"I don't remember signing anything."

"It's a formality. You can sign later." Gen shifted away from me. "He's a legend in the field, Shanti, we're lucky to have him."

We obviously had to bargain Apex up to the deal *we* wanted. So why weren't we talking to Confucius or whoever had greenlighted him to sign us? Why were Joaquin and Tad trying to sell the label to Asakawa-san, who should have already been on our side, if he was now *our* lawyer? I drew breath, then turned to Tad, who'd temporarily fallen silent as Shingo took over again. In my peripheral attention, I caught the gist of Shingo's argument: he was citing our numbers to prove that Cold Coeur Records was a potentially lucrative business venture. If *that* was what our hopes rested on, we didn't have any.

"They set us up," I whispered to Tad in English. "Gen's father and this lawyer. He's probably worked it all out with Apex already. No wonder he agreed to represent us. All he has to do is step in and collect his cut!"

"Not a setup. Good business."

"Is he on our side? Or isn't he?"

Tad didn't answer. He leaned forward, listening intently to Asakawa-san, who now seemed to be saying that Gorot's "tremendous opportunity" was a limited-time offer: it rested on the buzz that *U-Turn Day* had generated, the album's breakout airplay, and our chart position. I could only catch about one word in five, but I could read between the lines as well as the next person. Asakawa-san was trying to rush us into signing a deal that we would regret. Everything had happened so fast that we hadn't yet had time to discuss it properly, let alone figure out what it all meant, and that was part of the routine.

"We're your friends." Asakawa-san said it in language that even I could understand. "I'll tell you what we want from you, and I think it's the same thing that you want from yourselves. We want you to keep on making music the way you know, the way your fans want. That's the bottom line."

As he'd probably said to hundreds of suckers over the years.

But OK. If we were all on the same side, I didn't have to sit here in silence with my doubts. "Asakawa-san," I said, projecting my voice to cut across everyone else's. "It's nice of you to say the music is the bottom line. But I think there are elements in this negotiation, that aren't present today, that have a different view of what the bottom line is." I was pleased with that bit of Japanese: nice and vague. Unfortunately, I couldn't keep it up. I started mangling Japanese into the shape of the English in my head. "So let me ask you. On the basis of your experience and professional judgement, if we're willing to sacrifice on our side, would that make our terms more attractive to Apex?"

Everyone was staring at me. The attention jazzed me, but for some reason I was suddenly aware of my vulnerability as the only female at the table.

"Let me clarify," I said. "Why are they pushing for this three-album deal? Because I have a sense that the main reason is because it's their boilerplate, and they like to do things the established way."

Asakawa-san and Hiroyuki Tajitsu exchanged a glance and laughed.

"I fully understand that if we take a hit in the paycheck, you do, too. But if that's what we want, it seems as if you're obliged, as our legal representative, to at least make an effort to get it for us." *A good faith effort* was what I wanted to say, but I didn't know the term in Japanese. I wouldn't have been surprised to learn there was no equivalent: in Japanese business negotiations, good faith tends to be, well, taken on faith. Straining for some way to get to Asakawa-san, I tried to tap his cultural sensitivities. "You have to be aware that we've got obligations to the other acts on our label, just as you have obligations to us. We're not prepared to sell out and leave them behind."

Looking at Asakawa-san's face, and thinking about Suicide Bomb Bear and Bon Kyoki And Sayaka and The Deadenders and all the others, all of them trusting that Joaquin would do what was best for the label, I thought I'd said the right thing.

Until Shingo said, "Shanti, who appointed you our representative? Prepared to take a hit in the paycheck? Speak for yourself." He tacked on a smile, but he'd dropped the hyperpolite diction, and he called me *kimi,* signifying at once that I was on his side and that in the last few minutes he'd changed sides. He was loyal to CCR, but the salaryman in him knew when to re-up, when to quit, and when to get while the getting was good. He was the one who'd thought of the album title *U-Turn Day,* I remembered.

Tad said, "I think what Shanti wants to say is the financial issues are obscuring the real issue, which is creative control. The boilerplate contract would give them a license to mess with our shit, Miya-ch – Miyazaki-san, you know that."

Joaquin said doggedly, "We shouldn't have to make any sacrifices. We have an attractive business proposition."

"No, you don't," said Hiroyuki Tajitsu. We all looked at him. He looked at me. "Hazard-san, I hope you'll accept my opinion for what it's worth, as the opinion of an impartial outsider."

I cringed. What was it about Gen's father that shut me up every time?

"You don't have as much bargaining power as you seem to think. At this stage in the evolution of the Japanese music industry, Apex is the only major likely to take a chance on Gorot, and you can be sure they know that. What's more, there are certain considerations that you don't even seem to have thought about. Gorot-kun, you aren't Japanese. Even if you were to transfer ownership of the label to Kuroiwa-kun or Miyazaki-kun or my son – which I *don't* advise…"

He got a laugh for that. Gen the loser. It was the equivalent of a political joke around here. People laughed automatically, even when it wasn't funny.

"They're already aware that you're the key person in the operation. If you had to leave the country for any reason, that would be the end of Cold Coeur Records, Cold Coeur Productions, the whole show. And I didn't see anything in your presentation about your visa status."

No one spoke. We all knew that Joaquin's self-sponsored visa status as the owner of a kabushiki gaisha, or incorporated company, depended on his consistent overreporting of his income to the immigration authorities. I reflected panickily on my own visa status. I had a working visa from the Meguro Language Academy, but every yen that I made as a singer was technically illegal.

Tad broke the silence. "We understand that Apex doesn't discriminate on the basis of race, creed, or—"

"Don't worry," said Hiroyuki Tajitsu with a smile. "They won't be running to the cops, if we're not."

I realized with a sense of wonder that Confucius might have fucked up. In the conversation he'd had with Joaquin and Tad after our Oasis gig, which now seemed to have been pivotal, the question of visa status hadn't even arisen. Yet another example of the weird way that people latched onto us for being a Band With Gaijins In, and then forgot that Joaquin and I weren't Japanese. The weirdness cut both ways, of course: I constantly forgot that the people around me were Japanese, and then got blindsided by Japanese shit like hyperpolitesse. Or aging jazz guitarists who had a better grasp of reality than the pros who were paid for it.

"I don't think these considerations are dealbreakers. I'm only saying that Apex will be taking them into account." Hiroyuki Tajitsu leaned over his scruffy denim knees and took a sip of coffee that must have been stone cold. "Back to you, Asakawa-san."

"Those were very valuable comments, thank you, Tajitsu-san." The lawyer produced a fulsome smile and glanced at his Cartier watch. "Now, Fujita-san and Nakanishi-san should arrive in approximately thirty minutes. So if we intend to make a counterproposal, we would be well advised to clarify our demands." He swept together his copy of our presentation and stashed it in his briefcase. It was literally off the table. He opened a fresh page of his leatherbound notebook and looked at the five of us, all in a line around two sides of the table, with Gen stuck on the end like a piece of junk DNA. "I suggest you let me do the talking," he said kindly.

"Confucius is coming *here?*" I whispered to Tad in English, as Joaquin began to modify his non-negotiable requirements. I could have spoken out loud, I guess, but I'd had enough of feeling vulnerable. "These are just blatant pressure tactics!"

"If you want to be a rock star, get used to it." Tad looked unhappy. He probably felt like he wasn't living up to Joaquin's expectations of him.

"And who's Nakanishi-san?"

"Confucius's boss. Head of A&R."

Great. "Tad, can I ask you something? What I just said, was it all stuff that had been covered already? Before we arrived, or—"

"More or less, yeah. But you have such a unique way of putting things. I think you made an impact."

On the band's united front, I thought dismally. Greater and greater. "I didn't understand everything Asakawa-san was saying," I confessed. "I mean, I literally can't understand his Japanese when he's not speaking directly to me."

Tad squeezed my knee. Did I imagine that the conversation faltered for an instant? We'd all been so focused on the negotiations that Shingo and Gen might not yet have realized I wasn't just staying at Tad's house, in the same way I'd stayed there many times before. How do you let people know these things, anyway? In America, it would have been easy,

I thought. Tad would have been openly hanging all over me. In Japan, that's a big no-no.

He scooted closer to me and whispered, "Sometimes I forget you're not Japanese."

I whispered, "Sometimes I forget you *are* Japanese."

"And sometimes I'm ashamed of it," he said even more quietly.

"Do you want the bad news first, or the good news?" I hopped up and down in front of Alastair. Joaquin bumped into me as he twirled Nina off her feet and staggered with her into the crosswalk. That was a big chunk of good news right there. He dipped her like a tango dancer and kissed her on the mouth, the rain falling around them, sparkling in the headlights of a car that waited for them to finish instead of blasting its horn.

"You know me," said Alastair. "Bad news first, every time."

"OK. Well, we signed!"

"A contract?"

"A deal memo. But it's legally binding."

"I'm trying to guess what the good news could be."

"We got everything we wanted! It's better than we ever could have hoped for! We not only got our P&D deal, we got them to invest directly in the label! They're going to give us a massive cash transfusion, so we can record a single and start working on our next album, and there'll be plenty of money left over for our other artists. They're going to rush out another pressing of *U-Turn Day,* and it's still going to be a CCR record. We're licensing the masters of *U-Turn Day* and *Xenophobia* to them. Operative word, licensing, not selling. And the label gets the proceeds from that, too." I capered, trying to coax his smile wider. "Oh, Alastair, I'm so happy. I don't think I've ever been this happy."

Tad came up beside me and slipped his arm around my waist. I twisted around and kissed him on the mouth. The rain pattered down on our joined faces. Right now, I felt American. The world was mine.

Alastair said, "Sounds to me like you've been bought out."

Joaquin, still holding Nina's hand, said in French, "Very astute. Are you sure you're Shanti's brother?"

"I've spent my whole life trying to keep her out of trouble."

"I'm afraid this time you've failed. Mais bien, fifty-one percent, it doesn't make us wholly owned, and where there is money there's a way!"

"Very astute," Alastair shot back.

Joaquin laughed. He stepped forward and embraced Alastair. They kissed on both cheeks. Joaquin, I realized, must have temporarily relapsed to his preferred version of my life story, in which my family was French. "A brother of my chanteuse is a brother of mine. Come on, let's celebrate!"

Nina said, "I'm surprised they aren't taking all of you out to dinner."

"That'll be next week, when we sign the actual contract," Joaquin said. "Really, people, it's not so bad. This way, we keep our creative control!"

"And an extra layer of management between us and our royalties," muttered Shingo. "And we'll have to pay for our own marketing. I wonder just how long that cash transfusion will last?"

"We held out for our bottom line, and we won through," Joaquin declaimed as we started to walk. "Thanks in large part to Shanti!"

I was no longer so sure I wanted the credit on this. "It wasn't me. It was all him," I said to Shingo, indicating Joaquin. "They'd never have agreed to our demands unless they figured it would work out cheaper."

"Yeah, to let us do all the hard work while they sit back and collect the profits." Shingo's face set into lines of aggravation. In front of the lawyer, Confucius, and the heavyweight A&R exec, Nakanishi-san, he'd backed Joaquin and Tad, but maybe he'd only intended it as a show of solidarity. He'd been ready to accept Apex's original offer. He hadn't thought they would compromise. And maybe, in reality, they hadn't compromised.

"Well, you can't put a price tag on artistic integrity," I said.

"I'm going home. Kaori's waiting for me." Kaori was Shingo's girlfriend.

"Call her," Joaquin said instantly. "Tell her to come over. Tonight we party! And tomorrow you'll look authentically unwell." He clapped Shingo on the shoulder.

"Speaking of which, I need a drink," said Gen. His face was pale, his hair more wildly tousled than usual. Throughout the entire meeting, he'd barely said a word. "Scratch that. I need several drinks."

"You don't fool me. I know you drank a whole bottle of Black Nikka in the station toilets before you came to meet us," Joaquin started in on him. I shook my head at Joaquin. He stopped.

As we rounded the corner past the Seiyu department store, Gen said stiffly, "I apologize for my father."

An outcry erupted. If anyone really had been on our side, it was Hiroyuki Tajitsu. Gen had no call to apologize.

He shook us off. "I've got to call Chiharu."

"Ah, you don't need to do that," Joaquin said with an unconvincing grin. "She's coming over, too."

A song is an alternate reality that lasts three, four, six minutes.

Musicians are famous for trying to live in one or more of those alternate realities all the time. But now, at the stroke of a pen, an alternate reality had become as concrete as the walls around us. Money is the real magic.

We spent the evening spreading the news around by phone and wallowing in congratulations from all sides. Alastair was seeing my friends at their best, and I was relieved to see that their approval of him seemed to be mutual. Reverting to East Village party mode, I sat on Tad's lap with a bottle of wine and decided I'd been wrong about the music industry and life in general: it was benevolent and saturated with love.

At one in the morning, Nina and I dragged Alastair's suitcase along the upstairs hall from Tad's room to the master bedroom. The last train had gone and Gen and Shingo were still here, so we had to create enough floor space in Tad's room for the two of them plus Joaquin and Alastair. I kicked Alastair's suitcase over the threshold. "What the fuck does he have in here? I'm tempted to peek."

There was an odd pause before Nina said, "Didn't he tell you?"

"Uh… no."

"All his worldly goods. Mostly books, I think."

"Oh God." My thoughts whirled. The answer came to me so fast that it must already have been formed somewhere in my mind. "Maisie."

"Yeah." Nina giggled. She was drunk, and she thought it was funny, or maybe that was how Alastair had presented it to her. "He said he was afraid she'd throw all his beloved art books out on the sidewalk while he was gone."

The enormous Samsonite sat on the carpetless floorboards beside the bed that Nina and Joaquin still officially shared, looking at home amidst the other objects that haphazardly furnished the room: the three-quarters-lifesize bureau and ornamental dressing-table that had belonged to Tad's dead mother; towers of cardboard boxes filled with CDs, squirrelled away in here so that visitors to the studio couldn't count our returns; a pair of clapped-out JBL speakers; Joaquin's old synthesizer, which he hadn't played since he got the Korg but couldn't bring himself to sell. As I'd often observed, Nina's knack for domesticity stopped at the door of her and Joaquin's own room. And now it had become the repository for the shards of *another* broken relationship.

"It's so awful for him," Nina said, still sounding warm and gossipy. "But I think it's great that he's taking a vacation. Reconnecting with family. And since he's so interested in Japanese art… well, I think it could be really healing for him!"

I wondered if the breakup story was actually just Alastair's alibi. Smiling. I said, "Did he tell you anything else? About how they… broke up?"

"Oh, well, he didn't really go into detail. He just said they've been having problems for a while, and it all came to a head recently. I didn't want to ask too many questions. I mean, you don't pry into someone's pain, right? But it all just kind of..." Nina sat down on the bed. She flopped onto her back, picked up a pillow, and held it at arm's length above her face. "I guess I said something about me and Joaquin. So that was when he said, hey, what a coincidence, I've just broken up with my girlfriend. And he said it was helpful to talk about it with someone who could understand what he was going through." She tossed the pillow aside and rolled onto her stomach. "So he told me about how she always put her acting first, and they could never really have a life together because of that..." She laughed. "I was like, shit, we have a lot in common."

Laughter gusted from the kitchen downstairs. It was a boys' club down there, now that Kaori had gone home. Even Tad's father had emerged to share the booze and the self-congratulatory atmosphere. I leaned against the jamb of the door and lit a cigarette. "Nina, you know I'm always here if you want to talk," I ventured.

"Always here... and now you're always here with Tad." She sighed dramatically.

I shrugged. The general assumption seemed to be that I must have moved in with Tad because I'd lost my job. I'd been hoping Nina would be less cynical.

"Let me say this, he's my most favorite elf in the whole world." She arched her spine and bounced on the bed. "But Shanti, he's *so* passive-aggressive! And obstinate. It's that whole Japanese thing about face: once he takes a stand on something, he'd rather die than back down. And I just wonder if those are the qualities you really want in a boyfriend?"

"My brother's on the fence about him, too," I said, mentally crossing my fingers that Alastair had warmed up to Tad in the course of the evening. It had looked that way, but with Alastair, it was hard to tell if he liked someone, or if he was just in a good mood. "Tad made a pretty bad first impression. I should have told him to dress more conservatively."

"Oh, I'm sure Alastair's not that shallow!" Nina gave me one of her luminous smiles that betrayed pain even as she intended to convey brightness. "Honestly, Shanti, your brother is extremely cool. He's smart, he's funny, he knows all about art... he's almost too good to be true!"

She was right about *that,* I thought sadly.

My dreams lurched in and out of nightmare territory. In episodic chase sequences, I struggled through a baroque landscape of castles and cliffs. The sea glittered miles below, while a seagull flapped around my head, screeching in some language I was supposed to know but couldn't understand.

Inevitably, I fell, and woke up.

I fought the covers for an instant before the tickle of Nina's breath on my shoulder oriented me to where I was.

The room was no longer quite dark. I got out of bed, padded over to the window, and twitched back a corner of the curtains. Dawn, or a little after. The quietest time of all.

So how come I could hear the faint sound of conversation from downstairs?

I changed out of Nina's shortie pyjamas into my jeans and sweater and let myself out of the room. Tiptoeing downstairs, I was conscious of trying for stealth. I must have succeeded, because when I opened the kitchen door, Tad literally dropped his coffee cup. He was sitting at the table with Alastair.

"You gave me a fright," he said, rising.

I beat him to the sink, grabbed a dishrag, and mopped up the coffee before it could drip off the table. Alastair had snatched up the book that had lain open between them. It was the Mapple street atlas of Tokyo. "The conspirators surprised," he said. "A fine gang of international criminals we'd make."

I laughed. "You can't be a gang with only two of you." I threw the dishrag across the room. It splatted against the window and slid down into the sink. I stared at them, hands empty. "If you let me be in it, we'd have a gang worthy of the name, and you could tell me all about your conspiracy."

"A tempting offer," said Alastair.

Tad said, "No."

"While I'm thinking about it," said Alastair, "why don't you have some coffee? Tad's made a kick-ass pot of java, but the milk tastes strange. I suspect they feed the cows on miso and raw fish."

"It's probably just sour. Nothing gets put away in this house." I poured myself a cup of coffee, sniffed the milk, and added a drop of it. "When did you guys suddenly turn into conspirators?" I said in French.

"But it's simple," said Alastair in the same language. "I woke up at about four in the morning. Jetlag's a bitch. Tossed and turned for a bit and then decided to get up. Picked my way over the sleeping bodies; stepped on one of them. I said sorry, go back to sleep, but he said he'd get up, too. He wanted to talk to me... You said he didn't know anything."

"So what are you smirking about?"

"You underestimated him. He knows more than you do."

"I'd appreciate it if you guys speak English," Tad said.

"Sorry." Alastair grinned. "Bad habit."

"What do you know, Tad?" It was a funny way of putting it, but my ears had started to ring, and I didn't want to look at him, in case the answer should turn out to be *everything*.

"I know that the world is a dangerous place. I know you don't trust me." He was moving towards me. "But I also know that I love you." He squeezed me around the shoulders with one arm. His kiss landed half on my hair, half on my cheek. "Trust me a bit more, huh?" he said in my ear. "I'm just trying to look out for you."

"Awww," said Alastair. "Shanti, can I put my two cents in here? Mr Right," he mouthed exaggeratedly, nodding hard at Tad.

Tad and I both laughed, although my laughter was strained, because I was thinking about what Nina had said to me last night about Alastair and Maisie. That wasn't a topic I wanted to broach with Tad around. Certainly not until I got this conspiracy business cleared up.

I sat down at the table, gulped coffee, and stole one of Tad's cigarettes. "OK, guys. Talk." The ringing in my ears had moved into the base of my skull, like a faroff alarm.

"Well, basically," Tad said, and looked at Alastair.

"Basically," said Alastair, "Tad knows where Neddo's buddies live. He found out all about them during your tour. So if Ned's still staying there, we've got him."

Our eyes met. Alastair's eyes were hazel like mine, but brighter than mine, closer to yellow than green. Right now, they had a forbidding look, as if to warn me not to ask too many questions.

But there was one question I had to ask. "Were you going to leave me out?"

They denied it simultaneously, which suggested that they *had* been going to leave me out. Tad's excuse would be that he was thinking of my safety. The thought nearly choked me. I was supposed to be protecting him, not the other way round. And Alastair?

I met his eyes again, and in their depths I saw something shift: an evasion.

"Try and leave me out," I said, putting on an exaggerated scowl. "Just try. You won't get very far. So, when's zero hour?"

"Whoa, whoa," spluttered Alastair. "Don't you want to hear the details of my brilliant plan? Tad, let's have that map."

From: xenophobiash@docomo.ne.jp

To: optimist76@softbank.ne.jp
Subject: Sorry... about Tuesday. I'm free tomorrow if you want to meet up & talk. Shanti

From: optimist76@softbank.ne.jp
To: xenophobiash@docomo.ne.jp
Subject: Re: Sorry...
DONT WORRY ABOUT TUES :) ID SOMETHING TO GIVE U THATS ALL BUT RECKON U DONT NEED IT. ANYWAY LETS HAVE A DRINK. WHAT TIME TOMORROW?

Alastair's brilliant plan had a role for me, after all. I was the bait.

Dub Shibuya II, tucked away in an alley behind the Mark City shopping mall, belonged to a chain of "Irish" pubs that attracted mostly gaijins and the Japanese girls who loved them. "Go Slowly Round The Bend," read the road sign nailed to the panelling in front of my face. I had my hair up in a knot, and I was wearing black jeans, my Pumas, and my brown hoodie, with my little saddle-leather belt pouch substituting for my shoulderbag just in case I had to do some running. I'd arrived half an hour early, and now Ned was late. Whitesnake filtered through the hubbub. I stirred the dregs of my G&T.

There never was a pub like this in Ireland, and I ought to know: Alastair and Ned and I had spent enough nights in the genuine Irish pubs of Bantry, waiting for Nigel to drive us home. He always knew everyone, and every newcomer was another excuse not to leave yet. We would read in the poor light, eat sweets and crisps, and seethe with impatience.

But it wasn't all bad. Friday nights, in particular, could be fun. Friday was fair day in Bantry, when June sold her paintings in the square in collaboration with another artist, Fiona, an Englishwoman. Fiona's teenagers usually came into town with her. Stephen, Aisling and Conrad were homeschooled, so they didn't know to hate us the way our classmates did. All three of them had silky dark ponytails to their waists, just like their father, Rhys, and a standoffish manner that I felt I understood. We would huddle in a corner of the pub, trading insults, and it felt more flirting. And then as the evening hotted up, a guitar would appear, and a tin whistle, and a bodhran, and sometimes a mic: instant ceilidh. Squatting on a hard black bench in my school uniform, licking sugar from the corners of my mouth, I memorized a whole repertoire of folk standards. *Oh saddle for me my milk-white steed, with a tooray ah and a faddle diddle dah, any day now, any day now, I shall be released –*

Often, June and Fiona would arrive after they'd packed up the stall and get sucked right into the merry company. On those nights we wouldn't get home until one or two in the morning. As Nigel drunkenly piloted the Land Rover along the coast road, he and June would make fun of everyone who'd been at the pub, their opinions, their personal lives, and their appearances. She didn't mean any of it; he meant all of it. She thought he was terribly funny, and he thought so, too. All I heard was his cruelty. Once, when I couldn't stand it any longer, I started bouncing on the back seat and singing *Blowin' In The Wind.* I was only twelve, but I already had an incredibly loud voice, as everyone around me knew to their cost.

That was the kind of thing I kept on doing, even though I knew in some part of my mind that it was going to get me killed.

I abandoned my barstool and skirted the cluster of people around the bar. Bodies buffetted me as I craned over the glass of the jukebox. The Rolling Stones. Tom Petty. U2. With or without you… Back to the beginning. The Beatles. The Best Of Bob Dylan. Guns 'n' Roses! Not *Use Your Illusion I* or *II,* but *Lies,* which told you how old this jukebox was. I fed a ¥100 coin into the slot and punched in the numbers.

"Hey."

I turned around, pressing my back against the jukebox. Ned wasn't alone. Beside him loomed a large young man with a belly that tented out his FUBU sweatshirt. "You're late," was all I could think of to say.

"This is Mike Schultz. Mike, this is Shanti." Ned glanced around with a shudder of happiness mingled with pain, as if he'd just plunged into a 40° bath. "Like a fucking rush hour subway! Shall we have a drink here or go somewhere else?"

"Dude, it's Saturday night."

"So you're the legendary Mike," I said. My thoughts churned. Alastair's strategy hinged on the not unreasonable assumption that no one would be home at 4-16-3 East Nakano on a Saturday night. I was responsible for ensuring that Ned wouldn't be. I hadn't expected to have to keep tabs on this Mike, too.

"So have you been in Japan long?" Instead of looking at me, Mike was scanning the crowd in a casually predatory way.

"Almost five years," I said. "What about you?"

"Too long. I'm getting out of here next year. Going back to Thailand."

"Oh, so maybe Ned can return your hospitality," I said emptily.

"Yeah, my house should be finished by then," said Ned. "Come stay, man, we'll party."

"Dude's my role model." Mike grinned at Ned. "Living off the fat of the land, whoa dawg."

"Don't listen to this guy. He's full of shit."

I smiled painfully. Fear hammered away inside me. At the same time, I wanted to reach out and touch Ned's lips with my finger: *Sssh.*

Alastair's plan really was brilliant: it combined revenge and expediency with more restraint than I'd dared to expect from him. Theoretically, I had no problem with what I was doing. I just hadn't foreseen how tough my own role was going to be. Well, actually, I had foreseen it, but guilt is like pain or cold: you never remember what it's like until you feel it again.

A table opened up. We dived through the crowd and claimed it. Ned went off to buy drinks.

"So you're the one that's in that band?" said Mike, focusing on me at last.

I pulled a *U-Turn Day* promo postcard out of my belt pouch and gave it to him. "Soon to be on sale at a Tower Records near you."

"Gorot, yeah." He mispronounced it: *Gawrot.* "You play Western music? Japanese music?"

"Hard rock. Most of our influences are American—"

"That's the trouble with this country. Too many Western influences. They've forgotten their culture. Basically, they all want to be American. Worshipping Disney and shit. I'm like *dawgs,* you know what I'm saying? Thailand's different. They've still got monks running the country."

"Do you enjoy teaching English?"

"Fucking hate it."

"I used to be an English teacher, too," I said, thinking of Meguro Language Academy, which already seemed to have receded into my distant past.

"You quit?" Mike raised his hand. "Put it here, sister."

Ned came back with two beers and a G&T. When I tried to pay him, he pushed my money away. "This one's on me. To celebrate the end of Cold Coeur Family Vol. I." He added awkwardly, "Since I didn't get to buy you a drink at your homecoming party."

Mike chugged his beer, wiped his mouth with the back of his hand, and stood up. "Well, I'm outta here. You guys don't want to come to Xanadu? Might meet up with Gav."

"Nah, I guess we're going to hang out."

"Catch you later then, dawgs. Nice meeting you," Mike added to me. "Hit me off with some tickets, huh? If you give them to Ned, I'll definitely be there."

As Mike shouldered towards the exit, the first of my selections came up on the jukebox. That first riff of Slash's always jerked my heart like a whip. "You're Crazy" was practically my theme song. It was in Gorot's tiny repertoire of covers, along with classics like "Piece Of My Heart" and Placebo's "Without You I'm Nothing." I'd chosen it to give myself a boost. Now I wondered if I'd ever be able to listen to it again. I made myself look at Ned, reminding myself, as I'd been reminding myself all day, that he'd tried to kill me.

"Shanti, I…" He dropped his gaze and pushed his beer glass around. "I'd better say it straight away. I'm sorry."

A tiny thrill of triumphant contempt evaporated, leaving me feeling dizzy. "Sorry for what?"

"For what happened up in the mountains. I scared you, didn't I? That's why you freaked out on Tuesday night. I realized that afterwards. Sorry."

"I almost drowned," I said.

"I'm sorry. It was an accident."

"An accident!"

"Yeah. Sorry. I dunno, what else can I say? Sorry."

And I couldn't say anything, because I knew it *might* have been an accident, didn't I? Mentally reconstructing that moment when he swung me off balance, I'd been unable to exclude the possibility that he'd meant to throw me into the bushes, not into the river. The last time we fought, we'd been kids, and he might have forgotten how much bigger and stronger he was now. So a little had gone a long way, and my own momentum had carried me into thin air - and he might have been as surprised as I was. But I'd decided this was so unlikely, on balance, that I hadn't even mentioned it to Alastair as a possibility.

I'd suggested that Tad play decoy tonight instead of me. That would have kept him out of trouble and spared me from coming face to face with Ned again. Alastair had told me he didn't trust Tad enough to give him such a pivotal role. It was a plausible argument, but I didn't believe it. The truth, I thought, was that Alastair had discovered, or rediscovered, how much fun it was to have another boy to play with. The two of them had kitted themselves out with surgical gloves and stocking masks and a nifty little glasscutter. They were like a pair of Tintins gone to the bad. There are no girls in that world, and they were determined to keep me out of it. I couldn't change their minds, so I'd reluctantly accepted my assignment.

And now I knew there was something worse than feeling sorry for Ned.

Ned saying sorry to me.

"You could have stuck around to say that at Kusatsu!" I told him.

He colored and scrunched his head down between his shoulders. "I know, but... I went down and looked for you. You weren't there, and I thought... I thought you were under the water. So what was I supposed to do? Sure, maybe I should have called the police, called Joaquin, gone back to the hotel to get help... but all I could think about was getting out of there."

"And so you went back for your stuff and caught the train?"

"Yep."

Was there a hint of relief in his eyes? Was he glad that he didn't have to spell it out for me? Or did he think I'd overlooked the possibility that he'd planned his getaway *in advance?*

"All I could think about was getting back to Tokyo," he repeated. Then, oddly, he laughed. "If you *had* drowned, I'd have looked guilty as fuck, wouldn't I? Fleeing the scene."

"Yeah. I figured if you'd really meant to hurt me, you would have planned it better than that."

There was a brief pause. The air seemed to tremble with some unbearably pure sound just beyond the range of human hearing.

"Jesus, Shanti, it was an accident! It was an *accident!"*

"I believe you," I lied.

"So..." He looked up at me, his mouth slightly open in a way that made him look very young.

"It's OK. I forgive you," I said woodenly. The words should have resonated through the world. They were words to end a war and heal ancient wounds. Instead, I sounded like I was writing them with a dried-out biro that had no ink.

But Ned seemed to take them at face value. "That means a lot to me. You're the best, Shanti! I admit I had my doubts a few times, but I never really thought you were a, you know what, rhymes with witch. I knew you'd understand, if I could get you to stay in one place for long enough so I could explain—"

"I'm listening!" I almost shouted.

"No! I want to move on." He spoke frantically. "I don't want to start raking up the past again. It's no good. It doesn't work. Can we move on? Is it wrong of me to say that? Can we put it behind us?"

I started stammering. *But you haven't forgiven me yet. Or did you just want me to forgive you? Is that why you hurt me? So I'd have something to forgive you for? Ned, that's so fucked up –*

I couldn't get it out, and he wasn't listening, anyway. He was digging in the pocket of his denim jacket. "Hey, I almost forgot! I bought this for you. You sent me a text message, so I guess you don't need it, but what was I going to do, throw it away? You might as well have it, anyway." He laid a glossy white cell phone on the table. "I know it doesn't make up for… for what I did, but it's got a camera. You can take videos with it."

I took out the phone that I'd bought last week and showed it to him. "I replaced it. But this one's really nice. It must have cost a lot, Ned!" And if he'd really bought it new, where was its box and manual and charger? It wouldn't be much use without that when its battery ran down. "Thank you!"

"Don't worry about it. I just wanted to make it up to you. I was thinking of flowers, but…"

"If you'd brought flowers on Tuesday, I might not have run away."

"Oh!" His eyes widened. "What did you think I had in my pocket?"

I shrugged.

A shadow crossed his face, and then he chortled. "It's like, hey, is that a cell phone in your pocket, or are you just happy to see me?"

"Ne-ed."

"But I thought: she's practically a famous singer, she probably gets flowers all the time. It wouldn't mean anything to her."

"Oh, come on, you were on the road with us. Did anyone give me flowers even once? In fact, I can't remember the last time anyone gave me so much as a… a cactus!"

Ned made an elaborate show of licking his fingertip and pretending to scribble on his palm. "Memo for the next time I screw everything up with my clumsiness. Cactus, one. With baby's breath or that ferny green stuff?"

"Ned… *was* it just clumsiness? Really?"

His smile faded. He took a gulp of beer and set the glass down carefully. "I'm fucking clumsy. I know that, Shanti, it's one of the things I'd change about myself if I could. That whole scene… from beginning to end: Ned being clumsy. But some things you can't change, can you? All you can do is try not to hurt people, and apologize when you do."

I nodded, even as my memory offered disproofs of his claim. I thought he'd grown out of his clumsiness. But maybe he was still clumsy when he was trying too hard. That happens to most of us. Only a very few people – I could only think of Alastair and Joaquin – never seem to lose their balance, never spin out of control. It's like they have an extra gear.

I had an extra gear of my own, but it only ever kicked in when I was onstage. When I was just being myself, I lacked that spontaneity. I could have used it now.

Because now I knew what I had to do. I had to sabotage Alastair's brilliant plan.

I still didn't believe Ned was telling me the whole truth. But the thing was open to reasonable doubt. More importantly, I'd forgiven him. Hadn't I?

I struggled with myself for a long minute. At last I spoke from behind my G&T. "Ned, I'm glad we're having this talk, because I need to tell you... uh… you might be in danger."

"Sure, you've no need to fret on my account." He smiled, but it wasn't the genuine smile I'd seen a minute ago, it was the smile that belonged behind a merchandise table, the one with the zip up the back. "The danger's only there if you don't know what you're doing. If you don't believe me, ask Mike. Ask Joaquin. He'll tell you I don't go looking for trouble. I'm not into aggressive sales strategies. I just supply an existing market. Doing my bit for the global economy…"

Or something like that. Halfway through, I stopped listening. I almost stopped breathing.

Alastair had walked into the bar.

He shoved through the throng to our table. He was pink and rumpled, as if he'd come at a run. "Hey, Shanti. Ned, holy shit! Well, this is a reunion to celebrate. Hell of a venue for it. We'll just have to maintain an ironic frame of mind." He raked his hair back with both hands. "I'll start, shall I? That glass looks half empty to me. You OK with a generic brewski, Neddo, or will you have a Guinness to remind you of the auld country?"

The change that had begun to come over Ned when I mentioned *danger* now amounted to a transformation. His shoulders were rigid, the set of his head unnatural, and his hands looked big and awkward where they lay on the table. His eyes glowed their brightest shade of blue.

He thought I'd betrayed him. He thought I'd set him up. Guilty as charged. But I hadn't set him up for *this!* Had Alastair and Tad finished in Nakano already? Impossible! It was barely eleven o'clock. Had Alastair's brilliant plan gone wrong? Where was Tad? I kicked Alastair in the leg. He took a step back. He was talking about some vile yet humorously named cocktails he'd had at an art gallery somewhere.

"I don't need anything," Ned said at last. "I'm fine. Will you have a seat?"

"Yes, sit down, Alastair," I squealed, willing him not to go off to the bar and leave me and Ned alone again. We all looked around for an extra chair. There wasn't one.

"Oh, the hell with this," said Alastair. "Let's just get out of here."

"I chose this song," I said. It was my third selection, "Paradise City."

Ned cleared his throat. "Lead the way." He stood up. He was taller than Alastair. I'd known that, but it was still a shock to see it. "We've a lot to say to each other, haven't we? And I'd just as soon not say it in public."

Shibuya is a carnival of seedy distractions. American rap thumps from African boutiques, sex industry scouts lie in wait for schoolgirls, sedans with tinted windows crawl along the curbs, and old wrecks in pachislot sandwich boards shuffle their feet and share cigarettes. Ned and Alastair passed through it all like neutrinos going through solid matter. They were catching up, hitting the highlights of the last sixteen years with a lot of bragging and financial exaggeration on both sides. Scurrying behind them, I dialed Tad's number. It went to voicemail.

I was afraid of giving away the plan, but maybe there was no plan left to give away. "Alastair! Is Tad OK?"

"He was fine the last time I saw him," Alastair threw over his shoulder.

"So you've met the whole gang," said Ned. "Joaquin's a great guy, isn't he?" There was a hint of wistfulness in his voice. "His wife's a babe, too. Nina. You met her?"

"I sure have," said Alastair.

At the top of Dogenzaka we turned right on 246, a four-lane highway that lies in the shadow of the Keio Inogashira line and the Shuto No. 3 Expressway. Traffic thundered overhead. The crowds had thinned out. I caught up with the boys and walked on Alastair's other side. Did he have any idea where he was going? Even I was pretty much lost on this side of Shibuya. But I didn't say anything to interfere with whatever Alastair might be planning. Old habits die hard.

We turned off 246, plunging into the hush of an expensive residential neighborhood, and we might as well have been walking straight back into the past.

Ireland is a lonely country. From our front garden, on a nice day, you could see clear across the bay to the opposing headland. On a rainy day, there seemed to be nothing out there but clouds.

The lane continued to drop steeply past Fuschia Cottage, but only for about fifty metres. It deadended in a disused pier. Storms had gnawed at the old masonry. Beneath the encroaching trees, a small boat stood upside-down with weeds growing through its ribs. There was no beach, just cliffs enclosing a small rocky harbor, but we used to swim off the pier on summer days when we were too lazy to bike to the cove at the end of the point. The sea below the pier was as clear as green bottle glass when the sun shone, solid black when it didn't. Even at low tide, it was very deep. Ned claimed to have dived all the way to the bottom, but when we challenged him to do it again and bring up a trophy to prove it, he cheated, attempting to jump into the water with a seashell already in his fist.

The partial renovation of the cottage told you a lot about its owner, the artist Monsieur Duvalier. He didn't have children (the upstairs rooms had been draughty and carpetless when we moved in), he didn't care much about his own comfort (June's room, off the kitchen, was jammed with a bewildering assortment of junk including a spinning-wheel and an antique printing press), but he did care about his food. The wall between the kitchen and the parlor had been demolished, creating an openplan room that had one end in the twentieth century and one end in the nineteenth. The kitchen had pine counters, an electric cooker, and an American-size refrigerator. Three strides took you from these mod cons to the poky stone hearth. All the chairs in the house tended to collect around the fireside, winter or summer. June aspired to paint outdoors, but given the Irish weather, she ended up doing most of her work at M. Duvalier's easel in the living-room. She'd never felt the need of a sanctum; she preferred to have life happening around her.

In Paris she'd had her paintings professionally framed, but at Fuschia Cottage she taught herself this craft and became adept at it. She installed a second worktable in the living-room for the purpose. Once framed, a painting has to be left untouched with weights on its back while the glue dries. June used whatever came to hand - stacks of books, at first, but Alastair and I kept forgetting that they were acting as weights and taking them away. By way of combining an apology with something to do, we collected stones for her from the garden and the pier. We picked out nice heavy ones with flat bottoms, and the three of us spent a Sunday painting them. June wrapped them in leafy mandalas, I did splodgy sunsets and stiff-legged animals, and Alastair worked for hours, using June's smallest sable brush, on a microscopically detailed black-and-white picture of St George weeping over a dead dragon. I think that was the first time I ever saw Alastair draw or paint anything, except at school, which didn't count.

Once they were varnished, they looked like objets d'art - the ones June and Alastair had done, anyway.

We kept walking, and I couldn't see how things might have worked out differently. Nothing is inevitable until it happens, but as soon as it does, it grows reasons out behind itself, like a plant sending its roots into the darkness.

In the summer of 1988, Nigel taught Alastair to drive the Land Rover. It had dodgy brakes and the lane was perilously steep. Alastair picked up the basics before the odds caught up with him. But what could Nigel have been thinking? Alastair was years too young for a driver's license. Was Nigel trying to win him over with this quintessentially male activity? Or was it simply a whim?

Nigel always gave the impression that everything he did was according to the rules - *his* rules. When these conflicted with other people's rules, as they usually did, he could convince you that they were stupid and he was sane.

But early in the spring of 1989, on one of those raw drizzly nights when the damp lodged indoors and my nose ran constantly, this logic of his failed him. Only for five or ten minutes, maybe fifteen.

But that was enough. It was our chance.

If we'd only seen it that way.

We're all sitting around the crackling fire. Nigel is working late on a consignment for some shop in Dublin, so Ned is down at the cottage with us. He and I are solving a Choose Your Own Adventure book, looking for the endings and unravelling the stories backwards. June is reading a book that has a stylized naked woman on the cover. Alastair is doing his homework. He should be lurking in his room, but it's so cold upstairs that his fingers won't grip the pencil. Or maybe he's sticking close to us on purpose, slightly nervous about whatever it is he's done - always supposing he has done something. He'll deny it afterwards, but I'll come to suspect he played one of his jokes on Nigel that day, something too embarrassing to admit, something with a rotten egg or Supaglue. Nigel has reduced us to behaving as inappropriately as he does. But Alastair looks very innocent now, with the firelight all red in his hair and pink on his cheeks.

Not that this does him any good.

Nigel storms into the cottage. Textbook, copy, and pencil scatter to the floor as he frogmarches Alastair outside.

June and I dash out after them. I scream in terror. Alastair is fighting back.

One of the rules is that if you take your punishment "like a man" - that bizarre euphemism for stoic submission - he won't really hurt you. But apparently Nigel has forgotten all the rules, and Alastair has, too.

They grapple on the overgrown vegetable patch in the triangle of light from the front door, dewy grass up to their knees, the skinny teenager struggling madly to get away, the big man trying to pin his arms and hit him at the same time. I jump up and down and scream, "Hit him, Alastair! Hit him!" Nigel is one of the most powerfully built human beings I've ever seen. He can lift the smaller of the two kilns in his studio. Alastair is six inches shorter, a bendy straw of a boy. *"Hit him!*

Stop it, Jesus Chriiist! Love!" June and I are screaming a chorus of mixed messages.

Nigel lands a punch above Alastair's eye, a sound that will continue to echo in my memory for years. Alastair doesn't seem to feel it. He sinks his teeth into Nigel's bare forearm. Blood wells around his lips. Blood is streaming down over his right eye.

June screams louder. She flies at them, thrusts Alastair away, and backs Nigel into the shadow of the sycamores, both of them protesting in tones of aggrieved confusion.

I catch phrases I've heard at other times, during rows of normal intensity, and that's when I believe everything is going to be OK.

Alastair crumples to his knees. I reach him just in time to stop him falling flat on his face. Blood smears off his face onto my neck. Some of it's probably Nigel's, but most of it is coursing down his face from the gash that Nigel's hard-as-clay knuckles opened in his forehead. It gets on my hands and makes them slippery. "Ned," I gasp, "help," because I can barely hold Alastair up. He sags like the dead in my arms, and his face keeps bleeding.

But Ned stays where he is on the doorstep, his lips drawn back in a frozen grimace, like a Neolithic explorer trapped in a glacier that hasn't moved for thousands of years.

The little eejit.

The little boy lost.

The useless little coward.

He should have stayed away.

The street snaked between compact fortresses with walled gardens. Some of these "houses" married Japanese and Western motifs beautifully, but most were eyesores. It was hard to imagine anyone living in, for example, an asymmetrical tower with a waterfall incorporated into its slanting side. They did, though. The tails of imported cars gleamed through barred gates. Splinters of light fell from upper windows festooned with plants.

This wasn't the way to anywhere, as proved by the total absence of other pedestrians. I no longer had any idea which direction Shibuya station was. We might have been walking in circles. We might have been walking along any street in the world, for all Alastair and Ned seemed to care. What were they talking about now? China, and before that it had been Russia, and before that it had been Iraq. Ned was hotly espousing the anti-American platform, while Alastair interpolated the *Yes, but*s that tied those arguments in knots. What really surprised me was that Ned *could* argue. He was taking Alastair seriously, listening to him in a way he'd never listened to anything I had to say.

Memory lane has so many forks, but all of them are dead ends. Whichever way you go, you end up at the same place. And how clearly I remembered the smell of dead grass baking in the summer heat (Nigel had recently macheted back the weeds in our garden), the taste of the eraser on the end of my pencil, and the *tap tap tap* that the legs of my chair made on the floor of uneven stone flags.

We arrived at a T-junction. A park loomed in front of us, trees solid in the night, a path winding away between them. Houses tessellated the skyline to the left, but ahead and to the right the park merged into the darkness with no end in sight. Japanese landscaping genius at work. The illusion that we'd reached the edge of the city was damn near perfect.

Alastair crossed the road and halted on the skirt of brick paving underneath the first trees. "Nabeshima Park," he read off the bilingual signboard, with satisfaction. I realized this had been his destination all along. There never had been a brilliant plan, only a simple one. But all the same, I was unprepared for him to say, "OK, Shanti. You know the way, don't you?"

"The way to where?" I said brightly.

"Wherever you like. But I think the station's over that way. If you get lost, just ask a policeman," he added as a policeman glided past, a fat man on a white bicycle lighting his course down the center of the road. Alastair nodded after him: "That's why they call this a safe country," and he and Ned both laughed.

"Don't blow up now, Shanti," added Ned, "but your brother and I need to talk in private."

Somehow, after a gap of sixteen years, Alastair had got Ned in his power again. Or had he? Ned was lounging against the low brick wall with that annoying pretense of confidence I'd observed in him so often on tour. I realized that he thought it was the other way round. He thought he had Alastair in his power.

"You're both being stupid," I said. "Whatever you have to say to him, you can say in front of me."

"Nah." Ned shook his head. "Can't say anything in front of you. You just take it the wrong way and get all defensive."

"Excuse me, a few days ago it was the other way round. You wanted to talk to *me.*"

"And you made clear it was Alastair I should be having that conversation with."

"I did not! I just—"

"I rest my case," Ned interrupted me. Alastair chuckled. They glanced at each other, the way Alastair and I used to do, only now I was the one getting left out. Somewhere along the way here, they'd forged an understanding. The frangible intimacy of enemies.

Alastair hadn't told me what he planned to do, in fact he'd lied to me pretty comprehensively, so I didn't *know* what he planned to do, but it wasn't hard to guess. I was ready to clown and mug and throw my dignity away, but I couldn't think of anything funny to say. "Try me," I said at last. "Talk about something that really matters and see if I get defensive or not."

"You're saying Iraq doesn't really matter?" Ned scoffed. "Close to a million dead, to secure America's supply of cheap petrol?"

"Ah, but you see, most of them were just little brown people," Alastair said, deadpan. "And there's so much more to it than cheap oil. Look at the way the invasion revitalized the stock market. That's what we need now, actually: another war."

"Of all things, I never thought you'd grow up to be a conservative," Ned chided him.

"Don't blame me, blame June. I've got classic Adult Child of Hippie syndrome."

"Have you now!"

It pained me to see Ned taking Alastair seriously. "He doesn't really blame June," I said. "He's just embarrassed that his mother's an artist. Because then people start looking at him like, well, why aren't *you?* And—"

"Artist, schmartist," said Alastair. "She's a sentimental hack."

"That's not what Maisie said." I turned to Ned again. "He took his girlfriend to visit June in France, and she loved June's work, and *she* was the one that said to Alastair, well, I know you have talent, so why aren't you—"

"Girlfriend?" said Ned.

"Oops, I meant ex," I said.

"Don't go there, Shanti," Alastair said.

"What's this I hear?" said Ned, grinning. "Trouble in paradise?"

"Fuck off," said Alastair.

I realized I might have gone too far. "Just don't blame June for our problems, that's all I'm saying…"

"Oh, I don't blame her for our problems. I blame her for being a dilettante without a principled bone in her body. Is that better? Sorry, Neddo, it's hard for me to remember not to use the big words. Let me simplify. Our mother's life is structured around two lies: that she's a good artist and a good person. She's neither. To put it even more simply, she's a fake. That's why she got along so well with your father, in fact. They were both raving fakes. They were made for each other."

"That's going a bit fucking far," said Ned.

"Well, are you going to defend him?"

Without thinking about it, I hopped between them. Alastair carried on talking past me.

"He treated those fucking goats that you kept better than he treated you. He acted like the dictator of his own little country. And I think I have a right to say that, because my sister and I lived in that country, too. You and I were boys, so there's some precedent there. English public schools, like Nigel wished he'd gone to. But no one, *no one* is going to tell me that a grown man has the right to beat a little girl! Jesus Christ! Again and again! And who was there to stop it? Her mother had no time for anyone except her muse. Didn't have a fucking clue. So who did that leave?"

"Well, you made him sorry, didn't you?" said Ned.

"It's a position of responsibility, being the oldest," Alastair said lightly.

"That's a good one. Responsibility. I'd like to see you take some."

"Oh, I take full responsibility for protecting my little sister."

"You drove him insane."

Alastair barked a laugh. I think Ned had surprised him. "If so, it didn't take much. What's the distance between borderline and full-blown psychotic? Mind you, I'm not admitting anything."

"You don't have to admit it. I know what happened, and I'm not the only one who knows. I've got evidence that'll stand up in court!"

Alastair shrugged. "Think what you like, but you might also want to think about this: it was just a matter of time before he hurt someone seriously. It might have been Shanti. It might have been June. It might have been *you.*" He smiled widely. "We might have saved your life, Neddo."

I said, "Yeah. Him or us. It was him or us."

Ned looked at me as if he'd forgotten I was there. Then he looked past me at Alastair again. "And you had no right to drag her into it."

"But I was the one who started it," I said.

"Oh Shanti, protecting you is a full-time job," said Alastair, and brushed past me, heading into the park entrance where the gravel path ran into darkness around a thicket.

Ned moved after him.

I sprang around Ned, getting in his way. He turned his shoulder into me. Alastair grabbed me from behind and thrust me off the path.

A metallic clatter rang through the trees. "Hold it right there! Hands up! Out on the street!"

A beam of light dazzled me. On a reflex that I hadn't known I possessed, I obeyed the voice, gabbling a translation to Alastair and Ned. It was unnecessary. They'd already followed suit, jerkily. With our hands in the air, we trailed towards the curb, where the policeman had jumped off his bike in such a hurry that it had fallen on its side. Its rear wheel spun round and round, clicking. The policeman shone his torch in our faces. "What's the problem here?"

"Nothing," I said.

"All right, you can lower your hands." The policeman didn't have his truncheon out, but he was plainly nervous. It wouldn't be every day that he had to break up a fight among a bunch of gaijins. "Let's see some ID."

"They're not being uncooperative," I said. "They just don't speak Japanese."

"So ka. Well, *you* speak Japanese, don't you?"

Fishing in my belt pouch, I translated.

"Fucking hell," said Ned.

"Tell him to stop shining that shit in my face," said Alastair.

Static blared from the radio on the policeman's belt. Backup, I gathered, was on its way. "And be quick about it," he ordered.

"This is probably the most excitement he's had all year," Alastair said scornfully, but he kept one hand in view while he dug in his jeans pocket with the other. He handed over his passport at the same time as I handed over my alien registration card. I waited for the policeman to notice that we had the same last name and write it down. But maybe the proffering of documents constituted the formula. After a cursory examination, he handed them back.

"All right. Now you, blondie! Where's your ID?" Waving his torch in Ned's face, he clarified in broken English, "Iden-chi-fi-ca-tion doc-u-mento. Understand? Pasuporto. Cardo. Driva licensu!"

Ned shook his head. "Left it at home."

"What's he say? You! What's he say?"

Alastair's hand tightened on my shoulder. He was shaking with silent laughter.

"**A**nd so justice is served. Albeit temporarily."

"Well," I said, "they'll have to get onto the Danish embassy to confirm his identity and visa status. But no one will be there at this time of night. So I guess they might stick him in a cell until morning. That's if he doesn't act up and get himself arrested for real." Ignoring the red walk light, I dragged Alastair across the street, past Don Quixote, the discount emporium. The crowds clotted around the outdoor displays of stuffed toys and household appliances and everything Made In China.

As soon as Ned vanished from view between the policemen, I'd stopped caring about him. Maybe my guilt hadn't been about him in the first place. Now it raged inside me, intensified by fear… for Tad.

Tad had had a key role in the "brilliant plan" within which Alastair had concealed his simple one. This afternoon, he'd gone to Ikebukuro and talked Hori-kun into selling him ¥20,000 worth of hash from his personal supply. Tonight, while I kept Ned distracted, Alastair and Tad had been going to break into Gavin and Mike's house, plant this "evidence" in Ned's room or bivouac, and make an anonymous phone call to set the machinery of the law in motion. Tip-offs are hugely important in the Japanese war on drugs, since the police can't get search warrants on suspicion alone: they need informants. One phone call can ruin someone's life. The "evidence" was just in case Ned had already sold all of his own supply.

If the house had been empty when Alastair and Tad arrived, the whole operation would have been straightforward. I supposed it might even have had some function in Alastair's mind as insurance, in case Nabeshima Park went FUBAR, as had in fact happened.

But Alastair had told me on our way back to Shibuya that against all expectations, the house had been lit up like Lincoln Center. He and Tad had sheered off and returned twice; still no luck. And so Alastair had ditched the stakeout and come to intercept me and Ned.

"What did you tell Tad when you left?" I demanded.

"The truth."

"The *whole* truth?"

"That's your job. But I wouldn't, if I were you. Murder tends to be a deal-breaker." Alastair laughed. I could see that he was still elated by the irony of Ned's being taken into custody. "No, I said I was worried about you. I didn't like to think of you dealing with Ned alone, so I was going to check up on you. He agreed to that straightaway. Said he'd be less conspicuous without me; undoubtedly true. And one could do the job as well as two. Also true."

"But one *couldn't!* One of you was going to be the lookout while the other one planted the evidence."

"A lookout is a luxury, but Shanti, here's the likeliest scenario. The house never did empty out. Gavin decided to order in and watch a ball game on satellite. So Tad gave up and went home."

"Then why isn't he answering his phone?"

Alastair had no explanation for that.

"I still don't understand why you had to go and involve him in the first place!"

"I thought that was obvious. He knows too much." Alastair sobered.

He hated having to defend his own actions. "You would go and pick a guy with more than his natural share of curiosity. So I get here, and I'm facing a damage control situation. What was I supposed to do? I had to improvise. Think of some way to stop him from asking more questions. And since he already knows too much, I had to think of some way to make sure he keeps his mouth shut. Well, there was only one thing for it." Alastair spoke with relish, and I saw that he was still pleased with this aspect of his own planning. "Give him a damn good reason to keep his mouth shut."

"You deliberately set him up to incriminate himself!"

"Set him up? I beg to differ. Breaking and entering, framing a guy for possession, doesn't that sound criminal to you? It sure does to me. He knew what he was getting into."

The crowd surged over the Scramble crossing in front of Shibuya station, carrying us with it, through the blare of commercials from competing thirty-foot TV screens.

"You could have just trusted him," I said.

"No one is a hundred percent trustworthy," Alastair said flatly. "Not even you. Not even me. People are essentially unpredictable. The only thing that endures is good old self-interest. That's not a reflection on anyone's character; it's just the human condition."

We hurried into Shibuya station, through the JR wickets, and upstairs to the teeming Yamanote line platform. A train swished in. We crammed onto it. The crowds squashed us together, face to face. Alastair braced one hand on the door above my head. In this uncomfortably cramped position, I whispered into his face, "You should have just told me your *real* plan."

"I thought you'd catch on."

"I did."

"So why didn't you *go* when I said…" He sighed, then did something unexpected: he stroked the top of my hair with his fingertips. "Never mind. Let's save the post-mortem for later."

In French, I said, "I couldn't leave you. He might have killed you."

"Not a hope."

"He was going to try."

"But try is all he would have done." Suddenly, Alastair reached down for my hand and guided it around his back, under his sweater. He placed my fingers on a flattened cylinder tucked into the waist of his jeans. Warm, textured plastic… three dents…

I whipped my hand back to my side. I didn't dare say anything, but I guess my face said it all.

"See? It *was* a good plan."

"Did… did you get that in Shanghai?"

""Nope. America. Gotta love a country where you can buy an M-16 through the mail. And for your discerning international crook, there are other options. This is a ceramic blade, guaranteed not to set off metal detectors. I checked it with my luggage in one of those anti-X-ray boxes that look like cigar cases. Nifty, no?"

The look in his eyes broke my heart. "It just seems a little bit crude for you," I said, because I had to say something. "Lacking in tactical refinement."

Alastair dropped his voice even lower. "That was kind of the guiding principle. Crude but effective." He paused. "One of the things I've realized as I get older, I guess, is the utter pointlessness of dicking around with half-measures."

At Shinjuku we changed to the Chuo line. We spilled out of the station at Nakano. I set the pace as we scuttled around Sun Plaza, a gigantic shopping mall / wedding hall / hotel that looked as if it had been built by a cult to commune with aliens. Ahead of us stretched a dark sea of tightly packed houses. Alastair guided me around turning after turning, between houses aligned corner to corner, tiny gardens behind high walls, and the rear bumpers of cars fitted into garages like shoes into shoeboxes. The real estate developers had made little headway here. We were walking between squat old wooden houses with their eaves pulled down over their windows like coolie hats. Of one of these Alastair said softly as we passed it, "That's it. *Don't be so obvious!*"

But I'd got a good look. The whole house leaked light from behind blinds and curtains. We kept walking. I said, "Maybe it's not it. Tad might have got the address wrong."

"Yeah, I thought of that, but he was sure. He'd mailed a postcard for Neddo in Hokkaido."

"I've got to know," I said. "You stay here. Be my lookout. I'm going in."

"No. Shanti, don't be crazy."

Alastair followed me back along the dark street, trying to talk me out of it. I told him that wasn't an option. He had two options: to come with me or not. He settled for the former. I was glad, because I'd already begun to shake with fear.

Up close, the house wasn't as dilapidated as it had looked at a glance. The roof of heavy overlapping tiles sagged in the middle, but these urban log cabins were built to last until the next apocalyptic earthquake. I rang the bell. The street was so quiet that I could hear TV voices and applause not only from this house but from the ones on either side.

"All right. Fuck it," said Alastair, elbowing me aside. "If we're doing this, let me do it."

I recovered my footing on the narrow steps just as the door opened a crack. It closed again. I heard the chain coming off, and the door swung wide. "Fought you might be someone else. Sorry. Help you?"

It took me an instant to translate *fought* into *thought.* Gavin, for Gavin this presumably was, had an accent as heavy as coal. He was taller than Alastair and older than I'd expected, closer to forty than thirty, judging by the grey hairs speckling his narrow head. His face was all forehead and beaky nose, the scraggy chin starting to fall into wattles.

"Wondering if Ned Gallant was anywhere around," said Alastair, looking suitably abashed. "We kind of arranged to meet him…"

"Oh, I see! Well, he's not in at the moment. But come in if you like. You'll have to excuse me." Gavin lolloped back down the hall, towards the English-language sports commentary that was crackling from deep in the house. He was wearing sneakers, I noticed as I was about to take mine off. Alastair had no such reflex. We both kept our shoes on. The scuffed grey carpet stuck to our soles. There was a poster of a surfer on one wall: *Aloha.* A pink coin-operated telephone stood on a side table. The smell of stale fried food curled my nostrils. We were in a guest house. And Gavin's manner had left little doubt that he ran the place. Oh, poor Ned, always telling it like he wished it was.

Gavin added over his shoulder as he vanished through a door at the end of the hall, "As a matter of fact, I'm keen to talk to Ned myself, whenever he can tear himself away from the bright lights and the native beauties."

"Native beauties?" whispered Alastair. "My word!" He was taking off Gavin's accent. I elbowed him.

The kitchen proved to be the source of the rancid takeout odor and the sports commentary. A flat-screen television stood on a cabinet full of DVDs. Alastair had been half right: Gavin was watching a game on satellite, but it wasn't baseball, it was club football. On the other side of the formica table, looking fragile and uncomfortable, sat Tad. He didn't get up to greet us.

"Do you support Arsenal? Or West Ham?" Alastair's question sounded ludicrously eager to me. But Gavin answered readily.

"Man United, actually. But this is a fairly interesting game. Ref's on crack; they all are." He swigged from a bottle of Yebisu that had been standing on the table. "You may as well make yourselves at home. No knowing when Ned'll be back."

Alastair warmly accepted the offer. "I'm Sebastian, by the way, and this is Rachel."

I'd probably have said *John and Jane.* Or simply blurted out our real names. Thank God for Alastair.

"Pleasure to meet you. I'm Gavin. Can't introduce this bloke," Gavin jerked his thumb at Tad, "because he hasn't told me his name. Have you? Are you going to change your mind now we've got company? No? He speaks English. Better than most of them do, anyway. *That's* not the problem."

I supplied the question. "What is the problem, then?"

"I caught him breaking in here, is the fucking problem." Gavin took another swig of beer. "You think I'm having you on? I'm not."

"What the hell?" said Alastair. His timing was a little off, and mine was even worse as I chimed in, "Unbelievable," but maybe Gavin had had too much beer already tonight, because he merely nodded.

"Un-fucking-believable. But true. Just when you think you've got this country sussed. You want a beer, by the way?"

"Sure," said Alastair.

"In the fridge. No, that one."

That one was on the other side of the table, behind Tad. I went around the table to open it. Tad was tied to his chair. A thin nylon rope looped around his torso, with a couple of extra loops for his wrists, through the rungs of the chair's back. His legs were free, but he obviously couldn't stand up without taking the chair with him, and the knots looked solid.

"Bottom shelf," said Gavin. "With my Post-Its on them. I've got a rule that we all label our stuff. Saves trouble in the long run."

The fridge door screened me from the room. I watched the side of Tad's face twitch. He was barely holding it together. Well, if Gavin had overpowered me and tied me to a chair, I'd be frightened out of my wits, too. But it was bad news. It meant that it was up to me and Alastair to get us out of here.

All I could think of was to try and get Gavin even drunker than he already was, so I took three bottles of beer out of the fridge. "Don't you have any glasses?"

"Sure, but you'll have to wash them." As I squirted detergent into tumblers, Gavin confided with a chuckle to Alastair, "Three blokes living here, and none of us ever does a stroke of housework. We just wait for a bird to come over. And I must say we never have to wait very long. That's one good thing about this country… Thanks, love," he added as I poured out for him.

We all sat down at the table. Gavin discoursed about football. Alastair had still had no opportunity to see that Tad was tied to his chair, and I didn't dare to say it out loud, because I was afraid Gavin was a little bit mad. I reached for Alastair's hand under the table. Who cared if

Gavin noticed? He probably assumed we were boyfriend and girlfriend, anyway. Just another pair of American drifters on the scent of a high. Yeah. I uncurled Alastair's hand and wrote on his palm with my index finger. We'd practised this many years ago, as a game rather than a system of communication. *T,* I wrote, *T, I, E, D, U, P.* When I ended the message, Alastair grabbed my hand, but he didn't write anything. He just squeezed and let go.

"Yeah, I caught him breaking in," Gavin abruptly got back on topic. "Biked over to the station, didn't I? Had to meet up with a potential tenant. Ned's leaving the country soon, as I'm sure you're aware, and this bloke was thinking of taking his room." He pointed at the door to the left of the television. Through the crack, I could see Ned's red and white parka crumpled on the floor. "Not very large, but I don't charge very much. Anyway, the bloke was a fucking waster, as it turned out. No money, no visa, and he hadn't showered in a week. Told him to go and get himself repatriated. If you want to live here, you've got to have either a job, that's Mike, or other means of support, that's Ned, and I'm sure I make myself clear."

Alastair and I laughed.

"Not to say that Ned's means of support aren't various and mysterious. He even went on tour with a rock band recently. I'll say this for the bloke, he knows how to network. But you can't be too fucking careful who you pick up with, can you? In this country. See exhibit A." Gavin tossed a bottlecap at Tad. It hit him in the chest and clinked to the table. "So I get back from the station, put away my bike, and there's a light in Ned's room. That's funny. Well, maybe he's home early. 'Ned?' No one in Ned's room. Then I hear this noise in *my* room. It's the one on the left as you come in. What the fuck? I go in there and here's this motherfucker opening the window to jump out into the side bit. Do you know how he'd got in? He'd cut a piece right out of the fucking window glass. Well, I mightn't have tackled him if I'd known he had a glasscutter. But he didn't know I'm a black belt, second dan."

"Shit," said Alastair.

"Kyokushin karate." Gavin nodded and drained his beer glass. I refilled it. "You know what that means?"

"Ultimate truce," said Tad, breaking his silence. Truce? *Truth.*

"Yeah, but you know what it means? It means I could have killed you as easily as *that.*" Gavin threw another bottlecap at Tad. "However, I don't want to give the fucking pigs a reason to take an interest in me. Your lucky day. So you've decided to talk, have you? Then maybe you can tell me what I ought to do with you. By rights, that's Ned's responsibility, but I'm not sure I want to sit here looking at your ugly Jap face until he gets back from wherever he is."

Alastair said, "I know Ned pretty well, and... you said this guy was in *your* room, didn't you? So why do you think he's anything to do with Ned?"

"Well, I did think at first that he was after the TV and DVD player. But the light was on in Ned's room, wasn't it? And for another thing, he had some of Ned's personal possessions on him. Found them when I frisked him."

"Personal possessions?" I squeaked, wondering if this was some kind of off-the-wall euphemism for hash.

Gavin gave me a long look. "As in photographs."

"Yeah, Ned's into photography, isn't he?" said Alastair.

"True. He's got a nice digital camera. A Sony. But these were your ordinary family snaps or what have you."

Tad made a small movement. Our eyes met across the table. Before I could stop myself, I said, "Can we have a look at them? The family snaps..." My voice trailed off. Gavin was gazing at me consideringly.

"Don't think that would be appropriate. They're Ned's, aren't they?"

"But we're his oldest friends," I said.

"Are you now! Congratulations."

Alastair kicked me under the table.

For some minutes we all gazed at the television. Gavin supplemented the commentary with his own criticisms. It was raining on the football pitch in England. The crowds in the stands heaved.

"What goes in must come out," said Gavin at last. "Keep an eye on the perp." With a stern look at Alastair, as if to impress him with the weight of this responsibility, he headed for the annexe beyond the kitchen, where the bathroom presumably was. The door closed behind him.

Alastair and I rose simultaneously. As I slipped into Ned's room, I saw the knife in Alastair's hand. I'd thought a ceramic blade would be bisque-colored, like Nigel's pots before he glazed them. It wasn't. It was blackish-grey.

Ned had been living in a four-mat tatami room. The furniture consisted of a futon piled against the wall and a bureau whose oak-look veneer was peeling at the corners. I ignored it and went for Ned's knapsack. It was the same hiker job he'd taken on tour – had we really only come back four days ago? I pulled out his fleece, his crumpled t-shirts, the *Rough Guide to Japan, Rich Dad, Poor Dad, The Seven Habits of Highly Successful People, Xenophobia, U-Turn Day, Nevermind,* and *Get Behind Me Satan.* We were keeping good company, as least as far as the music went. A manila envelope held a bunch of Cold Coeur Family Vol.

I flyers, plus a few of our *U-Turn Day* promo postcards. I found the evidence, in a ziploc baggie. Tad had completed his mission. Back in with that. It would be some compensation for all the grief we'd put Ned through, if he ever returned here. Finally, I extracted a handful of Fujifilm and Kodak envelopes. If these were what I was looking for, Gavin had considerately tucked them back to the bottom of the knapsack. I strewed photographs across the tatami. Beaches, temples, dark club interiors. My own face blinked up at me. Here I was onstage, a howling closeup, and there I was in the back of the van, leaning against Gen's shoulder. Ned was a pretty good photographer. But were these what Tad had gone to the trouble of attempting to steal?

One of the remaining envelopes, a Kodak one, was much older and tattier than the others, as well as slightly shorter. Thick rubber bands held it shut. I stuffed it into the back pocket of my jeans.

Shouting erupted in the kitchen, followed by a crash. Before I could react, the door slammed all the way back along its grooves.

"The fuck are you doing?"

I stumbled to my feet, reeling back to the far wall. There was a window high up in it, but there was nothing to stand on. Behind Gavin, I could see Tad helping Alastair up. Gavin had knocked him down.

"What are you fuckers? Some kind of terrorist cell?" Gavin advanced on me. He was so tall, and the way he was moving now, I could see that that black belt, second dan, was no lie. "Fuck that." His voice was heavy with anger. "I don't want to know. Do you hear? I don't care if you're Ned's friends or you're here to sort him out. I don't want to know the first fucking thing about you."

"Don't hurt me," I said. "Please."

"Oh, I'm not going to hurt you." A smile flickered on his lips, and he swept my legs out from under me. I don't even know what he did – some kind of kick? All I know is that I was on the floor, desperately scrabbling away from the blow that I knew was coming next.

And then Gavin fell on top of me, and Alastair was on top of him, and the only reason I didn't scream was because I'd been winded. My vision went grey. I hacked and couldn't breathe. It was like being under the waterfall again.

The weight of Gavin's body came off me. Tad dragged me clear. I breathed.

Gavin writhed face down on the floor, clawing at his shirt collar, as Alastair braced his foot in the middle of his spine. Stumbling and swaying, Alastair hauled back.

It took many subjective years, the balance of an entire lifetime, for Gavin to stop moving. He flopped onto his face. The blood seemed to have curdled under his skin, turning it the color of a bad bruise. His mouth sagged open, lips engorged, tongue stiff. I understood why he hadn't made any noise. Alastair had strangled him with the thin nylon rope that had tied Tad to the chair.

Straightening up, Alastair stared at me and Tad. "God. Look at the pair of you. You'd think I'd murdered him or something." He giggled.

"S-s-so much for ultimate truth," I said.

"Yeah. These martial arts freaks never expect you to have an equalizer."

Tad held up Alastair's knife. "You had this."

Alastair half-smiled. "Hang onto that. It would have been the bloodbath of the century. Pretty messy. Lucky I remembered how to tie a slipknot."

I followed them into the kitchen. I was about to shut the door to Ned's room, shutting out the sight of that sprawled horror and the blood seeping from its head as it breathed, no, of course it wasn't breathing, and there wasn't any blood; what was wrong with me? Alastair said, "Catch." He threw a dishcloth at me. "Wipe down everything we've touched. Start with the beer bottles and glasses. And don't forget the window Tad got in at."

"I was wearing my gloves," Tad said. His face was grey. He looked hostile and twitchy.

"Where are they now?"

"He put them in the trash."

"Well, get them out. That's exactly the kind of clue we don't want to leave."

I thought about DNA, filaments of fabric, microscopic flakes of skin, fallen hairs. We would have had to bomb the house to be absolutely sure we'd erased all traces of our presence. Without a handy supply of Semtex, the best we could do was make it look as if Gavin had been here by himself all night.

At last Alastair called a halt. We turned off all the lights, wiping the switches afterwards, and left with no pretense of stealth by the front door.

The street was even darker and quieter than it had been when we arrived. All the televisions in the neighboring houses had gone off. It was two thirty in the morning.

"Not out of the woods yet, I'm afraid," Alastair said quietly. "How are we going to get back to your place, Tad? No trains at this time of night, am I correct? And I don't feel like taking a taxi."

"No," said Tad. "But we could take those." He pointed down the crevice that Gavin had called "the side bit." Two bicycles leaned against the wall.

"Well, I don't know about that," said Alastair. "That would be stealing, wouldn't it? And stealing is against the law." He frowned reproachfully at Tad, who stammered that it had only been an idea. Then Alastair doubled over, his face darkening with laughter. "Oh boy," he gasped. "We'll make a criminal of you yet."

One of the bicycles was fitted with standing bars. Alastair and Tad took turns on that one while I balanced behind them, holding onto their shoulders.

We sped through the silent streets. Tad's knowledge of Tokyo led us south as surely as a compass. But you never realize how big a city is until you have to cross it under your own steam. Soon, Alastair and Tad were tired enough to let me take a turn pedaling.

We kept to back streets but followed the loop of Kannana Dori, which arcs south all the way to Omori. Before it got there we parted from it, veering east to Shinagawa, where the JR station straddles a sprawl of tracks and sidings. We abandoned the bicycles among dozens of others in a multistorey parking shed, taking care to wipe their handlebars.

"Heigh ho," said Alastair. "And now for a nice stroll."

But even he was near the end of his flippancy. None of us had much to say as we trudged on southwards. It was still only four in the morning, so the streets were mercifully free of traffic. I felt shaky and sick. I longed for a hot drink, but it would have been too risky to go into a convenience store. I bought a bottle of water from a vending machine and drained it at a gulp.

Dawn broke slowly, bringing the green back to the trees, the birds back to the air, and the trains back to the railway. We stumbled at last into the Kuroiwas' dining-room. I breathed in the familiar scent of the incense that Nina was always burning in the kitchen.

"You can have that hot drink now, Shanti," said Alastair.

"Quiet," whispered Tad. "My dad's home. So're Joaquin and Nina. Probably."

"I don't want a hot drink anymore, anyway," I said. "All I want is bed. Well, I want a shower. But I want bed more."

Halfway up the stairs, I glanced back at them. They were muttering about the way we'd cleaned up the house in Nakano, speculating how it would look to the police. I continued up the stairs.

As I took my jeans off, the Kodak envelope fell out of my back pocket. I'd forgotten all about it.

I glanced over at the bed. Nina breathed deeply, one arm flung over her face, as if even in sleep she was trying to hide from reality. I knew how she felt.

I weighed the envelope in my hand. Gavin had died for this. Gavin what? I didn't even know his last name. Could it possibly have been worth it? We'd forgotten to ask Tad why he'd taken it, and it no longer seemed important.

I tucked the envelope, unopened, back into my jeans. Then I crawled into bed beside Nina and pulled the covers over my head.

Noise woke me. No, not noise, faint bass vibrations leaking from the studio down the hall. The pieces of my life closed around me. Bon Kyoki And Sayaka, a compellingly weird pop duo – she sang, he played the electric violin, and Joaquin added the drums on his computer. They'd had an appointment at eleven. I rolled over and grabbed my phone out of the pile of clothes on the floor. *My* phone? It was the other phone, the one Ned had given me, but it still told the time.

A quarter past noon.

I didn't meet anyone on my way to the bathroom. On my way back, with my hair in wet strings because I had more important things to do right now than blow-dry it, even if I didn't know what they were, I met Tad coming downstairs. "Where's Alastair?" I said.

"He went out."

"Where to?"

"Ueno, I think. He said there was an exhibition he wanted to see."

I flopped dramatically against the banister, then straightened up as I realized this was a typically Alastair thing to do. It was probably his way of cleansing his soul. I touched the Kodak envelope, which was still in the back pocket of my jeans. For some reason, I didn't want to be alone when I opened it. "Are you busy in the studio?"

"Yeah. Just fetching perks for the talent."

I followed him into the kitchen. He took a bottle of green tea out of the fridge, poured three glasses, and set them on a tray. I said, "That was pretty crazy last night, wasn't it?"

"If you need something to do, you could work on the merchandise reorders."

"Where's Nina?"

"Oh, she went with Alastair."

"No way! They could have woken me up. I'd have gone, too!"

"What about me?" Tad said, mock-offended.

I crossed the kitchen. He put down the tray. I fell into his arms, and he hugged me until pain flashed around my ribs. We kissed.

The doorbell rang.

Tad groaned. "Probably Shu-chan and the rest. We scheduled them for two o'clock. Now you've got your work cut out for you: entertain them while Joaquin and I wrap up this session. And if they ask you if we have any weed, well, we don't."

"Well, we *don't,*" I said with a big-eyed look of innocence that made him laugh. It almost sounded genuine.

The doorbell rang again. I went to answer it.

"Good afternoon." The man on the doorstep did a polite bob, starting in the middle of his back, which made his shirt front appear to cave in. A younger, handsomer man in the street behind him seemed to be guarding the dark blue Toyota sedan that had managed to insert itself down the cul-de-sac. Neat trick. The man standing in front of me consulted the inside of a manila folder. He had unfashionably short hair and he was so thin that his plain black suit hung in pleats. Gas meter reader, I thought, NHK dues collector, door-to-door salesman, Jehovah's Witness, reporter. He said, "Are you Nina Gorot?"

"No, I'm Shanti Hazard."

He recited the street address and asked if he could speak with Seiichiro Kuroiwa.

Parking violation, I thought, problem with the taxi company, personal finance agency, that's it. Kuroiwa-san's secretly racked up gambling debts, and now they've come to break his legs.

"No, you can't," said Tad, coming up beside me. "He's at work." That was a lie. Today was Kuroiwa-san's day off, so he'd be at the racetrack. "I'm his son. Can I help you?"

"Maybe you can. We'd like to have a talk with the members of Gorot," the man pronounced it correctly, "a rock band. I understand this is their residence."

Right on cue, the drum track from upstairs broke through to audibility. Someone had opened the door of the studio.

"Just a few questions. We apologize for any inconvenience." The man's voice held a tinge of authority.

But! If he had a warrant, he'd have produced it by now. So he didn't have one. We could refuse to let him in. But then we'd look guilty. And what did we have to hide? Nothing. Nothing, nothing.

"Have there been complaints about the noise?" I said.

"Come in," Tad overrode me. "Yes, of course, do come in. But could you – would you mind moving your car? The neighbors…"

"Of course! I'm very sorry. We'll move it right away." He called back to the other man, who jumped into the sedan at the same time as a third man got out of the back seat, and I saw one of the cute little old ladies who lived next door dithering in front of the sedan's bumper, trapped there with her Black Watch plaid shopping trolley. The neighbors might be old and deaf, but they had eyes, and tongues.

The third man was also in plainclothes, a chic grey suit with a pale yellow shirt and dark yellow tie, but I would have known him for a policeman anywhere. He had a hard still face and eyes that ticked openly from side to side, like an unmanned spy plane cruising through enemy airspace. We got the two of them inside the house just as Joaquin, Sayaka, and Bon Kyoki came downstairs. Joaquin said with automatic belligerence, "What do you want?"

"Pleased to meet you." They introduced themselves as Inspector Something and Detective Something Else of the Shinjuku Something Police Station. They flashed their badges, but they didn't give us their business cards, and they didn't sit down.

"Tad, what have you done now? Forgotten to pay your taxes?" Joaquin laughed, but no one joined in. Standing close to him, I saw a tremor in the corner of his smile. Oh, hell, maybe he *did* have some weed or hash in the house, just not enough to give away to Shu-chan and his boys.

Inspector Something, the hard-faced one, had a gravelly moo of a voice that made me think of a tenor saxophone. "Have any of you turned on the television today? Looked at a paper?"

Tad started for the kitchen, where the TV was. I grabbed his hand to stop him. "No, should we have? I'm afraid, inspector, we're just musicians…" I made a helpless gesture with my free hand. "Is Japan at war with the United States again? It's nice of you to notify us in person."

Neither of them so much as smiled. I remembered a different policeman, an Irish garda ten feet tall who'd entreated me to stop crying, and gone out to his car and fetched me a Kit Kat. I'd stopped crying then because I felt so bad for him. Recovering, I'd said without premeditation, *I was crying because my mummy doesn't love me,* and after that he'd been on my side. But I wasn't thirteen anymore, and being funny and cute wasn't going to work.

The saxophonist slid a newspaper out of his briefcase. "Quite a shocking story," he informed us. "A British man has been murdered in Nakano ward."

Sayaka screamed. I looked at her and Bon Kyoki. Fear and confusion chased across their faces, which were the naïve, attractive faces of musicians who really do live for their art. No one else had reacted. Was that right? Probably not. "That is absolutely tragic, Inspector," I gasped. I squeezed Tad's hand. His palm stuck to mine, clammy with sweat.

Joaquin said, "Anyone we know? It can't be. What was his name?"

The saxophonist perused the page that was already folded open, as if to refresh his memory. "The victim's name was Gavin Uintaazu."

Uintaazu? Winters. Gavin Winters.

A cool name for a shithead.

How did they get to us so fast?

I thought: Ned.

Pulled in for lack of ID, sitting pretty at some police station in Shibuya. Hauled out of the tank to have the news broken to him. And what does he do? He points the finger at me and Alastair.

Not because he knew we planned to kill Gavin. Because we didn't.

Just on general principle.

He'd turned Alastair's brilliant plan around on us like high-velocity karma.

"Winters? Gavin Winters?" said Joaquin, sounding more relaxed. "Don't know him."

"Officers, may we go?" Bon Kyoki hugged his violin case in one arm, Sayaka in the other. "We didn't know this guy, either. It's nothing to do with us..."

"Are you members of Gorot?"

"No!"

Sayaka said, "We're just on their label." I could see that in her mind, being on CCR had suddenly become the next closest thing to a crime. "They've got a studio upstairs... we were rehearsing... mixing some of our tracks..."

"Did you participate in the tour that this group, Cold Coeur Records, recently conducted?"

"No!"

"Take their contact information," the saxophonist ordered. The handsome young policeman led Bon Kyoki and Sayaka into the hall. Joaquin helplessly watched them go. The saxophonist moved around the dining-room table, glancing over the debris that littered it. He picked up a copy of *U-Turn Day* and looked around at the three of us, matching our faces with the jacket photograph. "Where are the rest of you?"

But not *where is Alastair.* Why not? Had they already pulled him in? No, we'd have heard about it from Nina.

"I don't keep track of them every minute of the day!" Joaquin sounded angry now as well as frightened. He probably understood that he'd just lost Bon Kyoki And Sayaka forever. "Do you suspect one of them of this – of causing this tragedy?"

"We don't have a suspect at present. We're seeking information from a variety of sources." The saxophonist put down the CD and started to leaf through our press pack materials. I felt a pang of outrage at the way he was handling our stuff. After another instant, I realized that I was *meant* to feel outraged. I was *meant* to lose my cool. I straightened my back and readjusted my blank face. No matter what Ned had told them, he didn't have any proof. This game wasn't over yet. The saxophonist said to Joaquin, "We'd like to have a look at your payroll," and that was when I remembered the flyers and CDs in Ned's backpack.

I was the only one who'd seen them, and then Gavin had been dead. So there they'd remained, linking Gorot to the murder scene.

The room started to close in on me like the garbage compactor in *Star Wars.*

A few flyers! What does that prove? It doesn't prove anything. Breathe.

"I don't have a payroll," Joaquin said. Manufacturing a scowl of boredom and disgust, he pulled out a chair and sank down.

"Oh?" Detective Something Else took out a notebook. He had long, strong hands, I noticed, much like Joaquin's own. Maybe he played the piano in his spare time. "Do you pay your employees under the table?"

Joaquin laughed. "I don't have any employees."

"We all work together," I said. To my amazement, I sounded flippant and in control. "We share the pain, the pleasure, and the profits. When there are any."

"We've got a d-d-deal with a major record label," Tad said. "I expect our c-c-compensation structure will... will alter significantly in the coming... in the future. But for now, we're just... I work for the label on a v-v-volunteer basis."

Shut up, Tad, I thought. Or at least control that stammer. You sound guilty as fuck.

"You conducted a domestic tour recently, I believe." The saxophonist.

"It helped your label to attract the attention of an important corporate investor." The pianist.

"That's a nice way of putting it," I said, still channeling Alastair. "The music industry is a Darwinian environment: anything that moves will be eaten."

"'A Darwinian environment.'" The pianist.

"You have a bleak view of the world." The saxophonist.

"Then we ought to understand each other well," I said. "Your jobs can't leave you much in the way of optimism."

"Oh, I don't know about that." The saxophonist smiled for the first time. "I'm always optimistic that we'll catch the bad guys."

The handsome young policeman had come back into the room. He in his turn was examining a copy of *U-Turn Day.* I said, "Would you like to take that with you? I'll autograph it. A token of our appreciation for the fine work you do."

"That would be strictly illegal." The young policeman put the CD down.

"It could be interpreted as a bribe," the pianist explained.

"However..." The saxophonist held up our standard publicity eight-by-twelve of me. "I'd like to have this, if I may. Would you mind autographing it?"

As I scrawled my name across the bottom of the photo, Alastair warned me in my head, *Don't sign anything!* Too late. Now they could compare my signature with the one on the CD in Ned's backpack – I distinctly remembered signing it for him, *Plus ça change, Shanti*. Fuck my signature, they now had my *fingerprints*.

And speaking of incriminating evidence…

The Kodak envelope in my jeans pocket seemed to vibrate against my ass like a phone with a unique ringtone: *Guilty! Guilty! Guilty!* Sweat coursed down my back. I squashed the impulse to touch the envelope and make sure it wasn't about to fall out of my pocket. Mercifully, I had on one of Tad's t-shirts, which covered my hips. I said, "Hang onto that photo, Inspector, it might be worth something someday."

"I'll frame it and hang it in my office," the saxophonist said without a trace of humor.

Slouched at the table, Joaquin said, "Can we quit playing these games, please? You aren't here to collect autographs. If you have questions, please ask them. If not, my next clients are due at two o'clock…"

"Then stop lying!" the saxophonist suddenly shouted at him.

Joaquin flinched. I think we all did. He resorted to everyone's last line of defense: "I don't know what you're talking about."

Tad said, "We're n-not answering any questions without our lawyer present."

"Where did you get that?" the youngest policeman sneered. "American TV?" His gaze flicked from Tad's face to mine, then dropped to our joined hands. I stared back at him, but it didn't work. All that happened was that his handsome face dissolved into a collection of abstract angles as incomprehensible as the routine they were running on us. He was the flautist, I decided. He had the lips for it, and I'd always hated the sound of the flute.

"Your lawyer would be Shuichi Asakawa?"

"How the fuck do you know so much about us?" Joaquin said.

"That's our job."

"And Asakawa-san's job is negotiating contracts. Not defending homicide suspects."

It was out. I felt almost relieved.

"He'd be worse than useless to you at present."

Joaquin gave them a look so scathingly superior that I wanted to applaud. "You can't arrest us for the simple reason that we have done nothing wrong. We didn't know this guy. It's tragic that he is dead but we had nothing to do with it. I assume that even in this country, you are required to *prove* your misguided suspicions?"

The saxophonist held Joaquin's gaze for a moment. Then he turned away. He was smiling. He put the photo I'd signed for him into his briefcase. "No one is going to be arrested here. As I said, we do not have a suspect at present. Your cooperation is appreciated, but not compulsory."

Relief elevated me like a hit of oxygen. All they'd had was a bluff, and Joaquin had called it. They didn't have anything on us, or at least, they didn't have anything more than a bunch of flyers. They'd just been administering shocks to see how we'd react, *just on general principle!* So fuck you, Ned, fuck you and your sad little revenge ploy.

"I'd like to have a look at your studio," the pianist said pleasantly. "Would one of you show me around?"

"Sure," said Tad, breaking away from me. "It's upstairs. This way, please."

Shit, I thought. Maybe Tad had the right attitude to begin with. We shouldn't have been so hostile. How are they to know that's normal where we come from? I said, "Can we offer you something to drink? Tea, coffee…" That wouldn't be construed as a bribe, would it?

The saxophonist said he would accept a cup of tea. Joaquin followed us into the kitchen. He hovered over the table for a moment before going to the cabinet for the teabags. The flautist had disappeared. I hadn't noticed him leaving the room. He was either out in their car or snooping elsewhere in the house. What a shitty job, I thought, pouring hot water from the electric urn I'd switched on about a thousand years ago.

"I request you to leave us," the saxophonist said to Joaquin in English. "I have some private questions to ask Shanti."

Hot water overflowed the teapot and splashed my hand. I swallowed a cry.

Like a robot, Joaquin moved to the door. As he left, he said in French, "Don't cooperate. Give him your alibi if he asks for it. But don't answer any other questions. They don't need to know."

Call Nina, tell her to tell Alastair, warn him – I swallowed the words just in time. The pleasant blankness of the saxophonist's expression told me that he didn't speak French, but he didn't look as disconcerted as he should have, and that told me something else I should have been aware of from the start. He was wearing a voice recorder inside that nice suit jacket, and back at Shinjuku Something Police Station there were people who could translate French into Japanese.

Steadily, I poured the tea. "Milk?" I said. Since he'd started speaking English, I did, too, hoping it might give me an edge. "Sugar?"

"No thank you."

I sat down. The saxophonist sat down. He instantly seemed more human. Scratch that thought.

"Where were you last night, Shanti?"

I had an instant of wanting to laugh, because he sounded like he'd got that off American TV, and then I had another instant to think of a lie, and what I thought of instead was Mike Schultz.

"I was out," I said. "I had a couple of drinks at a bar in Shibuya, and then we went to hang out at the park."

I sipped my tea and burned my mouth.

"Who were you with?"

"My—" I caught myself. Mike had left before Alastair arrived.

I made a snap decision. I was neck-deep in shit here and sinking, but Alastair still had a chance. At the museums at Ueno on a Sunday? No detectives on the planet could track an individual through those crowds, especially if they didn't know he was there in the first place. And if I could leave him out of my alibi, then I would be in the clear myself, because I was five foot four and Gavin could have snapped my arms like disposable chopsticks. The autopsy would reveal, *must* reveal, that Gavin's murderer had been several inches taller than me and a lot stronger.

I thought all this in the time it took for me to put my cup down. "I met a friend at Dub. He brought another friend."

"Their names?"

"My friend Ned. And his friend's name was Mike." I forced a smile. Calm, but not too calm. "Aren't you going to write that down? Ned's full name is Edward Gallant and I think his friend's surname was Schultz."

"We are aware of that. Mr Schultz and Mr Gallant are residents of the house where Mr Winters's remains were discovered."

"No! Oh my God. I knew there was another guy - oh shit, they did say his name was - oh my God," I repeated. I raised a tortured face to him. "Do you mind if I smoke?"

"Please."

I took a Lucky Strike from a pack Tad had left on the table. The saxophonist extracted a pack of Larks from his shirt pocket and held his Bic out to light my cigarette. "So that's why," I breathed. "Oh God. Why didn't you say… Was it one of them who… who found him?"

"Mr Schultz discovered remains of Mr Winters at seven o'clock this morning."

"No."

I waited, smoking my cigarette in a distraught manner.

"At twelve seventeen a.m., Mr Gallant was taken into custody in area of Nabeshima Park, near Shibuya, for failure to produce identification when requested to do so by police officer. At that time, you were with him. Another Caucasian male was with him also. That was not Mr Schultz. Who was it?"

Ned hadn't talked. "Some guy we met in Shibuya after we split up with Mike." I shrugged distractedly, as if barely able to remember. "A friend of Ned's."

The cops who'd been in on Ned's arrest could probably pick Alastair out of a lineup. But I was stuck with my lie now, and all I could do was pray that they hadn't already pulled Alastair in. And that we got a chance to coordinate our stories before we contradicted each other.

We should have done that last night. But I'd been so tired.

What if Tad and I had already contradicted each other?

The saxophonist was talking again and it was washing over me like jazz, but I understood what he wanted.

"We went to a club. Womb," I named the biggest club in Shibuya that wasn't Xanadu, where Mike had presumably been picking up girls while we were murdering Gavin. "I'd missed the last train and it was Saturday night. And the guy… God, what was his name? Something unusual. Sebastian? Anyway, he was pretty hot…" I managed a rueful grin. "I didn't get home until dawn." The story unspooled in my mind. Shanti the slut, got a boyfriend but she can't resist a sexy pair of cheekbones, not giving a shit that her friend's been taken into custody, dancing the night away with a stranger – very rock 'n' roll.

The saxophonist examined his cigarette. "Mr Gallant accompanied your band on tour in capacity of," he coughed, "'roadie.' Why did Mr Gorot lie about that?"

I said in astonishment, "You didn't ask him."

"'No payroll,' Shanti? 'No employees'?"

I laughed. "Oh God. None of us thought of Ned as an employee. I guess he technically was one, but he never got paid."

"Did that inconvenience him? Or did he have alternate sources of income?"

The proverbial lightbulb flashed on over my head.

"Well," I said, twisting my body and taking a nervous sip of tea, "I did kind of notice that he seemed to have… well… a lot of money to throw around…"

The saxophonist stubbed out his cigarette. He hadn't touched his tea. He opened his briefcase and took out the stomped-looking notebook that appeared to be standard issue. "Did you observe incidents when he accept payments from strangers?"

"Well..."

High-velocity karma, I thought. Coming right back at you, Ned. Let's see you dodge this one.

After dark Alastair came home with Nina, although I'd begged him on the phone to stay out and meet me somewhere in the city. He said if we did that, we'd be acting suspiciously. Maybe he was afraid I would be tailed. Or maybe he wanted to hear Joaquin's side of the story as well as mine.

He did agree to give the jazz band plenty of time to get clear, so by the time he and Nina arrived at the house, the warm April night had gathered. On their way back, they'd ascertained that the street wasn't being watched. "At least, not by a fat man gobbling doughnuts in a stakeout car," Alastair said.

"Filthy racists! Fascist whores!" Joaquin put down his can of Sapporo and launched into another string of Quebeçois swears. When Alastair started laughing, Joaquin leaned against the table and grinned. He passed Alastair a beer. "We had one very close call. Shanti offered the senior fascist a cup of tea. *A cup of tea,*" he trilled in falsetto.

"Elementary psychological warfare," I shouted. "I was fighting back."

"And when she did that, I remembered that I had a smoke in here, oh, at perhaps three o'clock in the morning, and the roach was still in the ashtray. Well, I managed to slip it up my sleeve before they spotted it. But it was close! Very close!"

Tad bowed over the table, laughing so hard he could barely speak. "And the studio stank." He lifted his face and morphed into the pianist, sucking in his cheeks and flaring his nostrils to sniff out the illicit goods. Joaquin and I convulsed again.

"You have to burn incense," Nina exclaimed. She'd dressed up to go to the museums in beige leather trousers and a white shirt, with a silk scarf and her pearl earrings. More than at any time since I'd known her, she looked like the Upper East Side fashionista she could have been in an alternate life. And now she was reacting like it, too. "How many times have I told you? It's just basic courtesy!"

Tad gasped, "I think it *was* the incense."

Alastair turned his unopened can of beer in his hands. I prayed he could make all the variables add up, because I couldn't. While Joaquin and Tad were autopiloting through their session with Shu-chan and his boys, aka The Deadenders, I'd called Gen and Shingo to warn them, but had only succeeded in infecting them with my own confusion. Now my sense of victory was alternating with paranoia. Even though I had the advantage of knowing what had happened last night, when I tried to breathe deeply and think like a policeman, I couldn't get past the dissonance of Ned blaming me and Alastair… and the jazz band failing to give the slightest indication that they knew such a person as Alastair existed.

We had both the TV and the radio on, which made it even harder to think. Twice since the jazz band left, we'd seen the same footage of 4-16-3 East Nakano. The front of the house strung with yellow crime scene tape. The side bit, with more tape covering the hole Tad had cut in the window. The networks had also got hold of a snapshot of Gavin, tanned and grinning, toasting the camera, elbows planted on a rough wooden bartop. "Police suspect a botched robbery," the reporter had announced. That was more than they'd told us – so who was lying to whom?

"So they asked you about Ned's, uh, sales activities?" Alastair prompted me. His eyes were half-lidded. The scar over his eyebrow stood out bright and shiny, his forehead glossed with sweat.

"Oh, that's right. You also know that piece of shit!" Joaquin said before I could speak.

"We were friends as children," Alastair nodded.

"Well, forgive me, but I'm not very happy with him right now. First he ditches our tour. Did Shanti tell you about that?"

"The tour was *over,*" Nina said.

"He got himself into trouble in Utsunomiya, now it's quite clear. That's a yakuza city. He must have stepped on someone's toes. He doesn't know Japan, he doesn't know the language, and it's very easy to provoke misunderstandings. Isn't it, Tad? He returned to Tokyo to stay with his friend. He probably thought he was safe. But they tracked him down! And his unhappy friend…" Joaquin drew the side of his hand across his throat. That gave me a start, because neither the jazz band nor NHK had shared that Gavin had been strangled. "And now we're caught in their net! And they will shake us to see what falls out! That's what they did today. Only they didn't shake hard enough." He turned his palm over and let the infamous roach fall to the floor. Everyone laughed except Nina. White-lipped, she snatched it up and threw it in the trash. "Soyez calme," said Joaquin under his breath.

Oh yes, Joaquin had a story that accounted for all the facts. Or rather, all the facts he knew.

Did he really hold Ned to blame? I couldn't tell. I got the feeling that he half-sympathized with Ned on the basis of the business relationship they'd established on tour. A gaijin's gotta do what a gaijin's gotta do. Fuck tha police. There was also some twisted guilt in there, I thought.

"So Shanti, they asked you about Ned," Alastair pursued. At that moment Joaquin's phone rang, so I got to answer the question myself.

"Yeah. I actually got the impression that they were leading up to that from the start, and everything else was just tinsel. Like Joaquin said, they already have Ned tagged as a bad guy. The evil alien corrupting the innocent Japanese yoof."

Tad snorted laughter. I spared him a worried glance. He, even more than Joaquin, was running on fumes and his sense of humor.

"They asked me what I'd seen on tour," I said. "What I'd—" I giggled— "smelt. I kid you not, they did. And so, well, I wasn't going to lie, was I?"

Joaquin snapped his phone shut. I stopped laughing at the look on his face. Until now, I hadn't admitted that I'd confirmed the saxophonist's guesses about Ned. Naturally, I'd also insisted that the Cold Coeur Family was so clean we could advertise breakfast cereal. I got ready to explain away my cooperation in terms of leading questions and a girly compulsion to please. But Joaquin just gave me a nasty look and said to the room at large, "I've got to make a run to the station. I'll take the van, so I'll be back in fifteen minutes."

"Are you picking someone up?" I said.

"Chiharu," he said, halfway to the door.

"My God," I said. "Here? Now? *Why?*"

"I forgot she was coming over. Completely forgot. Now she's at the station, and I can't just leave her there." The last words came from the hall.

"Wait, Joaquin, I'm coming," Nina said. "I need to grab a couple of things at the drugstore. They're open until—" The front door closed on her voice.

"Hoo boy," said Alastair, running one hand through his hair. He popped open his beer and took a long drink.

"For fuck's sake," I said. "Can't she walk?"

"At night? Alone?" Tad laughed. "No, I bet he wanted to tell her the story himself. Instead of letting her get it from us."

"Tad, speak English," I said.

"Sorry." He lit a cigarette. "So Alastair, you know the maximum penalty for murder in this country?"

"Sure," Alastair said. "I did my research."

"It's death," I said. "Medieval style. Hanged by the neck until you are dead. We have a proud and ancient culture, we don't need no steenkin' lethal injections."

"Why are we talking about this?" Alastair's eyes went to the TV on top of the fridge. "And why are we watching this crap?" It was an NHK talk show, not a panelist under fifty.

"It's kind of boring, but it's better than MTV Japan," said Tad.

"We don't know that they didn't bug the house," I said. "There could be a microtransmitter in here. But now, all they're getting is the crossfire between NHK and Bay FM."

"OK, I know this is a pretty science-fictional country," Alastair said. "But guys, seriously – "

"I'm going to get a portable RF detector tomorrow," Tad said. "Sweep the whole house."

Alastair moved around the kitchen, looking into the cabinets and under the table, ironically checking for bugs. He peered at the opaque black windows, then leaned his hip against the sink. "Have you called your label? Your A&R rep?"

"No," said Tad. "We're hoping they won't find out."

Alastair said strongly, "That's crazy. You've got to call them. Get them on your side. What you need is allies! Christ, you're a bunch of smart, internet-savvy – Things happen to people who are afraid to speak up. Bad shit happens all the time to people that nobody knows or cares about. But bad shit does not happen to rock stars. Or if it does, they get out on bail inside of twenty-four hours, and their sales go up on the publicity. *Call* them! You haven't got anything to hide!"

"We're not rock stars yet," said Tad. "We haven't even signed our official contract. If Apex backs out of the deal – "

"I think that's a risk you're just going to have to take."

I understood what Alastair was telling us: we couldn't cling to the lunatic hope that the jazz band would preserve some kind of confidentiality agreement. We had to get our story out first. And to do that, we had to psych ourselves into the mindset of innocent victims.

Easier said than done.

Sorrow brimming up in me, I said, "But we do have something to hide, Alastair. I'm talking about Joaquin. He and Nina messed around with hard drugs in the past. They've put that behind them. I don't know why he's never given up weed – "

"He's a hundred and ten percent all the time," Tad said. "Sometimes he needs to relax."

"Whatever. He knows how it is in this country, he knows that a tenth of a gram of hash could jeopardize everything we've worked for, but he still won't give it up. But he *knows* that if we were linked with some yakuza cartel, or even just an evil alien like Ned, our careers, such as they are, would be over." I looked at Tad for support. He nodded.

"Japanese culture is behind America. Weed is taboo."

"So he's freaking out, and he's thinking like a junkie," I said. "Hide it! Flush it! Deny it!"

"So, I take it he doesn't know that Ned is already in police custody," Alastair said. "I think he should know that. I can tell him, if you don't feel up to it."

I bounced onto my toes. "No! Have you forgotten? You weren't there! You were exploring Ginza by yourself! I was with Ned and some guy named Sebastian—"

"Yeah, and you told me about Ned just now," Alastair interrupted, but I knew he'd forgotten. Distracted by his own thoughts, he hadn't yet fixed our alibis in his mind as solid facts. I suddenly felt more frightened than I had all day. The front door rattled. Alastair said, "He's back; either you tell him, Shanti, or..."

But it was a gravelly "Tadaima!" that came from the hall, and Kuroiwa-san who entered the kitchen. He playfully covered his ears, drawing attention to the noise. I leapt to turn down the radio and TV. "Good evening to you! Not very many of you tonight, are there? Not lonely?"

"Okaerinasai!" I said. "So did Senzo Bulk win?"

"Romped home with three lengths to spare." Kuroiwa-san's face glowed with the memory, and maybe a few drinks shared after the race with his betting cronies. "What a lovely colt. The withers on him."

"Dad," Tad said, rising. "Dad, I've got to tell you something."

"Has he popped the question?" Kuroiwa-san drolly asked me. I startled at the revelation that he'd noticed that Tad and I were involved at all. He chuckled.

"No, Dad. It's not good. But I have to tell you." With a quick ashamed glance at me, Tad guided his father out of the room.

Alone with the radio and the TV, Alastair and I looked at each other. "They get along really well," I said. "Isn't it amazing? A father and son who aren't in conflict." As I spoke, I thought about how Kuroiwa-san would likely react to the news that his home had been invaded by a homicide squad.

"Shanti," Alastair said. "Look at me. I'm sorry. I never meant for any of this to happen. But it's going to be all right. I promise you."

"Oh Jesus," I said, stabbing the volume button on the TV remote control, turning it most of the way back up. "How is it going to be all right?"

"Well, I haven't got a magic wand. But if you do as I say, and if you can make the whole gang do as I say, I think I can stop it from getting any worse. One thing I do know is how to use the media."

He began to explain. The front door opened again, this time with a crash. "But he was so gentleman," Chiharu said incredulously as she,

Nina, and Joaquin entered the kitchen. "He help me with carry stuff, he always take care – "

"Yeah," Nina agreed, "and personally, I don't think he was involved in any way. The cops are just fixating on the drugs angle because, well, they're cops! But it was probably, I don't know, a fight over a girl, or..."

"You women," Joaquin said, "you think everything is about you!"

Chiharu screamed faintly and pointed at the TV.

"Oh, we've already seen this," I said, glancing at the familiar footage of East Nakano.

"But it say - now, it say – " Chiharu's English was deserting her.

Ned's face filled the TV screen.

"Tad!" I shouted.

"I can't hear! Shut up," Joaquin begged.

It looked like a mugshot, but it was probably an old passport photo. Ned's hair came to his shoulders, and he wore a vacant, stoned expression. The voiceover said *...Danish citizen... believed to have...*

The camera cut back to the news anchors in their gaudy studio. Her concerned frown fading from her face, the female anchor said, "And now, the Hanshin Tigers..."

We all closed in on Chiharu. "What did they say? We couldn't catch it. You must have. What did they say about Ned?"

"Yes, yes, I hear, it say - it say this is share house man – "

"Roommate."

" – of victim. Police want he cooperate with - with survey – "

"With their inquiries."

"They're looking for him," Joaquin said. "We knew that."

"No!" Chiharu shook her head. "They - this – "

"Take it easy," said Alastair. "Take your time."

"It is form. Custom. To broadcast the photo of man on television. They don't say yet, but it means this is - they think he do very bad thing."

Alastair said, "I believe the word you want is murder." His face reddened; he took a deep breath and half turned away.

Joaquin said, "It's a manhunt." He flung himself into the nearest kitchen chair. "Turn it off. I've heard enough."

"Chiharu," I said. "Did they *say* it was in connection with... with the murder? Because..."

"Yes, they say. Or no, they don't say, but this is topic of segment." Chiharu looked excited rather than afraid. Ned was nothing to her, of course; this was just another test. The Cold Coeur Family, now accepting applications. Chief qualification, Good in a Crisis.

Personally, I was fast approaching my limit. Ned was out loose in the city. Maybe he'd only been taken into custody for a few hours. And now the police were looking for him. Because… "Because I laid it on pretty thick. When they asked me about Ned's, uh, sales activities. I kind of, uh, used my imagination."

"Shanti," Joaquin said. "What did you tell them?"

"I kind of said that I wasn't sure, but I thought he was, uh, well, this was the truth, I said I heard him talking about smack." I covered my face with my hands, remembering how the saxophonist had taken down every word.

"Jesus H. Christ," Nina said. "Shanti, that's not funny. If you'd ever been around heroin addicts—"

"I have. And sometimes you've got to laugh to keep from crying. I'd expect you of all people to know that!"

"Don't be too hard on her, Nina," Joaquin said. "She was interrogated by herself for almost an hour. I expect any one of us would have told them what they wanted to hear. Still," his voice hardened, "Shanti, you've complicated our position nicely. If they catch him now, we are in very deep trouble."

"It's so unfair," Nina cried. "I'm sure he didn't have anything to do with it!"

"He picked his enemies badly. One false step, that's all it takes! In a town like Utsunomiya. Isn't that right, Chiharu?"

Or a green corner of nowhere, I thought. In a country like Ireland.

"Shanti, can I talk to you for a minute?" Alastair said.

I followed him out into the hall and whispered, "I thought he was still in custody! I was trying to get him locked down for the rest of his life!"

"Which proves that you still don't get it. I never planned for him to go to jail."

"I know, but since they already *had* him—"

"Let me spell it out for you: he *mustn't* go to jail. And above all, he mustn't go on trial for murder. You might as well give him a microphone and ask him to tell the whole world about us."

"He wouldn't."

"He most certainly would."

It flashed before my eyes, a globally reported soap opera with a tragic ending. I felt dizzy. I said, "Well then, I guess we've just had another lucky break."

"The lucky break of the century. Provided he doesn't get himself picked up again—"

"Do you think he escaped?"

"Either that, or they let him go before the left hand figured out what the right hand had arrested."

"Oh," I said, "and this is what we pay taxes for. Oh, that's fucking classic."

I was so dizzy I had to double over and grab my shins. I heard Alastair panting his crazy laughter for a moment. Then, perhaps realizing that I wasn't laughing, he laid his hand on my back. "Is it all getting a bit much?"

"Touch of dizziness," I said to my knees. "Remember, I used to get this in high school."

"And the doctor said it was low blood sugar. Here." Alastair heaved at my shoulder, unclamming me, and pulled a box of matcha-flavored Calorie Mate out of the pocket of his cords. "You haven't eaten anything all day, have you?"

"This stuff is disgusting."

"Sure is. Nina insisted I had to try it. But go on. For me."

For me. Mother's words, but all our lives, it was Alastair who'd been saying them to me. He knew my self-destructive pattern of forgetting to eat when I was stressed, only to grab the nearest unhealthy junk when I reached my physical limit. My eyes filled with tears, and I filled my mouth with Calorie Mate, a dense chunk of carbohydrates that tasted like flavored styrofoam.

The doorbell rang. Instead of dying away, its electronic chime repeated, as if a giant DJ had his finger on the vinyl disk of the world, scratching a two-note loop. I swallowed and coughed. Alastair went past me. I pressed behind his shoulder as he opened the door.

"Let me in," Ned said. In the dim light skewing out from the hall, he looked the very picture of a fugitive, unshaven, in last night's denim jacket and jeans, his face shadowed by a Yankees baseball cap. The Band-Aid on his chin buckled when he spoke. "You've got to help me."

"Are you aware that you're one of Japan's Most Wanted?" Alastair said.

"Let me in. I've been shitting myself all day. Good old Mike. He called me, warned me to keep my head down. Not very fucking easy in this city. Holed up in an internet café. Started to walk when it got dark. I've walked all the way from Shibuya."

Joaquin shouldered past me. "You maniac. They've been here, they've given us all the third degree, it's not safe!" His flailing arms encompassed the neighboring houses battened down behind their garden walls. At this hour many windows were still lit.

"It's not safe for me out there." Ned took a step forward, as if he might barge into the house by force. Alastair blocked his way.

"Listen, Neddo, how about we take a walk? It's a hell of a situation. I need to hear your side of the story. Then we'll work out what we're going to do, OK?"

Ned fell back. I saw that Alastair had hold of his elbow in a grip that had to hurt. Ned's face was grey and his movements lacked precision. He was clearly so tired that he could hardly keep his feet. I ducked around Joaquin. The steps were so narrow I almost slipped into Kuroiwa-san's potted shrubs. "Don't go anywhere," I said. "You'll be seen, if you haven't been seen already. Ned's right, it's not safe." I darted past them and stood in the gap in the garden wall at the bottom of the steps, which would have been a gateway if there'd been a gate in it. There was only me. Ludicrously, I spread my arms. "I say no. Think of something else."

"Whatever, but you can't just stand out there all night!" Nina shrieked from the doorway.

"Shut up! Tad's father!" Joaquin said urgently. "Ned, did you ever meet him? A lovely old gentleman. If he sees you he'll call the cops. Go with Alastair, I know! Shanti's apartment. You can stay out of sight—"

"All right, but how is he going to get there?" I said. "You'll have to drive him."

Joaquin cursed us all and hurried off down the street. Nina and Chiharu piled out of the house. We knelt behind the garden wall, out of sight of the street. The prickly pompoms of the topiary cedar plucked at my hair. I mindlessly smoked a cigarette while Ned recounted the story of his "arrest" last night.

After making a few telephone calls, the police had confirmed his ID and let him walk within the hour. "They must have a night clerk at the Danish embassy, or they've got some central data retrieval system." By that time the last train had gone, so what had Ned done? Headed for central Shibuya, where he could have scraped together an alibi? Not he. He'd gravitated back to Nabeshima Park and napped on a bench for the rest of the night. Around eight in the morning, he'd eaten breakfast at McDonalds, then headed for the train station, and that was when Mike had called him and warned him not to come home.

"Well hey, I guess Mike isn't such a bad guy," I said.

Nina said, "You've met him?"

"Uh, long story. I'll explain later."

The van's headlights arrowed down the street, bringing to life the toothy candidates on the local election posters affixed to the wall of the Armageddon Institute.

"You guys are the best," Ned said brokenly. "Friends in need! It's when the shit hits the fan that you find out who's really with you, who's against you."

"It ain't over till it's over," said Alastair with a smile.

"Wasn't talking to you, asshole," Ned said.

"Oh my God," I said suddenly. "We can't leave without telling Tad. He'll freak."

I dashed back into the house, kicked my sneakers off, and slithered through the dining-room. The door to the annexe was tucked in a triangular nook under the stairs. TV voices blathered within. I knocked.

I waited.

"OK, well, it's me, Shanti, I just wanted to say we're going out—"

Tad opened the door. Past his shoulder, I saw that Kuroiwa-san's TV was also tuned to NHK. So he must have got all the bad news at once. Tad said in Japanese, "Come on in, it's OK."

"Ned's here," I whispered in English. "We're taking him over to my place. I think everyone's going. Just to let you know." I backed away.

"*What?* Shanti, wait."

He turned back into the room, leaving the door open. I caught a fragment of what Kuroiwa-san had to say to him - *if your mother…* and bolted.

Tad caught up with me in the genkan as I was putting my sneakers on. We sprinted down the street to the van's taillights. Ned lay in the back while Nina and Chiharu arranged over him the floral velour blanket that had lived in the van since our tour. An old Doors CD churned out of the stereo. Ray Manzarek, one of the all-time great keyboardists. Joaquin turned left and right and left. I clambered over Ned and plonked my elbows on the back of Alastair's seat. "Know where you're going?" he was saying to Joaquin.

"Shanti's apartment, of course. You went over there with her on Friday, didn't you?" A stop light washed Joaquin's face glassy red. "We'll be there in twenty minutes if I take the expressway."

"No offense, but that's the dumbest idea I've heard all day. If he's found there, it'll implicate her. And that would implicate the rest of you."

"Well, if you have a better idea, please share it!"

The fish-tank interiors of the liquor mart and the Honda dealership ticked past. Joaquin drove beneath the colossal flyover of the Keikyu railroad and turned north on Keihin Expressway No.1, the artery that fed southern traffic into Shinagawa.

Alastair said, "We need somewhere to talk. Everyone's panicking. Not ideal conditions under which to, uh, make life-and-death decisions."

Tad crouched beside me, braced against the sway of the van. He said, "The wharves."

I'd been coming to Tad's house for more than a year before I found out that Omori was on the coast. The kanji for *Omori* read "Big Forest," but this had been a seaside village before it got swallowed up in Tokyo… long before. The one Omori landmark that all Japanese people seemed to know about was the museum that sheltered a midden of seashells from a prehistorical Jomon settlement. Since then, the coast had moved farther off as more and more land was reclaimed from Tokyo Bay. The second most widely known Omori landmark was now probably the racecourse, built on a landfill. Beyond that, factories and warehouses sprawled out to meet cargo wharves that had lost much of their business in the last couple of decades, maybe because they were so damn hard to find. Every time water glittered down below the guard rail of the road, it turned out not to be the sea, but just another canal.

The traffic had thinned to zero. We coasted down yet another empty street, under widely spaced streetlights, between warehouses set amidst low hedges. Along the sides of the road lay silent convoys of trucks. Joaquin said, "Long-haul drivers sleeping in their cabs. No good!"

"Keep going," Tad said.

We rounded a corner and the road ended in a barren expanse of concrete. The van's headlights picked out a few containers in the distance. Beyond them, long-legged loading tackles guarded the invisible edge of the wharf. Joaquin drove out across the concrete and parked behind one of the containers, a rusty brown metal box the size of a double-wide trailer. He turned the engine off. Suddenly, it was silent and dark. "Bien, we're here. Now what?"

Ned sat up and said, "Where are we?"

Like he'd been asleep.

I followed the others out of the van. Wind tossed my hair. The harbor smell of salt and rot pervaded every breath I took. We stood in a huddle. Ned said, "Are we here for any particular reason?"

"The scenic view," said Joaquin.

On the opposite shore of the bay, the neon of Odaiba twinkled, as seemingly close and as illusory as a TV commercial. I thought about all the dark acres of water between there and here. Somewhere out there, far beyond Tokyo Bay, this very sea was smashing into the cliffs where Ned and I used to play chicken with the waves.

"Look," Nina said, "you can see the Ferris wheel going round."

Ned said, "I never realized how important freedom is. Just the freedom to be here, to breathe the sea air, to…"

"Well, enjoy it while you can," said Alastair. "Because we're going to kill you and dump you in this handy container here. Next stop, Buenos Aires."

No one laughed except Tad.

"Alastair, that's so not funny!" Nina's voice whipsawed between registers.

"How about it, guys?" said Alastair. "Nina, you could just get back in the van and block your ears."

"Just fucking try it," Ned said. His fists were clenched and he was swaying on his feet. "Come on! One on one." He spat sideways. "Nah, I forgot, you're too pussy for that." He swiftly glanced around at the rest of us. Then he shambled towards Alastair. "You'll jump a man from behind, but let's see how fucking confident you are in a fair fight!"

Joaquin grabbed Ned's wrists and walked him away from Alastair. Although Ned was the bigger man, he let himself be carted backwards. Joaquin threw him against the side of the container. It boomed hollowly, and Nina did scream, but only under her breath. Joaquin pinned Ned's shoulders and got up in his face. "Who do you think you are, my friend? Jean-Claude fucking van Damme? You're in the land of samurais and ninjas here. But we're not samurais and ninjas, so we stick together. We have safety in numbers. Bon! You see the wisdom of this policy? So calm down! We're only trying to help you! Alastair," he added in French, still blazing his words into Ned's face, "I think you should apologize for your extremely sick sense of humor. Since our friend here seems to have lost his along the way."

"Oui, ç'est égal," Alastair said, shrugging. "I was only throwing out suggestions. Since no one else seems to have any. Sorry, Ned; I know you've had a rough night of it."

Sagging with relief, I covertly checked the reactions of the others. My gaze snagged on Chiharu's face. She didn't look disconcerted at all. She stood on the perimeter of the group, her black eyes bright and thoughtful. Maybe she just hadn't understood what was being said.

"Are you OK, Ned?" Nina pleaded.

"Never been better," Ned spat, feeling his chin. The Band-Aid had come loose at one end, and the cut underneath was bleeding.

Tad offered him the pack of paper tissues that he always seemed to have in his pocket. "Cut yourself shaving?"

"Police brutality." Ned dabbed, winced. "I didn't understand what was happening at first. Thought they were arresting me for - well." He looked at Joaquin. "You know. So they had to forcibly restrain me until an English-speaker showed up and explained the situation."

"They restrain us every way they can," Joaquin said, gazing out at the black sea and the distant shore. The wind ruffled his cowlicks into a brown crest. "They restrain us with their laws, with their customs, everything designed to protect the status quo. I don't think it is any coincidence that this shit blows up just as I am on the verge of becoming the first gaijin to break into the Japanese music industry!"

"Yeah, it's totally ironic," Nina said, and Ned smiled hopefully at her, scenting sympathy.

Heart thudding, I said, "Here's what I think. Yeah, it was on NHK, but the average viewer has the attention span of a cockroach on crack. And pretty soon they'll catch the real criminal. I mean, they always do." *God, please no.* But Alastair was looking at me in admiration, and that gave me courage, although he was going to hate what I had to say. "They'll forget all about Ned. It'll just take a little while—"

"They won't forget what you told them," Joaquin said.

"We can worry about that later! I'm just saying, Ned just has to wait this out, just until the average TV viewer forgets about him…"

"Yeah," Tad said, supporting me. "But if not at your apartment, where?"

"I've got a bit of money," said Ned meekly. "And I might be able to get my ID back, my passport and everything. Mike has it."

Chiharu blurted, "Please we let him go!" Without any warning she started crying. She wrapped her arms around her middle and doubled over. Every other sob was a scream.

She *had* understood what was going on, I thought. She'd understood more than anyone else. She'd understood that when Alastair suggested killing Ned, he wasn't being funny, he was dead serious.

Quicker than a thought, Joaquin went to her and lifted her upright, begging her to calm down.

"Let him go," Nina said. Her hands fluttered up to her face; she looked like Münch's *Scream.* "Let him go!"

"Yeah," Tad said, gabbling. "They're right, Ned. I really think it's best for everyone if you just, you know. Go. Before anything else happens. It's best thing. Because if we don't know where you are, we can't tell anyone. Of course, we won't tell anyone. And you won't tell anyone either. Right?"

"You're saying you can't… you won't help me?" Ned sounded stunned. He paused. Tad said nothing. "Well, I can't expect you to put yourselves in danger for me. Fair enough. I'll go."

He turned and started to walk away towards the sea, the emptiness.

Joaquin patted Chiharu on the back, straightened up, and called out in ringing tones, "Wait, Ned! Don't be a fool, we can give you a ride back into town. I have to drive Chiharu to Shinjuku, anyway, she's staying with a friend. We can let you out in Shin-Okubo, Ned. It's a good place to spend the night, heh? Little Korea. Lots of illegal immigrants and hookers."

Ned checked, wheeled. "Little Korea? Hey, I like kimchi. Actually, I like hookers, too." He sat down with his back to the nearest container.

"Don't mind me, I'm just going to have a rest."

Joaquin heaved him to his feet. "Do it in the van."

Another twenty-four hours passed, and another. Ned had walked away into Little Korea, and that was the last we'd seen of him. The police continued to search for him without success, judging by the TV news bulletins. The whole thing hit the newspapers, it even made Reuters, and Gorot was there in black and white, filling out the triad of sex, drugs, and rock 'n' roll that turned Gavin's murder into a human interest extravaganza. We got calls from reporters speaking several different languages. We got a call from Confucius saying his boss was concerned.

In the afternoon sunlight, Yoyogi Park teemed with bikers, skateboarders, amateur actors rehearsing, small children dodging their mothers, and a team of junior high school kids playing badminton on the lawn in front of the gazebo where Alastair and I sat with Mike Schultz. We'd had to walk half a mile from Harajuku for even this much privacy. It was one of those unseasonably warm days you sometimes get in March. The spring breeze blew the sunlight through the trees and into the gazebo, dusting bright sprinkles over the table between us. It lifted Mike's blond hair, revealing a thinning patch on top of his skull.

"So you met up with him in Shin-Okubo," Alastair repeated. "Did he tell you where he was staying?"

"In a love hotel by himself. That's what he said, anyway... Naw, I believe him. Poor guy's sweating bullets." Mike aimed a reproachful look at me, reminding me that as far as he knew, I was supposed to be Ned's friend.

"He's not the only one," I said. "My bandmates are worried that all this publicity is going to screw up our relationship with our backers." *Our backers.* I didn't even have the right to call Apex that until we'd formally signed our deal.

"Yeah, I'd be worried about bad publicity in your shoes, too," Mike said, with an edge to his tone.

"There's no such thing as bad publicity," Alastair said robustly.

"But we're worried about Ned," I said. "Didn't he give you any idea of what he was planning to do? Apart from keep his head down?"

Mike had called me to set up this meeting, using the cell phone number I'd scribbled on that promo postcard. I didn't believe he'd insisted on coming out here just to inform us that he'd met up with Ned. He kept glancing nervously at the badminton players, and when he finally spoke, he lowered his voice.

"He said he might be going back to Thailand."

"I knew it," Alastair said.

"You're fuckin' A. Best place for him. No one looks at you twice over there. But what I'm saying is, I had to front him the bucks for his plane ticket. That shit's not cheap, when you're paying cash at the last minute."

"So you want us to reimburse you," Alastair said, smiling.

Mike sat back, obviously relieved. "That's straight up, dawg. I knew you'd come through. Ned said you guys were his best friends. I'm his friend, too - and poor fucking Gav - but the cops took all Gav's shit." His pudgy brow clenched. "I'm like, whassup with that? You got a license to rob and steal, and then say it was a robbery?" He laughed, by himself. "Which I'm saying it had to be, they really fucked the place up, but they didn't find Gav's cash. He used to keep it in a Ziploc bag inside the top of the toilet."

I said, "Wait. How is Ned going to buy a plane ticket, let alone get out of the country? They're definitely going to have his name on a list, even if he's not recognized at the airport."

"But he might just be stupid enough not to think of that," Alastair said bleakly.

"Aha." Mike sat forward, his smile too wide. "But he did think of that. Which is why I would like to also ask you to refund me the cost of one American passport. I also threw in one attractive, stylishly laminated alien registration card, but we can call that a freebie."

I looked Mike up and down and laughed hopelessly. Sure, he and Ned were both blond and blue-eyed, but the resemblance stopped there. Mike was no longer quite young, overweight where Ned was lean, pale where Ned was tan, denim-blue eyes puffy from a lifetime of nights before.

"It's an older passport. The photo was taken before—" He slapped his stomach. "Before my latest personal health disaster. Dude, it's a total lie about Japanese food being healthy. Tempura, Yoshinoya—"

"You're about the same height, same coloring, and they never look at your passport, anyway. Holy shit, it just might work!" Alastair looked at his watch. "Hey, I bet he's safely on a plane by now!"

"I bet he is. Nothing stops that dude when he decides to get shit done." Mike made an admiring little *tch'* noise. "So how about we all share the financial burden? Believe me, I wish I could've done this out of the goodness of my heart. But you know how it is."

Alastair gazed at Mike, appraising him, until the other man started to pout. Then he smiled again. "I know how it is." He reached for his wallet; paused. "How much were we thinking of?"

I lit a cigarette as they haggled. Mike laid Ned's Danish passport on the picnic table between us, as if this was what we were buying. I flipped it open and stared at the same picture that had been flashing on TV screens all over the nation with gradually decreasing regularity for the last thirty-six hours. Issued five years ago. What had been running through Ned's mind as he sat in the booth with this blank and weary expression on? Had he been stoned, or just depressed? *(like images in a fucking temple)* What had he been thinking about? *(and I want to burst in there like Indy Jones and blow it all away)*

Alastair was an art dealer; Mike didn't have a chance. In the end he settled for five hundred dollars cash. We watched him stomp irritably away across the grass, buttocks swaying.

"Do you think Ned really might have got away with it?" I said.

"I think…" Alastair stretched his arms over his head. "God, that guy is a piece of shit. I'll tell you what I think after we have lunch. I'm ravenous. Do you want to grab sandwiches and bring them back here? Not much privacy to be had at Tad's house, with everyone running around like chickens with their heads cut off."

I nodded. As I stood up, I snaked my hand into my bag and felt paper corners and rubber bands. "And I actually have a surprise for you, too," I said. "I've been putting it off. But you're right, we may as well take advantage of the privacy."

I hadn't wanted to be by myself when I opened the Kodak envelope, and my premonitions had been justified.

Dapples of sunlight swayed across the photographs spread out on the table. The sun fell at a lower angle now; the badminton players had been replaced by a group of three gaijin guys playing Frisbee. My half-drunk bottle of green tea weighted down the wrappers from our sandwiches. Now that I'd seen the photographs, I was glad I'd eaten first.

"You know what's funny, though," I said. "Tad's already seen these. But I asked him last night, and he was just like, oh, they're nothing much, haven't you looked at them yet?"

"Maybe he didn't realize what they were."

"If he hadn't, he wouldn't have taken them."

"Maybe he wanted them as souvenirs."

"Oh Alastair, come on, he obviously thought they were evidence that had to be destroyed. Well, they *are.*"

"Evidence of an ambiguous kind with a broad variety of possible interpretations. I'd say he probably thought they were important at the time, but after Mr Ultimate Fucking Truth bit the dust, they suddenly didn't seem so important anymore." The wind lifted the top photograph and skimmed it across the table. Alastair slammed his hand down on it as if he was squashing a bug. He replaced all the photographs in the envelope. "Still, they're important enough to destroy."

"Can I hang onto them for a bit? I promise I'll burn them."

"Why?"

I made a pleading face. Alastair seemed about to tease me, but instead he handed the envelope over. "Just make sure they're not there to be found if and when the police come back."

Anxiety trickled through me. He was deliberately trying to frighten me, because he thought I should be frightened. But how many things could I be frightened of at once? I burst out, "I know I was the one who said to let Ned go, but what's going to happen if they catch him? Even if he makes it to Thailand, they could still catch him there. They've got agreements. There's Interpol. This is turning into a big embarrassment for Japan; did you see the interview with Gavin's mum in the paper this morning…"

I trailed off, because Alastair wasn't reacting. A pigeon hopped across the floor of the gazebo. He stared at it and whistled a trill that set off a descending run of minor notes in my head. Reaching into the sandwich wrappers, he tossed a crust of bread down beside the table. We both watched the pigeon peck at it.

"Fuck, fuck, fuck," Alastair muttered under his breath.

"What?" I said. "What?"

He stamped suddenly on the floor of the gazebo next to the pigeon. It flew away. He straightened up. "Shanti, I'm going to Thailand."

"You're *what?*"

"I'll give Neddo another twenty-four hours. If he hasn't got himself caught by then, we've got to assume he made it. But if I wait any longer than that, he'll have a head start."

And if you wait any longer than that, you won't make it back to Shanghai before the end of the antiquities fair, I thought. Oh hell. I understood. He'd lost Maisie, so he had to hang onto his job at all costs. But his job alone wouldn't be enough to bring him back safely. I said, "All right. But I'm coming with you."

"No, you're not. Look how well that went last time. Besides, you need to stay here and look after Tad." He smiled.

"And let you risk your life for both of us?"

"Just like you did when you didn't call me until he almost killed you, huh?"

"Alastair, I know it sounds stupid now, but I thought I could deal with him—"

"And that's exactly what he was counting on! Why do you think he came after you in the first place? Regardless of who is or isn't on the internet, he could have found me if he really wanted to. He could have called all the Hazards in the Philly phone book - there aren't that many of them - and found Uncle Red. It would have been a little more challenging, but not beyond his intellectual capacity, limited as that may be. I was pretty sure that if he ever… that he'd come after me. But he came after *you*."

"I was closer. Geographically."

"Or he saw you as a softer target." Alastair smiled. "Here's how it is. He tried to hurt you. So I'm going to hunt him down. I'll rip his guts out and make him eat them. Then I'll cut his balls off and leave him to bleed out. And they'll never find his body." A wider smile. "This is Thailand we're talking about. Much easier than staging his disappearance in the middle of Tokyo. Neddo is going to vanish like a vehicle left on Phang Nga Road with the key in the ignition. Do you still want to come?"

"I think maybe not," I said, because it was what he wanted me to say. I couldn't tell how serious he was. Then I burst out, "Alastair, what happened to Maisie? I mean, with Maisie."

"Oh Christ. She's got a temper, you know, or rather you wouldn't know." He grimaced. "Poor bloody dogs, their world's fallen apart. She's threatening to take me to court to keep both of them. I guess when I get home I'm going to be staying with Oswald for a while—"

He grunted and jumped away from me. The Frisbee had skidded into the gazebo, sending the pigeons up into the roof.

"Yo hey! Sorry 'bout that!" shouted one of the Frisbee players, jogging towards the gazebo. A stocky blond, he had his shirt tied around his waist in anticipation of summer.

Alastair picked up the Frisbee and threw. It hurtled in a wide curve around the blond and fell like a red flower into the hands of another guy. They whooped. "Nice throw! Y'all wanna have a game?"

Alastair said, "My glory days are behind me. But I think I'm going to play for a bit."

He loped across the grass to them.

After a few minutes I went to join in.

Joaquin strode around the kitchen, talking about the synergy between Cold Coeur Productions and Cold Coeur Records, the importance of creative control, and our debt to our fans. Tad and Shingo sat drinking beer and heckling him to get to the point. He'd come back from his meeting with Apex looking grim, and his voice had cracked with insincere jollity as he called the others to announce this impromptu band meeting, so I had a pretty good idea what he was eventually going to get around to telling us, and I wasn't really listening. I was thinking about Alastair, who'd gone straight from our Frisbee game to reserve his ticket to Thailand.

Nina whispered to me, "He went to look at apartments today."

"Who? Where?"

"Near here, so he can keep on using Tad's studio. Shanti, you're not mad, are you?"

My confusion coalesced into alarm. "Has Tad's father said something to you?"

"It's not really that he's *said* anything," Nina said, and then Gen arrived, late as usual.

"Hey, Chiharu," he said, as if the rest of us weren't here. I'd almost got used to Chiharu's presence myself. But obviously, Gen was never going to forgive her.

"Hey, Gen," she muttered, cringing. She was like the cord of an overhead light swaying in an earthquake, shaken by every emotional nuance.

"So, you're moving in with him, are you? I wish you well." Gen plopped himself down and cracked the can of Sapporo that Tad pushed over to him. From the way he indifferently tipped it up to his mouth, I saw that he was already drunk. "Honestly. I really hope everything goes well for you."

Looking for apartments. It all fell together in my mind. "Oh my God," I said in French. "Joaquin, is *this* what you got us all here for? You're unbelievable!"

"You know, Shanti, sometimes fate pushes us in surprising directions." Joaquin dropped back into English, smiling around at everyone. "I am a songwriter and a performer, but I think I am primarily a producer. In this day and age, production is artistic creation. The producer's role is the most influential of all. It makes me very happy to take the raw material and transform it into an artistic product. And that's why I have decided to direct a greater effort towards Cold Coeur Productions. I'm going to rent an office – today I looked at some places near Omori station, one of them even has a studio attached. It will improve my professional image if I don't have to do sessions in someone's spare bedroom. Tad agrees, don't you, Tad?"

So Tad had known about this development for at least a few hours already.

"Would this place," I said, "would it have living quarters attached, too?"

"Oh, fuck it!" Joaquin gave a huge shrug. He said in French, "You know as well as I do that Tad's father doesn't want us here any longer!"

"That's an excuse," I snapped. If I hadn't known what was going on, one glance at Chiharu would have told me. "You're blaming it on Tad's father because you're ashamed, aren't you? And so you should be."

Joaquin reddened. "Don't you know that there's such a thing as civilized adult behavior? It's easiest this way for all of us!"

"Don't you mean it's easiest this way for *you?*"

Gen laughed harshly. He understood a decent amount of French, especially when he was drunk.

"Shanti, don't be mad," cried Nina, understanding only our tones.

I cried, "I don't understand why *you're* not mad!"

"No one is mad! We merely express ourselves in the European fashion!" Joaquin shouted with a broad grin that betrayed how mad he was.

"You could call it that," said Gen. "But she was asking him why he was moving out of your place." He spoke in Japanese, ostensibly to Tad. "And he said it was something to do with your father."

"My dad's cool," Tad protested in English. "He hasn't said anything."

"Oh, I know," Nina broke in, "but it's the way he's been *looking* at us! Or actually, the way he *hasn't* been looking at us. You must have noticed. I understand how he feels, I mean I know it must be humiliating for him, but it really… it's just kind of like, oh *God,* you know? On top of everything else."

"But it's not your f-fault," said Tad. "Everyone knows it's n-not your fault."

"Well, exactly! That's why it hurts! I mean, I wasn't the one who hired him, was I? I was the one who said we had enough drivers in the first place!"

"We would have had enough drivers if you'd passed your test," hissed Joaquin.

"I screwed up, OK? That's established! But you would have hired him even if I'd passed the damn test! You hired him before I even *took* it!"

"As backup. If you'd passed, I would have told him: thank you but we do not require your services!"

"Oh, crap. Crap, Joaquin! You wanted him to come because he flattered your ego. And you were feeling insecure about the tour, and you wanted a yes man."

"I don't believe I am hearing this. It was you that he flattered outrageously. And you responded to him. You encouraged him!"

"That was all in your imagination! Jealousy comes in handy sometimes, doesn't it? I never did anything I shouldn't have. But you convinced yourself - you wanted me to be slutting around with him! Because you wanted an excuse to sleep with her."

A small noise drew my eyes to Chiharu. She stood in the corner of the kitchen with her hands over her face.

Joaquin licked his lips. "You're oversimplifying. There are many considerations. The future of Cold Coeur is a responsibility that I take very seriously. I have many people depending on me. I have to do what's best for all of them."

"If you really love her," Gen said, "just go ahead and say it. It's the lying I can't stand."

Chiharu squeaked, "I'll say it. This is so horrible. I'm so sorry we've caused everyone so much trouble. I'd get down on my knees and apologize if I thought it would do any good. I guess it won't do any good, either, to say that I never planned for any of this to happen. But it has happened. And now I can't help it. *I can't help it.* I love him. And he loves me. When the real thing comes along, you can't deny it, can you?" She appealed to me, of all people. I didn't know what to say. "It took both of us by surprise," she wailed.

Joaquin slid his arms around her and pressed a kiss on her forehead, staring balefully over her feathery black head at the rest of us.

"This is so fucking wrong," Shingo said. He unfolded his long legs and stood, touching Tad's upper arm. "Later, man. I'm out of here."

"Hey, you can't go yet," Tad said with uneasy geniality. "We still haven't heard about Joaquin's meeting with Apex this afternoon."

"Haven't we? I bet *you* have. And I can guess. They've canceled the deal. Don't blame them, either. They may be daring and innovative, but who'd want to associate their good name with a murder case? Not me. I've been getting shit at work about it, too." Shingo waited for someone to contradict him or sympathize with him or something. When we all just gaped at him, he nodded heavily and shrugged his canvas jacket on. "Who needs a bunch of fucking gaijins, anyway," he muttered, and I couldn't tell if he was parodying Apex's attitude or speaking for himself.

"Oh, you," Joaquin said. "Miya-chan, it's a temporary setback, that's all!"

I'd guessed as much, but hearing it out loud, the truth washed over me like cold salt water. Confucius - an abandoner. All our anxiety and frantic work, all that backing and forthing between Asakawa-san and Apex and Joaquin - for nothing. The triumphs of Cold Coeur Family Vol. 1 - an illusion. The Cold Coeur Family itself - the biggest illusion of all. "In America, it's different. There's no such thing as bad publicity. The majors would be breaking down the door to get a piece of us," I said bitterly, thinking: Alastair had *promised.* Yeah, but even he was wrong sometimes, wasn't he?

"Well, Shanti, this isn't America." Shingo turned to Tad. "And before you say anything, yes, it's because they're gaijins. I know it's not right, but we have to accept that that's how it is."

"No, we don't," Tad said loudly. "We don't have to accept it."

"That's right," Joaquin said. "We can make our own rules, just as we have been doing for the last three years! Miya-chan, let me tell you - you were right all along: Apex is not the ideal partner for us. Part of the deal obligated us to use their recording facilities in future, and we would have lost the very thing that makes us different: our sound! Those fossils! They think their equipment is the state of the art, but it's obsolete! The world has left them behind. They just don't know it yet. In North America, most recording and mixing is already done on computers. This is my field of expertise, and my studio in Omori will be digital only. You could spend millions of yen on DAT and MIDI equipment and you would not have any more functionality than I have with Pro Tools! I stand by every track that I have recorded in the last four years! This is the music that's being requested on every call-in radio program, this is the music that's climbing the indies charts. OK, so I don't have the power to crack the chain stores or the ringtone market yet, but when Cold Coeur Records is the hottest indie label in Tokyo, the story will be different! Then they will laugh on the other side of their faces!"

Shingo looked down at Joaquin with his head slightly cocked. He said, "Kuroiwa, did you tell him Naoya's news? No? Oh yeah, Joaquin, Kinderbox has scored an opening slot at Punk March. I'm surprised they didn't mention it to you. They've asked me to play with them on the day. Of course, I'm sure it won't lead anywhere: they're unsignable unless Naoya can screw himself up to dump the junkie."

Punk March was only one of the biggest music festivals in Japan, due to annihilate Makuhari Messe three weeks hence. As Joaquin struggled to take this news in stride, I saw Nina standing by herself near the sink. I edged over to her "Are you OK?" What a goddamn stupid thing to say.

"Of course I'm OK." She looked down and drew a peace symbol with her finger in a spill of coffee grounds on the counter. I added two more lines to turn it into an anarchy symbol. She smiled ruefully at me. "That's what I was trying to say all along. I'm not going to be here, so why should I care what - I mean, of course I care about Joaquin. And of course I care about Gorot." Her eyes glowed dangerously. "But I've invested enough of my life in this band. It's time for me to start living for myself, instead of through you guys."

"Wh-wh-where are you going?" I couldn't imagine. Back to her parents in Connecticut? To throw herself on the mercy of some sketchy acquaintances in Europe?

"Don't you know?" Seeing that I didn't, Nina glanced past me. She was hoping, I thought, for a larger audience, but Joaquin and Shingo had stolen her thunder. "I'm going to Thailand. With..." She winced in embarrassment. "Oh my God, I can't believe he didn't tell you. With your brother."

It appeared that Alastair had called Nina to invite her along on the second leg of his "vacation" at four o'clock this afternoon. That was about an hour after we'd parted at Yoyogi Park.

He'd got a tour package of two tickets for the price of one, flying out of Narita tomorrow.

The evening passed in false colors, everyone pretending. The collapse of our deal shouldn't have been such a huge tragedy, since it left us exactly where we were before - but that wasn't all that had collapsed, I thought. Whatever it was that had held us together, the thing we called our synergy, had separated into its constituent parts. It felt as if the music had stopped and left us all sitting in the wrong chairs, and none of us knew how to start it up again.

The next day, I planned to see Alastair and Nina off at Narita, but Alastair deterred me. "It's not as if we're saying goodbye, after all." We hugged on the platform at Nippori station. "Don't forget to destroy those photos," he whispered.

Tad and I returned to Omori in silence. Neither of us had anything else to do. We were both out of a job. The house was unnaturally quiet.

"Nina doesn't have a clue, does she? She thinks they're going to ride elephants and take moonlight walks on the beach," Tad said.

"They probably will," I said. "Alastair is great at compartmentalizing." This was the best, in fact the only way I could explain why he'd taken Nina with him. "It's like when he's with someone who doesn't know his quote unquote, dark secrets, he doesn't have to deal with them, either. And I know it sounds twisted, but I think that's how he stays sane."

"Someone like his ex-girlfriend?"

I sighed. "Yeah. You've seen that picture I have of him and Maisie? Nina even looks like her. Well, not her individual features, but they're the same physical type. And a little bit similar in... well, I think it's the idea of normality he's attracted to."

"But he's taking her into a dangerous situation. Joaquin would have something to say about that, even if they are splitting up."

"They *have* split up. Tad, don't tell him. It wouldn't do any good."

For a moment, Tad looked exactly like his father. "I think Joaquin has a right to know that your brother may be planning to use Nina as his alibi."

I gabbled, "OK, I admit that that's not impossible. But that's exactly why she won't be in danger. He'll keep her out of it."

"Just like he kept you out of it."

"He tried to keep me out of it. Tad, can we not fight? OK?"

"If it was me," Tad said. "If it was me…" He shook his head.

We were sitting in the kitchen, munching the bentos we'd grabbed on our way home. Our chewing sounded loud in the empty house. I was so tired I could barely taste the difference between potato salad and inarizushi.

Tad got up to turn on the TV.

I said, "No. OK, I know we should be following the news, but I want to talk to you."

"Oh yeah?"

"Sometimes it's really hard for me to tell what you're thinking," I said.

"I'm thinking about my dad. He didn't mean that Joaquin and Nina should leave. He's really upset that they took it that way."

"You're lucky," I said. "You've got a great dad." I pushed away the remains of my bento, dragged the Kodak envelope out of my bag, and spread its contents on the table. I turned one of the photos so it was facing Tad. "What does this look like to you?"

Tad barely glanced at it. Crunching into a piece of tempura, he said, "The guy is dead."

"C-c-can you tell that easily?"

"Sure. It jumps right out at you."

I lined up a couple of other photos. "Anything else?"

"The dead guy is the same guy who's in this one. Helping you make a clay giraffe. You were a cute kid."

"My mother gave Ned this camera for his eleventh birthday," I said. Even back then, Ned had been a good photographer. And we'd never suspected that he had his camera with him that afternoon, up in Alastair's room. His camera, with half a roll of film left on it.

I gathered the photographs up. Twilight filled the kitchen like cool blue water, but I was sweating. "I guess Alastair was right: these *are* important enough to destroy—"

Tad grabbed my wrist. "First, you talk."

"You've already guessed."

"I'm still waiting for you to tell me why." He let go and went to the fridge for a refill of orange juice.

"He was only a dumb gaijin," I whispered.

"Who?" Tad came back to the table and shuffled through the photographs until he found one of those which Ned must have taken from the window of Alastair's room as we struggled towards the Land Rover. It showed two foreshortened figures lugging a third by armpits and ankles. Maybe the print had lain in sunlight at some point, because its bottom half was discolored with a reddish haze. A mephitic odor seemed to rise from it, and I knew it was only my imagination, but it seemed to me that this was actually a picture of Hell, where all the paths of memory come to a dead end. "Who was he?"

"Ned's father," I sighed.

Tad set down his glass without looking where he was putting it. Orange juice slopped onto the photographs. "Shit. What was it, some kind of ancestral blood feud?"

I laughed politely. Something else had occurred to me. I said, "Gavin saw these, didn't he? When he took them from you."

"What? Yeah, but he didn't look at them very closely."

"But you said you wouldn't *need* to—"

"Well, he thought there was something funny about them. I could see that."

I replayed those minutes? seconds? in my mind. How long had it taken me to empty Ned's backpack? How long had Gavin been in the bathroom? While Alastair stooped over Tad's chair, cutting him loose?

Tad said, "They seemed important at the time. But now..."

Oh God, sometimes I felt like I was perceiving reality on a grotesque factor of magnification, so I could no longer see its constituent atoms, only the gaps, the vast grey domains of uncertainty.

Tad folded his arms across his chest. "I want to know *why.*"

I thought about playing Frisbee with strangers in the sunset, our voices curling up into the sky like birds. I thought about Alastair and Nina boarding the Keisei Skyliner without looking back. I started to talk.

I turned thirteen three days ago. My birthday is the first of August, right in the middle of the summer holidays. I'm in love with a boy. His name is Conrad and he's the son of my mother's friend Fiona. He used to have a brother and sister of his own to hang out with, but their father has taken them to England. "For the summer holidays," is what Conrad says, but June says that Rhys and Fiona have split up. Anyway, now it's just Conrad and his mum, and he hangs out with us on the days we go into Bantry.

Last week, a travelling funfair set up in the field next to the old Protestant primary school. We went on the dodgems and the magic teacups with the money that Nigel gave us to keep away from O'Leary's until closing time. Lots of kids from school were there, too. Alastair talked to a couple of the other rising fourth years - they're all dying to find out how they did on the Intercert. But none of the girls in my year said hi to me. They just eyed us in that supercilious way that the Irish have, and for once I didn't care, because now it wasn't just me and my brother and Neddo. It was me (and them) and Conrad. The music thumped, the rides clattered, the smell of candy floss mixed with the smell of petrol from the generators, and I threw up on the Viking Longship.

After spending all our money, we wandered down the road, around the harbor. High tide lifted the seaweed skirt of the pier. The funfair's lights twinkled across the black water. It was like Odaiba last night, but Bantry Bay... well, you could fit it into the mouth of the Sumida River. Ireland is a *small* country. And the funfair's music drifted across the bay: Duran Duran, Martika, Tiffany, Wham! Go right ahead and laugh, and then tell me how Boøwy and Unicorn sound to you today. When you're thirteen and in love, every song is the best song in the world.

We sat on St. Brendan's plinth. Alastair and Ned started quarrelling about something. The breeze off the sea blew Conrad's long black ponytail around his face. He was watching Alastair with the same awe that Ned sometimes did. I sank my fingernails into the soft part of his thigh. He sprang up. "Oi, eejit!" I jumped onto the harbor wall and ran along it with my arms outspread like a tightrope walker. He came after me, and we all ended up chasing each other around with slimy limbs of kelp that we ripped off the side of the pier.

Why am I telling you this? I guess I want you to know it wasn't all bad. We had our normal days. The day when I made that clay giraffe, that was a normal day, too.

The other thing you should know is that Ned's father used to beat up on us. He would have killed Ned sooner or later, if not for Alastair.

He would have killed *me.*

We had a truce in place, and we were trying to enjoy our summer holidays. But all summer long, I felt like I was running along that harbor wall, trying to keep my balance, always on the verge of losing it. Alastair had withdrawn, cutting me off in an attempt to preserve himself as a person. He'd found a way to do that through his drawings. I didn't have anything like that. I could only look forward to meeting Conrad in Bantry. The rest of the time, I had no one to hang out with except Ned, and that was like hanging out with my own shadow. I used to go for long walks and think about dying.

What? You, too?

Well, I never thought about playing the guitar, and I couldn't draw, so I wrote poetry.

There was a man lived in the moon, lived in the moon, lived in the moon

There was a man lived in the moon
And his name was Aiken Drum
And he played upon the ladle, the ladle, the ladle
He played upon the ladle
And his name was Aiken Drum

I was prolific. I filled notebooks with rhyming verses populated by the people around me in clever disguises. But all of them have been lost, and now, whenever I try to recollect my own poems, my head just fills up with Aiken Drum.

Like most songs, this one ends tragically. Aiken Drum plays upon a bunch of different household objects, and then he starts eating things: roast beef and cream cheese. And the last verse goes:

And he ate up all the haggis bags, the haggis bags, the haggis bags
And he choked upon the haggis bags
And that ended Aiken Drum!

But that's not what I hear inside my head. I don't hear the words, I just hear the rhythm. *Tap tap tap-tap.*

Ned must have had his camera in the kangaroo pocket of his sweatshirt when he came down to Fuschia Cottage that day, and I can even guess why. He wanted to take a picture of the intergalactic cruiser he was building with my Space Lego, which Uncle Red had sent me for my birthday, apparently forgetting I was thirteen and not eight.

Unfortunately, the only place to play with the Space Lego was Alastair's room. They were already fighting - I could hear them through the ceiling - when Nigel walked into the cottage. "Where's your mother?"

It was sunny outside. I told him that June had gone over to Ballydehob to deliver some paintings to The Celtic Knot. I knew she and Nigel were supposed to have gone together in the Land Rover, but they'd had a fight the night before, and I figured Nigel could put two and two together for himself.

"Are you sure now?"

"She said she was probably going to stop by Peter's for some tomatoes, too. I don't think she'll be back until evening." Over the summer, I'd developed a tremulous, compulsive, knuckleheaded defiance that took the form of what Nigel called cheekiness. It wasn't courage. I believed that Nigel had mended his ways under threat of losing June's love, and so to a certain extent, it was safe to taunt him.

"Peter! Can't bloody endure the man. The next time you see him, ask him why." The noise of hostilities upstairs saved me from having to respond to this. Nigel shouted, "Do you little sods want sorting out?" Without waiting for an answer, he started up the stairs.

I skittered back to the kitchen table, knotted myself into my chair, and drew stars and planets in the margins of my poetry notebook. I was doing Saturn's rings when Alastair came flying downstairs, clamping an armful of sketchpad and pens and pencils. He dropped into the chair across from me and resumed drawing with ferocious intensity, not saying a word. Neither of us flinched at the sound of the blow, a single dull slap muffled by sweatshirt or jeans. Nigel hitting Ned was like Irish rain – not even June could stop it, although sometimes it seemed as if she could persuade it to lighten up with the sheer brilliance of her smile. This time, I knew that Alastair had saved Ned from a real beating by sacrificing his right to draw in his own room.

A few moments later, Nigel stomped back downstairs and sprawled into one of the chairs by the cold, empty hearth.

Can you see us now? Alastair has his back to the window, drawing as if his life depends on it. I rock in my chair and try to go on with my poem, but my spine tingles with anxiety and I rub out as much as I write. From the utter silence behind me, I know Nigel is immobile, staring into space, his face as blank as unfired clay.

Alastair calls these moments "Nigel's autistic breaks." I'm not sure what *autistic* means. All I know is that he's been having them more often, and they creep me out. It's as if he's switching himself off to save the battery. Recently, he's even started to do it in front of June, but always late at night, when he's got the excuse of being tired or stoned. His logical cunning still works for him... but when it's only us, he doesn't bother anymore. He's given up his attempts to intimidate us and make us think he's funny and great. He no longer cares what we think.

What I think is what I imagine. And as I stare blindly at the lines of my poem, I imagine that I'll run away with Conrad. *I love you*

tap

I love you

tap

I love you

The somnolent hum of heat from the open windows has the texture of a bass line. It's actually the sound of the sea, but it's not cold like the sea, it's hot like the sunlight soaking into the garden. The swoopy scratch of Alastair's pencil delineates the fruit bowl between me and him on the table, which holds two bananas that smell overripe, a broken calculator, a nutcracker, and a small colony of ants. I flick one of them off my notebook.

Tap tap *tap!*

That's the sound of the legs of my chair on the stone floor.

Tap tap *crrrreak!*

My pencil stills. I stiffen. Alastair doesn't move, but his eyes dart past me.

Nigel grabs the back of my chair and pulls it out from the table, nearly jolting me off it. "I've told you I can't abide that bloody noise." He rocks the chair to emphasize every syllable. "Is it more," bang, "than you can do," bang, "to bloody well sit," bang, "still?"

It's been months since we played Aiken Drum. But the thing about Aiken Drum is that it comes so naturally, you can do it without even thinking about it. You can do it unconsciously. "I wasn't doing anything," I howl. "I didn't do it on purpose!"

"Wasting your summer holidays. Mouldering inside." My notebook jumps into his hand like a lame white bird. "I'll look after this. Go outside and play."

"No, let me have it! I promise I'll put it away!"

He'll read my poetry. And he won't be fooled. I've disguised him as a cruel king, an evil sorceror, a bawling generalissimo. But now I understand that I haven't been careful enough. I haven't been very clever at all. He'll see how cheeky I've been, and then he'll - he'll –

Alastair knows what my poetry is mostly about, and his calm amazes me. "Better give that back, that's her creative writing. Her English teacher at school said he'd enter her for a competition, it was that good."

"Like fuck," says Nigel. But he's slightly daunted, and he makes a show of scanning the poem I'm working on. *"Tree, be; might, fight; threat... rigret? Invocation, impercation?* Methinks the poet could use a dictionary."

I hop off my chair and make a grab for the notebook. Nigel jerks it away and lifts it high, out of my reach. He smiles down at me: *this is all in fun* says his mouth, and *suck it up, kid* say his eyes. I'm expected to jump for my notebook like a dog jumping for a biscuit. My pride stings, my eyes water, but I have no choice. I spring into the air, and manage to tear half a page out. Nigel jerks the mutilated notebook higher. Alastair rises and sidles around him, giving him a wide berth. That distracts Nigel for just long enough. I jump onto my chair and make a panther leap, grabbing my notebook a split second before I slam into Nigel's chest. I'm not heavy enough to knock him down. But he grunts and staggers.

I fling my notebook over his head. I see Alastair picking it up and flinging it away again, into the empty fireplace, just before Nigel sweeps me off the floor and clamps me against his side as if I was four years old. "Cheeky little cow. You never fucking learn, do you?"

"Let me go! June will kill you!" I scream, kicking the air.

"We'll see who kills who," says Nigel, and flips me upside down. He's holding me by my ankles as if we were going to play Wheelbarrow, but only my fingertips and the ends of my hair brush the floor. Blood rushes to my head. I thought I knew what was coming, but I was wrong. How wrong, I don't realize until the floor hurtles up at me. I just manage to fend myself off with my hands. Nigel lifts me up and then drops me again. This time my forehead makes contact with the stone flags. I'm screaming as fast as I can draw breath. Nigel is playing Aiken Drum. He's playing Aiken Drum with my head.

"Let her go, you fucker," Alastair is shouting, but Nigel doesn't. I can hear him laughing, the low, unamused laughter that is normally a signal to take cover. But it's too late now. Again he hoists me up and lets me fall, keeping his grip on my ankles, letting gravity do his work for him. The strength has gone out of my arms. I'm falling into a galaxy of grey stars and moons. Saturn's rings wheel around me.

I crumple to the floor and roll away under the kitchen table. When I scramble out the other side and claw my hair out of my face, I see Alastair clinging to Nigel's back as Nigel blunders this way and that, cannoning into the furniture, trying to shake him off. Alastair's arm rises and falls. A rhythm emerges from the commotion. Nigel doubles up in jerky slow motion. The next time Alastair draws his arm back, I see what he has in his hand. It's one of June's frame weights, aka a large heavy stone.

I dart over to her worktable and grab a stone of my own, the one with St. George and the dragon. I dance around Alastair and Nigel, landing my own blows. Thunk! Square on the skull! Hit him, *hit him!*

"Ned," says Alastair between his teeth, riding Nigel to the floor. "Don't let him see."

Ned! I race for the stairs. Alastair's bedroom door is closed. I fling it open. Ned is sitting on the carpet in front of his half-constructed intergalactic cruiser. "You stay here," I tell him. "Don't come out until we say. Promise? You've got to promise!" Through the floor I can still hear: *thunk! thunk!*

"Don't," begs Ned, his voice high and thin. "Don't hurt me, Shanti, please!"

He's staring at the stone in my hand. I glance down at it. It was originally black and white, but now its sharp end is stained red. There are a few hairs clinging to it. As I stare at it, I feel something crawling down my face, and a drop of blood splashes on the floor.

I back out of the room and drag the door shut. Spotting that crummy little bolt, I fumble it home.

When I get back downstairs, Nigel is lying on the floor, sprawled on his face with his arms flung out. Alastair is kicking him in the ribs. I kick him, too, but it soon stops being fun. He's no longer reacting. His eyes are open, but he doesn't try to move. He's having the autistic break of all time.

And here we are lugging him out to the Land Rover.

It looks like we're carrying him, but he was too heavy. We're dragging him. His backside is scraping along the ground. You can't tell from this angle. From Ned's angle.

This is me pushing him into the passenger seat. Even after we put the seatbelt on him, he kept flopping sideways.

This is Alastair backing the Land Rover around the side of the cottage. I'm opening the gate. That was always my job. The gate sagged at the end, so you had to get your shoulder under the top bar and lift it. You can see the blood all over my face. It was pouring out like a tap. Alastair had assured me that I wasn't going to bleed to death, but I think I probably had a mild concussion, and I certainly should have had stitches—

Yeah. No, that's OK. I didn't expect you to believe me.

Alastair drives out of Ned's viewfinder, into the lane. I drag the gate shut again, run around the Land Rover, and hop into the back seat. This is our procedure whenever we go anywhere. But this time we're not going very far. Alastair has a plan. He filled me in on the details as we lugged Nigel out of the house. It's such a great idea that I don't think he can have come up with it on the spur of the moment; but he swears, then and afterwards, that that's exactly what he did. He engages the clutch and we coast downhill in first gear.

The Land Rover has been sitting in the sun all afternoon, so its interior is warm. A fly buzzes against the windscreen. I lock my hands over Nigel's collarbone. Blood trickles down his neck, staining the headrest and my sleeves. My arms tremble with the effort of holding him upright. I wonder if he'll wake up and bite me. His skin is warm, but it doesn't feel like skin, more like kneaded clay. The stuff that God made Adam out of. I learned that in religion class. I feel sick.

"Tourists," says Alastair, banging the steering wheel. "What if there are tourists?"

There sometimes are, on sunny days. They drive out from Bantry, turn down our lane without knowing it's a dead end, and get out of their cars on the pier to stretch their legs. They usually end up buying something at Allihies Ceramics.

"I'll go see," I say, and jump out of the Land Rover, stumbling as I hit the ground. I run down the lane. All clear. Even the sea is empty of yachts and fishing boats. I dash back uphill, meet the Land Rover, and beckon it on with big gestures like a mechanic at a petrol station. Alastair is having a tricky time of it, fending off Nigel's slumping body with one hand while he steers with the other, but I pretend not to see that. I jog along in front of the Land Rover, and at the bottom of the hill, Alastair puts the handbrake on and jumps out.

The pier stretches ahead, a wide grassy ledge carved out of the cliff. Waves lap against its weathered stone sides. The tide is in. We drag Nigel out of the Land Rover and around the Land Rover and wedge him in again behind the steering wheel, and this is where Alastair's plan goes wrong. He's brought along a stick of driftwood, one of the bits that accumulate around the front door of the cottage because they're pretty. He tries to use it to jam Nigel's foot down on the accelerator. But Nigel's legs are all heavy and floppy, like the rest of him, and they won't stay put. The engine is still in neutral, and it roars every time we push the pedal down. Alastair starts cursing in frustration.

"My head is killing me. I feel sick to my stomach." I start to cry. "I think I'm going to *die!*"

Alastair is still in control. "You're not going to die," he says. "You couldn't blub like that if you were dying." *Blub,* a Nigel word; we've killed him, but we'll never get him out of our minds, I confusedly realize at that very moment, and I cry harder. Alastair pulls me into a hug, the kind I haven't had from him in ages. He hesitates to nuzzle my face because of the blood on it, which is stupid because Nigel's blood is already smeared on his T-shirt and his bare arms, and maybe the same thing occurs to him, because he gives me a kiss on the nose, and then he stands me up straight. "I'll put a bandage on it later," he says, now looking like a vampire, with blood on his chin. "Now stop it, OK? I need you to help."

"But what are you going to do?"

"I've got another idea. But you have to be ready to jump." He explains to me, and then he bangs the driver's side door shut, crunching Nigel's head against the headrest. We open all the other windows. Alastair settles face down across the passenger seat, pushes his head into Nigel's lap, and reaches down to depress the clutch with one hand. I hop into the back seat and hold Nigel up against his seat. "Ready," Alastair gasps. I lean forward between the seats and yank the handbrake off. Then I shove the gearstick up and across, under Alastair's body, into fifth gear.

Alastair takes his hand off the clutch and presses the accelerator down to the floor. The Land Rover shoots forward. With his other hand he grabs the bottom of the steering wheel, not trying to steer, just holding us straight.

His feet are sticking out of the open passenger door as we rocket along the pier. My door is flapping open, too. Alastair twists his head between Nigel's knees and shouts over the engine, "Jump! What are you waiting for? Jump!"

But I've fallen into a trance. I'm staring at the grass blurring past at thirty miles an hour. Alastair's shout triggers a response, but not the right one. I reach out and drag the door shut.

The Land Rover goes off the end of the pier.

The water meets us with a crash like an explosion. My head cracks against the ceiling. The sea floods the interior, gulping me up.

Alastair swims out of his open door - I'll learn afterwards - and hangs onto the frame of the sinking vehicle, feeling for the handle of the back door. The wheels judder on the bottom. This is deeper than any of us have ever dived. But Alastair holds on. Somehow, he gets the back door open, grabs me by the ankle, and kicks for the surface.

When I open my eyes I'm floating on the broad cold back of the sea, coughing.

Below us, the Land Rover is settling onto the sea floor.

We swim back to the pier, haul ourselves out of the water, and stagger home. Halfway up the hill, Alastair has to stop and throw up. The gravel in front of the cottage still bears the Land Rover's tyre tracks. Superstitiously, we circle around them. That's this picture. I guess it was the last in the roll. Don't we look terrible? At least our swim washed the blood off.

Alastair crunches ahead of me, around the side of the cottage, and stops dead. He scrubs his foot over the doorstep, working it back and forth like he's trying to get dog poo off his shoe. It leaves a dark wet smear. Blood! The doorstep is smeared with it. It must have dripped from Nigel's body, and maybe from my head, which has finally stopped bleeding, although the salt water stings horribly on my scalp.

We stand in silence, surveying the wreckage of the living-room. Every chair is overturned. So is June's easel. Alastair's sketchpad lies on the floor amid shards of broken glass. What got broken? When? It seems as though all this must have happened while we were gone, maybe while we were underwater. I remember the blood, of course, but I didn't remember there was so much of it.

June will probably stay in Ballydehob until evening, but we can't count on it. We strip down to our underpants, sling our wet clothes into the washing-machine, and start its cycle. Then we get to work with the mop, J-cloths, and the bottle of Fairy Liquid from the sink.

Scouring, mopping, returning the room to its normal state of squalor, has a restorative effect on us. We start to think we've been very clever indeed. We've got rid of Nigel, and now we're getting rid of any trace that he was ever here. The stone flags are easy to clean. In the days that follow, we'll continually spot stray drops of blood in places they shouldn't be: on the walls, on a sketchpad of June's that had lain open on her worktable (Alastair will rip the whole leaf out and pocket it while her back is turned) – even on the ceiling: how did it get *there?* But once it dries brown and crackly, it will be indistinguishable from the other substances that have been flung about in this room – paint, brush-washing water, dinners that went badly.

Normality is something you work for. And the work is never done. But at thirteen, I don't know that.

At last Alastair rises with a sigh. He goes to the sink, rinses out the J-cloth he's been using, and splashes his face. Outside the windows, the sun is setting over the bay in an explosion of pink and orange clouds. "I wouldn't mind a swim right now," he yawns.

"Get off! I never want to go swimming again." I giggle. "Nigel always used to hate swimming, he never would go in, would he?"

Alastair starts laughing silently. I pirouette on the part of the floor that's still wet, doing an impression of Nigel swimming.

Overhead: *bump bump.*

I freeze, staring idiotically at the ceiling.

Alastair brushes past me and takes the stairs two at a time.

Ned is sitting where I left him. Nothing has changed, except that he's almost finished his intergalactic cruiser. He sees us in the doorway, both of us in our underpants, our hair in damp strings, and he startles just perceptibly. Then he goes back to manipulating the two pieces that he holds in his hands, trying to fit them together. One is a Lego brick, but the other one is the cap of a ballpoint pen.

The Gardai were in no hurry to get involved in Nigel's disappearance. It was June who hounded them to investigate. I think she blamed herself for that last fight she and Nigel had. To us and to anyone else who would listen, she bitterly expressed the belief that Nigel had lit out for a warmer climate, dumping his son on her.

There were huge problems with this theory, of course. Allihies Ceramics. The farmhouse that Nigel had built onto over the years. The goats. The Allied Irish account with thousands of untouched pounds in it. But as the Gardai pieced these facts together, they must have decided that it *was* all a bit fishy. Ten days after we drove the Land Rover off the pier, "Mysterious Disappearance of Bantry Craftsman" appeared in the bottom corner of page two of the *Cork Examiner.*

Two guards questioned Alastair, Ned, and me. All together, not separately - maybe they didn't take us seriously as individuals, or maybe they were just working the Irish way. We said that Nigel had come down to the cottage on the afternoon of the fourth, stayed a while, then left in the Land Rover. That was perfectly true as far as it went, easy to remember, and easy to stick to. Alastair worried that Ned might crack, and I think now that the danger was greater than we knew. One of those guards was big and kindly, with a rumbling voice like Nigel's. But Ned had no chance to tell him anything, because I started crying, and a new storyline emerged: irresponsible hippies, neglected children. And then from somewhere, maybe Peter, maybe Fiona, maybe another of the myriad people whom Nigel had fallen out with over the years, arose the suggestion that Nigel had been mentally ill.

Another week went by, with June getting ever more frantic, and then the guards came back in a van with two scuba divers.

In the end, they had to get a truck-mounted crane down from Cork. Almost a month had now passed since we drove the Land Rover off the pier, including several days of high winds and stormy seas, and the currents had tumbled it some distance into the bay. The men in charge of the winching operation said to Alastair, Ned, and me - we were hanging around the pier, hypnotized by the spectacle of the frogmen and the heavy machinery - that in another few days it would have been irretrievable.

That was another day when Ned could have squealed on us. As a matter of fact, he could have squealed on us at any time. But is it any wonder that he didn't? For one thing, Alastair had intimidated him with gruesome threats. And for another, the awful truth, as far as any of us knew, was that we were all he had left.

Alastair and I hadn't taken *that* into account. The joke was on us.

We learned to our (well-concealed) astonishment that Nigel had *drowned.* The hairline cracks in his skull were deemed to be consistent with injuries sustained in the crash. Our kindly guard told June there would be no inquest: it was obviously a case of death by misadventure. Like a sheet draped over a corpse, the generous contours of this verdict outlined the Catholic horror of suicide. They were giving Nigel an ecumenical dispensation.

The coroner's report shattered the last of June's equilibrium. She cried for a while, then launched into a frenzy of packing. Her tears alarmed us and her excitement compelled our obedience. Alastair and I knew this routine of old. Ned didn't. I made several trips up to the farmhouse with him. He wanted to take a ridiculous amount of stuff, including many of Nigel's display pieces, which included not just pots but sculptures. I got mad at him. He started crying, and that set me off, too. We sat on the bench in Nigel's deserted studio, blubbing like babies.

"Where are we going?" Ned pleaded through his tears.

"Probably Paris," I said. "You'll like it. There's a merry-go-round near where we live. It's better than the magic teacups were at the funfair. And you have chocolat chaud and pain in the morning instead of cornflakes. And we'll probably have a TV. They have 'The Transformers' and 'Knight Rider,'" I said, trying to cheer him up.

"I bet everything is in stupid French!"

"You'll learn it at school. It's just like English."

"Alastair says I'm too stupid to learn anything."

"*Alastair's* stupid. Don't cry!" I hugged him, taking the opportunity to wipe my eyes and nose on his shoulder. "We'll look after you, Neddo. You'll be OK with us."

The next morning we loaded up our old Renault 4 and set off for Bantry. But instead of taking the road for Cork, June turned the other way, towards Glengarriff. The sea sparkled in the sun, glinting between the fronds of palm trees. We reached the lane that led to Fiona's house. I hadn't seen Conrad or thought about him since Nigel's death. "This is you, Ned, baby," said June. "Alastair, help him get his stuff out." We stood around the car in mute confusion. June hugged Ned, then tucked an envelope into his shirt pocket. "That's for Fiona. Make sure you give it to her. It's to explain… well, just give it to her."

Will I ever forget Ned's face as we drove away? He stood in the dappled shade of the trees beside his stack of cardboard boxes, hopelessly following the Renault 4 with his eyes.

"**A**nd then we flew to Thailand. Where my father lived at the time… He's dead now. Committed suicide."

After a minute, Tad said, "That's ironic."

"Yeah, tell me about it. Cosmic payback!" I shrugged. "But we never really knew him."

My story had taken two hours, a whole pot of coffee, and half a pack of cigarettes to tell. Quite early on, I'd grown frustrated by the difficulty of putting into Japanese things that I'd never thought about in that language, and I'd dropped into English, not even adding sidebars to explain what kind of a country Ireland had been, although everything hinged on that. I said, "It's OK. I don't expect you to understand."

"I *do* understand. I just wish you hadn't waited so long..." Tad sighed and lit yet another cigarette. He seemed exasperated, as if my story was something other than he'd expected or hoped for.

"Isn't it obvious why I waited?" I said. "I didn't want you to hate me."

He left his cigarette smouldering in the ashtray and paced aimlessly around the kitchen.

I said, "Of course, you can hate me now. That's your right." More than a right, I thought, it was almost his duty. Although he'd still have to stand by me, out of self-interest. Alastair's plan had worked perfectly in that respect.

"I don't hate you," he shouted. He punched the wall. I yipped a scream. He said, "Shit," and examined his hand, as if it had moved without his permission. I jumped up and went to him. The wall hadn't taken a scratch, but beads of blood were springing out on his knuckles. He said, "It's cool. It's not my fretting hand... You thought I couldn't handle it."

"No," I said. "I wanted to protect you. Because I love you."

"You're tripping."

"I do," I said, feeling as if I was falling into another of those gaps in reality. "I love you," *tap,* "I love you," the rhythm of life imitating art, things I thought I meant getting confused with dramatic effects.

"And so you wanted to *protect* me? Look, I'm Japanese. We don't say things that would make the other person uncomfortable. But... but fuck that."

He picked up his cigarette, scattering ash on the photographs, and inhaled deeply.

"My mother died when I was five. She was in hospital for months, but at the end they let her come home. My dad took time off work to nurse her, but I guess he exhausted himself, because that night he was out cold. I woke up. I don't know why. I don't even know why I was home – I'd been staying with my grandparents. That was before Granddad died and Grandma came to live with us. Anyway, I remember it clearly. I went into Mom's room – that's Nina and Joaquin's now. She looked awful. She was crying. But she wouldn't let me fetch Dad. She had me climb up on the bed, and I stayed there until she died. When I remember it, it seems like hours, or maybe even days, but it was probably only a few minutes. Do you know the last thing she said to me? 'Grow up strong.' And I said, 'I'll try, Mom,' but I drifted off to sleep again, and the next thing I knew, I was lying next to her cold body."

He stubbed out his cigarette.

"So why did I start talking about this? Oh, yeah. Don't tell me that I don't know about death."

"I'm sorry," I whispered.

"And don't flatter yourself that there's anything you can protect me from. I know about it all. *All!*"

"But Tad, what a terrible thing to happen to a child."

"And it happens all over the world, every day. That's what I always used to tell myself. You're not unique and you're not alone."

I came up behind him and put my arms around him. He was as stiff as a board. I didn't know what to do, so I lifted his right hand to my mouth and licked the blood off his knuckles. He groaned. I drew back.

"Oh, Shanti."

We fumbled upstairs, kissing all the way, and fell on his bed. The sheet pulled free of the mattress and our clothes flew. This was the real Tad, I thought, spilling drops of cold sweat on my face, here in the house where he'd grown up and I'd parked my shit like an unsafe little travelling funfair. *You're not unique and you're not alone.* He had this way of phrasing clichés so that they struck me like revelations.

He crashed on top of me. We lay in each other's arms, brokenly apologizing.

But in my shallow dreams, he raised his hand to strike me, and I ran away. Through fading walls I plunged onto the grass. The pier stretched before me, deserted in the velvety Irish sunlight. High tide lapped at the masonry. In my state of dawning terror it made perfect sense to me that the sound of the sea should be mechanical. It was the Land Rover's engine still running beneath the water, I realized. Trundling along the sea floor with not-yet-dead Nigel at the wheel. Coming back.

My plan had been to burn Ned's photographs, but on second thoughts, another strange smell in this house was the last thing we needed. I wanted to keep some of the snapshots on the first half of the roll – Alastair feeding the goats, June sunbathing on the pier – but Tad convinced me it wasn't worth the risk. So we cut all twenty-four of them into slivers and flushed them down the toilet.

From: *shanti@coldcoeur.co.jp*
To: *alastairh@gmail.com*
Subject: *Koh Samui ETA*
Hi Alastair, I was just wondering if you and Nina decided to stay another day in Bangkok?? It's just that you were supposed to be in Koh Samui two days ago, but I haven't heard anything from you. I guess you're planning to catch N off guard – THE ELEMENT OF SURPRISE! – but you don't want him to get a head start, do you? Anyway, let me know the revised itinerary.

Love, Shanti

From: *shanti@coldcoeur.co.jp*
To: *alastairhazard@windroseandsons.com, alastairh@gmail. com*
Subject: *ALASTAIR! GET IN TOUCH!*
Where are you??? I haven't heard from you! I've been mailing your gmail address EVERY DAY for the last WEEK (exaggeration but almost). If you never got to Koh Samui, as I'm assuming you didn't for some reason, then PLEASE DON'T GO because it's just not worth it. Actually come to that, N might have KNOWN that you'd follow him and devised some VILE SCHEME! He might be LYING IN WAIT! So don't give him the satisfaction!
As for me, I'm supposed to be jobhunting but I haven't really gotten it together. I'm still staying at Tad's since I had to give up my apartment because I couldn't pay the rent, thus confirming everyone's cynical suspicions, but that's not really how it is. The FLICS came back once to ask us if we'd seen N, and it was lucky I was there because T went all stammery and I was afraid he might mention THAT NIGHT. But we didn't tell them anything!! In other news we may have to look for a new drummer since our drummer, Shingo you remember him, has jumped ship for this appalling little bunch of punks called Kinderbox. But I'm really more worried about you. T says maybe Nina has been kidnapped by bandits and you're mounting a heroic rescue? J says, "Je comprends três bien quoi qu'elle fait! Elle se venge de moi!" I'm afraid he thinks the whole thing was just cover for you and Nina to elope together. So you've got to come back and prove him wrong!!
I really don't care what's happened as long as you're OK. So GET IN TOUCH!!!!
Love, Shanti

And all the time Ned was singing in my mind. We were on tour, in the scuzzy living-room of someone's apartment in Morioka. An overflowing gig behind us, several bottles of nihon-shu down, and now for the handful of people who remained awake Ned was singing his own song.

"I worked my way up. I started off as a mule. That's the lowest of the low. It's like working in the mailroom of the Trump Tower. I was down and out when Jeremy found me, didn't have the clothes on my back, I'd been robbed of my last baht. So I had to work my way up. It would make the hair stand up on your head. Swallowing twenty thousand euros worth of heroin. Getting on the plane. Getting off the other end. Amsterdam: it's known as the drug trafficking capital of the world. And with good reason! But once you get through, you can sell the stuff in the open air on the fucking street corner. Well, we never did that.

Jeremy's local contact would meet us. Dispose of it as rapidly as possible. You get paid for your trouble then, just about enough to stay high for a week, and that's what the rest of them would do. Fucking shit-for-brains junkies. Me? I'd get on the train and go to visit my grandmother in Copenhagen. She used to say, boy, I'm not believing that you live in the Far East, because I'm seeing you more often than I see my other grandson, who lives in Odense!"

Laughter.

"She was a great lady. I'm telling you, she was the reason I never went down that road. I knew what it would have done to her. And Jeremy knew that, too. He saw that I care for my loved ones, I don't get high, I don't get wasted, and I come back. Most of them never make more than a couple of trips. Can't handle it. Lose their nerve. Or lose consciousness in some fucking nightclub and wake up in Heaven." Ned grinned and flapped his elbows like wings.

"Or they get arrested," I said crossly.

"Occasionally, but not our people. You've got to understand that Jeremy is smart. He only uses EU nationals. That makes all the difference. Backpackers with no money left, tourists who want a free flight home… of course we'd modify their luggage to hold the goods. Ingrid and Klaus from Frankfurt don't want to swallow condoms. But you'd be absolutely astonished what people will do for a couple of hundred bucks. And how many of them do it just for the *thrill.*" Ned made a sound of disgust in his throat. "Notwithstanding, they're all liable to lose their nerve. That's why you need someone reliable along for the trip. Mules are perverse animals, they need a good herdsman!"

The Art Of Drug Smuggling, by Ned Gallant, I thought, looking at the bleary amiable faces of Ned's listeners. They were all pretending to follow him, but how much did they really understand?

"You also need someone to turn the operation around on the other end. Half of the money goes into the bank, half buys E for the tourist trade in Thailand. You need someone to transport that product home. And Jeremy saw that I had the potential to take on that responsibility. So I became his right-hand man. His conductor."

Aka his fall guy, I thought. Sitting in business class in your expensive suit, waiting for Ingrid or Klaus to stagger up the aisle and die in your lap.

Ned didn't have the imagination to invent someone like Jeremy Siek, complete with a flaky girlfriend who read palms and interpreted dreams – and besides, his supply of product had to come from somewhere. But I'd assumed he was exaggerating his connection with Jeremy. Far from being like a brother to him, Jeremy was probably no more than his wholesale supplier. I'd said as much when I described the scenario to Alastair, and Alastair had agreed with me, dismissing Jeremy as a relevant factor.

But what if Ned hadn't been exaggerating at all?

What if every last detail had been true?

From: *shanti@coldcoeur.co.jp*

To: *alastairh@gmail.com, alastairhazard@windroseand sons.com*

Subject: *(none)*

Dear Alastair, I'm really worried now. Where are you? What's happening? Why aren't you getting in touch? afraid you might be If you weren't you would have Well, I guess maybe you're just BUT IT DOESN'T MAKE SENSE but I just can't believe OH GOD OH GOD

I thought you were invulnerable

Alastair I just can't

just vanish like it's like what the FUCK oh GOD

Part 3:
You're No Fun

A cool sea mist hazed the skyscrapers of Makuhari Messe, early on Sunday morning when the only traffic was the elevated trains. Alastair would have liked it here, I thought. A cluster of highrise office buildings surrounding a convention center and a mall, with an outlying stadium, built halfway between Tokyo and Chiba City on what probably used to be an inoffensive little patch of coast, Makuhari Messe epitomized the wacky excesses of postwar Japanese urban planning. And this weekend it hosted Punk March, an extravaganza of all things angry and loud, with headliners from the USA and UK underground scenes… and Kinderbox in an opening slot at 10 am.

It turned out that Naoya and the boys had inherited their good luck from a band that cancelled at the last minute. Confucius had seen them opening for us at Oasis and tipped them off when he heard about the slot. That made it all the harder to bear. But still, we had to go and support them, especially since Shingo would be performing with them. It was the only way left for us to prove that we were still the better band.

The boys didn't say much as we signed in at International Exhibition Hall. and got our wristbands and backstage passes. They craved success, and Apex's betrayal must have been hitting them all over again here, as the glowering posters and cornucopic merchandise stalls drove home exactly how much we'd lost. In contrast, I'd discovered that I didn't really care about success for its own sake. All along - I now understood - it had been Alastair who I wanted to wow with my achievements. Without him, there would have been no point being a rock star, anyway.

I left the others talking with the Kinderbox boys in their dressing-room, which was obviously a breakout session room with mirrors temporarily replacing the conference table, and tracked the echoing wheels of the gear dollies to a badly lit backstage area. About two dozen people buzzed around in an organized frenzy, unpacking hard cases and reviewing checklists. A familiar smell pervaded the place: dust burning on the floods, duct tape, fried plastic, cigarette smoke, overloaded circuitry… Something quivered beneath my breastbone. I slipped through the wings to the stage.

I'd been to Makuhari Messe before. I remembered this hall. But I didn't remember it being this big. Out in the center of the otherwise empty cavern, a handful of technicians loitered inside a cage full of mixing desks and monitoring equipment. I waved. They waved back. I shouldn't have been here, but they didn't seem to realize that.

A mic had already been set up for Naoya in the middle of the stage. I tapped it. The power was on. I hummed a few scales and started singing - thirds, fifths, random snatches of melody, and then I segued into a *Xenophobia*-era Gorot number, "Rage."

"Say you're gonna go today. Too late to do it all over. You waited and your time has come. Today you're gonna cry: Lift me, lift me up on high!"

(Why didn't you take me with you?)

"You say you're glad to go? That attitude is you all over!"

(How did he do it, Alastair? Did he trick you, outwit you, or just get lucky?)

"You never turned your back until the drama was all over! You chased the devil's tracks while he was sitting on your shoulder! Oh no! Time to say goodbye. Oh no! Time to go down fighting!"

I stopped in the middle of my a-cappella performance and stood with my hands braced on my thighs, fighting to breathe normally. Maybe it looked like I was taking a bow. Out in the hall, a couple of people clapped, and I looked up to see that the punters had started to filter in. Clinging to the picnic mentality of an outdoor festival, they were staking out their patches with backpacks and bottles of water. A few groups had even spread tarpaulins on the concrete floor.

"Shanti!"

I turned around at Tad's scandalized voice. He hurried between the technicians who were scurrying around the stage, installing and checking Kinderbox's equipment.

"You're not supposed to be out here! What's everyone going to think?"

"Mic check," I said. "One two. Check one."

"Come on." Tad's face creased with helpless anger.

"It's just not fair," I said, fighting tears. "Why him? Why not me?"

"I know," Tad said. "I know," but he didn't.

Kinderbox dispatched their show with feverish energy. Shingo's drumming improved the familiar racket immeasurably. Afterwards they joined us in the front of the hall, exploding with joy that it was over. They had an autographing session in the HMV booth, with product supplied by Cold Coeur Records - probably the first and last time CCR discs would ever find their way inside a chain store. Their table wasn't exactly mobbed, but Joaquin took command in the role of producer and schmoozed the fans who showed up. The rest of us went to grab lunch.

By now the midway teemed from wall to wall with yoof. A manzai duo insulted each other on the sideshow stage. Arty geometry flickered on the giant VJ screen in the improvised picnic area under the stairs. We sank to the concrete floor and scarfed crêpes and yakisoba. None of the punters camping around us paid us any attention. Even Naoya with his tiger-striped hair and Sato-kun with his tattoos looked conservative in this crowd, where punks in tartan plumage rubbed shoulders with supertanned yanquis and their hooker-chic girlfriends. I went to buy a pineapple-flavored cocktail from the Hawaiian bar. As I carried it back through the crowd, a gaggle of high school girls recognized me and got me to sign their thighs and shoulders in red magic marker. Happiness sparked, turned grey, and went out.

I finished my cocktail and curled up on the floor beside Tad. "We're losing her," someone said over my head.

"I'm taking a nap," I said without opening my eyes. Me and Snow White. "Is that OK with you?"

"Let her sleep," said Tad. "If she forces herself to stay awake, someone'll get hurt."

I uncoiled one leg and aimed a horizontal kick in his direction, making the others laugh. As drowsiness overtook me, my thoughts melted into a whorl of fantastical imagery: spotlights crisscrossing on black water, a train that I was missing, an army of killer palm trees advancing on me along a deserted beach.

I woke up with folds of cloth pressing into my cheek and a familiar scent in my nostrils. Tad had folded his shirt under my head. I sat up. The boys had subsided into sprawling postures, tall paper cups of beer at their elbows. Gen lazily raised his cup to me. "Welcome back to the festivities. You've got warpaint."

This struck me as gibberish until I realized my left cheek was creased from sleeping on Tad's shirt.

"Don't worry. It's cute."

"You guys are drunk off your asses," I said, rising. "But don't worry. It's cute."

Gen laughed. "You've been asleep for hours. Tad's gone to wait in line to see The Heights."

"And I'm just, *why,*" Kiichi said. "When he's got a pass?"

"Because that's how Tad is," Gen said. He glanced at me. "He's big on fairness."

I put Tad's shirt on over my own t-shirt and trotted off. The public entrance to the Mountain Stage had turned into a bottleneck besieged by about two hundred people. Ushers stood on stepladders, begging everyone to be patient. In most other countries that I could think of, the crowd would have rolled straight over the ushers, or at least given them a hard time. But this was a Japanese crowd. Chatting, smoking, and text-messaging, it waited patiently, so dense that not even a child could have squeezed into its midst. I fingered the all-areas pass in my pocket. *He's big on fairness.* I tacked myself onto the back of the crowd. At last someone up ahead gave the green light. Inch by inch, we shuffled through the funnel formed by the crowd control barriers.

The Heights were onstage. The beefy drummer bashed out their trademark two-buckets-and-a-dustcan rhythms, the vocalist fellated his mic, the guitarist wah-wahed, and the bassist poom-poomed. I found Tad in the hall's acoustic sweet spot right in front of the mixing cage. Eyes closed, he rocked gently from foot to foot while teenage goths pogoed around him and the occasional mosher shot past like a comet.

"Tad."

"Hey! I didn't think you liked this kind of thing."

I threw myself into his arms. He patted my back.

"I don't know what to do, Shanti. It's killing me, too—"

"I just know he's dead," I sobbed.

He pulled the ever-present packet of paper tissues out of his jeans pocket. My tears flowed as fast as he dabbed them off my face.

"He's dead, and it's all my fault."

Tad dropped the tissue, grabbed my shoulders, and shook me. I was so startled that I stopped crying. "He's OK! Something's just happened to stop him from answering his email. It's Thailand. Connections can be unreliable over there. What has it been, two weeks? You shouldn't be this worried yet. Fuck, I've seen him in action. He could go through a whole posse of lowlife drug dealers with his bare hands!"

"Tad, I've decided. I'm going after him. It's the only thing I can do."

I wondered if he'd heard me over the music. Then he said, "Give it another week, and I'll come. After all, it's not like I have anything pressing to do here."

"You - you - we've got that gig at Izm..."

"Big deal. It's just another shitty little live house. Who cares if we cancel? And how could we do the gig, anyway, without you? And you're not going to be here mentally, even if you are here." He gave me another shake. "See how I feel? You're the only thing left in my life that's any good. It would literally fucking kill me to lose you, too. Do you realize that? No, of course you don't! You don't have any idea how much I love you."

This rant fell oddly flat, collapsing under its own weight like a human pyramid on a bicycle. Tad's head drooped.

"I'm sorry. I've been acting like a complete child," I said.

"Oh, Shanti." He let his forehead fall onto my shoulder. He whispered, "Hey, I just noticed. You're wearing my shirt."

"It was a good pillow."

"I bet it wasn't. But you looked so uncomfortable curled up on the floor."

My phone vibrated in my pocket. I loosened his arms enough to dig it out.

"Ah, the lovey-dovey couple," Ned said dryly. "Don't stare around like that, will you? I was right behind you but I've moved. And I'd rather not have Tad know I'm here, if you don't mind."

Tad was right in front of me. I could hand him the phone. That would prove how loyal I was.

But something stopped me: the last scraps of my integrity.

Tad wasn't like me. If I said the word, he would try to deal with Ned for me, just to prove how loyal *he* was… but it would cost him, mentally and spiritually. He'd as good as told me that he was at the end of his tether. He couldn't take any more drama. Everyone in his life casually took advantage of his good nature. I couldn't be another of them. Especially when I was the only one who knew how fragile he really was.

A fury of self-loathing and determination filled me. I had to protect him. In a sense, we'd come full circle. Only now I knew, instead of just fearing, what the consequences would be if I failed.

It was like stepping onstage. Like water reaching its level, my tension stabilized. The world outside of my body faded into a blue screen. I was one with the air I was breathing. Sound is just wavelengths; so is light, when it's not being particles. And our entire universe is supposedly made of vibrating superstrings, so *everything* is just wavelengths, I thought.

Ned was telling me a disjointed story whose gist seemed to be that he'd somehow gotten into Punk March without a ticket. I rolled my eyes humorously at Tad. "Joaquin," I said. It's never too early to start covering your tracks.

Descending the steps of the perspex-roofed walkway from the convention center, I saw Ned before he saw me. He wore a grungy white t-shirt and baggy jeans with a pair of bright red Nikes that caught my eye from afar. He'd buzzed his hair close to the skull. A surprisingly effective disguise, it made him look like a young Marine from Iowa or Kansas. Yet, for the first time, he seemed to be at home in a Japanese crowd. He stood outside the entrance to the mall in front of the station, quietly waiting with his backpack next to his feet, very nearly blending in. I got the impression that he'd retracted the boundaries of his personal space until all that remained was a Teflon patina on his face and head.

But when he saw me, his old demonstrative manner revived – astoundingly, despite everything. He greeted me with a hug. "So how did you get away?"

"Everyone was heading over to the stadium to see NOFX. I just said I wanted to buy a Coke and I'd catch up with them later…" I shrugged, noticing that he had a grubby gauze bandage on the first two fingers of his right hand. It looked like they were splinted.

His eyes sparkled. "I knew you'd manage it. Will you have that Coke now? Or something else? Have you had lunch?"

I glanced around the little plaza in front of the mall. The sun had gone in, and a gusty wind blew the budding branches about. The temperature had dropped to the point that I was barely comfortable in my blouse and cardigan. I caught sight of a Veloce sign above the walkway that I'd just come along. "How about a coffee?"

"Good. Good. Sounds good."

We threaded between the tables to sit at the counter facing the window. Ned leaned his backpack against his chair. It was the identical cousin of his old one, a North Face model suitable for a Himalayan trek, with one of those padded waist harnesses. Voices around us drowned out the tepid muzak. My phone vibrated in my pocket again. Probably Tad, again. I ignored it, dumped creamer into my coffee, stirred. Ned counted his change and pocketed it, awkwardly because of his bandaged hand.

"Three hundred yen for a few coffee beans and a bit of hot milk," he said. "This fucking country."

"Ned, what happened to your hand?" I was stalling.

"This? I guess it looks pretty bad." His spoon clinked into the saucer. He laughed. "But you should have seen the other guy."

"Not Mike?" I thought with a kind of sad wrath about Mike Schultz, who had so completely misled us.

"No. I'm not in touch with Mike at the moment; it's safer. This guy was another friend of – well, you can't say that poor old Gav had any real friends. But one of the Israelis he used to do business with. We had a dispute. Your man was trying to rip me off."

"The Israelis?" These glimpses into Ned's life disoriented me, like snapshots taken from an unfamiliar angle. "Don't tell me you've got mixed up with the Mossad?"

Ned didn't smile. "Just the street vending mafia. You know they've got a monopoly on those stalls that sell jewelry and incense. They're all over here dodging the draft, and making a pretty penny while they're at it. Well, I've been working at one of their stalls in Ueno –"

"You've *what?*" I squeaked.

"Ah, nothing could be safer. It's like hiding in plain sight!" Ned chuckled. His chair rocked, toppling his backpack. He picked it up and apologized to his neighbor in broken Japanese. "Everyone took me for an Israeli! The police and our friendly local yakuza, too; they can't tell one gaijin from another!" His laughter resounded through the café. He was red in the face.

"But," I said, unable to contain myself any longer, "I thought you'd gone back to Thailand. That's what Mike said."

"And you believed him? Are you off your head? I couldn't go back yet. In fact, that's why I'm here."

I took a swallow of tasteless coffee, remembering: *don't come to the airport, Shanti, it's not as if we're saying goodbye.* And Nina's foolish smile. Alastair must have been in touch with Ned all along, he must have had a plan in mind, but that it had gone wrong was obvious from the fact that Ned was sitting here talking to me.

"So where have you been staying?" I said.

Ned shrugged. "Around." I saw that the logistical complexities of his own survival actually bored and irritated him, and that stoked my anger. Gaijins - farangs, incomers, étrangers - survive at the cost of accepting incongruities in their lives. It's that or don't survive at all. Ned's incongruities had always been amplified across an unusually broad spectrum, but the texture of his existence was familiar to me, even at this extreme. Everyone I knew in Japan was basically a foreigner, living two or three incompatible lives at once, even if they were Japanese. I'd never been able to decide whether this was due to the abolition of something called traditional Japanese culture, or simply because there was a selection principle at work. But in either case, how dare Ned act as if he deserved better?

"Eeto... sumimasen... Shanti-san desu ka?"

I whipped around and clicked on a smile. A couple sporting Birkenstocks and clothes with expensively frayed edges. It was she who'd spoken, and she was clutching a copy of *U-Turn Day* the way people often did, as if I was a monster who needed to be approached under a treaty flag. I chatted with her about the festival and signed the CD: *To Ayako, Love from Shanti,* inside an icicled CCR heart. Her boyfriend tried to talk to Ned in English. Ned just scowled. As soon as they'd gone, he said darkly, "You've got a lot of fans."

"That was the first lot today."

"I should have known better. We shouldn't have met in public."

"You were the one who suggested it." I watched him gather up the debris of sugar and creamer packets.

"I forgot you were so fucking famous."

"We lost our deal with Apex," I said softly.

"*Shanti-san!* And now they're going to be saying to each other, who was that with her? He must have been *somebody.* He was so handsome. Blue eyes and blond hair, that's all it takes to be handsome in this country."

"They'll probably think you were Joaquin."

He shot me a suspicious look. "You didn't say anything to them, did you?"

He meant the boys. "Of course not," I said, laughing.

"Good. I wouldn't want to confuse anyone." Ned stood up. "Well, I know somewhere we can talk in private. If you don't mind a bit of walking."

Anxiety made his face look pinched and vulnerable. I glanced at the clock on the wall of the café. Ten past five. And what time was it where Alastair was now? What time is it ever in Hell?

Ned's spirits seemed to recover as soon as we left the crowds behind. He led me the long way around the convention center, circling the parking lot. We came out on the road that stretched back to the stadium. There were actually two roads that led to the stadium. The other one ran straight from the convention center. This one was for vehicles. It was deserted. The wind carried a faint thunder that I identified as NOFX. Slipknot, the day's headliners, had yet to take the stage. So I had at least another hour before there would be any concerted attempt to find me. Tad had called me several times. I hadn't answered, and then I'd turned off my phone. I didn't need the distraction.

On our right, tall grasses rose and dipped, giving an intermittent view of an abandoned golf course. The stadium loomed ahead. Closer at hand, a gray rectilinear inlet cut across the tract of wild grasses and trees that bounded the golf course. A hump in the road signalled a bridge ahead. The wind smelt of the nearby sea. It whipped around us, lashing the trees that marched along the line of the inlet. I said, "It's supposed to rain later."

"Oh yeah?" Ned was scanning the tall grasses that choked the verge of the road. "Got it! I thought I'd missed it. That would have been funny."

He dived into the grasses. I froze for an instant, then dived after him. "*Where* are we going?" I already knew, but I didn't know what kind of place it would be.

"Not far."

In fact, we hadn't gone three paces when the ground fell away. We staggered down into a gully, choked with pampas, that had been invisible from the road. Canted clumps of reeds nodded over its not-quite-dry bed. Despite his cumbersome backpack, Ned crossed the boggy bit in a couple of long strides. I jumped onto the nearest tussock. One of my boots plunged into freezing mud. "No way," I wailed, hopping. "I'm not dressed for this. These are my lucky boots." At least, they used to be.

Ned grinned back at me. "Come on, where's your sense of adventure? Surely a little bit of mud isn't going to stop you?"

I went for it. Two awkward hops and I was across. Ned caught my arm and hauled me onto dry ground.

On the level, the grasses gave way to a sea of kudzu that came up to Ned's waist and my breastbone. We waded along like swimmers heading out to where the water would be deeper. I barely noticed the ground rising until I glanced to my right and looked *down* at the derelict golf course. Looking back, I couldn't see any traces of our path. The kudzu had closed over it. I took a deep breath and made small talk, telling Ned about Kinderbox's show, their autographing session, anything.

Ahead lay the belt of trees along the inlet. The stadium bulged over their crowns like earthrise on the moon. When Ned stopped to tie his sneaker, all I could hear was the wind. No, that wasn't quite all. There was a faint hollow susurration. I'd taken it for the sub-bass of NOFX's sound. It was the sea.

Ned plunged into the trees, and I followed him. This seemed to be a remnant of an older patch of woodland. A lot of what had looked like foliage was kudzu. The vines were swallowing the trees from the roots up. They slished dryly as we waded through them. I kept on talking about nothing. I was no longer nervous. I would see what he wanted me to see, and then…

Then the sea.

I pictured a winding concrete path guarded by a seawall that I would playfully jump up on and run along, as I'd once run along the harbor wall in Bantry, and Ned would remember that night and pursue me. But here, the drop beneath the wall wouldn't end in water. One foot wrong and you'd crash down into a jumble of concrete tetrapods with waves boiling up between their limbs. These Japanese erosion defences were as vicious as the cliffs along Bantry Bay where we used to go climbing. In that moment when the sea seems to inhale, exposing its barnacled teeth, we'd dart out onto the reefs that had been underwater.

Streaming hanks of mermaid's hair turned even the barnacled bits slippery, and foam gurgled far down in the narrow crevices. Ned had never liked to venture as far as I did, but he responded beautifully to taunts. It would be best of all if there were a breakwater. Japanese breakwaters were great reefs of tetrapods heaped along a wall that jutted way out into the sea. When the waves smashed on the end of the wall, blasting clouds of spray into the sky, your very blood hollered back to that power and beauty…

The trees opened and we emerged into a clearing whose centerpiece was a low stack of breezeblocks. Ned plopped down on it.

I turned in a circle. The undergrowth had been hacked back to expose manky brown grass. Assorted junk lay about: chipboard cable spools, newspapers, a car battery, a pair of old shoes. There was nothing else. "This is just some homeless guy's campsite," I said.

"Oh yeah?" Elaborately, Ned swung his legs onto the breezeblocks and stretched out, head propped on his backpack, hands folded on his chest. He looked like a medieval knight lying on his tomb, with a big grin. "It's *my* campsite. Make yourself at home."

I blinked speechlessly. I'd been so sure that he was bringing me to see Alastair's body.

"How long… have you been staying here long?" I finally said.

"A couple of days. It's not so bad. Bit cold, but you can see the stars at night. I assume there was a previous tenant, but I've not had a sight of him. Maybe he's moved on to that great homeless shelter in the sky."

I flipped one of the cable spools on end and perched on it. It rocked under my weight. "I thought you were working for the Israelis in Ueno? Did you quit? It sounds like a cool job."

Ned sat up and swung his feet back to the ground. "You must be joking. It was a safe place to spend time, is all. They knew I was only there on a temporary basis."

"But what happened?"

"Need I remind you? I had my little altercation with my so-called boss. So, to cut a long story short, Ueno's not a very healthy location for me anymore."

A premonition dawned on me. Suddenly, I had the feeling you get when someone switches on the lights at a small live house, revealing cigarette butts on the floor, a barren mess of cables onstage, and coats piled on beer kegs against the wall.

"Then I guess you're out of money," I said neutrally.

"I had enough for a one-day ticket to the festival. But I guess I'll be hitchhiking back to Tokyo." He shrugged. "Never seen anyone hitchhiking in Japan. I guess it's another of the things that just isn't done in this oh-so-safe country!" He ended this sentence with a grin and an odd little dart of his head, never taking his eyes off me.

I reached into my pocket and pulled out its contents. "Four thousand," I smoothed out the bills, "six hundred," I counted the coins, "and eighty-three yen." I rose and held it out. "That's all I'm good for today. But at least it'll get you back to the city. I'm sure Mike will help you out until you find another job - I know you guys are *really* good friends; and if worst comes to worst, you can always rely on the National Police Agency. I know they'd be happy to put you up! So take this and use it for train fare back to Ueno. Or turn yourself in at the nearest koban. I don't care."

He shook his head. "Put that back in your pocket, Shanti."

"Take it." I pushed it under his nose. "If you don't want to waste it on train fare, use it to get a bath. You know about sentos? Public bathhouses? Not quite as deluxe as onsens, but if you can't be good, you can at least be clean, as Nigel used to say."

"I *said* put it back in your pocket." He reached for my wrist. I dropped the money on the grass between his feet.

"Take it or leave it, it's up to you." I knew he would take it once I was gone. He would take everything I had to give and come back for more, because that was the way he was, and money was all I had left to give. All I had left.

"You know that was fucking insulting, don't you?"

I swung around. "What's so insulting? I'm just trying to help you out."

"I don't need your help. And if this is Joaquin I'm talking to, if this was Joaquin's bright idea… the only idea Joaquin ever had. Tell him I don't need his help, either. I can make money faster than he can in his dreams. I'm the only reason he made money on tour." Ned rubbed his thumb and index finger together. "I've got the golden touch!"

"Oh yeah? I guess that's how come you're sleeping rough."

"I'm on the run from the fucking pigs. Where am I supposed to—"

"You could have taken a ferry across to Korea. You could have gone up to Hokkaido and hired onto a Russian ship! You know about electrics and stuff—"

"Might work. In a movie. I'm sick of this fucking country; they're all scared of anyone bigger than them, and don't get me started on the quality of life. But I can't get out of here without some fucking money—"

"So pick it up." I pointed at the ground.

"Four thousand yen. God, Gavin would have laughed his ass off. When I say *money,* I'm talking… Your album could go multiple platinum and you'd still not be able to imagine the kind of money I'm talking about. But you know what money does? It *corrupts.* It poisons people's hearts. It's the same everywhere. Asia, Europe... I've got the golden touch, but I haven't got a friend in the world!"

"Poor Neddo. What the fuck, do you expect me to feel sorry for you?"

Ned twisted his body from side to side, his face red with emotion.

"Ah," I said. I started pacing around the clearing, laughing. "So *that's* it! You came here to show me... to show me what I've done to you! You wanted to make me feel bad for you!"

He didn't want money thrown contemptuously on the ground. He wanted it wrapped in fluffy soft sympathy. And so he'd tried to play on my heartstrings with his tale of woe. Incredibly, he didn't understand that it was way too late for that.

"I feel for you, OK? You've screwed up your life, and that's a damn shame." I kept laughing.

His face contorted. He jumped to his feet and paced, scuffing my ¥1000 bills aside with his Nikes. "I'm here to give you one last chance," he ground out.

"Oh yeah?" I blinked rapidly. I couldn't see him properly. What was happening? The sky had turned indigo. It was only the same thing that happens every day around this time. "One last chance? That's funny. Me, too." I giggled.

"Maybe you don't remember. So let me remind you. It was on the tour, I forget which city. You were drunk, but that could have been anywhere, couldn't it? You said, 'For once in my life I'm going to tell the truth.' That's what you said. And then you said that you... you *cared!"* He stopped pacing. Shadows lay thick in the trees behind him. "What happened to that? Where did it go? How can I get it back?"

"You can't," I said blankly. I didn't remember any such conversation, although it was quite possible I *had* been that drunk.

"So it wasn't true, after all? I should have known! You're incapable of speaking an honest word, you are."

"Ned, are you accusing me of lying to you?"

"Sure, I'm not accusing you. I only want to know—"

"Good, because hello! Remember what else happened on tour? You may say it was an accident, but I don't believe you. I'm sorry but I don't. And then you—"

"Is that really what you think of me?" he said, his voice suddenly breaking. "Do you really think I'd ever hurt you?"

He rubbed his cheek with the back of his hand. Déjà vu: little Neddo rubbing tears off his face with the same gesture, as if he thought I wouldn't notice that I'd hurt him. Alastair and I had been so cruel to him. He asked for it, we'd told each other in confusion. It had been years before it occurred to me that he asked for it because that was the only kind of love he knew.

Paralyzed, I was too slow to resist when he lunged towards me and enveloped me in his arms. His tears wet my cheek. I wriggled loose. He stood with his arms hanging by his sides. "I love you, Shanti, don't you know that? I've loved you ever since I was eleven fucking years old. I wrote 'NG loves SH' and 'NG plus SH forever" in a heart with an arrow through it on the wall of the hayloft, down by the floor, about six hundred times. I used to hope you'd find it. But you never did."

NG. His initials were the Japanese slang for No Good. I'd never noticed that before.

"We were *enemies,*" I said.

"That's the preteen boy's way of expressing affection." Ned chuckled through his tears, sniffled, and wiped his nose on his sleeve. "God, this is classic. You really never knew, did you?"

"Of course I didn't."

"Did you…" His face got a hopeless look. "Did you ever love me? Even a little?"

"Sometimes," I said, and then started again, trying for honesty, because that might be the only way to get the truth out of him. "Do you remember the time I fell on the cliffs? And my knee was bleeding all over the place, and you kissed it better? Times like that. We took care of each other, didn't we? But I don't know if you can call that… Christ. OK… Half the time we were enemies, and the other half of the time I took you for granted, but I would have been really… really… even lonelier if you hadn't been there. And that's the truth. But I don't think you could call that love. But you never loved me either, I mean really. Did you? You're just messing with my head. Aren't you?"

"I am not, so!" The Irish came through in that phrase, as clear as a note from a pitch pipe. "Boys that age, they're obsessive about sex. And they're also great romantics. That goes away later in most cases, but when you're twelve, thirteen, fourteen, it all fits together in a beautiful way. That's not news to you, is it? You had a brother, for Christ's sake."

"Speak for yourself," I said, all my warmth gone. "Alastair wasn't like that."

"Yeah, Alastair was different, I'll give you that. Alastair was something else."

"He was putting it on," I said, trembling. "He was just pretending to be scary, but no one ever called him on it. Not even me, because I thought it was cool."

"It's all right, Shanti. He's not here. You can tell the truth now."

I rolled my eyes stagily, because it was that or launch into him with my fingernails. "This from someone who's still in denial that his father was a psycho!"

Ned sighed. The look on his face was strangely close to relief. "Not anymore. Nigel abused me. You and Alastair had only the first taste of what I went through. He said it was to make me a good boy, but… He broke my arm when I was six. He threw me out of the Land Rover and made me walk home from Bantry when I was seven. I've still got the scars from where he shoved me into a barbed-wire fence when I was nine." He recounted the incidents in a rapid monotone. "It was child abuse, and I've finally come to terms with that."

"Huh. I guess you've been doing some thinking."

"It's taken me all these years. So I completely understand the process that you're going through. There's nothing as frightening as freedom. It's ironic, isn't it? I certainly didn't appreciate it at first. So why would I have thought you'd appreciate it? Just naïve, I guess. But I'm here if you want to talk, or even if you just want to sit and be quiet!"

He gave me a hopeful look. Maybe he didn't understand that he'd just given himself away.

"You've got a hell of a nerve," I said. A single raindrop hit me on the forehead. I jumped, and then I was screaming. "My life is totally meaningless without him! How dare you talk crap about healing to me when *you killed him!"*

Ned reared back. "Pardon?"

"You killed him!" I faltered, hearing the rain coming through the trees an instant before it struck. One second we were standing in the open air, the next we were getting drenched. I swiped at the droplets, refusing to be fazed. "He never got to Thailand! I haven't - haven't heard from him in two weeks—"

"Oh Christ, Shanti! He went to Thailand? I didn't even know that. The fact is—"

"You're lying! Where's his body?"

"This is the craziest shit I've ever heard," Ned muttered. He was cringing, sheltering his face with his bandaged hand. "Goddamn rain. It comes on so suddenly. Let's get under the trees."

"To hell with the fucking rain." My stomach was quaking. "I haven't heard from him in two weeks! If he's not dead, where is he? *Where is he?"*

"How should I know? Laos? South Africa? LA? He's wherever he is, and I'm here!" Ned gave up trying to shelter himself. He glared around at the watery shadows and said mordantly, "He always did have all the luck. He'll be sitting on a yacht somewhere, sipping champagne. While I'm left to take the fall. With you and poor old Tad held in reserve, in case I finally manage to make it out of this country before they catch up with me."

He was still talking, but I didn't hear him, because I was falling to the ground. The emptiness inside me forced its way out of my mouth in a silent scream. Singer or not, I didn't have the range for this scream. All that came out was an irregular panting. No tears. Crying would have been like spitting at an earthquake. I curled into a fetal ball with twigs digging into my hip and side. The knuckles of my right hand went into my mouth and my left hand went into my hair, because it was either that or break my fingernails on the wet ground.

Ned knelt over me, patting my back, telling me it was OK. I jerked away from his hands and scrambled to my feet. "It's your fault," I screamed over the noise of the rain and the wind sweeping through the trees, sounding as if the sea had come closer.

"You loved him that much?"

"We loved each other that much." I involuntarily echoed Ned's use of the past tense, and screamed again when I heard it. "Oh God! Don't touch me! What do you know about love? We would have died for each other. *That's* love." I screamed again, long and raw, before finding the inadequate words, "I hate you!"

He reeled back. "Ah, Shanti…"

"I hate you! Motherfucker, I hate you!"

"Then I won't bother to deny it anymore! You're right. It was all my fault."

"It… was?"

"I killed him." Ned's face twisted into an ugly grimace. "I didn't know he was going to Thailand, but I found out when he got there. Jeremy called me, didn't he? Told me there's some fucking American guy looking for me. With his girlfriend. So I told Jeremy I knew who that was, and he's the type of guy who carries cash on him!" The words jerked out; Ned slammed his fist into his palm to emphasize them. At the same time he was backing away from me. "Jeremy did the rest. He's a good lad, when he makes a promise, he keeps it. Whenever I get back home, I'll get half of the cash. Because that's all your precious brother was worth to me. A few measly grand in used banknotes!" He kicked the stack of breezeblocks. "Cry all you like," he shouted, "but you'll never get him back! And I'm happy about that!" He kicked the breezeblocks again. "I'm happy, happy, happy!"

I suddenly felt very calm. The emptiness inside me had spread throughout my body, leaching my strength. When Ned stopped shouting, I said steadily, "Did you really?"

"Sure I did! For your own good. You were never going to amount to anything as long as he controlled your every move. So I took the necessary steps to free you from his influence. And now you're famous. You've got everything you ever wanted. So what are you crying about?" He spun, waving his arms. *"Why aren't you happy?"*

A short eternity seemed to pass. I just stood there, getting wet.

Ned swayed slightly on his feet. Catching himself, he knuckled rain out of his eyes with his bandaged hand. "OK. You don't want to believe me, that's up to you."

He went over and started fishing around in his backpack. I regarded the hunched white expanse of his back. I believed him all right. The story was too messily plausible not to be true.

It was raining so heavily that we might as well have been under the sea, and I thought about my first home, the cottage in County Sligo with the stand of seven pine trees that June had painted from every angle and in all lights. She never had known how to deal with me, even when I was three years old. I'd been a hyperactive bundle of nerves with a default volume setting of 100 decibels. It was Alastair who'd been my substitute parent. He was the one who applauded my wild enthusiasms, comforted me when I despaired, and let me crawl into his bed when I got night terrors. We'd squabble over the covers and sometimes get into shoving matches that ended with me crying. Occasionally, however, he would unbend so far as to put his arms around me, and that was the only true peace I'd ever known.

I stooped and grasped the old car battery with both hands. There was a sticker on it that said in Japanese: "Read manual before use." It was half-embedded in the ground, so I had to work it free. I kept my head at an angle, watching Ned. He was still pawing through his backpack, dumping changes of clothes on the wet grass in search of whatever he was after. The battery was a lot heavier than I'd expected. But it made no sound in my hands. Ned turned his head only as I reached him, and the only difference that made was that instead of hitting him on the back of the head, as I'd intended when I brought the battery down with all my strength, I hit him in the temple and the side of the face.

Pale scraps tore loose from his cheek, and then the blood came, and then I heard the sound, the sound of Alastair hitting Nigel in the head, the echo finally coming back. The battery jolted out of my hands, bouncing off Ned's shoulder and thunking to the ground. Ned fell and caught himself on one elbow. His bandaged hand fluttered around the mess I'd made of the side of his face. The rain seemed to be turning black where it hit his face and flowed over his fingers. I kicked him. I shouldn't have taken the time to do that. I was just bending for the battery again when he slammed into me. The ground hit me in the back. I barely managed to get my knees up between our bodies. I wasn't Alastair, but Ned was Nigel. He was stronger than me, he outweighed me by about eighty pounds, and the rage in what remained of his face was not human. I bucked, trying to kick him in the balls, and only succeeded in getting one of my legs trapped between his. Simultaneously I was trying to hit him in the throat with the heel of my hand. None of my blows landed. Seizing my wrists, he pried my arms apart, and all the time the blood was pouring down from his face onto mine, getting in my eyes along with the rain so I could hardly see.

He was making some kind of noise, but I couldn't get any words out of it.

He pulled my arms all the way apart, and for a surreal instant I thought he might kiss me. Maybe he meant to rape me. I could probably survive a rape. As that thought flickered through my mind, his ravaged face struck down at my neck. He meant to bite my throat out.

I clamped my jaw to my shoulder. He went for the other side. I felt the warmth of his mouth on my neck right before his teeth sank into my flesh.

I shrieked, the pain excruciating, the fear worse. I kept on shrieking as a jolt travelled through Ned's body to mine, and his teeth stopped tearing at my neck and I rolled away, spitting blood and finding out that my legs still worked.

But I didn't run away.

Someone had Ned face down, straddling him in a crouch, stabbing him in the back with a blade that shone in the wet.

I was probably bleeding to death, but it didn't hurt much anymore. I just felt cold and spacey, and there was something I wanted to do before I signed out of the world for good. I heaved the car battery up off the ground, balancing it on one knee, staggering under its ever greater weight. "Get out of my way," I said to Tad.

And dropped the battery onto the back of Ned's skull.

We collected Ned's possessions and put them in his backpack. That is, Tad collected Ned's possessions and put them in his backpack. I stood nearby, holding Tad's wadded-up tank top to my neck, watching Ned to make sure he didn't start moving again. "Get my money, if you can find it," I said. "Four thousand yen. It's lying around here somewhere. I dropped some change, too, but I guess that doesn't matter." I was just talking to reassure myself that my voice still worked. In my free hand I held the ceramic-bladed knife Alastair had given Tad, and in the waistband of my jeans I'd stuck the bowie knife that Tad had found in the bottom of Ned's backpack underneath some dirty socks and a magazine that gave directions to Punk March. The weaponry made me feel safer. But I already understood that Ned wouldn't be trying anything, not now, not ever again. Up close, I'd seen his remaining eye and it was open, with dirt mashed against it. Blue, blue, but nothing has colors in the dark and the pouring rain, not even blood. Good thing, too. I'd already thrown up once, when I saw the dent in the back of Ned's skull, and if I could see the colors of the stuff that had come out of it, I'd probably throw up again.

"Tad? How did you find me?"

Hunting over the wet ground, he looked up. "You said you were going to catch us up at the stadium. I thought that was kind of weird, but I just went over there with the others. We were hanging out in the bleachers. It was noisy once they got started, so I went out on the walkway to call you again. You know, the walkways run around the outside of the stadium on the upper levels? Well, I was staring out at that bit of wilderness near the old golf course… and I saw you. And him."

"Oh God. Could you tell it was us?"

He shook his head. "I wouldn't even have been able to tell whether you were Japanese or not. I just… knew."

And very soon after that he'd slid through the trees, tracking us like some kind of a guerrilla, armed with the knife that my brother had left behind, that was guaranteed not to set off metal detectors.

He didn't need to tell me why he'd hidden in the undergrowth until it was almost too late… until, for Ned, it *was* too late. I knew what he'd thought he was seeing. And I could guess why he hadn't intervened until we started trying to kill each other.

If only he'd intervened sooner. But I wasn't going to tax him with it. He *had* saved my life.

He found the banknotes and returned them to me. As the rain got heavier, we conferred. I wanted to leave Ned where he was. The clearing showed no signs of being regularly visited. The rain would wash away the evidence. Besides, my neck had begun to hurt. But Tad shook his head.

"I fucked up before. I'm not fucking up this time."

"I," I said, "you mean *we.* I killed him, thank you very much."

"It was probably me. I stabbed him pretty hard."

"Chill," I said. "We can fight over who gets credit later."

"Well, we need to do this now, or there won't be any later." Tad hefted a breezeblock off the end of the pile and slid it into Ned's backpack. He extended his hand. Reluctantly, I passed him Ned's bowie knife. "The other one, too."

"We might need it again."

"What for?" He put both knives in the backpack, then closed the catches and held it out to me. "Think you can carry this? On the side away from your neck?"

"Sure."

The weight of the backpack practically pulled me over sideways. By the time we reached the inlet, my knees were buckling. Tad, bent over like a peasant, naked to the waist like a laborer, had dragged Ned behind him, his elbows hooked through Ned's knees. He let him fall and stayed bent over for a minute, hands braced on his thighs. "Well, I'd rather be completely out of sight," he said. "But no one looks at anything but the road when it's dark and raining."

About two hundred metres away on our left, the streetlights at the center of the bridge twinkled through the rain. The upper storeys of the stadium blazed beyond the trees on the other side of the inlet. The rain didn't seem to have stopped the show. Long white middle fingers jabbed into the night. "Look," I said. "We're missing Slipknot."

A couple of metres below our feet, choppy waves splattered the concrete retaining wall of the inlet. This was no city river, no oversized gutter that rain would swell to a torrent. It was the sea.

We put Ned's backpack on him. The catches were heavy-duty, they wouldn't come undone. The straps were nylon, they wouldn't rot, or at least not for a very long time. When we'd finished, Tad just stood there looking down at the body. I said, "D-d-did we forget something?" My teeth were chattering.

"I feel like I should say something. Like at a funeral."

"Well, I know something to say. Sayonara, motherfucker."

Tad didn't react.

"OK." I spoke past the pain in my neck. "At Christian burial services, they say, 'Ashes to ashes, dust to dust.' But that's totally inappropriate. The human body isn't made of ashes or d-d-dust. It's made of," I pointed down at the inlet. "Ninety-four percent, or something like that. So—"

Tad laughed. "Water to water."

He shoved his foot under Ned's body and tipped him off the edge. The splash came immediately. We looked down. The surface of the water glinted dimly, rippling.

"And now it's our turn," said Tad. I didn't understand what he meant until he started to take off his boots.

The icy Pacific swallowed me and bounced me back up. Wavelets smacked my face. The world seemed to be made of cold water, colder than any Irish sea had ever been. Tad bobbed nearby. "Wash your hair," he called. "Wring it out. It was full of mud and blood."

I obeyed, ducking under the water and swirling my fingers through my hair. My neck hurt with every movement. Abruptly, I felt lightheaded. I could no longer tell if the water was up or down. I floated, taking shallow breaths in between waves.

"Are you OK?" Distant words."Say something."

"Sayonara, m-m-motherfucker," I croaked.

"Stay with me. I've got you." Tad wrapped his arm around my neck in a lifesaving hold. I screamed. "Shit!" I felt him floundering away in the water. "I'm going to tow you. Don't pass out." His fingers fastened like a slimy handcuff around my wrist.

Sloped at an eighty degree angle, the wall was a raised lattice of ridges. I draped myself against the concrete. When I could speak, I said, "Thanks for being there."

Tad levered himself waist-high out of the water, then dropped back with a splash. "Just like climbing a ladder," he muttered, looking up into the dark.

"Right then, up we go." I grabbed a ridge and tried to lever myself out of the water. My arms gave. I dropped back with a cry.

"Don't hurt yourself! I'll think of something."

"It's my neck." The pain filled me with helpless fury. It seemed too farfetched to say aloud, but deep down I knew that Ned hadn't been trying to kill me, or hadn't *only* been trying to kill me. He'd been trying to steal my voice. It was the single most valuable thing I possessed, and he'd tried to rip it right out of my throat.

"Just think, it could have been much worse. If his knife hadn't been right down at the bottom of his backpack—" Tad's words broke into a yell. He flailed at the water. Beneath the surface, something curled around my hand. I jerked back, my whole arm tingling with shock. *Ned.* One breezeblock hadn't been heavy enough. He was drifting to the surface, reaching for us through the water with dead hands.

I climbed the wall, hauling myself from ridge to ridge, bare toes scrabbling on the concrete.

Up on the bank, I fell face down on the ground. Tad tried to pull me upright. "I just want to rest for a while," I said into the wet grass.

"It was a fish. Only a fish."

"It grabbed hold of me."

He snorted laughter. "Shanti, it was a fish." I made him out as a shadow in the wet luminescence from the stadium, crosslegged beside me, reaching inside one of his boots. "Shit, my cigarettes are wet."

That reminded me of something, and I stirred myself to reach for my cell phone. If it was dead, that would be my third cell phone in as many months. I held my breath. "Thank God," I said when the backlight came on. "I'm going to call Joaquin and ask him to pick us up."

Tad reached out. "Better not."

"I… I don't think I can walk very far."

"Then we'll stay here until you can."

The rain continued to pour down steadily. I hugged my shivering body, thinking that I shouldn't have been so quick to leave him behind at the stadium. I'd wanted to spare him, but for all that, it hadn't been so different from sliding home a cheap lock on a bedroom door. I hadn't wanted him getting in my way.

I'd learned my lesson now. Too late. Tad had his own need for resolution, some gigantic resolution that would put an end to the whole world. Of course he did. I'd seen it dozens of times, in front of dozens of audiences, when he would slide to his knees like a rock god and shatter his plectrum. When we played the bigger live houses, he'd never miss a chance to scramble up on top of a speaker stack and stage dive. And at the end of a song he would sometimes deadpan: *I know there has to be somebody in the house who was having fun there.*

We plodded out of the forest, waded across the gully that Ned and I had crossed earlier, and walked to the station to catch the train. It was nine o'clock. Joaquin had left an annoyed message on Tad's voicemail to say that he assumed Tad and I were travelling home separately. It was just as well, really. But the Keiyo line presented its own risks.

The Punk March crowd thronged the platform in such numbers that it felt like an extension of the midway. Tad and I skulked behind the shuttered news kiosk. Drunken bellows of laughter erupted from knots of festival-goers who'd been caught in the rain, too.

Tad had washed the blood out of his tank top and put it back on. The wet fabric bagged in folds above his belt buckle. His hair stood out in spikes. His face looked as if the top layer of skin had been rinsed off, leaving the cheekbones stark, the eyelids scraped back, the brown eyes bright yet dazed.

"I think we're OK," I said. "You look like you've just come out of a mosh pit. I've seen you looking worse than this after our gigs."

But as the train rattled through the Chiba sprawl, and regular passengers diluted the carnival atmosphere, I started to feel conspicuous.

I huddled against the door of the carriage, face to face with my own reflection. My hand gripped the collar of Tad's shirt, holding its points closed. I was also wearing his sunglasses, which had miraculously survived in his pocket. The carriage was air-conditioned to just above freezing. I slumped more and more of my weight against the door as my knees progressively gave way. Behind me, Tad kept turning his head, scanning the other passengers. I roused myself and plucked at his arm. "Don't do that. You look nervous," I muttered in English, not so much for security as because I was too wrecked to speak Japanese.

"You look like shit. You're *blue.*"

"At least I'm not acting like a suspect. I don't want to get caught just because you can't handle yourself. We should have travelled separately."

Tad slid his left arm around my waist and hooked my right arm across the back of his neck. My head sagged. His sunglasses fell off my nose. A man picked them up off the floor and gave them to him. "Sorry," Tad said. "She's not feeling well. Please excuse us. Sorry." He faced us into the door and whispered, "Hold your fucking collar closed."

The long walk from the Keiyo line platform (three stories underground on the east side of Tokyo Station) to the Keihin-Tohoku line platform (elevated, central) passed in a blur. So did our ride to Omori. When we got back to the Kuroiwas', after another nightmarish trudge through the rain, I collapsed on a chair in the kitchen. Tad vanished upstairs. Memories floated through my mind: times when the kitchen had been filled with the smell of food or incense, and voices would greet you at the door, and someone would be noodling in the studio upstairs, and you would just grab a beer or a cup of coffee and lay back into the groove. The good old days. My throat was parched, but it felt like too much trouble to get up and get a drink.

I heard Tad coming back downstairs and running a bath. He reappeared in the kitchen. "Can you walk, or shall I drag you?"

Painfully, I levered myself to my feet.

The steam from the bath had fogged up the medicine cabinet mirror. I peeled Tad's shirt off my neck millimetre by painful millimetre, then wiped a circle on the mirror with my hand.

The left side of my neck looked like it had been savaged by a wild animal. A quarter-sized piece of skin was plain *gone,* leaving a raw red wound that had now begun to ooze blood all over again. Luminous bruises surrounded it, pocked by the bloody imprints of teeth. "Oh, that looks even worse than it feels," I said faintly.

"Pity no one believes in vampires. Although I think maybe I do now."

"Then we should have put a stake through his heart."

"I put a knife into his back. It seemed to work."

"Can we get one thing straight?" I said, turning from the mirror. "I killed him. You saved my life. And I killed him."

"Whatever you say." He turned away and picked up a plastic bucket from the corner of the bath. "Lie down. Take off the rest of your clothes and lie down on the floor." He spread a towel on the tiles.

"Oh no. I'm sorry, Tad, but no," I cupped my hand over my neck.

"The only first aid I need is a hot bath."

"Do you want to fucking die? There are billions of bacteria in the human mouth. And then I made you go swimming in a sewage tank, give or take a few molecules. I ought to have taken you straight to hospital. I'm not going to insist on it now, but if that wound gets infected, you'll be inside of an emergency room before you can say, 'No, Tad,' 'I don't want to, Tad,' 'It was all my own fault anyway, Tad, so just let me die.'" He set the plastic bucket down on the floor so hard that liquid slopped out.

He was wrong. I had absolutely no intention of dying. "I just think you're making too much of a fuss," I said. "It's only a flesh wound."

But I stripped off my t-shirt and bra and lay down on the towel. Tad dipped up the iodine solution in the bucket with a toothmug. "Turn your head this way."

"Fuck, fuck, fuck. Shit, fuck, fuck."

"Grab onto me if you need to." His face hung in my field of vision, wearing a familiar look of concentration that reminded me of Kusatsu. He'd mothered me there, too, he'd held me and kissed my bruises. And a week later, when we were in bed for the first time, he'd done it again, stroking the discolored flesh and gently pressing his lips on it. I'd felt cherished and healed in some kind of symbolic way, and at the same time I'd vaguely understood that if it had been anyone other than Tad, I would have been creeped out. I was creeped out now, hiding it in my squeals of pain.

"What this really needs is stitches," he said.

"Can't you see there's nothing *to* stitch?"

"Yeah, there's a whole piece out. What a fucking animal."

And Alastair was still dead. The animal had got him, too.

We lay at opposite ends of the bath. On the washstand stood an ashtray, our phones, an empty bottle of Pocari Sweat, and bubble squares that had held three of the industrial-strength painkillers that Tad's father had been prescribed for his back.

I put out my third cigarette and slid down into the water.

"Careful, don't get your neck wet." Tad had improvised a bandage for me with antibiotic ointment and some ancient gauze and surgical tape out of the medicine cabinet.

"Don't worry. I don't want to go through that all over again." I surfaced as far as the tops of my breasts.

"Better check in with Joaquin, I guess." Tad reached for his phone. "He's not picking up… Hey! So where did you go after the gig? … Uh huh… uh huh. Starfucker. No, seriously, way to go. Guess what, though,

I'm home, too… yeah."

I drank the last few drops of Pocari Sweat.

"Remember when we were setting out to record Ravisher? Before we hit on the idea of using sheet metal to get reflections in the studio? We ran a cable downstairs and put Naoya's amp in the bathroom. Hung the room mic from the ceiling fixture. Gotta love that natural reverb…" Tad laughed. "You want to talk to her? No? OK then, see you."

He disconnected the call and set the phone on the washstand.

"He's home. Said come on over. He didn't sound mad. In fact, he sounded drunk. So now is probably a good time to establish our alibi."

Joaquin's new office-cum-apartment occupied the second floor of a rundown office building this side of Omori station. Tad had a key. "Joaquin!" I shouted. "When are you going to put a light in the fucking genkan?"

In the outburst that came down the stairs, mingled with the sounds of Neil Young, I caught the word "priorities."

To reach the stairs, we had to go through the new studio. It had been Phaze Studios Inc. until the former owners ran out of money, and they'd left behind a perfectly good drumkit as well as walls full of graffiti: caricatures and gnomic taglines that gave me intimations of futility, like a live house with Jimi Hendrix and Nirvana posters on the walls. We picked our way between Joaquin's old computer, 32-track mixing console, stacks of effectors (mostly broken or superannuated) left behind by the former owners, and the new monitor speakers on high stands that formed the only evidence of Joaquin's vow to refit the place with up-to-date equipment.

I'd been psyching myself up to make a perfectly pitched entrance, but it had been a waste of effort: none of the dozen people in the upstairsroom noticed our arrival. After a moment I identified them, to my astonishment, as The Heights and some girls – to be precise, five girls, one for each guy, except for the lead guitarist, who had two. There's just something about guitarists, isn't there? On the other hand, Naoya and Hori-kun, who I belatedly spotted near the TV, had no girls at all. That didn't surprise me, either.

The room reeked of weed. Smoke hung in whorls beneath the stained styrofoam tiles of the low ceiling. A Japanese porn movie, complete with mosaics, played on Joaquin's 40-inch flat-screen TV (expensed to Cold Coeur, of course).

The last few hours felt like something I'd eaten that I would soon be vomiting back up. But I'd been through this before. I knew that I just had to hold on and it would pass. I sat down on the floor next to Joaquin and tugged on my turtleneck, trying to get more air down my throat. I was wearing the only turtleneck I possessed, a fuzzy mohair number, and the room felt stifling. "What are we celebrating?" I said.

Joaquin laughed and turned to Chiharu. "She acts as if she's never seen a groupie before!"

"I don't give a damn about the groupies, Joaquin. It's your place. You can have the whole Japan chapter of their fan club over if you like."

The joint reached Chiharu. She handed it straight on to Joaquin. He took a theatrically long drag, holding my gaze until the smoke got in his eyes. Blinking, he offered its remnant to me. I dropped it in my drink.

"Hey," said The Heights' drummer, who was on my far side. "You could've stuck that on a pin."

"Sorry," I said.

"Yo man, she drowned the joint."

"So, we got plenty left. Hey bro! What's his name?" The rhythm guitarist rose and stood over Hori-kun, telling him how to roll a joint, which was like Hori-kun telling *him* how to finger chords.

"We're staying clean and legal from now on," I hissed to Joaquin. "I believe those were your words!"

"Look at Tad," said Joaquin in a surprisingly mild tone. "No, look at him."

Tad was squatting beside the TV, talking to Naoya. As I watched, Hori-kun handed his joint to the rhythm guitarist, who with emphatic sign language pronounced it good and then passed it to Tad. Tad's cheeks hollowed as he took a deep drag; the smoke dribbled out of his nose.

"Well," I said, "I guess he's forgotten about *clean and legal,* too."

I'd never really believed that any of us would be able to break our bad old habits. That wasn't the issue. The issue was deniability. "It's raining," I said. "I've had a stressful day, I got up at six o'clock this morning, and I'm wiped out, OK? I thought I could come over here and *relax!"*

Joaquin smirked. "Well, it's a good idea: you'd better relax while you still can!"

"What?" I said suspiciously.

"Nothing's fixed yet," said Chiharu, leaning across him.

"Nothing what?"

"I didn't want to mention it with Gen and Shingo not here. But we discussed it with their manager, and he was very enthusiastic." Joaquin's grin dazzled me. "Alex and the guys want us to support them on the North American leg of their tour."

"Well, well," I said blankly. "Take that, Apex, huh?"

"Precisement."

My gaze went back to Tad. He was deep in conversation with Naoya and Hori-kun. We'd come here to establish our alibi, which was simple and easy to remember: Tad had found me down on the ground floor of the stadium, with several hundred other people. When the headliners' show ended, we'd realized the others must have left already, and headed straight for the train. No part of this sequence of events could be disproved. All the same, I'd been braced for Joaquin or Chiharu to confront me with the quintessential accusation: "We called you! Why didn't you answer?" And I would have had to pretend that Tad and I had been so absorbed in one another that we'd forgotten our duty to be available at all times, in case something came up.

Well, apparently something *had* come up… and Joaquin had handled it by himself. "That's great," I said. "No, seriously, that's fantastic."

"As she said, it's not confirmed yet." He preened, taking full credit.

I've had a stressful day… and that might be all the alibi I'd ever need, I realized. No one cared where Tad and I had been. We were celebrating the future now. No one cared about the past.

It should have been liberating.

"I believe in this band," I declared, leaning forward between Tad and Shingo. "I believe that when five people, who have every reason to hate each other, discover that they feel the same way about music, and they feel that something's got to be done about the way music is made and sold and thought about in today's world, then it's like a Promethean event on the spiritual plane. The fire starts spreading. And no one can stop it."

One of the cameras had crept in towards me as I spoke. Even though we'd been told not to look directly at them, I addressed my last words straight to it.

"If you've got the fire, you can join the revolution. The From A Great Tour, Gorot opening for The Heights, thirty dates in a month and a half. First show, September tenth at the Cobra Club in Los Angeles."

I finished up with a fixed grin, eyes too wide. I managed to hold it for about half a second before we all melted down.

"You were doing so well with that metaphor at first," Shingo sorrowed. "What happened?"

"It was the transition from the spiritual plane to the material one," said Joaquin. "Always a problem for Shanti."

"Ask us about the history of overdriven guitar versus clean," suggested Gen. "Or Fender versus Gibson. That's the kind of thing we like to talk about. Except for Shanti; she doesn't have any opinions on gear, so she'll shut up for a change."

"I do, too! The more expensive the better. But wouldn't you really rather hear about my life on the *spiritual plane?"*

The way I said that made the boys convulse again. All except Tad.

Our interviewer, a handsome producer and pop culture pundit in a velvet blazer, was too professional to look desperate, but I felt for him. He'd perched himself enthusiastically on the edge of an armchair catacorner to the sofa where we sat, while two guys with shoulder cameras shuffled back and forth on their knees. Another guy crouched behind them with a boom mic. Beyond the photoreflective umbrellas, other people came, hung about, and went in the way I'd come to expect at TV studios: reverently silent, self-importantly busy.

Joaquin and Shingo started their perennial argument about the best way to mic up a drumkit. The interviewer coughed. "If I could pick up on something you said a minute ago, Shanti. You said that you five were 'people who had every reason to hate each other.' That's pretty strong, so could you elaborate on that?"

"She didn't mean it like that," said Gen. "Her Japanese sucks. She was just making a literal translation from English."

"Tajitsu-san, if her Japanese sucks, what does that make yours and mine?" The interviewer smiled ruefully, springing the modesty trap, and Gen fell into it with a self-deprecating laugh. "Shanti-san, when you said *reasons,* you must have been thinking of something specific?"

"Only that we're all five very different people," I said smoothly, and then I couldn't go on.

Joaquin came to my rescue. "She might have been thinking of the times, and there were many of these times, when I booked us into venues and no one showed up except our friends. Some nights I fully believed that when the gig was over, they would murder me and take what little money I had!"

Murder. In Japanese or English, it was just a word.

"Yeah, the money issue," Tad said, smiling. "These three here don't think it's fair that Joaquin is set to make as much money off our tour with The Heights as the rest of us put together. And then consider that he's also the CEO of our label. He owns all our rights. Well, as you know, rights are everything in this industry. So he's not only pocketing the lion's share of the cash, he's also the one who gets to decide whether our song is used for a soundtrack or a… a dogfood commercial."

"Chance would be a fine thing," said Joaquin.

"So you can see how some people would think there was every reason for the four of us to hate him. But personally, I've never seen anything wrong with it. He's a genius and we're mere mortals. He's the thumb and we're the fingers. Just look at the credits on our albums. He gave the rest of us arranging mentions, but he didn't really have to. Personally, I think we should all be grateful to him."

"'He's the thumb and we're the fingers'?" hooted Shingo. "Tad, I think that one's going to be immortal."

"Money is always an issue for bands," sighed the interviewer sympathetically. He had very small eyes, I noticed, and they seemed to be made of black vinyl, as if someone had smashed a record on his face and two splinters of it had lodged under his eyebrows. "But money disputes are often triggered by other issues, aren't they?

"I'd agree that's often the case with Gorot," Tad said. "Like with Miya-chan here, the issue is that he's hedging his bets. So the rest of us have to bend over backwards for him, rescheduling band stuff to fit in around his work commitments."

"I never *asked* you to reschedule anything for me," Shingo said.

"We do it of our own free will," I agreed.

"Oh boy, free will," said Tad, his voice cracking slightly. "Another contentious topic."

"Free will is like fractal geometry," said Gen solemnly. I racked my brains for the next line. If we could divert Tad into philosophy, we might be able to bore the interviewer to death.

But Joaquin leaned in from the end of the sofa and hissed, "If there is any trouble, and I don't say there is any trouble, but if there is, you and Shanti are the cause of it! And yet you pick on poor Miya-chan! It's not believable! No, it's unworthy of you, my friend!"

"Me?" I squeaked.

"Yes, you! The two of you! We don't know what to expect from one day to the next. Today they are joined at the hip? Or they don't speak to each other? Oh, I know that you *suffer,* but you make the rest of us suffer, too."

"Yeah," said Shingo indignantly. He nudged me in the side with his elbow, so gently that it would be invisible to the cameras. "Things don't always run smoothly for me and Kaori, either, but I keep it out of the studio and off the stage."

"Oh, come on, Joaquin," said Tad, still with a smile in his voice. "They don't want to hear any more about me and Shanti. We have our good times, we have our bad times, we struggle with our emotional baggage… Typical crap. They'd be much more interested to hear about how you pinched his girlfriend." He nodded at Gen.

No one outside the Cold Coeur Family knew that Chiharu had once been Gen's girlfriend.

Well, I guess they did now.

I restrained myself from peering into the gloom beyond the lights, where Chiharu presumably was. But I couldn't help looking at Gen. One of the cameramen crawled towards his end of the sofa like a fourlegged insect zooming in on its helpless prey. Gen ran a hand through his curls. "Ex-girlfriend," he said.

"I don't think I have done anything that I need to justify here," Joaquin said. "And Gen and I have already talked this affair through to our mutual satisfaction. We're all adults, and we know that when things work out a certain way, it can't be helped!"

The interviewer's voice made me think of spilt honey dripping off a table. "This occurred after your divorce, Joaquin-san?"

"There hasn't been any fucking divorce," I said. "Joaquin's wife is *dead.*"

Simultaneously, so that no one heard what I said, which was probably just as well, Tad said, "Oh yeah, you talked it through. I forgot about that." He crushed my right arm, craning past me to look at Gen. "You had a man-to-man talk, and Joaquin said, 'Sorry, my friend, I'm taking her, but you mustn't get too angry, because the band is more important than your feelings,' and you said…" He did Gen's voice, lower than his own. "'Oh, OK.'"

Beyond the lights, someone laughed out loud.

"Don't you think it's a bit weird that he would roll over like that?" Tad was addressing the interviewer now, still smiling. "You look as if you think it's a bit weird. As if we're all a bit weird. But it was only to be expected. I mean, look at the facts. What's Joaquin? A white guy, and a genius into the bargain. And what's Tajitsu-kun? A typical Japanese wimp."

"Fuck you, Kuroiwa," said Gen, half rising. The cameraman nearest him scrambled back. "I'm going to fuck you up."

Nervously, I laughed out loud. Then I did what I should have done before. I grabbed Tad's collar and pulled the mic off it. I jumped up and reached left and right, yanking the mics off Joaquin, Shingo, and finally Gen. I shoved him back down onto the sofa, and in the same movement I turned to stand over the interviewer. He sank all the way back into his armchair and gazed up at me with those vinyl splinters. "Tell them to cut." I glared at the men crouching near me, shooting me from a low angle. "Hey assholes, what part of *cut* don't you understand?"

"Cut," breathed the interviewer. "Don't you think you're overreacting?"

"This shit wasn't live." I stood back to let him resume his professional air. "And unlike real life, when a shoot goes wrong, you can scrap it and start over. Am I correct? So that's what we're going to do.

We're going to start over from, let's see, about twenty minutes ago. Is everyone cool with that?"

"Shanti," said Joaquin, "did I ever mention that I love you?"

"Oh, you're planning to take her, too, are you?" said Tad. "Believe me, you don't want the grief."

After a nanosecond of silence, even the interviewer laughed.

"But first I need a cigarette," I said. As I spoke, I remembered that I hadn't removed my own mic. I unclipped it from my turtleneck, trying not to wince too obviously.

Towards the end of the shoot, version 2.0, a girl from the marketing department walked onto the set and asked us to recreate our *U-Turn Day* jacket art. The cameras were still rolling. It was all part of the script. "Everyone's heard about it," the girl explained, feigning unawareness of the cameras behind her. "But hardly anyone's seen it, since the album is now, uh, a collector's item." Translation: we still didn't have the money for a second pressing. "So, uh… we thought this would be a good chance to show everyone what it actually looked like. If you've got a couple of minutes left?"

Of course we did.

Relaxed, joking, we got up and rearranged ourselves. Back in January, we'd been like kids on a dare. The boys had pretended to smooch each other, intentionally cracking Nina up. I'd mugged frantically, trying to look like somebody else. But now that breathless sense of taboo-busting was gone, replaced by weary tension. Tad hung his arm around my neck. He hadn't done that in the original picture, but no one said anything. The marketing girl presented Joaquin with a placard that resembled our original, except it was laserprinted, not hand-drawn on a piece of a cardboard box. A guy with a Nikon came and knelt in front of us. The cameramen kept filming. We sat still. *Flash.*

After the shoot we partied. Tad and I got home at one o'clock. While I wrestled with my sandals, he started up the stairs, but halted halfway up. He turned and slapped the banister. "I'm going back out."

"You're what?" I hopped on one foot. "We just said goodnight to them. They'll be going to bed."

"I didn't say I was going over to Joaquin's."

I lost my balance and sat down on the edge of the genkan. I was drunker than I'd thought. "Do you just want to get away from me or something?"

He sighed audibly. "No, Shanti, whatever gives you that idea?"

When I finally got my sandals off, he was no longer there. Faint guitar chords floated down the stairs.

"Fix your D string," I said, twining myself around the doorjamb. "It's flat."

The steel-stringed acoustic in his lap belonged to Gen. Tad was just playing random chords, but the curdled sound every time he plucked that D string set my ears on edge.

"Tad? That shit is flat."

He didn't look up.

"OK." I sat down on the edge of the bed. "So let me ask you. What the fuck were you thinking at the shoot? Did you think you were being *funny?*"

He ignored me.

"OK." I stood up again and took off all my clothes. Stark naked, I began to spin in circles. *This is Nigel swimming…* I did a dramatic crumple to the floor. *This is Ned swimming…* Tad's fingerpicking rhythmed my dizziness. I staggered upright and began to pirouette again, adding some arm movements, half dancing to whatever the hell he was playing. *This is Alastair swimming…*

"Shanti?" Tad cut the sounds and stood up, taking the guitar by its neck. "Go to bed."

"Only if you come with me."

He shook his head, not looking at me. "Got to go out."

I clumsily tried to throw my arms around him. He moved back so that I almost fell over. I said, "What the hell, Tad? What is your fucking problem? This afternoon you were all over me in front of everyone, and now—"

"Shanti—"

"Yes, Tad? *What?* Don't you want me? I'm here basically saying fuck me, I'm all yours, and I mean that, I'm all yours. You saved my life. You saved my life, and now you don't want me? What the fuck is that?"

Tad dropped the guitar with a discordant boom of strings. He took me by both arms and walked me backwards to the bed. I fell flat on my back, looking up at him. He looked down at me. "You want me to fuck you."

I pressed my lips together to keep from giggling.

He ripped his fly open and jerked his jeans and boxers down. "Say it," he demanded in English. "Fuck me, Tad. I want you. Go on. Say it."

I reclined at full length, tucked one hand behind my head, and reached out for him. He was already hard. Massaging him, I drawled flatly, "Fuck me. I want you. Your touch sends me to the heights of ecstasy."

His eyes kindled with the same light I'd seen during the shoot, the same light that had flickered on and off at various times during our afterparty, regardless of what was being said:. He slapped my hand away, and then he took hold of me and flipped me over bodily. I barely had time to get my elbows under me before he shoved my legs open and forced himself in from behind. I screeched and fought. It *hurt.* He pinned me down with the wiry strength of arms that had been playing bass and lugging heavy equipment for years.

This is a rape, I thought. I can survive a rape.

In what felt like a matter of seconds he thrust into me one last time and let his weight fall on me. I seized my chance to throw him off. Then I hit him. The impact of my fist on his shoulder startled me. I hit him again. He rolled on his back. I jumped on his chest, straddling him, and fastened my hands around his throat.

He wasn't struggling. He stared up at me, brown eyes wide with something that fell short of panic, more like acceptance.

I released his throat and covered my face with my hands. Then I tumbled off him, pulling in my limbs like a spider, curling into a fetal ball with my back to him.

Light came dull red through my eyelids. I could hear Tad breathing hoarsely, but otherwise I might have been floating in a medium other than air.

I've done a terrible thing, I remembered thinking, and now I'm going to drown.

After a few minutes I heard Tad get up and move around the room. A bump and an open echo of strings – he'd picked up Gen's guitar. Then the door opened. His footsteps receded down the stairs.

I lay there with my eyes closed, remembering. Alastair's brilliant strategy hadn't been quite without flaws. The Gardai had asked us particularly about the Land Rover. They even got us to draw it, putting in all the details we could remember. I drew arrows and explanatory bubbles for the interesting round holes in the doors where I used to post dead insects and scraps of paper covered with rhyming curses in mirror writing. I drew the rust holes in the floor and the broken left rear door latch that you had to hold shut on bends.

Alastair drew a detailed cutaway view of the engine, a cross-section, and a schematic of the chassis.

Ned drew a box on wheels with a sad-faced Nigel in the driver's seat.

The Gardai praised our drawings and took them away, and we never heard anything more about them. But years later, Alastair and I realized that the problem must have been the doors. When the frogmen found the Land Rover, they must have wondered why Nigel had opened two of the other doors, not his own door, and then stayed in the car to drown.

I guess they ultimately decided that the sea had poured into the Land Rover through its open windows, negating the pressure differential. That would have allowed the doors, with their faulty latches, to pop open when we hit the bottom. And that was right, to an extent. I saw the air going out. Alastair told me afterwards that I'd been unconscious, so I couldn't have seen it. But I *had* seen it, wobbling up and away like a swarm of jellyfish the size of dogs. I could see it now.

Twelve hours later, I lay on my stomach, examining my neck in the mirror propped on the nightstand. The afternoon sun gave me more light than I really wanted. Gusts of warm dusty wind blew across my back from the open window. I'd woken up and gone back to sleep several times, drifting in and out of nightmares. Now my phone said it was getting on for three o'clock.

Maybe I should just go back to sleep.

I heard Tad moving around downstairs, his brisk tread as familiar as his voice.

The scab on my neck, in its disgusting pit with the tightly curled rim, had come up at one edge. When I prodded it, imagining that it might be ready to come off altogether, pain spiked up into my temple and down into my shoulder. The imprints of Ned's teeth around the scab also hurt to the touch. Was it inflamed? Infected? The tenderness and sickly reddish-purple hue of the skin around the marks might just be bruising. I couldn't tell. All I could do was slather on some more antibiotic cream. But if it didn't start healing in earnest soon, I was going to take myself along to Omori Hospital, that dinky little for-profit facility where a grey-haired doctor had once prescribed me three different kinds of antibiotics for a cold. I could say it was a love bite.

I took a square of gauze out of the package and started cutting pieces off the new roll of surgical tape, sticking them on the side of my hand. My phone burred on Tad's desk. A Tokyo number. At any other time I would have let it go to voicemail. Now I answered, snappishly.

"Let me guess," said Alastair. "You're having a bad day."

I flew downstairs. "Tad? Tad!"

I burst into the kitchen and stopped. He must have heard my cry of delight. But he hadn't reacted. He was just sitting at the kitchen table with his head in his hands.

We took the train to Shinagawa. The familiar landmarks rattled past, every rooftop a peak on the graph of my impatience. "Why *not* tell

Joaquin?" I said. "He's been worried sick about Nina!"

"And it would be really gratuitous to bring them together in front of Alastair. Wouldn't it?"

"Oh. I guess so." I hugged myself. "He didn't say anything apart from she's there, too."

We emerged from Shinagawa station in front of the Wings shopping complex and hurried alongside the traffic of the No. 1 Keihin Expressway, passing by on the other side from the bicycle parking lot where we'd dumped our stolen machines on the night we killed Gavin Winters. Five minutes later we reached the Prince Hotel, a smoked glass crescent twenty storeys high. Ginkgos towered on the rotary in front of the concave lobby doors, where sycophants helped doddering old executives out of black Crown Lincolns. It wasn't the type of place I would have expected Alastair to stay.

I marched past the front desk. Sleekly suited business travellers and uniformed clerks bobbled out of my way like spacewalkers in a vacuum. The cavernous lobby opened out, bisected by a curving rail, on one side of which lay a sunken lounge area enclosed by a wall of windows that looked out on a garden with a fountain. I turned, thinking that I'd ask the desk clerks to call up to Alastair and Nina's room. Tad blocked my way. I would have grabbed him and begged him not to leave me, but in that instant I saw Alastair stand up in the far corner of the lounge.

I reached him in one superhuman leap. We hugged. He peeled me off and held his arms out to Tad. "Hey man, good to see you."

They embraced, Tad obviously stiff and unprepared for it.

"I can see you did a good job of looking after my sister. And by the way, congratulations! We saw your CD on sale in Bangkok."

"We – we're not distributed outside of Japan yet," I said, struggling to come down out of the stratosphere. After all that, it was just – Alastair. But not quite Alastair as I remembered him.

"He means the pirates were selling it on the sidewalk," said Nina, standing behind a round table with two little armchairs. She grinned with one rectangular chrome eye. "See, you can't escape the paparazzi! Come on, for the record now, say *natto* – "

Other guests looked on indulgently as Alastair rested his arm on my shoulders. He was rigid with tension.

Nina clicked the shutter. I hugged her. "Oh my God, you're so brown! Have you been lying on tropical beaches all this time?"

"It only goes halfway up my arms." She rolled back her t-shirt sleeve to show me. "Relaxing on the beach? I wish. We've been having hair-raising adventures… but I should let Alastair tell you."

She wore a long Indian skirt and Alastair was in shorts. Cheap leather sandals completed the hippie look that I would never have expected my brother to sport unless someone took his credit cards away.

"But Shanti, you're so skinny!" Nina squealed.

"I'm just the same as ever," I protested.

"Oh, bullshit. You're a total waif. Look at you."

But I was less interested in looking at myself than in looking at Alastair. His eyes glowed amber in his tanned face. He was as brown as Nina, as brown as Tad, and the little smile on his mouth jolted me back to the very beginning of my memories. He used to smile like that when he was six or seven, before he developed the art of giving the impression that he was utterly sure of himself. A disarmingly shy little smirk, it said *please don't be mad at me.*

He lifted his eyebrows with his usual smile, challenging my stare. "I want you to get ready for a surprise."

"Alastair, I've just had a surprise. I've had the biggest surprise of my life. You vanished and I never heard a word from you. I thought you'd been killed! Didn't you get any of my emails?"

Then and there, his unhappy wince decided me: I would never tell him how close I'd come in the past day or so to believing Ned's alternate theory of his desertion.

"But you're here, you're alive and well, and you… how dare you just breeze in like you've only been away for a few days! I'm just so happy to see you." I sat down in the nearer of the blue leather armchairs and pushed the heels of my hands into my eyes.

"Oh Alastair, I told you so!" Nina sank to her knees beside me. She smelt of cinnamon and fatigue. I resisted her attempt to pry my hands away from my face. "I wanted to email you and tell you we were on our way back, but he wanted to surprise you."

"I just didn't know what to think," I said wretchedly. And I didn't know what to say now, or how much I could say, even if we hadn't been surrounded by dozens of strangers. I didn't know how much Nina had learnt about Alastair's mission. What had happened on Koh Samui? Or had they genuinely never made it there? Where could I start asking questions? And when could I tell Alastair that Ned was dead? Not in front of Nina. No matter how close they were, I didn't believe he'd shared the whole sordid story with her. Although how could he have kept it from her? I still didn't know how he'd kept it from Maisie.

"It was really dramatic, actually," Nina hissed. Her tone told me that Alastair was no longer listening. I took my hands from my eyes. Sure enough, he and Tad had moved away. They stood by the convex wall of windows, at the point farthest away from the grouped tables and chairs. Alastair stared out of the window as if the play of the fountain amidst the greenery fascinated him. They looked spookily alike, utterly indifferent to their plush surroundings. I'd never noticed before that they held their bodies in the same way, with a minimum of superfluous movement.

"I'm getting a bad feeling here," I said aloud. "What's the deal with this *surprise?*"

"Well, that's part of it. I mean, that's why we went north. Or part of why we went north. And that's why we got into trouble… but there's no lasting damage!"

That was an understatement. I'd rarely seen her so radiant. Her eyes fairly glittered. "Share, Nina," I said.

"I should let Alastair tell you," she protested. Then she said, "W-w-well, the first thing that happened, no, it was more like the seventeenth, was that we got taken prisoner by these… they were *tomb raiders.*" She laughed. Her mouth wobbled. I saw to my horror that she was about to burst into tears. I jumped up and put my arms around her. "I don't know what's wrong with me," she said, wiping her eyes. "We're fine. Your brother was amazing. Oh God, I'm sorry."

"I'm so glad you're OK." I rocked her. "I'm so glad to have you both back." My voice shook, too.

"We can't both break down!" Pulling back, she composed her face into an expression of absurd firmness.

"No, I guess we can't." After an instant, I started laughing. "Tomb raiders?"

"Yeah. But I don't want to talk about it. I mean, they didn't *do* anything to us… And that's not representative. I mean, the issue is not that a few antiques are getting ripped off. We were up in the hills in Chiang Rai province. They don't even have electricity in most of the villages. Or running water, or toilets. And the roads shouldn't be dignified with the name. It's seriously medieval. Can I just tell you, Shanti? You haven't lived until you've spent the night in a four-wheel-drive after you slid into a gully, and then woken up with local villagers banging on the window, offering to give you a tow… with their water buffaloes. They're so unbelievably kind, and they're so poor… and the Thai army is against them, and the DEA and the CIA are against them, and basically everyone's against them…"

"Sounds like it was a pretty crazy trip," I said.

"Yeah, well, you see poverty on TV, so you think you know what it's like… but then you come face to face with it yourself, and you realize, Jesus H. Christ. These people are just… the land is all they've got. And the fucking multinationals are trying to take that away from them, too."

"I can imagine," I said, although I couldn't. Malcolm's suburb of

Phuket was the poorest place I'd ever been, and everyone there had shoes and enough to eat, and there was neon on the bar fronts, and yeah, sure, there were multinationals. "But what about the tomb raiders?"

"Don't make me talk about it. Please. It wasn't *bad,* OK?"

I got the picture. She'd had a traumatic experience that she was blocking out with all this stuff about the Hmong or whoever. But why had they gone up to the hills in the first place? Something to do with Alastair's *surprise.* Something that was worth letting me think they were dead?

If it turned out that they'd been looking for Ned all this time, I really was going to cry.

"Actually, Shanti…" Nina sneaked a glance towards the wall of windows. I followed her gaze, and an alarm pinged in my brain. Alastair and Tad stood too far apart, and Alastair's pose was elaborately casual.

"I was going to ask you how Joaquin's doing," Nina whispered.

"He's good," I said, struggling with the change of subject.

"But… you know. How he's doing? I mean, I know the deal with Apex fell through…"

"Yeah. But we got a supporting gig..." I told her about The From A Great Tour.

"Wow! I'm so happy for you guys. But is Joaquin…"

I grimaced. "Well, he's living with Chiharu in his new studio. It's a total dump, but what can you expect for a hundred thousand a month?"

"Well, that's great." Nina slurped down the dregs of the tall glass of juice on the table. "I'm… I'm happy for him."

"But what about you?" I wiggled my eyebrows. "I mean, what about you and Alastair?"

"I don't know," Nina said to my astonishment. "As you know, Shanti, your brother is an absolutely lovely guy. And he was just amazing when we were… well. Basically, we've been through this incredibly intense experience together, and I'm always going to be grateful to him for taking me up there. But who knows what the future holds?"

I fumbled for a cigarette and lit it. Oh, poor Alastair!

Simultaneously I thought: He can't have told her, then. She wouldn't say he was *an absolutely lovely guy* if she knew he was a murderer.

"You're still puffing away on those things," she said. "If you'd seen the Akha children on the streets of Mae Sai, smoking the butts of cigarettes that they…" Her voice trailed off. Her gaze shot over my shoulder. I twisted around in my chair.

Two people were approaching us: a stringy white man in his sixties, wearing a panama hat with a khaki jacket and shorts, and a petite Asian woman of about my age. She wore a pleated pink skirt, white jacket with big gold buttons, and black high heels. Everything about them screamed *not from Tokyo.* Maybe because Nina had mentioned the CIA and the DEA, I thought of international law enforcement agencies and how they would probably pounce on you out of a blue sky.

"Can't sit around upstairs all day," the man said forcefully. "Brought plenty of work with me, but Ao—" that was what it sounded like to me, Ao— "wants to be up and doing. Rang our people in Kawasaki; we can go over there at any time. Got to visit the world-famous Ginza, as well, don't we? But tell me, Nina, who is this young lady? Someone I ought to know?"

"Uh," said Nina. "Uh, yeah, well, actually…"

Alastair skidded past her. "Oh Jesus," he said. "For chrissakes, Malcolm, you've spoiled my surprise. I told you I was going to bring her up."

So! Does anyone feel like eating?" said Nina desperately. "I went ahead and made reservations, Malcolm, while we were waiting for Shanti and Tad. If you don't mind Japanese food?"

"Of course not," said Malcolm with one of his unpleasant secretive smiles, as if he knew in advance that we wouldn't get the joke. "I'm certainly prepared to try it. Can't be worse than whatever foul imitation of Western food they generally cook up for people like us."

I could hear his Scottish accent now, although it had worn very thin.

"It's that place we went a couple of times after gigs at Voxpit," Nina muttered to me. "With the flaming cocktails."

No one should have to cope with their brother *and* their father coming back from the dead in one afternoon. I knew now where Alastair had been all these weeks… but that just raised a bigger question: where had Malcolm been all these years? The last we'd heard of him, he'd been ashes in our hands, gritty and slightly greasy. No one had said anything yet that touched on this point.

"So we go to eat sushi," said the woman called Ao, crisply. "I must get my purse. Give me the keys. Wait."

"Of course, darling. No one would dare move a step without you," said Malcolm, dropping the keycard into her palm.

Darling? Well, I'd guessed as much. But there was something else I had to know. I edged up to Alastair. "It's driving me crazy, but I can't tell," I whispered in French. "Is she the same one? She's not, is she? I can't remember what she looked like, but I think she'd be older, and I'm pretty sure she had a Western name—"

"Sandy. That's what she used to be called, but that was just her nickname, her professional name or whatever. Yes, she's the same one. I can't believe you don't recognize her. She's gone back to her real name. And I hope you spotted the wedding ring."

"What?"

"It was a village ceremony."

I bit off my next question as Sandy / Ao returned, lugging a capacious tote bag.

Outside, sunset sheeted through the ginkgos like a break in a pipeline of Fanta. Now that I knew who Ao was, I couldn't take my eyes off her. Thirty-five? Forty? There were no deep lines around her eyes, even when she squinted into the sunset. She couldn't be more than ten years older than me at the most. And that was extremely odd, because when I was thirteen, she'd been a fragrant and graceful adult, a contemporary of June's with flashier makeup and higher heels... or so I'd thought. But maybe she'd just been a teenager playing pretend for the benefit of her much older boyfriend. And his first family.

She struck me now as a woman who might have enjoyed making life unbearable for poor June in Phuket. But the funny thing was that I remembered her, in the fragmented way I did remember her, as warm and playful.

"Are you aware of the per capita fossil fuel consumption of Japan?" Malcolm had latched onto Tad. "You're living beyond your means. Living on the resources of other nations, which you buy with paper credits that represent the American military threat. Oh, I know it's hard to grasp the actual nature of the forces involved when you live in the heart of *civilization.*" He laughed; it was Alastair's barking laugh, the echo absolutely eerie. "It's the carbon monoxide in the air. Puts you into a complete bloody stupor."

Maybe all that had happened to Ao was sixteen years of Malcolm.

We were among the first customers to arrive at the restaurant. Over the table in our booth, a dim tasselled lamp hung low enough for Malcolm and Alastair to bump their heads. The menu featured burgers and pizza as well as sushi. Malcolm laughed, underlined something with his finger, and commented to Ao in a language that must have been Thai. That's what I remembered them speaking together, and when we arrived in Phuket I'd been all set to throw myself into it, diving into a toppling wave of new grammar and new friends, until it turned out that Alastair and I weren't going to start school or anything else. We'd escaped. To nowhere.

"No, you're quite right. My wife and I speak the Akha language," Malcolm told Tad, who he'd kept on his left, apparently finding him easy to talk to. As for me, his long-lost daughter? I didn't even get an including glance. "She is an Akha. Born in Burma that was; driven across the border by the junta; resettled in Thailand. Now subject to Western cultural and economic imperialism, along with the other hill tribes. Genocide, in other words."

"Our language is Sino-Tibetan," said Ao. "But we are not Chinese. Not Tibetan. Not Thai."

"That's funny," I said. "I always thought you were Thai."

"We are Akha. I have pictures. You look, very interesting." She started to dig in her bag.

Malcolm smacked her on the head. "For God's sake let them have a drink first. Yes, have you any decent single malts? I'm afraid I like to do myself proud when someone else is paying."

"I excuse?" said the waiter nervously.

Tad and I ordered for everyone. As the waiter departed, I caught Malcolm stealing a look at me. He immediately turned to Ao and delivered a remark that made her laugh. Did it amuse him to hear me speaking Japanese? No more than it amused me to hear him speaking Akha. Although I'd always assumed Alastair and I got our knack for languages from June, it now seemed as if we might have got it from Malcolm. What else had we got from him? I stared at the hooked nose, deeply set colorless eyes, and incessantly moving mouth. The ears were pink cabbage leaves. The hair that had once been the same color as Alastair's, falling in poetic curls to his shoulders, was now a grey crop. Yet I could see that my brother was this man's son.

"The greatest threat to the Akha way of life at the moment is foreign missionaries. The hills are lousy with them. New concrete compounds, new concrete orphanages, fleets of new trucks. Bloody empire-builders!"

Malcolm broke off for the obligatory toast, then picked up where he'd left off.

"They're in league with Big Timber and Big Agro. Shift the tribespeople off the land, rape the land, repeat. It's going on all over the border provinces as we speak, and needless to say, the elite in Bangkok are laughing all the way to the bank. Only awkward bit is, what do you do with the people after you've shifted them? What would you do with them?" he asked Tad. "Old people, young people, kids. *Lots* of kids. Average six per family."

Tad frowned. I wondered if Malcolm's colorful phrasing was too much for him. "I don't know what should do with them," he said awkwardly at last. "This is modern world, have no place for such people."

"Aha! Very good! You ought to be in government, lad. Unfortunately you can't just gun them down and bury them in trenches. Well, it's been known to happen in Cambodia, and it still happens across the border in Myanmar, but it tends to put a damper on foreign investment. So first you let the Taiwanese recruiters in. Cream off the young men. Then you let the missionaries have at the remainder. Convert the elders, use them to control the villages. Sterilize the women. Take the kids away from their parents, put them in orphanages. Use them to attract donations from bleeding hearts back in the States. Child farming."

"But what happens to such children when they leave orphanages?" Ao broke in. "This very interesting."

She dug a photo album out of her bag. We moved our plates and glasses to make room for it. The first pages showed photographs of bamboo huts on stilts, children swarming around women in colorful headdresses, terraced hillsides. Nina murmured to me, "This is the area where Malcolm and Ao live. We visited most of these villages."

"And many more," said Alastair. "If you like these, just ask Nina to show you her pictures. No picturesque village or scenic view escaped her."

"I have other pictures, too. I show these for comparison," Ao said. "It is traditional village life. Now we see orphanages." She flipped the page. Concrete bungalows stood in empty fields; signage ran to gilt and sanctimony; children rode bicycles and played in sandboxes. "I like to photograph missionaries with children. But they say they sue us." Children pressing their faces to wire fences, clutching the bars of gates. "Many children run away." Street scenes: tangles of wires overhead, a rickshaw crossing in front of a truck. The bottom halves of children sticking out of dumpsters. Children curled up asleep on the dirty ground. "But runaway children are mostly boys. Girls stay in orphanages. Until they are too old. Then where can they go?"

Ao turned the page again. Girls playing cards at a low table, girls lounging on drab sofas. Two whole pages of mugshots of girls with outdated hairstyles and pale faces. An eight-by-twelve of three more girls, these not "too old" by anyone's standards, barely more than children in miniskirts and frilly blouses, hanging on each other's shoulders like girlfriends out for a night on the town. "They become prostitutes," Ao said. "Go to Chiang Mai. Lucky ones go south to Bangkok, to tourist resorts. Then get AIDS, drug addiction, illegitimate baby, then die. But they are baptized in orphanages, so it is OK!"

She touched the eight-by-twelve. The gold ring on her finger flashed in the light.

"This is one very young prostitute. She stole money and went to Phuket. She had many nice friends. Also a pimp, not so nice. Friends now dead. Pimp, too. He is drug addict."

Even before I took a second look at the photograph, I knew what was coming next.

"This prostitute is me."

I captured a spring roll with my chopsticks and chewed it fiercely.

Tad exclaimed on cue, "No way! Ao-san, how did you survive?"

"I was saved. Not by Jesus. By man. This one."

"Little did I know what I was letting myself in for," said Malcolm. "Never trust a muse, lad. They're protean."

I twitched the album towards me and indicated the other two girls in the photograph. "Were these your friends?"

Ao looked reluctant. "She is my friend. Dead now, yes. And she is my cousin. We ran away together. For a long time we were together."

"And then what happened?"

"She went with a bad man."

The rest of our food arrived: a big platter of sushi and another of sashimi banked on shredded daikon, decorated with bamboo leaves and marigolds. We went through the ritual of pouring the soy sauce into the little saucers and mixing wasabi into it. Malcolm said, "That's more like it. Makes a change from sa pi tau, wouldn't you say, kids?"

Alastair and Nina laughed and nodded. "Sa pi tau is this spicy dish they eat in the villages," explained Nina. "Kind of like kimchi. It gave me awful stomach cramps, but they always want you to eat with them..."

"Yes," said Ao, clapping her hands, smiling satirically. "Eat, eat!"

When we'd made a collective dent in the sushi and sashimi, she got a second photo album out of her bag and laid her hand on its cover.

"I expect you're wondering at this point whether the Akha have any future as a people." Malcolm turned sideways to address Tad directly. "Well, the plot thickens."

Restored somewhat by the first food I'd eaten all day, I had the strength to view the situation with more detachment. Wasn't it odd, from this perspective, that instead of questioning Tad about his country, Malcolm was lecturing him about the country he'd just come from? Shouldn't it have been the other way round? Or to put it another way, if Malcolm had no interest in Japan, and no discernible interest in *me,* what had Alastair brought him here for?

"In the last few years, the Thai government has undertaken a massive opium eradication effort. Or that's the story, but follow the money and it all looks rather different. The campaign is funded by the DEA, and the picture is complicated by the CIA, which has killed and will kill again to protect its assets in the region. Meanwhile, the sharp end of the operation is the Thai army. Their orders are to wipe out poppy cultivation in the hills. From one point of view, it's just relocation by any other name, but the knock-on effects are catastrophic. At one stroke the Akha lose their land, they are criminalized for their use of opium, and they become vulnerable to far more serious addictions."

"You sound like you think the war on drugs is a bad idea," I said.

"My people smoke opium as traditional medicine, not drug," said Ao. "I have pic—"

"*Good* idea," said Malcolm. "But the implementation? Bloody disastrous. Which is why the Akha urgently need help. If the campaign continues unabated, they'll end up as collateral damage, every last man, woman, and child. Unfortunately, the response from the wider world is largely what you'd expect. Another indigenous people bites the dust? Pass the popcorn! The only organizations that have attracted substantial non-governmental funding to the area are the missions, and they're as likely to destroy the Akha as the army and the CIA combined."

"In my personal, unexpert opinion," said Alastair, "the worst they do is set an example of conspicuous consumption." He raised his eyebrows at Malcolm's whiskey.

Completely undaunted, Malcolm hoisted his glass with an evil smile. "Down the hatch! Give me time and I'll drink the rest of your bloody BMW and your objets d'art; although if you make the mistake of accompanying my wife to the Ginza, it'll be gone a lot faster."

"Well, why don't you show them the Institute? I expect the suspense is killing them," said Alastair, pouring himself more wine.

"Righty-ho!" Malcolm turned to Tad again. "Now lad, given all that I've told you, would you say there is any hope for the Akha?"

Tad chiseled his cigarette on the ashtray, stalling. At last he said, "Often it is not guilty who die. It's innocent. I think maybe what's important for them, it's their pride."

"Exactly," Nina exclaimed. "They feel very strongly about keeping their pride and dignity."

The two words were synonymous for her, I thought.

"Ye-es," said Malcolm. "And therefore what they need is a voice. When I first moved to Chiang Rai, fourteen years ago, I immediately saw that one of the main obstacles facing the Akha was that no one understands them. Few of them speak Thai. Almost none speak English."

Fourteen years ago. That must have been right after the letter from Sandy / Ao arrived at Uncle Red's house in Philadelphia. Such a weird letter, we'd all thought. Factual, almost dispassionate. We'd put it down to her being Thai.

"It may surprise you to learn that there are laws, even in Thailand. And there's the UN, for what it's worth. But for the legal system to do the Akha any good, they need advocacy. And on a daily basis, they need to be able to stand up to the missionaries, to resist unfair treatment by the police, to receive adequate health care. That's the work of the Institute for Truth and Justice."

Ao opened her second photo album. The first page bore a picture of a wooden sign: *Institute for Truth and Justice,* with the same thing in Thai, presumably, below. On the next page, a muddy Toyota pickup was parked outside a dilapidated bungalow.

"Home sweet home," said Malcolm. I half expected him to say *Next!* like a speaker ordering up PowerPoint slides. But Ao didn't need cues. "Our staff. Our office. Our mascot." A golden labrador puppy. "Some of our successes." Pages of photographed typewritten documents." But I would be lying if I said the bulk of our work was clerical. You're as likely to find us helping to build a house - transporting seedlings - digging irrigation ditches - thwarting marauding missionaries - coming bloody close to giving this backwoods Führer a punch in the gob!" The photograph showed Malcolm confronting a group of Thai soldiers outside a barbed wire gate. "We try to be where we are needed," Malcolm said. "It's a pity that we can't each be in a dozen places at once. But we are all the Akha have."

The album ended with a heartwarming shot of Malcolm and Ao in the midst of what looked like an entire village, children on their knees, a toddler chasing the labrador puppy in the foreground.

"So there you have it," said Alastair, draining his wine.

"Wow," I said, as I more or less had to. "You're saints."

"I think it is very good work you do," Tad said, staring into his glass.

"I'm delighted to hear you say that. It's a struggle to get our message out, but we are optimistic about the possibility of gaining wider support. You saw…" Malcolm touched the photo albums. They had cheap white plastic covers that said *Precious Memories* in gold lettering, like the signs in front of the orphanages. "The Akha have such appeal."

"Yeah, they do," I said.

There was a brief, strained silence.

"It happened for the Tibetans," said Malcolm. "They became trendy, and all at once everyone cared."

Suddenly, he looked defeated.

I said hastily, "You know, this place does these great flaming cocktails…"

"Let's go back by taxi," shouted Alastair. "You're going to love this, Malcolm: the doors of the cabs open and shut by themselves! A flagrant waste of nonsustainably generated energy!"

"It's only a ten-minute walk," I said.

"You can walk if you like. I'm a cultural and economic imperialist and I choose to savor my privileges."

"Where's your fucking stretch limo, then, lad?" sneered Malcolm.

We crossed the street and joined the line at the taxi rank in front of Shinagawa station. Tad sidled up to Alastair, who looked black for a moment, then shrugged. Tad came back to me and said in Japanese, "I'm going to head home."

I clutched his arm. "Please hang out a bit longer. I need moral support."

"You've got Alastair."

"I need you."

"You'll be OK."

Our eyes met. He plucked his sunglasses off the top of his head, settled them on his nose, and vanished into the throng as if he'd slipped through a chink in a wall.

In the back of the taxi, Ao cuddled up to me and squeezed my hand. "You drink very much. It's nice. In Lo Mai Akha we all drink very much. You come stay with me, we have fun!"

Ao was a lot different when she was having fun. She was the Sandy I remembered, melting my resistance with playful hugs and confusing me with utterances that couldn't, I felt, be taken at face value.

"We go sometimes to Mae Sai, but I don't like to go with your father there. He see bad man in bar, he fight." She curled my fist and made me punch air. "Pah, pah! He love fight."

"That's why they call it activism," said Alastair.

"Behind every man who stands up for the poor and downtrodden," said Malcolm, "is a woman who can't keep her bloody mouth shut."

Ao uncurled my hand and turned its palm to catch the multicolored lights whisking past outside the window. "Oh, look. Is very much change since we meet before."

I stiffened. Ao giggled.

"Before, head and heart don't touch. Now joining. This means you have passion for your work. Here, look. Nice and strong. But this heart line not so good. I don't often see like this. Breaking, breaking, breaking! Here and here and here! What happen?"

"But you used to be a poet," I said. "You published a book."

Malcolm and I were sitting on high stools in the bar and grill on the second floor of the Prince Hotel. In front of us were glasses of an expensive cognac that he'd induced me to try. Everything around us was made of tropical wood: teak, walnut, mahogany. The bartender performed with the cocktail shaker. The elegant women next to me smoked clove cigarettes. They probably couldn't tell that Malcolm and I were related. We didn't even speak with the same accent.

"I was never a poet," Malcolm said at last. "I had a way with words. But poetry was just… it was an obstacle that occupied the center of my life for many years. Have you read Nietzsche? Understanding is an obstacle to action. And I would add with the wisdom of hindsight that true understanding can only be achieved *through* action."

"You still have a way with words," I said, sucking up. *Did I get it from you?* But my lyrics weren't poetry. If they sounded profound, it was only because of the music.

"Oh, you mean my advocacy? Words are tools. They are useful insofar as they produce effects. That was a very belated epiphany for me."

I lit a cigarette. My better judgement told me to hold off, at least until I'd heard Alastair's side of the story. But I'd learned that Malcolm and Ao would be going back to Thailand in four days. And they'd revealed plans to spend those days in meetings with Japanese NGOs and other Akha sympathizers. This might be my only chance. Before I'd quite made up my mind, I heard myself saying, "Well, that letter of yours certainly produced effects. *I am sorry but Malcolm is dead.*" In my mind I heard the silence. The twinkling copper pots that hung over the counter were the loudest thing in the kitchen. Then a burglar alarm started up out on the street, and Katie, our cute little cousin, shrieked a perfect fifth below the burglar alarm. She sat down gracefully on the floor and started to bawl. Phoebe went to her. *They need to take that goddamn Volvo into the shop it goes off every time someone looks at it,* and I just stood there. *Shall I read you the rest?* June sounded like she was trying not to laugh, and Alastair just stood there.

"I come home and he hanging from ceiling by belt on his neck." I carried on quoting from memory. *"I sell house and go back to my village this week. If I can, I buy sutra and Buddha will care for his soul when he go up to Heaven with peace. He leave note, say goodbye, now I send it to you.* It was inside the box, on top of your ashes. *I have failed all of those whom I held dear to me. I leave nothing behind me but footprints along the ephemeral sand by the sea of my world. Now the tide is approaching, my dear, and I find that I'd rather be swallowed by flame than by brine."*

"It was a joke!" Malcolm's voice was too loud. Under my startled stare, he regained his composure. "Used to be a man in Chiang Mai who would recite 'The Love Song of J. Alfred Prufrock' for ten baht. 'The Wasteland' would run you twenty. Shakespeare sonnets for three; those were his bread and butter. Tourists would pay him to recite to their girlfriends. *How do I love thee? Let me count the ways…"*

"I can do you Yeats for free," I said. "I grew up in Ireland, remember? We had to memorize him at school. *Things fall apart; the center cannot hold; mere anarchy is loosed upon the world. The blood-dimmed tide is loosed* – "

"Melodramatic fluff."

"Not as melodramatic as a fake suicide note." My pulse throbbed in my neck. "Did you write it? Or did Ao?"

"Excuse me!" Malcolm called, hoisting his upper body across the bartop. "The same again." While the bartender poured the cognac, I lit another cigarette off my first. Malcolm accepted his refreshed drink and inhaled its fumes. "It was a joke," he repeated. "Surely you never assumed… The whole bloody thing is in anapestic tetrameter."

"In what?"

"Behold," Malcolm addressed the bartender, "my daughter, a product of the American – the Irish education system! Anapestic tetrameter. It was a practical joke."

After a beat, I started laughing helplessly. Malcolm misunderstood why, or chose to misunderstand why, and laughed with me. I felt contempt for him, deeper than any contempt he could feel for me, because I knew a better joke than any he could imagine. "That's something else you have in common with Alastair," I gasped. "He used to be addicted to practical jokes."

Malcolm pretended to find that funny, too, even though he couldn't, because I hadn't shared the punchline: Alastair's biggest practical joke had *also* ended with a "suicide."

"Of course, it was necessarily a once-off." Malcolm resettled himself to face me, giving an impression of honesty. "With that letter I killed off the poet I had been, or rather the man who had thought he was a poet. The joke, of course, is that the letter itself was probably the only real poem I ever wrote. Does the irony seem rather labored? You must remember that I am a product of the sixties."

"June is a product of the sixties, too."

"In an altogether different sense. Americans are so literal-minded."

Teenagers are literal-minded, too, I thought. Especially teenagers like Alastair and I were. We were very self-centered, which also goes with the territory, and we thought our father's suicide was cosmic payback.

At that memory dread slithered through me. If Malcolm's death had been our cosmic payback for Nigel – and now Malcolm wasn't dead – that meant… Our payback was still to come, like a Land Rover chugging inexorably over the ridges and across the rocky plains of the world's sea floor.

"After that, we upped sticks and moved to Lo Mai Akha. I should mention that the catalyst for this scheme was not, as you may think, my midlife crisis. It was Ao's - midlife crisis, if you will. She had reestablished contact with her surviving relatives. We'd made a visit, bearing gifts, and the conditions had appalled us. Her people had been swindled out of their land - that story which was to become so familiar to us. They were living in shacks on a hillside ruined by logging and erosion, for which they were blamed. The only building worthy of the name was a brand-new church. It wasn't long before our horror turned to outrage, and outrage turned to determination… and the Institute For Truth And Justice was born."

Malcolm's oratorial style made my teeth hurt. But more than that, wasn't the explanation a bit gratuitous? It gave me the same twang at the back of the brain that I'd got when I first heard the name of the Institute.

Malcolm's suicide note had arrived in the middle of our first winter in Philadelphia. So Ao's "midlife crisis" had to have erupted within months of our visit to Phuket.

At the time, Alastair and I had thought we were just fine. We'd even congratulated ourselves on executing a flawless getaway to sunny Thailand (conveniently ignoring that it had been June's idea). But the combination of boredom, nervous fantasies of pursuit, and uncertainty about the future told on us. We were soon plotting and scheming again. We spent our days out on the beach, striking up friendships with holidaymakers, Thai kids who spoke a few words of English, and the staff at the hotel where Malcolm worked. They would take us out on the scuba tour boats, and we would watch the divers go over the side, happy to know they would find nothing down there. The hotel manager's wife took me to a temple and showed me how to pray to the gold statue of Buddha. But in my heart, I was praying to the god of secrecy: "Protect me!"

That god, or something, protected us out on the beach. The worst that ever happened to us out there was sunburn. But at home in Malcolm's tumbledown concrete bungalow, it was another story. All three adults, or all two adults and one teenage ex-prostitute, must have realized that we were far from fine. June lied for us that we missed our friends, and Sandy / Ao read our palms and said that we would both be rich and successful, but her face said something else, and late one night Malcolm confronted us.

We'd felt safe because the walls were concrete, but we hadn't realized that our voices carried around the *outside* of the bungalow, through the salty breeze and the exhaust fumes and the mosquitoes that filled the tropical night - although we regularly heard shrieks from the bar down the road, which travelled as clearly as motorbike engines revving.

When Malcolm had gone, I crossed my arms over my head, sheltering my wet face. He'd reduced me to tears. The night smelled of the frangipani that grew outside the window. Alastair sat on the edge of his bed. One of those big heavy moths flapped near me - they infested the bungalow after dark. I hit out at it. Alastair shook his head at me. "Fear not. I don't think he'll tell anyone."

"He'll tell June."

"Especially not her."

But maybe he'd been telling the whole world, in his own way, ever since. There are denunciations and denunciations.

"Come." Malcolm had finished his cognac. He levered himself off his bar stool. "I'm starting to feel the weight of civilization. Let's get some fresh air."

The garden extended up the hill behind the hotel, landscaped with Zen rocks and solitary trees, studded with benches where VIPs could huddle for off-the-record conferences. It was quite cold. We walked round and round, through the musty scent of greenery, while Malcolm filled me in on the history of the Institute for Truth and Justice. I only had to put in the occasional "Uh huh" or "Wow." At first, I waited on tenterhooks for him to get onto the subject of our family, but I gradually realized that wasn't going to happen. My thoughts began to run out of synch with his monologue. While he roamed the streets of Chiang Mai looking for runaway children, I plodded the familiar route from Makuhari Messe station to the abandoned golf course.

"The things that we take for granted," he said as we descended a flight of stone steps frilled with delicate plants. "The obscene callousness of the privileged. The flight into *entertainment…*"

I burst out, "Well, of course I'd like to help if there was anything I could do! I think everyone feels the same, but…"

"But there is!"

Suddenly, I had his full attention. It was that easy.

"I said the same to your young friend. Hard to tell with the Japs, isn't it? But he seemed quite enthusiastic. Wish he hadn't buggered off…" Malcolm glanced into the dark, as if he expected to spot Tad amidst the foliage. "But I'm sure I'll have further opportunities to… You must introduce me to the rest of your group, too."

"But I don't really understand," I said cunningly. I was thinking in terms of a donation to the Institute, thinking in the back of my mind that this might be the only way I could make him happy, but I wanted to know what he would consider a decent sum before I made an offer. "What are your needs, specifically?"

"Er… well… I thought we would all discuss that together. Come up with a plan of action."

I said firmly, "I'm not sure I can involve the rest of my band. Even Tad… I can't put them in a position where they'd have to…"

Malcolm gave a sharp laugh. "I'm afraid you may have misunderstood me." We were walking along the paved path that wound back towards the hotel. Malcolm groped in the air with both hands, as if the night had grown darker, rather than brighter, as we neared the cliff of glass beyond the fountain. "I'm not asking you to contribute monetarily to the Institute. What I had in mind was rather… something that only you could do. Rock groups have such power for good or evil. Think of the Tibetans. The name of the group escapes me— "

"The Beastie Boys," I said heavily.

"That's right. They didn't give away their fortunes. They simply publicized their support for the Tibetan cause. Hung banners on stage at their performances, had themselves photographed with the Dalai Lama, that sort of thing. And I saw a film clip at one point. They had monks performing with them at one of those festivals. Not to my taste, but it made the world sit up, didn't it? And look at the exposure the Tibetans have gained since! Look at the grassroots support! All set in motion by publicity." Malcolm stopped and faced me, a hack politician's move. His smile was grotesquely self-conscious. "I may be an old fogey, but I know how the world works nowadays!"

I pictured Gorot performing in front of banners that said *Save the Akha;* Gen with *Akha Rights* painted on his Ibanez; me singing about truth and justice instead of blood, guts, and heartbreak. I walked the rest of the way to the fountain and braced my knees against its marble rim, which was tightly curled over like the rim of the scab on my neck. A quartet of dry nozzles poked from the center of the dark pool. I could see the small faces of Akha children down there in the water, their eyes closed as if they were asleep. But more vividly, I could see Nigel and Gavin and Ned. And then I saw Malcolm, his sallow reflection beside my own like a wizened gibbous moon.

"You know, you really ought to have a website," I said. "It would be a great way to get your message out. We could definitely put a link on our site…"

"Yes. That's what your young friend suggested." Malcolm dug in his pocket and threw a coin into the water: heads, tails, heads, tails, plop.

I pretended to leave the hotel, waited until Malcolm must have gone upstairs, and then went upstairs myself. I knocked softly on the door of Alastair and Nina's room. Cream and gilt and no peephole. Does anyone really think that just because you're in a hotel, you're safe?

Nina peered out at me, hair tousled, eyes swollen.

"Sorry," I winced. "Is Alastair…"

"Oh, *he* wasn't asleep."

I followed her into the room, where she immediately flopped down on the bed and pulled the quilt up around her ears. Alastair was sprawled in the only armchair, watching TV with the sound off and the English captions on. He tilted a tired smile at me. "So how'd it go with the paterfamilias?"

I shrugged. "I could use a coffee."

Alastair flipped the TV off and stuck his feet into his sandals.

Down in the lounge, the wall of windows had turned into a vast dark mirror. We ordered cappuccinos from a bow-tied waiter. The place had pretty much emptied out: only a few groups of exhausted tourists slouched around the little tables. I sank back into my chair and lit a cigarette. Through the smoke, I watched Alastair pulling himself together, erasing the traces of weariness from his face and posture. He scrutinized me in turn, his gaze lingering, I thought, on the area of turtleneck that encased the left side of my neck.

I broke the silence. "Tomb raiders?"

"Nicest guys in the world, once you establish a rapport with them. Unfortunately, that took a while. I'm sorry you were worried. What about you? Are you OK?"

"Yeah, I'm fine."

"That's good to hear."

"Yeah, I'm absolutely fine. I have a stepmother who's young enough to be my sister. I have a father who's supposed to be dead. And can you guess what he said when I asked him, so what the hell, because you were supposed to have been cremated fifteen years ago in Phuket? I wonder if it was the same thing he said to you? He said it was a joke."

Alastair's eyes widened.

"Yeah, and I was like, yeah, oh now I get it. Oh, I see, faking your own suicide, oh that's really funny. Har-de-har."

Alastair's face turned red and his eyes watered. His shoulders trembled. I let myself laugh with him.

Our cappuccinos arrived in minuscule cups.

"Well, I've had longer to work on him." Alastair tonged up sugar cubes. "At first he wouldn't tell me a damn thing. But eventually he confessed that it was more or less… yeah. He decided that was the only way he could make sure he'd never have to see us again. Phuket hadn't been far enough away, so he went further. In every sense."

Again I smelled the frangipani and felt panic overtake me as the door opened. Maybe I shouldn't be so quick to mock Malcolm. "And we sprinkled his ashes in the river," I said.

"The ashes of a bonfire and a few bits of chicken bone. And he's been hiding out ever since. Keeping off the radar. That Institute of his doesn't even have an internet connection. Come on, Shanti, it *is* pretty funny."

"I'll tell you what's even funnier. He asked me to advocate for his cause. He thinks Gorot could give the Akha some publicity!"

I'd thought Alastair would start laughing again when he heard this. Instead he said defensively, "Well, how do you think I feel? How much do you think this," he gestured around the lounge, "is costing me? I had to call my bank from Chiang Mai and get a cash advance on my credit card."

Oh boy. And was Alastair still employed? Had he somehow managed to square his extended absence with Oswald? I didn't dare to ask. "Has he been mooching off you?"

"Not exactly. But I made a high four-figure donation to the Institute."

So we'd both been thinking along the same lines. It irritated me to know that Alastair was as vulnerable to Malcolm's tactics as I had been. "I don't see why you have to cater to his every whim," I said. "He's nothing but an old hedonist. Like a dry drunk: he may be doing the ascetic thing now—"

"Oh, they've got a satellite dish and above-average plumbing—"

"—but it hasn't changed him. And what's more, you've given him the wrong idea about me and Gorot. You let him think I was some kind of superstar—"

"Aren't you?"

"Look at me." Involuntarily, I touched my neck. "Our deal fell through, Alastair. We're still just an indie band trying to sell our shit online. All the publicity we've ever had is bad. So why did you let him think—"

Alastair's voice overrode mine. "—if there'd been any other way to lure him out of his fucking jungle!"

I sagged back, scowling. "We'll have to tell June. She'll be—"

"Annoyed." Alastair bared his teeth. "It would be kinder not to." There was some hidden factor in his mood, I thought. This wasn't all about Malcolm. Of course it wasn't.

"If only you'd come a bit earlier," I said. "I would have been slightly less... less... I would have been better equipped to... to cope."

"Tad told me."

"I'm sorry."

Alastair shrugged and sipped his cappuccino. "Saves me a lot of trouble."

I hadn't expected him to be quite this blasé about it. "See," I tried to joke, "I can look after myself."

"Evidently."

I longed to know exactly what Tad had told him. But the lounge hadn't been a safe place to talk this afternoon, and even now, it was still a public place. I leaned across the table and hissed, "He said he'd had you killed!"

"Oh Christ," sighed Alastair, raising his gaze to the distant ceiling. "Again with the justifications. What is it about you people? What are you so afraid of?"

"Everything," I said, hearing a faint roaring noise like the sea.

"Well, it won't help to look for justifications. Because there are none. Period." He added, "And if it's absolution you're after, you must see that it's pretty funny to ask *me.*"

I recoiled, dizzied by his bluntness. He seemed to be denying that my love of him could have justified me in killing Ned. To be absolutely honest, I was aware of the possibility that love of Alastair hadn't even been my motivation. And with that knowledge, I also understood that Alastair hadn't necessarily killed Nigel for love of me. But for seventeen years I'd taken it for granted that he had, and he'd gone along with that, playing his part in our baroque little drama. Maybe he'd been keeping this one last secret from me all along, and maybe my ignorance had helped him to keep it from himself. And if so, how did he really feel about the idea that I might now be in on the secret, too? Maybe it was fundamentally a lie that anyone ever kills for love. But without that lie, what would become of us? What would be left?

Alastair said, "Speaking of justifications, I guess it's my turn. Did Malcolm tell you how I found him?"

"Not a word. He was too busy giving me his sales pitch," I managed.

We both laughed, and I felt a little better.

"Well, it all began with Jeremy Siek, the notorious drug trafficker."

So they had made it to Koh Samui. "How did you find him?"

"Asked a few bartenders if they knew Ned. Within twelve hours, Jeremy found me."

"Wow. What type of a guy… is he?" Or should that be *was he?* I wondered.

"An interesting bundle of contradictions. Late thirties. Looks more Chinese than Thai. Not the type to bling it around town with a Hummer and a gold Rolex. He actually wore a Breguet; can't be five people in Koh Samui who know how much that costs. It's the girlfriend who wears the gold and diamonds. A walking bank vault. No wonder she hardly ever goes out. But Jeremy: he's not a bad guy. Only a bit of an opportunist.

Tells you, 'My hero is Manuel Noriega.' With a straight face. But that's the thing, he has this weirdly honest streak."

I laughed. "You liked him!"

"Kind of, yeah. I liked the fact that he was so upfront about what he is... I wonder if it's too late for another cappuccino?"

I took my phone out of my bag and glanced at the screen. I'd missed two calls, one from Joaquin and one from Tad. "It's only eleven." I signalled a waiter.

"Christ, I feel like I've been up for a week. But it's OK, I've got my second wind." Alastair closed his eyes for a moment. "So. Jeremy came and found us in Chaweng. That was a nasty shock. I'd wanted to keep Nina out of it, obviously. He offered to drive us out to his place, but I talked us out of it. Told him my girlfriend had already arranged to meet some friends, whatever. At that point I had to fill Nina in, much against my wishes…"

"What did you tell her?" I scraped the last blobs of foam out of my cup and sucked the spoon. I wanted to return Tad's call, but I was afraid that any interruption would shut Alastair down.

"The truth. Or most of it. I told her I was looking for Ned. I didn't tell her I was looking to kill him… Luckily, she didn't have time to get too mad right then, because we were due to meet Jeremy for dinner at his place."

"You went to his place? I wouldn't have."

"I thought Ned might be there. So we took a taxi out to Mae Nam. Jeremy's place was a luxury villa. His description. We got the grand tour and finished up with a barbecue on the patio by the pool."

"The de rigueur pool," I said, rolling my eyes. I could see Jeremy now, the small-timer who thought he was Manuel Noriega.

"Yes, but as I'm trying to explain, he was just that little bit different from what you'd expect. For one thing, that luxury villa was filled with *art.* Temple artifacts, ceramics, and one tremendous stone Buddha head. The Windrose doesn't specialize in Khmer art, but we get the occasional piece of statuary coming through. There are collectors who'll buy anything from that period. Of course, most of what's on the market is forged. But this piece… the serenity, the sensuality… it was a paradox in stone. There's no carver alive today who can pull that off. I said, 'Did this come from Angkor Wat?' and Jeremy said with that straight face of his, 'Somewhere near there.'"

"Aha. I begin to see. So Jeremy is a looter on top of everything else? A real Renaissance guy."

Alastair sighed. "Shanti, every artifact that is currently for sale in the world was looted from somewhere. And every artifact remaining at the world's archaeological sites is potentially for sale. The only brake on the market is provenance. And I've told you enough about *that* in the past. Basically, where there's a demand that exceeds the legal supply, there's a way."

Our second round of cappuccino had come. I held up my hands, cup and saucer, in surrender. "I know, I know, there's no such thing as art. Only artifacts."

"Exactly. And given the prices that genuine Khmer artifacts command? You have to hand it to a guy who chooses to keep a piece like that in his living-room."

"So did you offer to buy it off him?"

"Nope." Alastair grinned. "It's a bitch to ship anything that big. But I was buzzing… almost forgot why I was there. And now I've forgotten where I was. Oh yeah, we were out on the patio, listening to his sales pitch. He can't really have thought we were in the market for a luxury villa. It was more for the benefit of the hangers-on who were hanging around. They were straight out of Petty Crime For Dummies. IQs in the double digits. You could see where Ned would have fit in. There was actually a Japanese guy… he asked us how Ned was doing. It dawned on me around then that we were barking up the wrong tree. But I still thought Ned might be somewhere on Koh Samui. And then Jeremy introduced us to his girlfriend."

"Ruby," I said. "And let me guess. She read your palm."

"And Nina's."

"Was that when you remembered?"

"No. I hadn't forgotten."

"I had. Ned told me how she had this sixth sense, and she read his palm, and I knew it reminded me of something… someone. But I never made the connection."

"Why would you? There are millions of amateur fortune-tellers over there. Fair enough, the same thing was going through my mind… but it was something else that clinched it. Basically, Ruby gave it away. When she read our palms, she really got into it. Closing her eyes and swaying, humming to herself, tracing the lines with her fingers. She's very convincing. Got all the hangers-on under her thumb. Jeremy, too. And she told me that I had a complicated relationship with my father. And I said, '*Had,* yes. My father's dead; he committed suicide, lo, these many years ago.' And her eyes popped open and she said, 'No, he didn't.'"

"Oh boy. Open bag, release cat. So then what did you say?"

"Nothing. And Ruby moved on in a hurry. But Nina heard. And in the taxi on the way back, she came out with her new theory. We weren't there to look for Ned. We were looking for my father. She was ready to forgive me for keeping her in the dark, I think, if I'd have said she was right. She has a complicated relationship with her own parents..." Alastair massaged his face. When he took his hands away, his eyes were more bloodshot than ever. "So. The next day I left her at a café and went back to Jeremy's place. He was out at one of his construction sites. But Ruby was there. I took the opportunity to ask her a few questions, and that's when I found out she was Ao's, or rather Sandy's cousin."

"I knew it."

"They ran away together when they were twelve. It makes an interesting counterpoint to Ao's spiel about the evils of orphanages. Apparently they were never in an orphanage, but they had a patron. The refugees from Myanmar were so badly off that they were pimping out the orphans. And one day Ao and Bia, which is Ruby's real name, stole the old guy's valuables and headed south. In the last of many sordid episodes, Ao aka Sandy fell in with Malcolm—"

"You know, this is one point that bugs me. Our father is the kind of guy who patronizes underage prostitutes."

"Better not go there. The official story is that he rescued her. And there is an argument to be made that Ao got luckier than Ruby. Although Ruby seems happy, in her way. You should have seen her lounging on her patio in her designer robe and dark glasses and diamonds. Sparkling in the sun."

"Do they look alike?"

Alastair's lips quirked. "Not anymore. Ruby weighs about two hundred pounds. And according to both of them, they haven't spoken in fifteen years. But Ruby knew that Ao had gone back to the village with Malcolm."

I didn't want to bring Ned into the conversation again, but I couldn't help saying, "So Ned did find our father. He just didn't know it."

"Oh, he must have known that Ruby and Ao were cousins. Can't you just see him? Wandering around Phuket, asking everyone if they knew anyone who knew Malcolm... And he wanders straight into a nest of criminals."

"He was building a house for himself," I said. "By the sea. Did you get to see it?"

"Probably gone by now, if it ever existed." Alastair shrugged. "Ruby had a soft spot for him, I think. But obviously, she never saw fit to tell him that Malcolm was still alive. She only told me because, quote, God told me to, unquote."

"Whoa."

"Yeah."

"She told Ned not to go to Japan," I recalled.

"Oh, she's shrewd enough. She said to me, when we were talking about Malcolm: 'Be careful. One is too many. Two is the end.'"

I shook my head.

Alastair said softly, "*Nigel*. Only—"

"Oh, God! Ned told her! How could he?" I slammed my fist on my knee. "We'll never be safe," I wailed.

Alastair's gaze darted this way and that. He could regale me with stories of dining with notorious drug traffickers, but let me give way for one moment to emotion, and his paranoia kicked in. On the other hand, I knew he was right: nothing draws attention like an emotional outburst. I fought off the feeling that I was under the sea. Breathe, breathe, breathe.

"On the other hand," I gasped, "I guess it could have been God who told her."

"She needs to upgrade her connection, then. Any prophetess worth her salt would have known I was up to two already."

I laughed morosely, then startled as my bag beside me in my armchair vibrated. Probably Tad again. Was he feeling guilty about deserting me?

"Anyway, it was an interesting conversation. Then Jeremy came home for lunch, and that was even more interesting." Alastair grinned. "He said, 'I tell you the truth. Ned is a very good guy, one of my best guys, I worry about him,' etcetera. That went on for a while. We were in the dining-room, eating green curry and rice. When I got bored of hearing Ned's virtues praised, I said, 'I tell *you* the truth. I think you sent Ned to Ruby's cousin upcountry to keep him out of harm's way.' Well, then he got a bit dignified."

"Did he tell you he had? Sent Ned away?"

"No. But that's why I thought he had. It all fit together so beautifully." Alastair sighed. "And that's not all. We finished lunch and he said, 'So you like my antiques, uh huh?' I didn't give him the lecture on the difference between art and antiques. I just said yeah, he had a couple of impressive pieces. So he took me out to the garage and opened up a crate. Two more Buddha heads. He knew what they were worth. 'You want to buy like this? You go upcountry, don't you?' Wink wink. 'In Chiang Mai you can buy the best antiques, much better than Bangkok. I tell you the guy to contact.' And he wrote down the name and phone number. 'Tell him you know Jeremy in Samui, no problem, he make you a reasonable price.' And a bit later, when I was making my escape, who do you think came after me? God's own little ray of sunshine. All two hundred pounds of her. And she told me where to find the village."

"You could have emailed me," I said, wincing for him.

"Yeah. Sorry."

And I thought: You didn't email me because you knew I'd tell you not to look for Malcolm. You knew I'd tell you to leave him to rot.

"So we flew north, rented a Jeep, and spent a few days searching the jungle. But there was no trace of Ned – of course, there wouldn't have been – and as for Malcolm, Ruby's information was twenty years old. Relocation by any other name… The Akha aren't classified as Thai citizens, so no one keeps track of them. The bureaucracy is obstructionary, the roads don't exist…"

"But you did find them in the end," I said. "Obviously."

Alastair shifted in his chair. Then he grinned. "Enter the tomb raiders."

"Aka Jeremy's contacts?" I guessed.

"Yeah. We were back in Chiang Mai, and I decided it was worth trying that phone number. An excessively friendly guy met us and took us to his shop. It was full of crap forgeries, just as you'd expect. I said, 'Where's the real stuff?' He said, 'Oh, we don't keep here. You want to see? Special for friend of Jeremy. I take you to warehouse.'"

"Uh oh."

"I know. I shouldn't even have thought about getting in his car. Much less allowing Nina to come with us. But we'd been hitting so many dead ends, and I kept remembering that Buddha head – it was a vision of beauty, Shanti. I just…"

"It's OK," I said. "You don't have to justify yourself."

"If you'd seen it, you would understand. And when we got to the warehouse, they showed me half a dozen pieces that were even better. A kind of bunker in the jungle, with chickens running around outside, and they were sitting on inventory worth a million dollars! So I offered to buy the lot." Alastair drained his second cappuccino. "Not one of the best ideas I've ever had." He looked around. "Excuse me! Glass of water, please."

"Make that two," I said. I'd been smoking too much and talking too much, and my throat was raw.

When it came, Alastair drank off half the glass at a gulp. He ran a hand through his hair. "At this point the tale gets slightly medieval."

"How much did you offer them? How much did you have?"

"About ten thousand in cash." Alastair touched his stomach. For a strange moment I thought he'd swallowed it, like one of Ned's mules swallowing a condom full of heroin. But of course he meant he'd worn a money belt. "They got it all," he said, "when they drove us deeper into the jungle and threatened us at gunpoint."

"Oh my God."

"Yeah. And then, seeing how *rich* I was, they decided to hold us to ransom. They took us to an abandoned army encampment. Although I'm not sure it *was* abandoned; there were some uniformed drunks around the place who seemed to be soldiers - and the leader of our tomb raiders, Pitachorn, bragged that he owned the relevant officials on both sides of the border… But it was a strange place. A snarl of barbed wire around a few concrete blockhouses, stuck up in these breathtakingly beautiful hills. You could set your watch by the rain. And the *stars*… When they threatened to kill us, I remember looking up and thinking, I wouldn't mind, if this could be the last thing I ever see."

"Alastair, Nina said it wasn't that bad!"

"Oh, it wasn't. We weren't locked up, except at night; we could wander around the compound... Well, there wasn't anywhere to go except the jungle, and everyone except us had Kalashnikovs. But they weren't bad guys. I had some interesting conversations with Pitachorn about art, history, the ethics of plundering world heritage sites, that kind of thing. We developed a rapport. Unfortunately, he was under a lot of pressure to make the project pay… If I'd only had myself to worry about, I'd have broken a bottle over his head one night, stolen his Kalashnikov, and taken my chances. But Nina..." Alastair sighed.

He was glossing over it, too, I thought. It had been that bad. It had probably been worse, if even Alastair couldn't talk about it.

"So I told him: 'As a matter of fact, my father lives somewhere around here. Have you ever heard of a village called Lo Mai Akha?'"

"And they found Malcolm for you," I said, exhaling. "That's… I'm not going to say it's poetic justice."

"In less than twenty-four hours. And Malcolm being Malcolm, he exfiltrated us with relative ease. He even convinced Pitachorn to return what was left of my original ten thousand. Of course, the Akha got it in the end… But it was an impressive performance."

"No wonder Nina is crazy about him and Ao," I said emptily.

"Yeah. By the time we left the compound, everyone was the best of friends. And I'm still in touch with Pitachorn, as a matter of fact. As soon as I get back to the United States, he's going to send me some artifacts to sell on consignment."

I was too depressed even to smile. "So that's it," I said. "Your ticket back into Oswald's good graces."

"Fuck Oswald." Alastair ground his teeth restlessly. "I'm through with tying myself down in Boston."

"New York?"

"Where else? That's where the big players are."

Don't, I wanted to say. Not New York. The art world isn't the world of struggling musicians, but you can get high off the dust in the air at a gallery event, too. New York will kill you, like it almost killed me.

"Well, that'll be fun for Nina," I said. "Maybe she'll be the next one to have a family reunion."

"Don't bet on it. Officially, she hasn't made up her mind yet, but I think she may go back to Lo Mai Akha with Malcolm and Ao."

"What?"

Alastair shrugged. "She says she's always wanted to help people."

My phone vibrated. "Hang on," I said. "I've got to answer this. But Alastair, you can't let her go like that! You've got to try… moshi moshi!"

"Are you still in Shinagawa?" Tad said.

"Yeah. I think I'm going to catch the last train, though."

Alastair swirled the melting ice in his glass and drained it.

"OK. I just wanted to tell you, I might not be home."

"What? But… Tad… wait until I get back. Please."

There was a long silence. Alastair crunched ice cubes. The sound made me think of a frozen forest on a silver hillside, all glittery and dead.

"OK, I'll wait for you," Tad said at last. "But don't stay out too late." He sounded distracted. I could hear loud music in the background.

"OK. See you soon, then." I snapped my phone shut. All of a sudden I felt self-conscious. I gathered my hair back with one hand and let it fall. "That was Tad. I guess I'd better get home."

"What are you, his mother?"

"Alastair, he's stressed out. He's been acting weird! Really weird." I hung my head in remorse and confusion.

"Weird? How so?" Alastair didn't sound alarmed. I shot a glance at him through my hair. His eyes were shut, his hands splayed on the arms of his chair.

"As in picking fights." I described the scene at yesterday's TV shoot. "Everyone wants us to fail," I said hysterically. "And Tad is playing straight into their hands. It's so unfair to the others! It's just so unfair!"

"I know how much this band means to you," Alastair said. His eyes were still closed. Fearfully, I scrutinized him. The tips of his fingers had gone white on the arms of the chair. "I've seen you performing live, remember, and I understand about the… the sum of individual talents adding up to more than the parts. But is it really that tough to find a good bassist?"

At a quarter past midnight, the panic hour when every train is the last train to somewhere, people dashed madly in all directions across the concourse of Shinagawa station. I squatted in a corner with my back to the cool glass wall of an ATM cubicle. Hating what I was doing, hating what it said about me, I scanned through the lists of contacts on my phone, searching for someone who wasn't a part of the indie scene, someone who wouldn't spread rumors, someone who'd put me up for the night… someone who didn't exist.

Ned. The sight of his name on the screen gave me a jolt. It was his old number, not the one he'd used to call me at Punk March, but all the same, I had a crazy urge to dial it and see if anyone answered.

Ned? I'm still here. You went swimming and left me behind! I'm still here, motherfucker! Come back!

The screen swam. I dialed Tad.

The background noise on both ends distorted his voice to a crackle. *Shinde iru,* it sounded like he was saying, *I'm dying* or *I'm dead.* I pushed off from the wall in a bowlegged crouch.

"… in Shinjuku!"

None of the tension left me. "What's in Shinjuku?" I shrieked.

"Kinderbox… at Oasis! I didn't make the gig but I figured… celebrate!"

"I'll be there in half an hour!"

"You don't have to come out!"

"I'm already out," I reminded him. "Tell Naoya and the guys I'll buy them a drink if they'll forgive me for standing them up!"

"…here, too. You'll have to buy him *several* drinks!" Tad's laugh crumpled like cellophane.

As my train careened around the Yamanote loop, it dawned on me that Tad couldn't have got to Shinjuku and met up with Kinderbox and Gen in the thirty-four minutes since he called me last. He must have been in Shinjuku already. But when I assumed he was in Omori, he'd let my misapprehension stand. I would have been stuck home alone, wondering where he'd gone… again.

The train smelled putrid. When everyone surged off the train at Shinjuku, I saw a homeless man sprawled in the corner of the carriage, bearded and dreadlocked, extremities mummified in rags.

I called Tad. "I'm at the station. Where are you guys?"

"I'll meet you at the east exit."

I waited in front of the police box. The clatter of drums tugged my gaze to a band that was busking across the street, beneath the zelkova trees in the miniature rotary park. When Gorot busked there years ago, we'd drawn a better crowd than that, a full circle of innocently appreciative faces. Now, everyone loitering in the park looked like a pimp or a whore. In the police box, a girl sat huddled in front of the desk covered with laminated maps. Cops stood over her with folded arms. I could almost hear the mocking farts of the sax.

"Hey, sister. Waiting for someone?" Tad said in my ear.

He must have gone home to change: his plain sweatshirt and jeans had been replaced by black drainpipes with zippers across the thighs, a khaki wifebeater, and a short-sleeved baby-pink buttondown with a tiny FUCK YOU motif – the better to blend in with Kinderbox. Or maybe because it was sakura season. Or maybe for no reason at all. The light over the door of the police box dyed the tips of his hair bright. I twined my arms around his neck and kissed him. He clutched me for a second, then stepped back. I hung onto his hands. "Where are Naoya and the guys?"

He blinked and took a moment to answer. I was instantly suspicious. "They went on to a cabaret club."

"Shit! Gen, too?"

"He's finally accepted that he's single, I guess."

"Well, way to ditch me," I complained. I felt like crying. Now I would have no distractions, no excuse.

"Who cares?" He swung my hands in arcs, his eyes skipping past me. "You didn't bring Alastair, did you?"

"No."

"Well, then."

I swallowed. "OK. Let's, well, we had supper so early, and I didn't eat much, did you? So how about let's grab a burger."

We crossed the street into the park. As we neared the buskers, the rhythm sounded more and more familiar.

"I'm sure I know that," I said.

"Me, too."

"Oh my God," I said. Know it? I'd written it. "A Drop Of Poison." Track 6 on *U-Turn Day,* without the keyboards, with toothachingly shrill vocals that weren't improved by a cheap portable PA. The vocalist, a Japanese girl barely out of her teens, whirled from pose to pose on the dirty sidewalk while she screeched my lyrics in a barely comprehensible accent. No one recognized Tad and me as we circled the small crowd.

"Now I know we've made it," Tad said.

"They're not covering us," I said. "They're stealing our song, and they think no one will notice because we're so fucking minor."

"Maybe so, but can't you take it as a compliment?"

"They were crap!"

"Well, that guy had one fingering that I never thought of. That was always an awkward transition. So take the A up to the fifth fret…" He fingered air, head nodding.

They're like gold dust, I'd told Alastair. *Everyone wants to be the lead guitarist. So if you've got a good bassist, you hang onto him.*

We crossed Yasukuni Dori and walked down the main drag of

Kabukicho, between the pachinko parlors and the games centers and the bikers hanging out around their machines like shepherd boys with a sleek black herd. In the shifting light of the neon, Tad's face glowed as if his skin were coated with gasoline. We went into the McDonalds on the plaza. I got a chickenburger, fries, and a Coke. Tad got fries and a strawberry milkshake. We carried our trays to the fourth floor and found a table overlooking the plaza. Instead of starting to eat, Tad got out his Lucky Strikes, then crumpled the pack. "Forgot. Gen smoked my last one."

"I'm surprised Gen was even there. He doesn't usually support Kinderbox."

"I asked him to come."

"Why?" As I said it, I realized the truth. "Oh my God, you went to his place last night, didn't you? To give him back his guitar."

"Yeah. And to apologize for… for… you know. The shoot."

"So, what? I guess he accepted your apology?"

Tad momentarily gave me haunted eyes. He shook his head minutely.

The food in my mouth turned into clay. It took me an absurdly long time to get it down my throat, and then I had to swallow hard to stop it from reversing its trajectory. "Oh my God. Tad, you told him everything, didn't you?"

Tad played with the straw in his milkshake. Tiny pink dots landed on the window beside us. "I told him… too much. That's why I had to see him tonight. I tried to explain. But he wouldn't listen… He wouldn't even agree to come for a drink with me. Went on with Naoya and the guys instead."

"Why? I mean, why wouldn't he have a drink with you?"

"Obviously," Tad almost shouted, "because he's scared of me now!"

"Did you tell him I was coming out?"

"Yeah. I guess he… couldn't deal."

"Oh, Tad." I was still holding my burger. I put it down. "Motherfucker," I said emptily.

"What can I say?" Tad leaned back in a casual manner, gazing out the window instead of at me. "Sorry. Would that cover it?"

"Why?"

"Drunk. That shochu really does a number on your self-control."

"Why?"

"Can you believe he wasn't mad at me? At least, by the time I went over there last night, he wasn't mad at me anymore. He said he figured something was going on with me."

"So you told him."

"He thought it was something to do with you."

"And you told him—"

"I tried to convince him he was wrong. I told him..." Tad stopped and shook his head. "It felt like I had to. It seemed like, if he can see something's wrong, then everyone can see. And if it's only a matter of time until everyone guesses—"

"How the fuck would anybody guess!" I exploded. "I told you, you will get paranoid. It comes with the territory. But it fades with time! Nobody guesses. Nobody *cares.*" I blinked back hot tears. "But... oh fuck. Too late now."

"I might still be able to calm him down."

"No. No, that's not what I mean. I mean I've screwed up, too. I told Alastair—"

"So? I already told him. He had to know, surely."

"Yes, but that's not what - OK, well, that, too. I don't know exactly what you told him—"

"The truth," Tad said bitterly.

"OK, and that's the problem!" I remembered Alastair's suspiciously blasé reaction. I should have known a fake-out when I saw one. "He didn't think we would - *could* do it. Even if Ned was still in Japan, he thought we'd be OK, because he was sure none of us could really - he thought we didn't have what it takes." I was talking around the word *murder,* conscious of the people around us. They weren't listening, they didn't care, but I still didn't dare to say what I really thought, which was that in his heart of hearts Alastair had believed he was the only one of us who was capable of murder. He'd been prepared to kill Ned, but not because he thought Ned would do anything violent. And if not Ned, how much less me? How much less Tad, who'd been comparatively well brought up? "Now all bets are off," I said desperately. "Don't you see? He thought nothing would happen unless he made it happen himself. Now he knows that's not true."

"He was impressed. He said we handled it really well."

I let out a moan and rocked back and forth. "That was just to put you off your guard. Well, I don't know! He might just let it go and head back to America. He's so fed up with Malcolm and everything... But then I had to go and tell him you were stressed out. I didn't need to tell him; he could see it for himself. But then I told him... and I got him worried. That's what he said. *Now you've got me worried.*"

Rape. That was the word I'd used to describe what happened between me and Tad last night. That was when Alastair had said *Now you've got me worried.* And after that, we'd had a little clash over whether he was going to let me go home.

I'd insisted that I had to be there for Tad and stop him from doing anything stupid.

I guess I should have thought of that earlier.

Panicking, I said, "If Alastair finds out you've told Gen—"

"Why should he care? If Gen goes to the police, it won't be Alastair in trouble."

"To the… No! *No.*"

Tad gave that awful smile again, mocking himself. "Haven't you ever noticed? Gen's pretty conservative."

"Yeah. If you had to confess to someone, you should have picked Joaquin." I croaked a laugh. "But Gen… regardless of what happened at the shoot, he's still our friend! He wouldn't—"

"I don't know, Shanti, I don't know what he'll do. Today, he seemed like he'd calmed down a bit. But he might just have been controlling himself. I don't know! All I can do is keep trying to talk him around. Persuade him that he's wrong…" Tad slapped the table with his fingertips and leaned forward. "He said, 'I can't believe you did something like that. But Shanti? Yeah. She's the type, isn't she? She gets carried away, doesn't she?' He wanted me to say that it was all you, and I was trying to hold you back, or something like that. Complete bullshit! He wanted me to blame it all on you. He kept saying, 'She'd do *anything,* wouldn't she?'"

Personally, I couldn't believe Gen thought I was 'the type,' whatever that meant. I was supposed to be just this kooky rock chick with a neurotic streak. But I guess maybe no one had ever seen me that way. So maybe I should just quit lying to myself.

I reached for Tad's hands and rubbed my thumbs over his rings. Fleetingly, I remembered the way Gen had touched me beside the waterfall at Kusatsu, drunkenly fumbling after some distant ideal. He was so sweet in his utter thoughtlessness. And like many people with one outstanding gift, he was so weak in every other way.

I hitched myself to the edge of my chair, holding onto Tad's hands. "One thing about Gen that I've always thought. He scares easily."

"He's fragile," Tad agreed. "Can't handle reality."

"He's never had to work for his living—"

"Never paid taxes in his life."

"Yeah, and he's so alienated. He doesn't feel like part of this society. That's why I don't think he'd go to the… to the." I thumped Tad's hands lightly on the sticky formica tabletop. "Not if he's scared. If he's really scared, he'll be paralyzed, and he'll try his best not to think about it. To forget it. And we'll let him, won't we? We'll *allow* him to forget anything was ever said." But as I spoke, I saw that I was losing my audience.

"There's obviously only one thing to do," Tad said distantly.

"Oh," I said. "Do you think we should kill him?" My voice sounded childish. Tad freed his hands from mine and blinked at me. My question, which I'd asked earnestly, without any of the anguish I actually felt, seemed to morph in the silence, becoming its own answer.

Follow your heart, they say. All the movies you've seen, all the books and manga you've read, all the songs you've heard - including the ones I wrote - they all say: Follow your heart.

I fell for the propaganda. Hell, I contributed to the campaign.

I followed my heart.

And look where it got me.

Tad shook his french fries out onto the tray and ate them one by one. "I'm not going to make Gen pay for anything I did."

"No, of course not," I said hurriedly.

"It's not his fault."

What did that have to do with anything? Tad had forgotten the lesson he learned at Makuhari Messe, I thought. He was getting hung up on hypothetical questions, lost in the twists of an analysis that would lead him farther and farther away from reality.

He wiped his fingers on a paper napkin, gazing out the window as if he saw something interesting down there in the plaza. Impatience stung me. I said, "Looking at the whole situation, the only thing I can think of is for you to—" *Go into hiding?* No - echoes of Ned. "Go away for a little while. Go, I don't know, go to Guam and lie on the beach for a week." *Just until Alastair says* To hell with it *and goes back to America.* "Swim, go snorkeling, eat, recharge your batteries for the tour," which would put us all in the same country again. But America is big, and everyone would be distracted. The best antidote to danger is an ample supply of distractions. So maybe not Guam; nothing there but sand and sea. "How about Okinawa? You could hang with those surf-rock guys we met at Punk March." I sought to charge my voice with more persuasive energy. "I know you think CCR would fall apart in five minutes without you. But the rest of us can keep the show on the road for a week or so. Everyone would understand; you deserve a break—"

"And leave you here?"

"Well, not necessarily. We could go together!" For a moment, this seemed like the best idea I'd ever had.

"Running away is never the answer. What would Gen do if he thought we'd run away?"

"Oh," I said. "Oh yeah, I guess."

"And everything would just be waiting for us when we got back. No. I'm through with closing my eyes and hoping it all goes away. That didn't work before, and it's definitely not going to work now." Tad slouched sideways and leaned one elbow on the table. He pushed his remaining french fries around the tray, making a pattern. "You're not the type to get mixed up in this stuff, whatever Gen thinks. You've just been under Alastair's influence for too long. Whereas me? I've had this inside me all my life. Want to know what Alastair said?" He looked up at me. "'Well, I won't try to bullshit you anymore. I can see you've found out the truth.' And I think he was right."

"He was joking," I said, mouth dry. I wondered exactly what Alastair had been referring to. A private joke of his own; but sometimes Alastair's jokes were so black that you couldn't see them in the dark.

After a long pause, Tad said, "And do you know what I think? I was never really a musician at all."

"You *are* a musician. You're one of the best musicians I've ever—"

"Rock isn't real. It's just the soundtrack for the real thing. And now—" He broke a fry in half and added it to his pattern. "I can't feel the music like I used to. It doesn't get me in the heart anymore."

"I could kill fucking Alastair," I said, on the edge of tears. Then my whole body spasmed in protest at what I'd said. I shoved my chair back from the table and doubled over my knees. As suddenly as going over the waterfall, I'd tumbled into one of those gaps in reality where to say *I didn't mean it* would mean that I *had* meant it, because hyperbole was the same thing as danger and there was no such thing as a mere joke, but on the other hand everything was a joke and nothing really mattered. The darkness resounded with mocking laughter. There are doors that should never be opened, and I'd kicked them down one after another, until only one remained. On it hung a placard inscribed with black marker: The Truth.

"Shanti?"

I shook my head.

Tad scraped his chair around the table and slid his arm across my shoulders. He kissed my turtleneck, right above Ned's wound. I squeaked in pain. My head came up. He kissed me clumsily on the mouth. I resisted, aware of the people around us, the goths and ravers and tourists, all the sulky freaks who ate fast food in Kabukicho on a weeknight. "I want you to remember that I always loved you," he muttered into the side of my face.

"Tad!"

He let go of me.

"Wh-where are you going?"

He shook his head. Hesitancy overcame me like nausea. I sagged in my chair and watched him move away between the tables. There was nothing more I could do. He'd said he loved me. And even that wasn't enough to make him stay.

Then he vanished down the stairs, and I sprang to my feet. I wasn't defeated yet.

I was going to leave our trays on the table, but the french fries on his tray caught my eye. He'd arranged them in a pattern. Not a random one, either. I spun the tray around to see it the right way up.

死刑

The death penalty.

With one hand I scattered Tad's french fry kanji; with the other I dialed the Prince Hotel. Clattering down the stairs, I asked for room 719.

"Yes, hello?"

"Nina, I'm really sorry, but can I speak to Alastair?"

"Isn't he with you? Where is he?"

Oh, shit. "If he was with me, I wouldn't have fucking called you!" I barged through a gang of girls on their way up the stairs. A tray clattered, icy soda splattered my calves, and their voices followed me like the keening of seagulls. "Did he come back? When did he leave?"

"I don't know. I think I would have heard him come in, but I woke up half an hour ago, and he wasn't here. Jesus H. Christ, Shanti, your fucking family. I'm starting to think Malcolm is the most normal one of the whole bunch of you!"

"You're probably right. Listen, just do one thing for me. Don't open the door unless you're absolutely sure it's Alastair, or Malcolm, or whatever her name is." I wanted to say *Sandy,* but I knew that wasn't right.

That set Nina off on a new tack, as if she hadn't fully heard what I said. "They have an appointment in Kawasaki tomorrow with these big potential donors. It's at ten, and they can't manage the trains. If Alastair doesn't come back, I'll have to get them there by myself. I probably will anyway, because he'll be totally exhausted if he plans on staying out all night. I guess he's gone to see some of his raffish art dealer friends." She managed a pale gloss of irony on the last words.

"I guess maybe he has." I shoved through the lines at the registers on the ground floor. "Just do this for me, stay there until he comes in. Or if you can't stand it, go to Joaquin's… you know, the new studio. You'd be safe there."

I burst into the chilly night, staring around at the crowds on the plaza. Tad was nowhere in sight. I dialed his phone. It was turned off.

Calm down, I told myself. There are twelve million people in this city. You're not going to find anyone unless they want to be found. I walked in a purposeful way across the plaza. I had no destination, but my role seemed to require me to keep moving.

I entered an alley on the far side of the plaza and found myself frowning at a featureless metal door. I squatted down with my back against it. Dead and by my hand, but what does it matter in the end? If it's not one thing it's another. Death by paperweight, by rope, by car battery, by water. I tried Tad's cell phone again. It was still turned off. I absently tapped my fingers on my knee. Then, on impulse, I dialed a number I'd never used before.

"Moshi moshi."

"Kuroiwa-san! I… It's me. You know. Shanti. Can I ask you a question?"

"I may as well tell you I advise against it," he said good-humoredly.

I gasped and took a wild guess: "What did he want to know?"

"I thought you were with him." An edge of worry entered Kuroiwa-san's crackly telephone voice. "Aren't you on your way to Jonanjima Park?"

"Uh… Jonanjima Park. Got it." I pushed off from the door and hurried towards Yasukuni Dori, where I could pick up a taxi. "What… what time did he call you?"

"Why, only a few minutes ago. He wanted to know where it was that we went to dig for clams when… I was surprised he remembered that. He couldn't have been more than four years old. His mother was still alive… At any rate, they've terraformed the whole coast since then. It's just part of Jonanjima Park now. How times change!" Kuroiwa-san chuckled. "But I can't advise going out there at this time of night. He sounded… sentimental… Shanti-chan, I'm counting on you to keep him out of trouble."

If only it wasn't already too late.

Jonanjima Park. The whole Cold Coeur Family had come here once for a barbecue party. We built a fire in one of the little concrete hearths that you could pay to use for a few hours, and there were public toilets and an information center and an RV campground, and it hadn't occurred to me that a couple of decades ago none of this had existed. There'd been children running everywhere. Our conversation had periodically been extinguished by airplanes taking off from Haneda.

But at this time of night, the illusion that I'd left the city behind was complete. Hell, it wasn't an illusion: half an hour from the lights and noise of Shinjuku, I was out beyond the wharves where we took Ned that night, on a landfill island in Tokyo Bay.

I paid off my taxi at the park entrance. Mighty propane tanks reared behind the trees, and bursts of vapor shone gold above the streetlights. The nearby factories monologued in clanks and hisses. The barbecue area was fenced off and locked. As I crept around it, a faint *clah!* echoed through the night. I stopped in my tracks. Had that come from the factories behind me? Or from the seaward side of the park? Nerves tingling, I crept on through the darkness, beneath giant bonsai pines supported by wooden tripods. Their needles clattered in the wind off the bay. "God! God!" I used the syllable as a mantra to prevent myself from turning back.

As soon as I emerged onto the promenade, the wind clamped down, a cold pulsating torrent. I backhanded my hair out of my face and waded across it. As far down the promenade as I could see, the streetlights washed an empty expanse of bricks. The darkness on the other side of the railing was the artificial beach. The sea was too far off to be visible, but I could hear it, even over the wind, like the buzz from live speakers, rising and falling. On top of the deserted observation tower behind the promenade, an enormous letter F flashed in yellow bulbs. F for Failure.

I stared out at the distant shipping beacons and the standby lights on the runway at Haneda, a kilometre away across the water. Nearer by, faint white flecks danced around a dark ridge that reached into the sea: the breakwater at the corner of the island.

At the foot of the breakwater, something moved, black on black.

I vaulted over the railing and pelted down the beach. "Tad! *Tad!*" The wind muffled my voice. The loose sand slowed me down. I let my bag fall and abandoned it. "Tad!"

I reached the flank of the breakwater and the sea at the same time. The waves swirled around hunks of unhewn granite. Instead of settling for the ubiquitous tetrapods, the landscapers of Jonanjima Park had shipped in these rocks from God knows where. You get what you pay for. Authentic granite slimy under my hands, I hauled myself from stone to stone. A line of posts ran along the top of the breakwater, sunk in plugs of concrete that were already crumbling away, a rope strung between them. I used it to steady myself against the wind as I stood upright. Too breathless to shout anymore, I squinted into the darkness.

Not one, but *two* figures scrambling out along the breakwater.

The nearer one was Alastair.

The other one moved jerkily in and out of view, a few metres ahead of Alastair. Fleeing to the end of the breakwater. In about one minute he'd have nowhere left to run.

I leapt along the spine of the breakwater, bounding from stone to stone. The wind shoved at me with unpredictable force that increased the further out I went. The row of posts with their nylon rope ended, and I had to keep my balance without help as best I could. Once I fell and cracked my knee, but I started moving again before the pain could register. Out at sea, beacons rocked on the waves, flashing orange and green every few seconds. Without penetrating the darkness, they wrecked my night vision. The two figures ahead of me seemed to have vanished.

Waves scraped the rocks and burst into gouts of foam that rained on my face. As I neared the end of the breakwater, I could see arcs of white spray flying in a wicked jazzy rhythm. I filled my lungs and screamed Alastair's name. Nothing. Had I hallucinated both of them - and that sound I'd heard from inside the park? Had I come all this way only to die? One slip of the foot was all it would take. Hit my head on the way down and I'd be finished.

My foot slipped. I swung around a gigantic boulder, scrabbling at its edge, and fell on top of Tad, who sat in its lee, shielded from the spray. Alastair stood lower down, the sea splattering his back. Something in his hand—

"Shanti!" Alastair's voice struck into my wind-numbed ears. "Get away from him!"

I straddled Tad's lap, shaking him by the shoulders, asking whether he was all right. He pushed me off, half rising. "You're not supposed to be here," he muttered. "Let me go."

I clung to him. "I am not letting you go!" I screamed. "I am never, never letting you go again!" I'd let Ned go, down into the water, and that had been a mistake so stupendous that I could never make up for it, but I didn't have to repeat it again. "You'll have to kill me if you want me to let you go now!"

"Oh, Shanti," Alastair said. "Do you have to fuck up *everything* I do?" He grabbed my arm and forced me back against the rocks, but he used a clumsy onehanded grip that I eeled out of without difficulty. I dropped down another rock, which put me so low that the next wave soaked my legs, and also too low to get in Tad's way when he launched himself at Alastair. They toppled across the stones. Alastair flung out his arm to break their fall. But he was still using his wrong hand, because he had—

He slipped into a crevice with Tad on top of him. They struggled like spiders in the weak light of the beacons.

"If you hurt him, I'll throw you in the sea!" I screeched. "I'll kick you in the face and watch you drown!" My loyalties had crystallized in an exhilarating way, but when I found myself yanking violently at Tad's legs, that clarity vanished in a swirl of horror. My voice tore apart in mid-threat. Tad shook me off easily. He backed up, steadying himself on the rocks in the same clumsy one-handed way Alastair had, and for the same reason. He'd seized the gun that Alastair had had in his hand. So that was what I'd heard.

I got my arms under Alastair's armpits and helped him to haul himself out of the crevice. He swayed like a zombie rising from the grave. "Nice to know you care."

"Do you have to be in danger before I can prove it?"

"I wonder about everyone. And I'm right more often than I'd like to be. Witness your boyfriend here."

I tried to settle Alastair on the ledge where Tad had been, but he fought me, saying that he was going to kill Tad or die trying. I knelt on his thighs to hold him down. Wrenching my head back, I found Tad standing in the darkness above us. The wind whipped at his soaked shirt. The gun hung in his right hand, small and blunt, a semi-automatic, possibly. I'd never seen a gun before, except on TV or in a policeman's holster. God, my horizons were expanding tonight. "Throw that shit away!" I screamed. "Where did it come from? Did you *buy* it?"

"I liberated it from Malcolm's luggage," Alastair said. "He thinks the whole world is run on pretty much the same lines as Chiang Rai province. And I have to say I'm starting to agree."

"Just because I said—"

"No! I'd already seen enough. Look at the guy. We're talking about the rest of our lives, and he's already flaking out! Can't look me in the eye, can't keep his story straight—"

If Tad had looked shifty to Alastair this afternoon, no wonder: he'd been faltering under the burden of his confession to Gen. But I guess it didn't matter whether Alastair knew that little detail or not, because he'd already made up his mind.

"Guilt written all over his face. Keeps saying he's sorry. *Sorry?"* Alastair shouted up at Tad. "What the fuck is that? *Sorry?* Say that to the man you killed! Don't say it to me!"

"That's just a Japanese thing," I wailed. "Can't we be rational here?"

"Rational?" Alastair howled. "What the fuck is that?" He was panting with laughter, but the sound turned to grunts of effort as he tried to struggle out from under me. He'd said he wasn't hurt; he obviously was hurt, but even so, I couldn't hold him back indefinitely. He yelled up at Tad, "You're dead already! You can thank my sister - for this *short* - extension of your wretched existence - but better make it quick! Because you are *dead!"*

"How did you find him? How did he find you?" I starfished my body across Alastair to protect him from an incoming wave. Water doused my back, sickeningly cold, like being soaked in blood from the biggest wound in the world.

"Thanks," Tad said distantly.

He sounded rational. My relief died as the nearest beacon swung around and I got an orange flash of him. I couldn't be sure, but it looked like he had his finger on the trigger.

"You brought him to Shinjuku. Thanks. You helped me find out the truth."

"You followed me?" I recoiled from Alastair.

"Guilty - as usual. Take it up with me later. Right now - could you please fuck off? The object was - to keep you safely out of it."

I remembered that moment when I embraced Tad in front of the police box. He must have seen Alastair over my shoulder then, and again from the window of McDonalds. And all the time I argued with him over our meal, he must have been wondering how - *whether* - he would be able to get away from me. He hadn't really listened to anything I said, because he'd been thinking about Alastair. Wrapped up in their tacit conspiracy. They'd turned into mirror images of each other, two warped yet weirdly similar reflections of a dead man. Justice, Tad had said, but what he'd been thinking was 死刑.

I thrust Alastair back down on the rocks. I stepped on him. I crawled up towards Tad. Alastair exclaimed, "Crazy," and grabbed my left ankle. I pulled free but lost my sneaker.

"Tad! *Why?*"

"I wanted to know the truth," he said distantly.

"But he didn't know - I was armed and lethal!" Alastair shouted. "Operative word, was!" He giggled.

Tad shivered visibly, but didn't lower the gun. "Your brother's responsible. He started it all. Didn't he? In Ireland. Seventeen years ago. It's hard to get your mind around, isn't it? One accident, in a different country, and I was only a kid, but my life was already over." His teeth flashed in the light of the beacons. "Well, at least we had some fun along the way."

"You told him the truth, Shanti!" The boom of another wave failed to blot the pain out of Alastair's voice. He wasn't climbing after me. How badly was he hurt? Had I hurt him worse by trying to hold him back? "You told him about fucking Nigel. You can't trust anyone! How many times do I have to tell you? Oh God," he ended, the waves swallowing his voice.

"He's got to take responsibility," Tad said.

"Fuck responsibility!" I struggled to my knees. "It's all my fault, it's all your fault, it's all his fault, it's no one's fault. We're all guilty, so we just have to love each other, *even though* we're guilty!" I clutched his thighs and pressed my face to his hip.

The barrel of the gun lightly bumped the top of my head.

I peeled my arms away and staggered to my feet. I balanced on the edges of two rocks. Tad stood on the highest point.

He gestured with the gun at Alastair, who was sitting with his head in his hands.

"You can't love me *and* him. It's impossible."

I swayed. My voice was hoarse. "I didn't have enough love before, but I do now! I do now! I do! I love!"

The wind swatted at us; another wave smashed on the end of the breakwater; I grew self-conscious.

Tad lifted the gun – a little piece of Chiang Rai province, here in Tokyo Bay – and made it click. "There's only one thing left to do." He raised the gun to his own head, then lowered it. That awful smile touched his mouth again. "Don't you see?"

I sobbed, "I'm taking Alastair away, then."

"No." He sounded almost frightened. "No, you c-c-can't do that!"

At last I understood. He intended to kill Alastair and then himself. I lunged at him, clawing for the gun. He jerked back. We half stumbled, half fell down the side of the breakwater, holding onto each other.

It felt like a monster wave, the mother of them all. It slammed into me and spun me around. An instant ago I'd been striving for balance, but now I was falling into the water, sinking into the troubled blackness, where Ned was waiting for me.

Epilogue: Over Here

"Dig deeper at the bottom."

The foamy tongue of a wave coils into the lowest trench of our fortifications and soaks out of sight, leaving a dark imprint. I scoop the wet sand out, deepening the trench. The object is to get the sea to fill up all the moats we've dug before the entire complex is overwhelmed by the incoming tide. My thin, scabby, eleven-year-old knees leave their own prints in the sand on either side of the trench. This beach is usually stony, but today it's all sand, which is nice because it gives you more to work with.

Tad looks up from the round citadel he's shaping and brushes his hair off his face, wet hand spiking his bangs. "We need something for the tower. A flag or something."

"It's not a tower, eejit," Alastair says. "It's *The Fortress of the Clockwork Necromancer*. And the Clockwork Necromancer doesn't have a flag. There should really be gears and cogs all showing through the sides."

Tad nods thoughtfully, taking the idea on board. Then he stands up and carefully steps over the citadel, placing one foot in each trench until he's clear of the fortifications. He wanders off along the tideline of shells and seaweed, a brown twelve-year-old in faded shorts. Alastair puffs into the breeze and carries on packing sand over his own knee to create a bridge outside the citadel. At thirteen, he's gangly and so sunburnt you almost can't see his pimples, but inside, he's still the same schemer, as the Irish say. Presently his mind is full of the Clockwork Necromancer, whose evil torture machines and symbolical riddles fill several pages of his sketchbook at home, and his hands are full of sand.

"Speak, visitor," I say, firming the edges of my trench. *"Speak of the ordeal thou hast endured. Honesty will compensate for much. Innocence will not protect the weak; yet you may live on if you will speak. If you love yet fear to show how much, fate's satisfied; loyalty abjured."*

Alastair grins, chip-toothed. "I still think that's one of your best ones. I'm going to put it into the next panel of the set."

"How about this?" Tad is back. Smug with anticipation, he stoops over the citadel and fits bits of bottle-glass into its side to form a star-shaped window.

"Not bad," Alastair says. I giggle. Alastair knows perfectly well that most of his ideas would never come to anything if Tad wasn't around to implement them.

A wave licks cool around my knees, half swamping the trench I'm working on. Gritty water flows almost all the way through the system of fortifications before sinking back into the rhythmically sighing sea. "And," I say dramatically, "the Necromancer's time has come!"

I spring up and dance, shouting at the sea to come and face its foe. The arms of the cove break the force of the waves, so they barely curl over before breaking. The jagged steps of rock enclose a crescent of sand rimmed by cliffs. The sun is hot on my face, on my arms and legs stripped of sand by the breeze, but the light is gentle: I don't have to squint, unless I look all the way out to where the world ends in a line of white fire.

"I feel like going in again," I exclaim to the boys, and when the Citadel of the Clockwork Necromancer has suffered its inevitable collapse into the tide, it's a race to the water. We pound into the waves, shrieking and yelling. I widearm a huge splash in Tad's direction, and then I dive under the waves.

Sea in my hair, strong rills of sea between my fingers, a cool wash of sea inside my bathing-suit, oh how I wish I were a fish, and something grabs my foot.

I pop to the surface, barely drawing breath before I start screaming. Certain it's Tad, I'm ready to duck him back, but I'm out of my depth so I have to paddle around in a circle to find him, and it turns out he's nowhere near me. He's further out with Alastair, both of their arms flailing. Behind me? I paddle around again –

Ned bobs in the waves, his blond hair flattened dark, his grin triumphant. "Got you!"

I scream in sheer delight. "Ned! Were you here all this time?" I splash over and hug him, wet skin sliding on skin. "Alastair! Tad! It's *Ned!* He was waiting out here – "

"Under the water." Ned chortles in glee.

Alastair reaches us first. He spits water into Ned's face, then splashes him, causing Ned to honk with laughter. "What were you hiding from?"

"Nothing. I was just waiting for you."

Tad paddles up, all sleek with his black bangs plastered to his forehead. "You didn't have to hide, Ned!"

"There's nothing to be afraid of," I chime in.

"Nothing to hide from!"

Ned points a dripping arm at the clifftop where we left our bikes. There stands a ponytailed man, the largest man I've ever seen, his hands hanging empty by his sides, and the sun shines full on his face; the light is all around him.

Tokyo, November 2006

About the Author

Felicity Savage is a major award-nominated fantasy author. MUSIC TO DIE BY is her first suspense novel. Born in South Carolina, Savage lived until the age of two in rural France, and then in the west of Ireland. At six, she moved with her family to the island of North Uist in the Outer Hebrides, where she joined the Girl Guides and appeared in productions of Robin Hood and Peter Pan at the RAF base on Benbecula. Some years later she graduated from Columbia College in New York City and then moved to Japan, where she now lives with her husband, daughter, and two cats. When not writing, she works as a Japanese translator, sings Gregorian chant, and moonlights as a serial houseplant killer.

Visit the author at http://felicitysavage.com/

www.ingramcontent.com/pod-product-compliance
Lightning Source LLC
Chambersburg PA
CBHW061553170626
46811CB00001B/183

* 9 7 8 1 9 3 7 3 9 6 0 3 9 *